KU-175-098

Critical Acclaim for Robert Crais

'Crais tells a compelling tale that glints with wit, intelligence and expertise. He has also created a star in Elvis Cole, the best new shamus – brave, funny, humane – to hit these mean streets for many a year'
Literary Review

'Far and away the most satisfying private eye novel in years'
Lawrence Block

'The kind of bravura performance only a pro can give'
Kirkus Reviews

'Terrific . . . should be mentioned in the same breath as Robert B. Parker, Tony Hillerman, Sue Grafton and James Lee Burke'
Houston Chronicle

'Crais is in a class by himself – he is quite simply the best'
Eric Van Lustbader

'Crais knows his way around a wisecrack and a narrative sucker-punch . . . enormously appealing'
San Francisco Chronicle

'Oustanding characters, tight plot and scintillating prose style'
Mystery Scene Magazine

'Intelligent, perceptive, hard, clean'   *James Ellroy*

'Out on the West Coast, where private eyes thrive like avocado trees, Robert Crais has created an interesting and amusing hero in Elvis Cole . . . definitely new'
Wall Street Journal

'Crais is a terrific writer'   *Sue Grafton*

Robert Crais has thrilled mystery readers with his Elvis Cole series, winning awards and top-flight reviews. He is the author of seven previous Elvis Cole novels, and lives in Los Angeles with his wife and daughter.

L.A. Requiem

AN ELVIS COLE NOVEL
....

Robert Crais

ORION

An Orion paperback
First published in Great Britain by Orion in 1999
This paperback edition published in 1999 by Orion Books Ltd,
Orion House, 5 Upper St Martin's Lane, London WC2H 9EA

Copyright © Robert Crais 1999

The right of Robert Crais to be identified as the author
of this work has been asserted by him in accordance with the
Copyright, Designs and Patents Act 1988.

All rights reserved. No part of this publication may be
reproduced, stored in a retrieval system, or transmitted, in
any form or by any means, electronic, mechanical,
photocopying, recording or otherwise, without the
prior permission of the copyright owner.

A CIP catalogue record for this book is
available from the British Library.

ISBN: 0 75282 661 1

Typeset by Deltatype Ltd, Birkenhead, Merseyside

Printed and bound in Great Britain by
Clays Ltd, St Ives plc

For *Ed Waters* and *Sid Ellis*,
who taught more than words.

'And dat's da' name o' dat tune.'

ACKNOWLEDGEMENTS

Many people contributed to the writing of this novel, and to its moment of publication. They include: Detective-Three John Petievich, LAPD (Fugitive Section); Detective-Three Paul Bishop, LAPD (West Los Angeles Sex Crimes); Bruce Kelton JD, CFE (Director, Forensic Investigative Services, Deloitte & Touche); Patricia Crais; Lauren Crais; Carol Topping (for nights out with the girls); Wayne Topping (for putting up with it); William Gleason, Ph.D.; Andrea Malcolm; Jeffrey Gleason; April Smith; Robert Miller; Brian DeFiore; Lisa Kitei; Samantha Miller; Kim Dower; Gerald Petievich; Judy Chavez (for the language lessons); Dr Halina Alter (for keeping me in the game); Steve Volpe; and Norman Kurland.

Special contributions were made by the following, without whom this book would not exist in its present form: Aaron Priest, Steve Rubin, Linda Grey, Shawn Coyne, and George Lucas. Thank you.

Help, encouragement, and inspiration were given by many who requested anonymity. These secret creatures include TC, MG, TD, LC, and Cookie. Good to go on night patrol whenever, wherever.

This book is not solely mine; it also belongs to Leslie Wells.

Do you know what love is?
(I would bleed out for you.)
    – *Tattooed Beach Sluts*

I've got the whole town under my thumb
and all I've gotta do is keep acting dumb.

We say goodbye so very politely
Now say hello to the killer inside me.
    – *MC 900 Ft Jesus*

Mama, Mama, can't you see
What the Marine Corps has done to me?
Made me lean and made me strong
Made me where I can do no wrong.
    – *USMC marching cadence*

L.A. Requiem

The Islander Palms Motel

Uniformed LAPD Officer Joe Pike could hear the banda music even with the engine idling, the a.c. jacked to meat locker, and the two-way crackling callout codes to other units.

The covey of Latina street kids clumped outside the arcade giggled at him, whispering things to each other that made them flush. Squat brown men come up through the fence from Zacatecas milled on the sidewalk, shielding their eyes from the sun as veteranos told them about Sawtelle over on the Westside where they could find day labor jobs, thirty dollars cash, no papers required. Here in Rampart Division south of Sunset, Guatemalans and Nicaraguans simmered with Salvadorans and Mexican nationals in a sidewalk machaca that left the air flavored with epizoté, even here within the sour cage of the radio car.

Pike watched the street kids part like water when his partner hurried out of the arcade. Abel Wozniak was a thick man with a square head and cloudy, slate eyes. Wozniak was twenty years older than Pike and had been on the street twenty years longer. Once the best cop that Pike had then met, Wozniak's eyes were now strained. They'd been riding together for two years, and the eyes hadn't always been that way. Pike regretted that, but there wasn't anything he could do about it.

Especially now when they were looking for Ramona Ann Escobar.

Wozniak lurched in behind the wheel, adjusting his gun for the seat, anxious to roll even with the tension between them as thick as clotted blood. His informant had come through.

'DeVille's staying at the Islander Palms Motel.'

'Does DeVille have the girl?'

'My guy eyeballed a little girl, but he can't say if she's still with him.'

Wozniak snapped the car into gear and rocked away from the curb. They didn't roll Code Three. No lights, no siren. The Islander Palms was less than five blocks away, here on Alvarado Boulevard just south of Sunset. Why send an announcement?

'Woz? Would DeVille hurt her?'

'I told you, a fuckin' perv like this would be better off with a bullet in his head.'

It was eleven-forty on a Tuesday morning. At nine-twenty, a five-year-old girl named Ramona Ann Escobar had been playing near the paddle-boat concession in Echo Park when her mother, a legal émigré from Guatemala, had turned away to chat with friends. Witnesses last saw Ramona in the company of a man believed to be one Leonard DeVille, a known pedophile who'd been sighted working both Echo and MacArthur parks for the past three months. When the dispatch call had come about the missing girl, Wozniak had begun working his street informants. Wozniak, having been on the street forever, knew everyone and how to find them. He was a treasure trove of information that Pike valued and respected, and didn't want to lose. But Pike couldn't do anything about that, either.

Pike stared at Wozniak until Wozniak couldn't handle the weight any longer and glanced over. They were forty seconds away from the Islander Palms. 'Oh, for Christ's sake, what?'

'It isn't too late, Woz.'

Wozniak's eyes went back to the street, and his face tightened. 'I'm telling you, Joe. Back off with this. I'm not going to talk about it anymore.'

'I meant what I said.'

Wozniak wet his lips.

'You've got Paulette and Evelyn to think about.'

Wozniak's wife and daughter.

The cloudy eyes flicked to Pike, as bottomless and as dangerous as a thunderhead.

'I've been thinking about them, Pike. You bet your ass.'

For just an instant, Pike thought Wozniak's eyes filled. Then Wozniak gave a shudder as if he were shaking out his feelings, and pointed.

'There it is. Now shut the fuck up and play like a cop.'

The Islander Palms was a white stucco dump: two stories of frayed carpets, stained beds, and neon palms that looked tacky even in Los Angeles, all of it shaped into an L around a narrow parking lot. The typical customers were whores renting by the hour, wannabe pornographers shooting 'amateur' videos, and rent jumpers needing a place to stay while they found a new landlord to stiff.

Pike followed Wozniak into the manager's office, a skinny Hindu with watery eyes. First thing he said was, 'I do not wan' trouble, please.'

Wozniak had the lead.

'We're looking for a man with a little girl. His name is Leonard DeVille, but he might've used another name.'

The Hindu didn't know the name, or about a little girl, but he told them that a man matching the description Woz provided could be found on the second floor in the third room from the top of the L.

Pike said, 'You want me to call it in?'

Wozniak went out the door and up the stairs without answering. Pike thought then that he should go back to the car and call, but you don't let your partner go up alone. Pike followed.

They found the third door, listened, but heard nothing. The drapes were pulled. Standing on the exposed balcony, Pike felt as if they were being watched.

3

Wozniak took the knob side of the door, Pike the hinges. Wozniak rapped on the door, identifying himself as a Los Angeles police officer. Everything about Joe made him want to be the first one inside, but they had settled that two years ago. Wozniak drove, Wozniak went in first, Wozniak called how they made the play. Twenty-two years on the job against Pike's three bought you that. They had done it this way two hundred times.

When DeVille opened the door, they pushed him backward, Wozniak going first and pushing hard.

DeVille said, 'Hey, what is this?' Like he'd never been rousted before.

The room was tattered and cheesy, with a closet and bath off the rear. A rumpled double bed rested against the wall like some kind of ugly altar, its dark red bedspread stained and threadbare, one of the stains looking like Mickey Mouse. The room's only other piece of furniture was a cheap dresser edged with cigarette burns and notches cut by a sharp knife. Wozniak held DeVille as Pike cleared the bathroom and the closet, looking for Ramona.

'She's not here.'

'Anything else? Clothes, suitcase, toothbrush?'

'Nothing.' Indicating that DeVille hadn't been living here, and didn't intend to. He had other uses for the room.

Wozniak, who had busted DeVille twice in the past, said, 'Where is she, Lennie?'

'Who? Hey, I don't do that anymore. C'mon, Officer.'

'Where's the camera?'

DeVille spread his hands, flashing a nervous smile. 'I got no camera. I'm telling you, I'm off that.'

Leonard DeVille was five-eight, with a fleshy body, dyed blond hair, and skin like a pineapple. The hair was slicked straight back, and held with a rubber band. Pike knew that DeVille was lying, but waited to see how Woz would play it. Even with only three years on the job,

4

Pike knew that pedophiles were always pedophiles. You could bust them, treat them, counsel them, whatever, but when you released them back into the world, they were still child molesters and it was only a matter of time.

Wozniak hooked a hand under the foot of the bed and heaved the bed over. DeVille jumped back and stumbled into Pike, who caught and held him. A rumpled overnight bag was nesting in about a million dust bunnies where the bed had been.

Wozniak said, 'Lennie, you are about as dumb as they get.'

'Hey, that ain't mine. I got nothing to do with that bag.' DeVille was so scared that he sprouted sweat like a rainstorm.

Wozniak opened the bag and dumped out a Polaroid camera, better than a dozen film packs, and at least a hundred pictures of children in various stages of undress. That's how a guy like DeVille made his living, snapping pictures and selling them to other perverts.

Wozniak toed through the pictures, his face growing darker and more contained. Pike couldn't see the pictures from where he stood, but he could see the vein pulsing in Wozniak's temple. He thought that Wozniak must be thinking about his own daughter, but maybe not. Maybe Wozniak was still thinking about the other thing.

Pike squeezed DeVille's arm. 'Where's the little girl? Where's Ramona Escobar?'

DeVille's voice went higher. 'That stuff isn't mine. I never saw it before.'

Wozniak squatted, fingering through the pictures without expression. He lifted one, and held it to his nose.

'I can still smell the developing chemicals. You didn't take this more than an hour ago.'

'They're not mine!'

Wozniak stared at the picture. Pike still couldn't see it.

5

'She looks about five. She matches the physical description they gave us. Pretty little girl. Innocent. Now she's not innocent anymore.'

Abel Wozniak stood and drew his gun. It was the new Beretta 9-millimeter that LAPD had just mandated.

'If you hurt that child, I'll fucking kill you.'

Joe said, 'Woz, we've got to call in. Put your gun away.'

Wozniak stepped past Pike and snapped the Beretta backhand, slamming DeVille in the side of the head and dropping him like a bag of garbage.

Pike jumped between them, grabbing Wozniak by the arms and pushing him back. 'That doesn't help get the girl.'

Then Wozniak's eyes came to Pike; hard, ugly little rivets with something behind the clouds.

When the two police officers went up the stairs, Fahreed Abouti, the manager, watched until they pushed the blond man back into his room. The police often came to his motel to bust the prostitutes and johns and drug dealers, and Fahreed never passed up a chance to watch. Once, he had seen a prostitute servicing the officers who had come to arrest her, and another time he watched as three officers beat a rapist until all the man's teeth were gone. There was always something wonderful to see. It was better than Wheel of Fortune.

You had to be careful, though.

As soon as the upstairs door closed, Fahreed crept up the stairs. If you got too close, or if they caught you, the police grew angry. Once, a SWAT officer in the armor and the helmet and with the big gun had grown so angry that he'd knocked Fahreed's turban into a puddle of transmission fluid. The cleaning cost had been horrendous.

The shouting started when Fahreed was still on the stairs. He couldn't understand what was being said, only that the words were angry. He eased along the second-floor balcony, trying to get closer, but just as he reached the room, the shouting stopped. He cursed the fates, thinking he'd missed all the fun, when suddenly there was a single loud shout from inside, then a thunderous, deafening explosion.

People on the street stopped in their tracks and looked. A woman pointed, and a man across the parking lot ran.

Fahreed's heart pounded, because even a Hindu knew a gunshot. He thought the blond man might be dead. Or perhaps he had killed the officers.

Fahreed heard nothing within the room.

'Hallu?'

Nothing.

'Is everyone all right?'

Nothing.

Perhaps they had jumped from the bathroom window into the alley behind.

Fahreed's palms were damp, and all his swirling fears demanded that he race back to his office and pretend to have heard nothing, but instead he threw open the door.

The younger officer, the tall one with the dark glasses and the empty face, spun toward him and aimed an enormous revolver. Fahreed thought in that instant that he would surely die.

'Please. No!'

The older officer was without a face, his remains covered in blood. The blond man was dead, too, his face a mask of crimson. The floor and walls and ceiling were sprayed red.

'No!'

The tall officer's gun never wavered. Fahreed stared into his dark bottomless glasses, and saw that they were misted with blood.

'Please!'

The tall officer dropped to his fallen partner, and began CPR.

Without looking up, the tall officer said, 'Call 911.'

Fahreed Abouti ran for the phone.

7

PART ONE

CHAPTER 1

That Sunday, the sun floated bright and hot over the Los Angeles basin, pushing people to the beaches and the parks and into backyard pools to escape the heat. The air buzzed with the nervous palsy it gets when the wind freight-trains in from the deserts, dry as bone, and cooking the hillsides into tar-filled kindling that can snap into flames hot enough to melt an auto body.

The Verdugo Mountains above Glendale were burning. A column of brown smoke rose off the ridgeline there where it was caught by the Santa Anas and spread south across the city, painting the sky with the color of dried blood. If you were in Burbank, say, or up along the Mulholland Snake over the Sunset Strip, you could see the big multi-engine fire bombers diving in with their cargoes of bright red fire retardant as news choppers crisscrossed the scene. Or you could just watch the whole thing on television. In L.A., next to riots and earthquakes, fires are our largest spectator sport.

We couldn't see the smoke column from Lucy Chenier's second-floor apartment in Beverly Hills, but the sky had an orange tint that made Lucy stop in her door long enough to frown. We were bringing cardboard moving boxes up from her car.

'Is that the fire?'

'The Santa Anas are bringing the smoke south. Couple of hours, the ash will begin to fall. It'll look like gray snow.' The fire was forty miles away. We were in no danger.

Lucy shifted the frown to her Lexus, parked below us at the curb. 'Will it hurt the paint?'

'By the time it settles it'll be cool, just like powder. We'll wash it off with the hose.' Elvis Cole, Professional Angeleno, educating the recent transplant, who also happens to be his girlfriend. Wait'll we get a big temblor.

Lucy didn't seem convinced, but then she stepped inside, and called her son. 'Ben!'

Less than a week before, Lucille Chenier and her nine-year-old son had left Louisiana and settled into the apartment that they had taken in Beverly Hills, just south of Wilshire Boulevard. Lucy had been a practicing attorney in Baton Rouge, but was beginning a new career as a legal analyst for a local television station (a nouveau occupational fruit growing from the ugly tree that was the Simpson trial). Trading Baton Rouge for Los Angeles, she gained a larger salary, more free time to spend with her son, and closer proximity to *moi*. I had spent all of Friday, Saturday, and most of Sunday morning arranging and re arranging the living room. That's love for you.

The television was tuned to the station she now worked for, KROK-8 ('Real News for Real People!'), which, like every other station in town, had interrupted regular programming with live coverage of the fire. Twenty-eight homes were threatened and had been evacuated.

Lucy handed Ben the box. 'Too heavy?'

'No way.'

'Your room. Your closet. *Neatly*.'

When he was gone I slipped my hand around her waist, and whispered, 'Your room. Your bed. Messy.'

She stepped away and considered the couch. 'First we have to get this house in order. Would you please move the couch again?'

I stared at the couch. I had moved it maybe eight hundred times in the last two days.

'Which wall?'

12

She chewed at her thumb, thinking. 'Over there.'

'That's where it was two moves ago.' It was a big couch. It probably weighed three thousand pounds.

'Yes, but that was when the entertainment center was by the fireplace. Now that we've put the entertainment center by the entry, the look will be completely different.'

'*We?*'

'Yes. We.'

I bent into the couch and dragged it to the opposite wall. Four thousand pounds.

I was squaring the couch when the phone rang. Lucy spoke for a minute, then held out the phone.

'Joe.'

Joe Pike and I are partners in the detective agency that bears my name. He could have his name on it if he wanted, but he doesn't. He's like that.

I took the phone. 'Hernias R Us.' Lucy rolled her eyes and turned away, already contemplating new sofa arrangements.

Pike said, 'How's the move going?'

I walked the phone out onto the balcony. 'It's a big change. I think she's finally realizing how big. What's up?'

'You heard of Frank Garcia?'

'The tortilla guy. Regular, large, and Monsterito sizes. I prefer the Monsterito myself.' You could walk into any food store in Los Angeles and see Frank Garcia smiling at you from the packages of his tortillas, eyes bright, bushy black mustache, big smile.

Pike said, 'Frank's a friend of mine and he's got a problem. I'm on my way there now. Can you meet me?'

Pike and I have owned a detective agency for twelve years, and I have known him even longer since his days as a Los Angeles police officer. He had never once asked a favor, or asked for my help on a personal problem in all of that time.

'I'm helping Lucy set up her house. I'm wearing shorts,

and I've spent the morning wrestling a ten-thousand-pound couch.'

Pike didn't answer.

'Joe?'

'Frank's daughter is missing, Elvis. She's a friend of mine, too. I hope you can make it.' He gave an address in Hancock Park, then hung up without another word. Pike is like that, too.

I stayed out on the balcony and watched Lucy. She was moving from box to box as if she could no more decide what to unpack next than where to put the couch. She had been like that since she arrived from Louisiana, and it wasn't like her. We had had a long-distance relationship for two years, but now we had made a very real move to further that relationship, and she had carried the weight of it. She's the one who had left her friends. She's the one who had left her home. She was the one taking the risk.

I turned off the phone, went back inside, and waited for her to look at me.

'Hey.'

She smiled, but seemed troubled.

I stroked her upper arms and smiled back. She has beautiful amber-green eyes.

'You okay?'

She looked embarrassed. 'I'm fine.'

'It's a big move. Big changes for both of us.'

She glanced back at the boxes as if something might be hiding in them.

'It's going to work out, Luce.'

She snuggled against me, and I could feel her smile. I didn't want to leave.

She said, 'What did Joe want?'

'The daughter of a friend of his is missing. He wants me to help check it out.'

Lucy looked up at me, her face now serious. 'A child?'

'He didn't say. You mind if I go?'

She glanced at the couch again. 'You'll do anything to avoid this couch, won't you?'

'Yeah. I hate that damned couch.'

Lucy laughed, then looked into my eyes again.

'I'd mind if you didn't go. Take a shower and go save the world.'

Hancock Park is an older area south of the Wilshire Country Club, lesser known to outsiders than Beverly Hills or Bel Air, but every bit as rich. Frank Garcia lived in an adobe-walled Spanish villa set behind a wrought-iron fence just west of the country club. It was a big place, hidden by lush green tree ferns and bird-of-paradise plants as big as dinosaurs and leafy calla lilies that were wilting from the heat.

Forty minutes after Pike gave me Garcia's address, I followed an older Latina with a thick waist and nervous hands through Garcia's rambling home and out to where Frank Garcia and Joe Pike waited beside a tile-lined pool.

As I approached, Pike said, 'Frank, this is Elvis Cole. We own the agency together.'

'Mr Garcia.'

Frank Garcia wasn't the smiling man with the bushy mustache you see on his tortillas. This Frank Garcia looked small and worried, and it had nothing to do with him being in a wheelchair. 'You don't look like a private investigator.'

I was wearing one of those terrific Jam's World print shirts over the shorts. Orange, yellow, pink, and green. 'Gee, did I wear this on a Sunday?'

Garcia looked embarrassed, then raised his hands in apology. 'I'm sorry, Mr Cole. I'm so worked up about this thing with Karen, I'm not thinking. I don't care how you dress. I just want to find my daughter.' He touched Joe's arm. It was a loving gesture, and surprised me. 'That's why I called Joe. Joe says if anyone can find Karen, it's you. He says you're the best there is at finding people.'

15

Here's the scene: The three of us are by the Olympic-sized pool. The Latina with the thick waist is hovering in the shade of the veranda up by the house, her eyes on Frank in case he might want something, but so far he doesn't and he hasn't offered anything to me. If he did, I would ask for sunblock because standing here next to his pool is like standing on the sun side of Mercury. Gotta be ninety-six and climbing. Behind us is a pool house larger than my home, and through the sliding glass doors I can see a pool table, wet bar, and paintings of *vaqueros* in the Mexican highlands. It is air-conditioned in there, but apparently Frank would rather sit out here in the nuclear heat. Statues of lions dot the landscape, as motionless as Joe Pike, who has not moved once in the three minutes that I have been there. Pike is wearing a gray sweatshirt with the sleeves cut off, faded Levi's, and flat black pilot's glasses, which is the way he dresses every day of his life. His dark brown hair is cut short, and bright red arrows were tattooed on the outside of his deltoids long before tattoos were *au courant*. Watching Joe stand there, he reminds me of the world's largest two-legged pit bull.

I said, 'We'll do what we can, Mr Garcia. How long has Karen been missing?'

'Since yesterday. Yesterday morning at ten o'clock. I called the police, but those bastards wouldn't do anything, so I called Joe. I knew he'd help.' He patted Joe's arm again.

'The police refused to help?'

'Yeah. Those pricks.'

'How old is Karen, Mr Garcia?'

'Thirty-two.'

I glanced at Pike. Together, we had worked hundreds of missing persons cases, and we both knew why the police had brushed off Frank Garcia.

I said, 'A thirty-two-year-old woman has only been missing since yesterday?'

'Yes.' Pike's voice was soft.

Frank Garcia twisted in his chair, knowing what I was saying and angry about it.

'What's your point, asking that? You think just because she's a grown woman she'd meet some man and run off without letting anyone know?'

'Adult people do that, Mr Garcia.'

He shoved a piece of yellow legal paper into my hands, and now the nervous eyes were rimmed with frustration, like I was his last best hope and I wasn't going for it, either. 'Karen would've called. She would've told me if she had to change her plans. She was gonna go run, then bring me a bowl of *machaca*, but she never came back. You ask Mrs Acuna in her building. Mrs Acuna knows.' He said it as though if he could only get it out fast enough, it would become as important to me as it was to him. But then Frank wheeled toward Joe, and now his voice held anger as well as fear. 'He's like the goddamned police. He don't want to do anything.' He spun back at me, and now you could see the man he had been before he was in the chair, a teenaged gang-banger out of East L.A. with the White Fence gang who had turned his life around and made a fortune. 'Sorry I pulled you away from your donuts.'

From a million miles away behind the dark glasses, Joe said, 'Frank. We're going to help you.'

I tried not to look embarrassed, which is hard to do when your face is red. 'We'll look for your daughter, Mr Garcia. I just want you to know that the police have their policy for a reason. Most people we think are missing aren't. Eventually they call or show up, and they're embarrassed that everyone went to so much trouble. You see?'

He didn't look happy about it.

'You know where she was going to run?'

'Somewhere around Hollywood up by the hills. Mrs Acuna said she was going to this Jungle Juice, one of those little juice places? Mrs Acuna said she always got one of those things, a smoothie. She offered to bring one back.'

'Jungle Juice. Okay, that gives us a place to start.' How many Jungle Juices could there be?

Frank was looking more relieved by the second. Like he could breathe again. 'I appreciate this, Mr Cole. I want you to know that I don't care how much this costs. You tell me how much you want, it's yours.'

Joe said, 'Nothing.'

Garcia waved his hands. 'No, Joe, c'mon.'

'Nothing, Frank.'

I stared at the pool. I would've liked some of Frank Garcia's money just fine.

Garcia took Joe's arm again. 'You're a good boy, Joe. You always were.' He hung on to Joe's arm as he looked at me. 'We know each other since Joe was a policeman. Joe and my Karen, they used to see each other. I was hoping maybe one day this boy might be part of the family.'

Joe said, 'That was a long time ago.' He said it so softly that I could barely hear him.

I smiled. 'Joe. You never told me about this.'

Joe turned my way, the flat black lenses reflecting sun. 'Stop.'

I smiled wider and shook my head. That Joe. You learn something every day.

The old man looked up at the sky as the first flecks of ash swirled around us, the flecks catching on his hands and legs. 'Look at this mess. The goddamned sky is melting.'

The woman with the thick waist showed us out through the cool of Frank Garcia's home. Joe's red Jeep Cherokee was parked beneath an elm tree at the curb. My car was parked behind it. Pike and I walked down the drive without speaking until we came to the street, and then Joe said, 'Thanks for coming.'

'I guess there are worse ways to spend a Sunday. I could be wrestling that damned couch.'

Pike canted the glasses my way. 'We finish this, I'll move the couch for you.'

Friends.

We left my car where it was, climbed into Pike's Jeep, and went to find Karen Garcia.

CHAPTER 2

Frank Garcia had written his daughter's name, address, and phone number on the yellow sheet, along with a description of Karen's car (a red Mazda RX-7) and her license number (4KBL772). He'd attached a snapshot of Karen laughing about something as she sat at what was probably his dining-room table. She had a brilliant white smile, offset nicely against golden skin and rich black hair. She looked happy.

Joe stared at the photograph as if he were peering through a window at something far away.

I said, 'Pretty.'

'Yes. She is.'

'You had to be seeing her, when, before you knew me?'

His eyes never left the picture. 'I knew you, but I was still on the job.'

I remember Joe dating back then, but the relationships seemed as they were now, none more important than any other. 'I guess you were tight with this girl.'

Joe nodded.

'So what happened?'

Pike handed back the picture. 'I broke her heart.'

'Oh.' Sometimes prying is a lousy idea.

'A few years later she married and moved East to New York. It didn't work out, and now she's back here.'

I nodded, still feeling small for prying.

I used Pike's cell phone to call Karen Garcia's number. She didn't answer, but I identified myself to her machine, and asked her to call her father if she got this message. Frank had provided Mrs Acuna's phone, also, so I called her next, asking if she knew where Karen had gone to run. The dry winds were amping the air with so much static electricity that her voice sounded like bubbling fat, but I understood enough to get that the answer was no. 'Is it possible, Mrs Acuna, that Karen came home, then left again without your seeing her? You know, like maybe she came home long enough to get cleaned up, then went out with friends?'

'You mean yesterday?'

'Yes, ma'am. Yesterday after her run.'

'Oh, no. My husband and I live right here by the stairs. Karen lives right above us. When she didn't come back for the *machaca*, I was so worried. Her father loves my *machaca*. She always brings him a bowl. I just been up there again, and she still isn't back.'

I glanced at Joe. 'You see Karen much, Mrs Acuna? You two chat about things?'

'Oh, yes. She's such a sweet girl. I've known her family since before she was born.'

'She say anything to you about maybe getting back together with her ex-husband?'

Pike glanced over.

'No. Oh, no, she doesn't say anything like that. She calls him "the creep". He's still back in that place.' That place. New York.

Still looking at Pike, I shook my head. Pike turned to the window.

'What about other boyfriends?'

'She sees young men. Not a lot, you know, but she's very pretty.'

'Okay. Thanks, Mrs Acuna. I'll probably drop around later on. If Karen happens to come home, would you ask her to phone her father?'

'I'll call him myself.'

I ended the call, then looked over at Pike. 'You know she's probably with her friends. Probably went to Vegas, or maybe spent all night swing dancing and she's crashing at some guy's.'

'Could be. But Frank's worried, and he needs someone to help carry the load.'

'You really were close with these people.'

Pike went back to staring out the window. Getting him to talk is like pulling your own teeth with pliers.

The information operator told me that there were two Jungle Juice outlets, the original in West Hollywood on Melrose, the second on Barham in Universal City. West Hollywood was closer, so we went there first. Detective work defined by the process of least effort.

The first Jungle Juice was manned by a skinny kid with blue hair and Irish tattoos on his arms, a short girl with a bleach-blond buzz cut, and a guy in his early thirties who looked like he might be president of the local Young Republicans chapter. All three of them had worked yesterday when Karen would've been in, but none of them recognized her picture. The bleach blond worked every weekend and said she would know her if Karen were a regular. I believed her.

The Santa Anas continued to pick up as we drove north to the second Jungle Juice. Palm trees, tall and vulnerable like the necks of giant dinosaurs, took the worst of it. The wind stripped the dead fronds that bunched beneath the crowns and tossed them into streets and yards and onto cars.

It was a few minutes before noon when we reached the second Jungle Juice, just south of Universal Studios. It was set in a narrow strip mall that ran along Barham at the base of the mountains, and was crowded with Sunday shoppers and tourists trying to find the Universal City Walk, even with the wind.

Pike and I stood in line until we reached the counter and showed them the picture of Karen. The girl behind the register, all of eighteen with a clean bright smile and chocolate tan, recognized Karen at once. 'Oh, sure, she comes in all the time. She always gets a smoothie after her run.'

Pike said, 'Was she in yesterday?'

The girl didn't know, and called over a tall African-American kid named Ronnie. Ronnie was a good-looking kid a couple of inches over six feet whose claim to fame was six seconds in a Charmin commercial. 'Oh, yeah, she comes in here after her run. That's Karen.'

'Did she come in yesterday?'

Now Ronnie squinted at me. 'Is she okay?'

'I just want to know if she came in yesterday.'

The squint turned into a frown, went to Pike, then grew suspicious. 'What is this?'

I showed him the license. He squinted at that, too.

'Your name really Elvis?'

Pike stepped past me until his hips pressed against the counter. Ronnie was maybe an inch taller than Joe, but Ronnie took a fast step back. Joe said, 'Did she come in here or not?' Voice so soft you could barely hear him.

Ronnie shook his head, eyes bugging. 'Not yesterday. I worked from opening to six, and she didn't come in. I would've known because we always talk about her run. I jog, too.'

'You know where she runs?'

'Sure. She parks down here and runs up the hill there to the reservoir.' He gestured across Barham to the hill. Lake Hollywood Drive meandered up through a residential area to the reservoir.

The girl said, 'I'm pretty sure I saw her drive past yesterday. Well, it was a little red car. I didn't see her or anything. Just the car.'

Ronnie said, 'No way. Karen always comes in after the run, and she didn't come in.' Like he was disappointed that maybe she had come for the run and not stopped in to see him. 'No way.'

We thanked them, then went out to the parking lot.

I said, 'Well, that's something. She shows up for the

run, but she doesn't go in for the smoothie, which is her habit.'

Pike walked to the street, then looked back at the parking lot. It was small, and empty of red Mazdas.

He said, 'She runs, but maybe she remembers something and doesn't have time to get the smoothie, or she meets someone and they decide to do something else.'

'Yeah. Like go to his place for a different kind of smoothie.'

Pike looked at me.

'Sorry.'

He stared up the hill. 'You're probably right. If she runs to the reservoir, she probably follows Lake Hollywood up. Let's drive it.'

We followed Lake Hollywood Drive past upscale houses that were built in the thirties and forties, then remodeled heavily in the seventies and eighties into everything from homey ranch-styles to contemporary aeries to post-modern nightmares. Like most older Los Angeles neighborhoods (until the land boom went bust), the homes held the energy of change, as if what was here today might evolve into something else tomorrow. Often, that something else was worse, but just as often it was better. There is great audacity in the willingness to change, more than a little optimism, and a serious dose of courage. It was the courage that I admired most, even though the results often made me cringe. After all, the people who come to Los Angeles are looking for change. Everyone else just stays home.

The road switchbacked up the hillside, meandering past houses and mature oaks that shuddered and swayed with the wind. The streets were littered with leaves and branches and old Gelson's Market bags. We crested the ridge, then drove down to the reservoir. It was choppy and muddy from the wind. We saw no red Mazdas, and no one who looked like Karen Garcia, but we didn't expect to. The hill was there, so you climbed it, and so far I wasn't too worried about things. Karen was probably just waking up at wherever she'd spent the night, and pretty soon she'd go home or collect her messages, and call her father to calm down the old man. The burden of being an only child.

We were halfway down the mountain and thinking about what to do next when a homeless guy with a backpack and bedroll strolled out of a side street and started down the mountain. He was in his mid-thirties, and burned dark by the sun.

I said, 'Pull over.'

When Pike slowed, the man stopped and considered us. His eyes were red, and you could smell the body odor even with the wind. He said, 'I am a master carpenter looking for work, but no job is too small. I will work for cash, or books.' He managed a little pride when he said it, but he probably wasn't a master carpenter and he probably wasn't looking for work.

Pike held out Karen's photograph. 'Have you seen this woman?'

'No. I am sorry.' Every word like that. Without contractions.

'She jogged through the neighborhood yesterday morning. Blue top. Gray shorts.'

He leaned forward and examined the picture more closely. 'Black ponytail.'

Pike said, 'Could be.'

'She was running uphill, struggling mightily against the forces that would drag her down. A truck slowed beside her, then sped away. I was listening to Mr Dave Matthews at the time.' He had a Sony Discman suspended from his belt, the earphones hanging loose at his neck.

I said, 'What kind of truck?'

He stepped back and looked over Pike's Cherokee.

'This truck.'

'A red Jeep like this?'

He shrugged. 'I think it was this one, but it might've been another.'

The corner of Pike's mouth twitched. In all the years I had known him, I have never seen Pike smile, but sometimes you'll get the twitch. For Pike, that's him busting a gut.

I said, 'You see the driver?'

He pointed at Pike. 'Him.'

Pike looked away, and sighed.

The homeless man peered at us hopefully. 'Would you have a small job that needs a careful craftsman? I am available, don't you know?'

I gave him ten bucks. 'What's your name?'

'Edward Deege, Master Carpenter.'

'Okay, Edward. Thanks.'

'No job too small.'

'Hey, Edward. We want to talk to you again, you around?'

'I am but a Dixie cup on the stream of life, but, yes, I enjoy the reservoir. I can often be found there.'

'Okay, Edward. Thanks.'

Edward Deege peered at Pike some more, then stepped back, as if troubled. 'Release your rage, my friend. Rage kills.'

Pike pulled away.

I said, 'You think he saw anything, or he was just scamming us?'

'He was right about the ponytail. Maybe he saw a four-wheel-drive.'

We followed Lake Hollywood Drive down to Barham, and when we turned left toward the freeway, Pike said, 'Elvis.'

Karen Garcia's red Mazda RX-7 was parked behind a flower shop on this side of Barham, opposite the Jungle Juice. We hadn't seen it when we were at the Jungle Juice because it was behind a building across the street. We couldn't see it until we were coming down, and I wished then that it wasn't there to see.

Pike turned into the parking lot, and we got out. The Mazda's engine was cool, as if it had been parked here a very long time.

'Been here all night.'

Pike nodded.

'If she went up to run, that means she never came down.' I looked back up the hill.

Pike said, 'Or she didn't leave by herself.'

'She's running, she meets some guy, and they use his car. She's probably on her way back to pick up the Mazda now.' I said it, but neither of us believed it.

We asked the people at the flower shop if they had seen anything, but they hadn't. We asked every shopkeeper in the strip mall and most of the employees, but they all said no. I hoped they had seen something to indicate that Karen was safe, but deep down, where your blood runs cold, I knew they hadn't.

CHAPTER 3

With her father's money, Karen Garcia could've lived anywhere, yet she chose a modest apartment in a Latin-hip part of Silver Lake favored by families. The Gipsy Kings played on someone's stereo; the smells of chili and cilantro were fresh and strong. Children played on the lawns, and couples laughed about the heat storm. Around us, great palms and jacarandas slashed like the tails of nervous cats, but the area wasn't littered with fronds and limbs. I guess if you cared about your neighborhood you cleaned up the mess without waiting for the city to do it for you.

We left Pike's Jeep by a fire hydrant and walked into a courtyard burgeoning with hand-painted clay pots that overflowed with gladiolas. Apartment number 3 belonged to Marisol Acuna, but Pike didn't come with me to the door. We knew from Mrs Acuna that Karen's apartment was on the second floor.

A heavy woman in her late fifties stepped out of a ground-floor apartment. 'Are you Mr Cole?'

'Yes, ma'am. Mrs Acuna?'

She glanced at Pike. He was already climbing the stairs. 'She hasn't come home. Let me get the key, and I'll let you inside.'

'Frank gave us a key, ma'am. You should wait down here.'

A line appeared between her brows, and she glanced at Pike again. 'Why don't you want me up there? You think something bad is up there?'

'No, ma'am. But if Karen comes home I'd hate to have

28

her walk in on a couple of strange men. You keep an eye out. If she comes while we're up there you can tell her what's going on and bring her up.' What a fine and wonderful lie.

Pike wasn't waiting for me. Karen's door opened.

I gave Mrs Acuna a final smile, then took the stairs three at a time, slipping into Karen's apartment behind Joe. He stood in the center of the living room, holding up a finger to stop me, his gun hanging loose in his right hand. Pike carries the Colt Python .357 magnum with a four-inch barrel. Firing a heavy bullet, it will generate over fifteen hundred foot-pounds of energy and can punch its way through an engine block. Pike uses the heavy bullet.

He went through a short hall into the apartment's only bedroom, then reappeared almost instantly, the Python now gone.

'Clear.'

Sometimes you just have to shake your head.

I said, 'Can we spell "paranoid"?'

Karen Garcia's apartment was furnished well beyond the rent she paid. An overstuffed leather couch with two matching chairs dominated the living room. A modern desk was positioned under two casement windows so that she had a view of the street; psychology texts were shelved on the desk, along with three Tami Hoag novels, a Nunzilla, and an AT&T telephone/answering machine combo. The red message light was blinking. A framed snapshot of Karen wearing a silly crown and holding a glass of wine was tacked beside the window. She was barefoot, and smiling.

I said, 'You want the messages or the rest of the place?'

'Rest of the place.'

All of Karen's messages were from her father except the one from me and one from a man named Martin, asking if she wanted to go to a *quebradita*. Martin had a Spanish accent, and a mellow voice. After the messages, I went through the drawers, and found a Rolodex. We would bring it to Frank to see whom he knew, and, if we had to, we would phone every name to see if we could find someone who knew where Karen was.

Pike reappeared from the bedroom. 'Jeans on the bed, sandals on the floor. Her toothbrush is still in the bathroom. Wherever she went, she wasn't planning on staying.' You take your toothbrush, you're thinking you'll stay the night. You leave it, you're coming home.

'Okay. She changed into her running things and left the other stuff, figuring to change back later.'

'That's my call.'

'You see any notes, maybe a calendar that says her plans?'

I thought he was about to answer when Pike held up his finger again, then took three fast steps toward the door. 'Someone's coming.'

'Mrs Acuna.'

'Someone bigger.'

Pike and I set up on either side of the door as a large, ruddy-faced man in a gray suit made the landing and looked in at us. Two uniformed LAPD officers appeared behind him. The man's eyes widened when he saw us, and he pawed under his jacket. 'Police officers! Step away from the door and move to the center of the room. Now!'

The suit clawed out a standard LAPD-issue Beretta 9 as the uniformed cops drew their own weapons. Mrs Acuna shouted something down in the courtyard, but no one listened to her.

I said, 'Take it easy. We're working for her father, Frank Garcia.'

The detective had the gun on us now, and the two uniformed cops were aiming past his head. One of them was young, and looked like his eyes were about to do the Pekinese pop-out. If I was the detective, I would've been more scared of them than me.

30

The detective shouted, '*Step back from the door and move to the center. Hands from your bodies.*'

We did what he said. He toed open the door and stepped through, the two uniforms spreading to cover us from the sides.

'My name's Cole. We're private investigators working for her father.'

'Shut up.'

'My license is in the wallet. Her father hired us a couple of hours ago. Call him. Ask the woman who lives downstairs.'

'Shut the fuck up and keep those hands where I can see them!'

The detective told one of the uniforms to see the woman, then edged forward, slipped out my wallet, and glanced at the license. He was more tense than he should've been, and I wondered why. Maybe he didn't like my shirt, either.

He brought my wallet to the phone, punched in a number without taking his eyes off me, then mumbled something I couldn't understand.

'We entered the apartment with a key the father provided and at his request. Would you lighten up?'

The uniform reappeared. 'Hey, Holstein, they're cool. She says the father called her and told her to expect'm.'

Holstein nodded, but the tension stayed.

'Can we put our hands down, or you like the view of our pits?'

'Sure, smart guy. Might as well relax. We're gonna be here a while.'

Pike and I dropped our hands. I guess Frank had raised so much hell that Hollywood Division had finally rolled out.

'I'm surprised you guys are on this. She's only been missing since yesterday.'

Holstein painted me with empty cop eyes, then took a seat on the edge of Karen Garcia's desk.

'Not anymore. Karen Garcia's body was found up at Lake Hollywood about an hour ago.'

I felt my breath catch. Joe Pike might've stiffened. He might've leaned forward just a hair, but if he did I could not tell.

I said, 'Holstein? Are you *sure?*'

More voices filled the courtyard, speaking with the distinct cadence of police officers. Down below, Mrs Acuna wailed.

I sat on Karen Garcia's leather couch and stared at the picture of her in the paper crown.

'Joe?'

He did not answer.

'Joe?'

April, three months prior to the Islander Palms Motel

Karen Garcia said, 'I'm a freshman at UCLA. I study child development there, and work with the day care part-time.' She was almost a foot shorter than Pike, and he had to remind himself to step back. He had been warned that he tended to stand too close to people, and it made them uncomfortable. He stepped away. She said to one of the little boys, 'Daniel, stay with the others, please. I have to speak with this police officer.'

Daniel blurped his tongue like an airplane engine and flew back to the group. LAPD patrol officer Joe Pike had already jotted in his notebook that there were eleven children, ages three through five, in the care of Ms Garcia and her children's group co-teacher, a slim young man with round spectacles and curly hair named Joshua. Joshua appeared nervous, but Officer Pike had learned that people often tensed when dealing with the police. It usually meant nothing.

They were surrounded by children in MacArthur Park,

south of Wilshire by the lake in LAPD's Rampart Division. The day was warm and the sky overhead almost white from the smog. Pike's navy-blue uniform soaked up the heat and made the sun seem hotter than it was. The park was filled with women pushing carriages or playing with their preschoolers on the swings and slides. Homeless men were asleep on the grass, and some younger guys who were probably harmless but out of work had drifted away when the radio car had turned into the parking lot, responding to a see-the-woman call regarding a possible child molester. The woman was Karen Garcia, who had phoned 911 with the complaint.

Pike said, 'Do you see the man now?'

'No, not now.' She pointed to the brick rest rooms at the edge of the parking lot. 'He saw us watching him and went behind the rest rooms over there before you got here. I haven't seen him since. He had a camera with a long lens, and I'm sure he was taking pictures of the children. Not just mine, but other kids, too.'

Pike took notes. If the suspect saw her go to the phone, he'd be long gone. Pike would look, but the man was gone.

'Joshua asked him what he was doing, and he walked away the first time, but he came back. That's when I called you.'

Pike glanced at Joshua, who nodded.

Pike said, 'Description?'

'Pardon me?'

'What did the man look like?'

Karen said. 'Oh. He was shorter than you. How tall are you?'

'Six-one.'

'A lot shorter. I'd say five-eight or nine, but very wide and heavy. Fat, but he didn't look fat, just fleshy, with stubby fingers.'

Pike wrote. 'Hair, eyes, clothes, distinguishing characteristics.'

33

'Blond hair, but dyed. I mean, a real do-it-yourself job.'

Joshua said, 'Long and slicked back. Like, how many human beings still use Brylcreem?' Joshua grinned when he said it, maybe trying to feel out Pike's sense of humor or maybe just trying to dispel his own nervousness. He looked disappointed when Pike did not respond.

Ms Garcia said, 'He was wearing dark slacks and a white shirt with a kind of vest, a brown pattern of some kind, and he was carrying the camera.' She waited for Joshua to chime in. 'I didn't get close enough to see anything else.'

Joshua said, 'Zit scars.'

Ms Garcia stepped closer to Pike and touched his arm. 'Are you going to find him?'

Pike closed the notebook, and stepped away from her. 'We'll radio a dispatch to other cars in the area. If we spot him, we'll question him.'

Ms Garcia wasn't happy with that. 'That's all?'

'No. We'll also beat him to death.'

Joshua stared, uncertain, but Karen Garcia laughed, showing even white teeth and a strong laugh which Pike liked a very great deal. 'To protect and to serve.'

'Yes, ma'am.'

Karen Garcia said, 'You don't have to say ma'am, for God's sake.'

The little boy with the blurping sound raced away again, and Joshua chased him.

Pike said, 'We'll do what we can, but if you see him again, call right away.' Pike handed her a card. 'Tell them you spoke to car two-adam-six.'

Ms Garcia looked up at him with the dark brown eyes, as if she was trying to see through his sunglasses. Calm eyes that Pike also liked. 'I thought I was speaking to a man, not a car.'

Pike said, 'Two-adam-six. You have a good day, ma'am.'

Pike went back to two-adam-six, where his partner sat

behind the wheel, idling with the air conditioning on. Pike slipped into the shotgun side, putting his nightstick in its holder. Woz didn't look at him, smoking a cigarillo as he watched a group of Honduran girls in halter tops. Gang bait. Pike said, 'Suspected pedophile with a camera. Got a description.'

His partner shrugged. 'So fuckin' what.'

'We're on it.'

'Maybe you.' Hard, with an edge to it.

'You going to retire?'

Wozniak's jaw clenched. He shook his head once.

'Then we're going to work this.'

Wozniak glared at Pike another moment, then sighed and seemed to relax. Accepting it. 'The guy a weenie wagger?'

'Shutterbug.'

Pike recited the description and related what Ms Garcia had said. Halfway through, Wozniak waved him quiet. 'Yeah, yeah, I know the guy. Lennie DeVille. Another fuckin' perv, be better off with a bullet in his head.'

'Got a last-known?'

Wozniak was staring out the window again, watching the paddleboats on the lake. 'Creep like this moves around, livin' in motels and weeklies and jumping the rent when he can.' Wozniak drew deep on the cigarillo, then rolled down his window far enough to drop it outside. 'I'll ask around.' Wozniak looked past Pike, and scowled. 'Now fuckin' what?'

Pike turned, and saw Ms Garcia walking toward them.

Karen Garcia watched the officer walk back to his car, unable to take her eyes off the way his ass worked beneath the tight uniform pants, and the way the heavy John Brown belt rode his trim waist. His arms were tanned and muscular without being bulky, his hair short and thick, his face lean and handsome.

35

Joshua said, 'Better reel in your tongue before you trip.'

She felt herself flush. 'Is it that obvious?'

'Mm-hm. Maria, let me help with that, honey.' Joshua bent to tend to one of the children whose shoe had come untied. It was almost time for the van from the day care, so they needed to start back across the park.

Karen couldn't help but look back at the young officer. She liked the way he carried himself, and her stomach did a little flip when he'd stood next to her. She had called the police with serious concerns, but when he arrived it had been tough to keep her mind on what she wanted to say. He was older, but he couldn't have been any more than in his late twenties. She wondered if he thought she was a child. She'd said she was in college, hadn't she? The thoughts swirled in her head, and she smiled even wider.

Joshua rolled his eyes. 'Karen, please, not in front of the children!'

She laughed and shoved Joshua.

Watching Officer Pike slide into his car, she was suddenly overwhelmed with a fierce urge to see what was behind his dark glasses. She had tried to see his eyes and could not, but now she had to have a look.

Karen's pulse hammered all the harder as she fought the urge to do something she had never done before. In a moment the two officers would drive away and she would never see him again. The next thing she knew, she was walking hard toward their car, taking long crazy steps as if some secret creature had taken possession of her. The two officers within were watching her approach. Pike's window came down and he looked out at her. 'Yes, ma'am?'

Karen Garcia leaned forward with her hands on the window. 'I have a request.'

He stared at her, and her mouth went dry. She absolutely knew that she was making a fool of herself.

'Would you take off your glasses, please? I'd like to see your eyes.'

The older officer made a face like he wanted to spit; irritated, as if she had interrupted something. 'Oh, for Christ's sake.'

Officer Pike took off his dark glasses, and looked at her.

She felt her breath catch. His eyes were the most liquid blue, the blue of the sky over the high deserts of Sonora, the blue of the ocean where it has no bottom and is infinitely clean. But it wasn't the blue that stopped her breath. For just a moment when the glasses were first pulled away, she could have sworn that those eyes were filled with the most terrible and long-endured pain. Then the pain was gone and there was only the blue.

Karen Garcia said, 'Would you like to go to a movie with me this Friday night?'

Pike stared at her for so many heartbeats that she wondered if she'd really spoken the words aloud. But then, slowly, he fitted the dark glasses over the incredible eyes again and put out his hand for her to take. 'My name is Joe. May I have your phone number?'

When he touched her, she quivered.

CHAPTER 4

Pretty soon the entire apartment building knew, and word spread through the block. I wanted to ask Pike how he felt, but not in front of these other men.

'How did she die, Holstein?'

'I don't know.'

'Was she murdered?'

'I don't know, Cole. I get a call out telling me to come here and secure the vic's apartment until the leads show up. That's what I'm doing.'

'You must know something. You got a fast ID.'

'Whoever found the body pulled an ID off her before they called it in. Looks like she's been there since yesterday.'

Pike said, 'Has her father been notified?'

Holstein glanced at Pike's shoulder tats, then his face. 'Sonofabitch. You're Joe Pike.'

When Pike left the job it hadn't gone well. A lot of cops didn't like him. More than a few hated him.

'Has her father been notified?' Voice softer now.

I went over, stepping in front of Joe. 'Her father hired us to find her, and now that's done. We should let him know.'

Holstein went to the couch and dropped his weight on it. The leather sighed. 'We're gonna wait here for the leads. They're going to want to know what you know.'

Pike touched my shoulder. 'They can ask us later. Let's go.'

Holstein reached under his jacket. 'I don't think so.'

'What're you going to do, Holstein? Shoot it out? C'mon, does Lou Poitras have the table today?'

'Yeah.' Lou Poitras has been one of my closest friends for years, and had recently moved from North Hollywood Division to the Hollywood Homicide table.

'Then call him. Poitras and I are tight. The leads can catch up to us at the father's. They're going to want to see him anyway.'

We were still arguing about it when the phone rang. Holstein answered, trying to make his voice anonymous. He listened, then held the phone toward me, looking impressed. 'For you, hotshot. I don't know how you rate, but it's the watch commander.'

I took the phone and identified myself. A man whose voice I didn't recognize said, 'Hold on.'

Another man, this one with a slight Spanish accent, came on. He identified himself as Frank's lawyer, Abbot Montoya. 'Mr Cole, I'm here with the Hollywood Division watch commander at Mr Garcia's request, along with a representative of City Councilman Maldenado's office. You're aware that Mr Garcia and Councilman Maldenado are personally close, aren't you?'

'No.' He wasn't saying it for me. He was saying it for the people in the room with him at Hollywood Division.

'Frank would like you and Mr Pike to visit the murder site. He wants you to witness his daughter's situation.' Situation. There's a word for you. 'After, Frank would like you to go to his home and describe Karen's . . . this is awkward for me, too, Mr Cole. I'm Karen's godfather.'

'I understand.'

'He would like you to tell him whatever you've found out about what happened. I know you're not being compensated, but we'll take care of that.'

'There's nothing to take care of.'

'Yes, well, we'll discuss that later. You and Mr Pike will do this?'

'Yes, sir. If the police let us.'

'They'll let you. And after, you'll see Mr Garcia?'

'Yes.'

'The watch commander would like to speak with Detective Holstein now, please.'

Holstein listened for another minute, then said, 'Yes, sir,' and hung up. When he put down the phone, his eyes were thoughtful.

Without a word he went to the door, held it open, and said, 'She's on the west side of the reservoir. They're sealing the lake, but Lieutenant Poitras will be expecting you.'

We left, and Holstein slammed the door.

It was early afternoon by the time we once more wound our way up Lake Hollywood Drive. Uniformed officers were still clearing the park. We passed runners and walkers on their way out, but pretty soon we came to half a dozen radio cars parked in the middle of the road with four unmarked sedans. An Asian-American man was fishing a large tackle box out of the rear of a white station wagon with L.A. COUNTY MEDICAL EXAMINER stenciled on the side. He would be the coroner investigator. As he went through the gate and down along the trail to the water, a cop who looked like a miniature King Kong came up to stand just off the road, waiting for us with his arms crossed. He was so big from a lifetime of pumping weights that his jacket fit him like a sausage skin about to split.

I said, 'Hey, Lou.'

Lou Poitras put out his hand and we shook. He didn't offer to shake with Pike. 'Understand you were trying to find her.'

'That's right. You got a suspect yet?'

'Take it easy. I've been here less than an hour.' Poitras glanced at Pike. 'I hear you knew the girl. I'm sorry.'

Pike nodded.

'You sure you want to go down there, Pike? You could stay up here at the car.'

Pike walked past him and through the gate.

Poitras grunted. 'Same old talkative Pike.'

We followed a narrow, winding trail through the trees. The leaf canopy above us rustled from the wind, but down on the floor the air was still. Ash from the fires to the north filtered through the canopy, floating in the still air. Poitras swatted at it as if the ash was insects he could drive away.

I said, 'What about the cause of death?'

'Coroner investigator just went down.'

'We saw him. What's your take?'

Poitras tipped his head toward Pike, clearly uncomfortable, and slowed his pace to let Pike pull ahead. 'Unofficial, it's one shot to the head. Looks like a .22, but it could've been a .25. She was popped up here on the trail, then fell down into a little ravine. No sign of assault or a sexual attack, but that's just my eyeball. They'll have to take smears back at the coroner's.' Smears. Looking for semen.

'Any wits?'

'I've got people making a house-to-house up along the ridge trying to get names, but you know how it is.'

The trail ran along a ledge about fifteen feet up from the water, sometimes in dense trees, sometimes not. When we reached a barrier of yellow crime scene tape, we followed a freshly broken path down to the lake, then traced the shoreline around a small finger. That's where we found the crime scene.

'The vic is right over here.'

Pike took two steps up the slope and stopped.

Karen Garcia lay head down at the bottom of a narrow ravine, wild purple sage obscuring her body. Her right arm was twisted behind her, her left extended straight from her torso. Her left leg was bent at the knee, left foot under her right leg. What I could see of her face was discolored with lividity, and the ugly smell of decay gases hung at the waterline like a pall. Giant black bottle flies and yellow jackets swarmed around the body. The CI swatted at them with his clipboard, as a Hispanic detective said, 'Fuckin' meat eaters.'

If Pike felt anything I could not tell.

The CI, now wearing latex gloves, leaned over her to look at something that the Hispanic detective was pointing out. Her exposed hand had already been taped into a plastic bag to preserve evidence that might be under her fingernails. They would check later when she was at the morgue.

'Who discovered the body?'

'Couple of hikers. They found her down here, and called it in on a cell phone. You guys know Kurt Asana?'

The CI made a little wave. Asana.

Pike said, 'How'd you get an ID so fast?'

'Doofs who found her. She had her driver's license in her shorts.' Officers arriving on the scene wouldn't touch the body. No one was allowed to touch the victim before the coroner investigator had his shot. That way, when a suspect was brought to trial, the defense attorney couldn't argue that ham-handed cops had contaminated the evidence. If the hikers hadn't done their search, the police would still be wondering who she was until Asana emptied her pockets.

Poitras said, 'Hey, Kurt. Can you give me a ballpark on the time?'

Asana tried to bend her shoulder joint, and found it stiff, but yielding. 'Rigor's starting to let go. I'd say about twenty-four hours.'

'She came up here to run between nine-thirty and ten in the morning.'

'Well, I'm just guessing right now, but that fits. When I get the BT, I'll be able to calc it out pretty close.'

Asana took a scalpel and a long metal thermometer from the box and moved back into the weeds. Pike and I both turned away. Asana would be going for a liver temperature. When he had the liver temp he would chart it against the outside air temperature and be able to tell how long the body had been cooling.

We were waiting for Asana to finish when three men in good-looking suits came around the finger like they owned the lake. Lou Poitras stepped forward to block the trail. 'Can I help you?'

Behind me, Joe Pike said, 'Krantz.'

The one called Krantz held up a gold detective's shield about two inches from Poitras's nose. He was a tall, leathery man with a high forehead and lantern jaw. He looked like the kind of guy who liked to jut the jaw at people to show them he meant business. He jutted it now.

'Harvey Krantz, Robbery-Homicide. Detective Stan Watts. Detective Jerome Williams.' Watts was an older white guy with beefy shoulders and a round head. Williams was black, and younger. 'Are you Lieutenant Poitras?'

'That's right.'

'Hollywood Division is off this case as of now. RHD is taking over.' Robbery-Homicide Division is LAPD's elite homicide division. Based out of Parker Center downtown, they could and did handle high-profile homicides all over the city.

Poitras didn't move. 'You're kidding.'

This was probably the biggest case Poitras had on his table, and he wouldn't like giving it up.

'Pull your men off, Lieutenant. We have the scene.' Krantz tucked his badge away and jutted his jaw some more. I made him for his mid-forties, but he could've been older.

'Just like that?'

'Like that.'

Poitras opened his mouth as if he wanted to say something, then took a single step back and turned toward the crime scene. His face was as flat as an empty plate. 'Two Gun. Chick. We're off.'

The Hispanic detective with Asana looked over. 'Say what?'

'We're off. Robbery-Homicide has the scene.'

The Hispanic detective and another detective who'd been poking around in the weeds stepped away as Watts and Williams went over. Neither of the RHD guys seemed to mind the flies.

Krantz was moving past Poitras to join them when his eyes widened, and he said, 'Joe Pike.'

Pike said, 'When did they start hiring chickenshits like you on Robbery-Homicide, Krantz?'

Krantz's face went bright red. He glared at Poitras and shouted so loud that Asana looked over. 'Do you know who this man is? Why is he at this scene?'

Poitras looked bored. 'I know who he is. The other guy is Elvis Cole. They're working for the vic's father.'

'I don't give a rat's ass if they're working for Jesus Christ! They don't belong here, and your ass is gonna be in a sling for opening this crime scene to unauthorized personnel!'

A faint smile flickered on Poitras's lips. Poitras and Krantz were about the same height, but while Krantz was bony, Poitras weighed two hundred sixty pounds. I had once seen Lou Poitras lift the front end of a '68 Volkswagen Beetle and turn the car all the way around. He spoke quietly. 'The watch commander ordered me to give them full access, Krantz. That's what I've done. The vic's father has juice with the City Council, and Pike here personally knew the vic.'

Krantz wasn't listening. He stepped past Poitras and stormed up to Joe. Maybe he had a death wish.

'I can't believe that *you* have the balls to come to a crime scene, Pike. I can't believe you have the gall.'

Joe said, 'Step back.' The voice soft again.

Krantz stepped right up into Pike's face then. Right on the edge of the cliff. 'Or what, you sonofabitch? You going to shoot me, too?'

44

Poitras pushed Krantz back and stepped between them. 'What's with you, Krantz? Get a grip on yourself.'

Krantz's mouth split into a reptilian smile, and I wondered what was playing out here. He said, 'I want this man questioned, Lieutenant. If Pike here knows the vic, maybe he knows how she got like this.'

Pike said, 'It won't happen, Pants.'

Krantz's face went deep red, and an ugly web of veins pulsed in his forehead.

I moved close to Pike. 'Is there something happening here that I should know about?'

Pike shrugged. 'Nothing much. I'm about to put Krantz down.'

Krantz's face got darker. 'You're going in, Pike. We'll talk to you at the Division.'

Behind us, Poitras's Handie-Talkie made a popping sound. Poitras mumbled things that we couldn't hear, then held it toward Krantz. 'It's Assistant Chief Mills.'

Krantz snatched the radio. 'This is Harvey Krantz.'

Poitras led us back toward the trail without waiting. 'Forget Krantz. The only place you guys are going is back to Mr Garcia's. The A-chief is down there now, and the old man is asking for you.'

Pike and I followed the trail back up the slope and through the trees. When we were away from the cops, and there was only the sound of the leaves crunching beneath our feet, I said, 'I'm sorry about Karen, Joe.'

Pike nodded.

'You going to tell me what all that was about?'

'No.'

The drive back to Hancock Park took forever.

CHAPTER 5

An LAPD radio car was parked outside Frank Garcia's home, along with two anonymous detective sedans, a black Town Car, and three other vehicles. The older Latina opened the door again, but before we entered, a Hispanic man about Frank's age stepped past her, and offered a firm hand. Ancient pockmarks and steel-gray hair gave him a hard appearance, but his voice was gentle. 'Mr Cole, Mr Pike, I'm Abbot Montoya. Thank you for coming.'

Joe said, 'How's Frank?'

'Not well. His doctor's on the way.'

Somewhere behind him, Frank Garcia shouted, 'You cocksuckers as good as killed my little girl and I want you out of my house!'

He wasn't shouting at us.

We followed Montoya into a huge, arched living room that I hadn't seen before. Two command-level uniforms, a man in a suit, and an older man in a charming Nike tennis outfit were clumped together like a gospel quartet as Frank shouted at them. Frank's eyes were hollow red blurs, and every crease and line in his face seemed cut deep by something incomprehensibly sharp and painful. So much pain was in his eyes that it hurt to look at him.

City Councilman Henry Maldenado was standing as far from the cops as possible, but Frank shouted at him, too. 'I oughta throw your ass out with them, Henry, all the help I get from you! Maybe I should give my money to that bastard Ruiz next time!' Melvin Ruiz had run against Maldenado in the primary.

Montoya hurried to Frank, his voice soothing. 'Please calm yourself, Frank. We're going to handle this. Mr Cole and Mr Pike are here.'

Frank searched past Montoya with a desperate hope that was as hard to look at as his pain, as if Joe had the power to say that this horrible nightmare was not real, that these men had made a terrible mistake, and his only child had not been murdered.

'Joe?'

Joe knelt beside the chair, but I could not hear what he said.

While they spoke, Abbot Montoya led me across the room and introduced me. 'Mr Maldenado, this is Mr Cole. The gentleman with Frank is Mr Pike. We'd like them to represent Mr Garcia during the investigation.'

That surprised me. 'What do you mean, represent?'

The man in the suit ignored me. 'Letting in an outsider would be a terrible mistake, Councilman. If he were privy to our investigation, we would have no security control.'

The tennis outfit agreed. 'We're more than happy to work with families to keep them informed, Henry, but if someone like this were to interfere, it could hamper the investigation or even jeopardize the case.'

The man in the suit was Captain Greg Bishop, boss of the Robbery-Homicide Division. The tennis outfit belonged to Assistant Chief Walter Mills. I guess he'd been called off his Sunday morning tennis game, and wasn't happy about it.

I cleared my throat. 'I don't mean to be obtuse, but am I the outsider in question?'

Montoya glanced at Frank, then lowered his voice. 'Rightly or wrongly, Frank blames the police for his daughter's death. He believes they were unresponsive, and would prefer his own representatives to monitor the investigation and keep him informed. He told me that Mr Pike and yourself would do that.'

'He did?'

Montoya looked surprised. 'You wouldn't?'

Bishop and Mills were watching me now; the two uniforms sizing me up like a couple of peregrines eyeing a chicken.

I said, 'If the police are involved, Mr Montoya, I'm not sure what it is I can do for you.'

'I think that's clear.'

'No, sir, it's not. We're talking about a homicide investigation. Joe and I can't do anything that LAPD can't do more of. They have the manpower and the technology, and they're good at it.' The uniforms stood a little taller and the assistant chief looked relieved. Like he had just dodged a runaway pit bull.

Bishop said, 'Mr Montoya, I will personally stay in touch with you and Mr Garcia to keep you apprised of the investigation. I'll give you my home number. We can have a daily chat.'

Maldenado nodded, encouraging. 'That seems reasonable to me, Abbot.' As he said it, the Latina showed in Krantz, who looked neither relieved nor encouraging. He eased up behind Bishop.

Montoya touched the councilman's arm, as if neither of them understood. 'The issue isn't the department's willingness to keep Mr Garcia informed, Henry. The issue is trust.'

Behind us, Frank Garcia said, 'When my little girl went missing yesterday, I called these people, but they didn't do a goddamned thing. I knew where she was going. I told'm where to look, but no, they said they couldn't do anything. Now I'm supposed to trust these same people to find who killed her? No. That will never happen.'

Maldenado spread his hands, and there was a plea in his voice. 'Frank, if you gave them a chance.'

'They're with Karen right now, probably messin' things up like with O.J., and I'm stuck in this goddamned chair. I can't be there to watch out for her, and that means someone else has to do it for me.' He twisted around to

48

look at Joe. 'My friend Joe. His friend Mr Cole.' He twisted back to Councilman Henry Maldenado. 'That's the way it's going to be, Henry.'

Montoya said, 'We'd like Mr Cole and Mr Pike to have full access to all levels of the investigation. We wouldn't expect them to function as part of an official LAPD investigation, or to interfere, but if you allow them access, they can keep Frank informed in a way that lends comfort to a man who needs it right now. That's all we're asking.' Montoya turned back to me. 'You'd be willing to do that, wouldn't you? Just observe, and let Frank know what's going on.'

I glanced at Joe again. Joe nodded.

'Yes.'

Montoya turned back to Maldenado, and smiled like a priest explaining why you had to empty your pockets if you wanted to get to heaven. 'Frank will appreciate it, Henry. He'll remember this kindness come election time.'

Maldenado stared at the assistant chief, who stared back. They were looking at each other like a couple of mind readers, Maldenado thinking about campaign funding, and the assistant chief thinking that if he ever wanted to be chief, he'd need as many friends on the City Council as possible.

Finally, Councilman Maldenado nodded. 'That seems a reasonable position to me, Walt. I think that we can show Mr Garcia this small courtesy, don't you?'

Assistant Chief Mills offered his hand to Maldenado as if he were already being sworn in as chief. 'Councilman, we understand what Mr Garcia's going through, and we'll find a way to make this work.'

Montoya put his hand on my shoulder, and the soft voice was satisfied. 'It's settled, then. We'll work out the details and give you a call later this evening. Would that be all right?'

'That would be fine.'

Behind us, Frank said, 'Karen's still up there. I want somebody with her.'

Everyone looked at him.

Frank Garcia took my arm as he'd taken Joe's. He had a grip like pliers. 'You see that they take care of her. You go up there and watch these guys and make sure.'

Bishop looked as if someone had just suggested surgery. Krantz stared at Joe, but it was thoughtful and vague, not hard.

Montoya looked questioningly at the A-chief, who nodded, giving his permission.

I said, 'I will, sir.'

'I won't forget this.'

'I know. I'm sorry about Karen.'

Frank Garcia nodded, but I don't think he was seeing me. His eyes filled, and I think he was seeing Karen.

Krantz left before me. Pike wanted to stay with Frank, and told me that he would call later.

Montoya walked me back through the big house. 'Mr Cole, I know this isn't the kind of job that you normally take. I personally want to thank you for doing this.'

'It's a favor for a friend, Mr Montoya. Thank Joe.'

'I will, but I wanted to thank you, too. Frank and I have been friends for as long as I can remember. Brothers. Do you know White Fence?'

'Yes, sir. I know that Mr Garcia was a member when he was young.' The White Fence gang.

'As was I. We ran on Whittier Boulevard and Camulos Street. We fought the Hazard gang and the Garrity Lomas gang on Oregon Street, and we paid respect to the *veteranos*. It's a long way from the barrio to UCLA Law.'

'I imagine it is, Mr Montoya.'

'I'm telling you these things because I want you to know the depth of my loyalty to Frank, and my love for him, and Karen. If the police aren't cooperative, call me and I will take care of it.'

'Yes, sir. I'll call.'

'You are helping my brother, Mr Cole. If you need us, we will be there.'

'Sure.'

He put out his hand. We shook.

Latins.

I let myself out into the heat, and went down the drive to the street, ash from the fires still sifting down from the sky. Krantz and Stan Watts were standing by a clunky LAPD detective ride, smoking.

Krantz said, 'Where's your asshole friend?'

I kept walking. I wasn't happy about going back to the lake, and I wasn't happy about spending the rest of the day with a dead girl.

'Stop it, Krantz. It'll go someplace you won't like.'

Krantz flipped his cigarette into the street and followed me. 'See where it gets you. You'll go to Men's County and I'll own your license.'

I got into my car. Krantz stood on the street in front of me, ash collecting on his shoulders like dandruff.

'That old man might have the juice to jam you down my throat, but if you interfere with my investigation, I'll snap your license.'

'That old man just lost his daughter, you turd. Try being human.'

Krantz stared at me for about five centuries, then went back to Stan Watts.

I drove away.

I imagined that I could still hear Frank Garcia crying, even as I climbed the mountain to the lake.

CHAPTER 6

Robbery-Homicide worked at the Karen Garcia crime scene for the next six hours. Everyone appeared professional and competent, as I knew they would. Even Krantz. A young criminalist named Chen, consulting with the detectives, photographed the area around her body in minute detail. I knew enough about homicide investigations to know that they would map the area for physical evidence, then map her life for suspects to fit that evidence. Every investigation is the same that way because most homicide victims are murdered by people they know.

I tried making conversation with the detectives, but no one answered me. I swatted at the bottle flies, all too aware of where they had been. I didn't want to be there, didn't like it, and would rather have been wrestling Lucy Chenier's couch. When the shadows down in the crook of the mountains made it hard to see, Krantz finally released the body.

The medical examiner's people zipped Karen Garcia into a blue plastic body bag, strapped the bag onto a stretcher, then worked their way up the slope. When the body was gone, Krantz called out to me. 'That's all you're here for. Beat it.'

He turned away without another word. An asshole to the end.

I watched them load the body into the coroner's van, then drove down to the little strip mall at the bottom of Lake Hollywood, where I phoned Lucy.

She said, 'I moved the couch without you.' First thing out of her mouth.

'The woman we were looking for was found murdered. Her father wanted me to be there while the crime scene people did their jobs. That's where I've been. She was thirty-two years old, and going to school so that she could work with children. Somebody shot her in the head while she was jogging at Lake Hollywood.' Lucy didn't say anything, and neither did I until I realized I had dumped it out on her. Then I said, 'Sorry.'

'Would you like to be with us tonight?'

'Yeah. Yeah, I'd like that very much. Would you guys come for dinner?'

'Tell me what to bring.'

'I'll shop. Shopping is good for the soul.'

At the Lucky Market, I bought shrimp, celery, green onions, and bell peppers. I also bought one bottle of Bombay Sapphire gin, two limes, and a case of Falstaff beer. I drank a can of the Falstaff while I was waiting in line, and got disapproving looks from the other shoppers. I pretended not to notice. They probably hadn't spent the day with a young woman with a hole in her head.

The cashier said, 'Are we having a nice day, sir?'

'Couldn't be better.' I tried not to blow beer in her face.

Twenty minutes later I pulled into the carport of the little A-frame house I have perched on the side of a mountain just off Woodrow Wilson Drive in Laurel Canyon. A fine layer of ash had blown into the carport, showing a single set of cat prints going from the side of the house to the cat hatch built into my door. People in Minnesota see things like this with snow.

The cat was waiting by his water bowl. It was empty. I put the groceries on the counter, filled the cat's bowl, then sat on the floor and listened to him drink. He's large and black, the black shot through with gray that grows from the lacework of scars on his head and shoulders. When he first came to me, he would watch me when he drank, but now he ignored me, and when I touched him, he purred. We had become a family.

When the groceries were away, I made a drink, drank most of it, then went up to my loft and took a shower. I showered twice, letting the hot run until the water was cold, but the smell of the crime scene stayed with me, and even the rush of water wasn't as loud as the buzz of the bottle flies. I pulled on a pair of loose cotton pants and went downstairs, barefoot and shirtless.

Lucy was in the kitchen, looking over the vegetables I had left in the sink.

I said, 'Hey.'

'Hey, yourself.' She eyed my empty glass without expression. 'What are we drinking?'

'Sapphire and tonic.'

'Pour. What are we making?'

'I was hoping you'd teach me how to make shrimp étouffée.'

She smiled then, softly and to herself. 'That would be nice.'

'Where's Ben?'

'Outside on the deck. We rented a tape for him to watch while you and I cook.'

'Back in five.'

'You take your time.'

Her smile pushed the bottle flies farther away.

Ben was on the deck that juts from the back of my house, hanging over the rail to look for the blacktail deer that browse in the wild grass between the olive trees below me. Here in the middle of fourteen million people we've got deer and coyote and quail and red-tailed hawks. Once, I even saw a bobcat on my deck.

I went out, leaned over the rail beside him, and looked down the slope. I saw only shadows.

'Mom said the woman you were trying to find was murdered.'

'That's right.'

'I'm sorry.'

His face was concerned and sorrowful. Nine years old.

'Me, too, buddy.' Then I smiled at him, because nine-year-olds shouldn't have such sorrow. 'Hey, when are you heading off to tennis camp?' Lucy and Ben were serious tennis players.

Ben leaned farther over the rail. 'Couple of days.'

'You don't look happy about it.'

'They make you ride horses. It's gonna smell like poop.'

Life is tough when the world smells like poop.

Inside, I got him set up with the VCR, then went back into the kitchen with Lucy. 'He says tennis camp is going to smell like poop.'

'Yes,' she said. 'It will. But it gives him the chance to meet three boys who go to his new school.'

'Is there anything you haven't thought of?'

'No. I'm a mom.'

I nodded.

'Also, it gives us two weeks alone.'

'Moms know everything.'

It took about an hour to make the étouffée. We peeled the shrimp, then wilted the vegetables in canola oil, and added tomatoes and garlic. I found peace in the small motor activity, and in telling Lucy about Frank and Joe and Karen Garcia. To cook is to heal.

Lucy said, 'Here's the important part. Pay close attention.'

'Okay.'

She pulled my face down, brushed her lips against mine, then let them linger.

'Feel better?'

I held up my hand. She laced her fingers through mine, and I kissed them.

'Better.'

We were waiting for rice to cook when Joe Pike let himself in. I hadn't expected him, but he'll drop by like

55

that. Lucy put down her drink, and gave him a warm hug. 'I understand you knew her, Joe. I'm sorry.'

Joe seemed gigantic next to her, like some huge golem masked in shadow even in my bright kitchen.

Ben yelled, 'Hey, Joe! I've got *Men in Black*! You wanna watch?'

'Not tonight, little man.' He looked at me. 'Montoya worked out a deal with Bishop. We can report to Robbery-Homicide at Parker Center tomorrow morning. They'll assign a contact officer, and we'll be briefed.'

'All right.'

'They'll give us copies of all reports, transcripts, and witness statements.'

He was giving me the information, but I wondered why he had come. He could have phoned it over.

I said, 'What?'

'Can I talk to you about this?'

'Sure.'

Lucy and I followed Joe out onto the deck. Outside, the cat appeared, moving between Joe's legs. Joe Pike is the only other human being I've known who can touch this cat.

'How's Frank?'

'Drunk.'

Pike didn't say anything more. He picked up the cat, and stroked it. Lucy slipped her arm through mine and settled herself against me, watching him. She watches him often, and I always wonder what she's thinking when she does.

Finally, he said, 'The Garcias are my friends, not yours, but now you're going to have to carry the weight with the police.'

'You talking about Krantz?'

'Not just Krantz. You're going to have to deal with Parker Center. I can't do that.' He was talking about the entire Los Angeles police force.

'I figured that, Joe. It's not a problem.'

Lucy said, 'What do you mean, deal with Parker Center?'

Pike said, 'I won't take money from Frank, but I can't expect you not to.'

'Forget that.'

He looked at the cat, and I realized he was embarrassed. 'I don't want to forget it. I want to pay you for your time.'

'Jesus, Joe. How could you even ask that?' Now I was embarrassed, too.

Lucy said, 'Let's pretend I asked a question.'

I answered her just to change the subject. 'Parker Center is the LAPD headquarters. These cops we're dealing with, the Robbery-Homicide Division, they have their offices there. I'll have to go down tomorrow to get briefed on their investigation. It's no big deal.'

Lucy said, 'But why wouldn't they cooperate with Joe?' She wasn't making a point of it. She was just curious, but I suddenly wished she wasn't out here with us.

'Joe and LAPD don't get along. They'd freeze him out.'

Lucy smiled at me, still not understanding. 'But why on earth would they do that?'

Joe put down the cat and looked at her. 'I killed my partner.'

'Oh.'

The black lenses stayed on Lucy for a time, and then Joe left. The winds had died and the smoke hung over the canyon like a curtain, blurring the lights that glittered below us.

Lucy wet her lips, then had more of the drink. 'I shouldn't have pried.'

We went inside and had the étouffée, but nobody said very much.

Nothing stops a conversation like death.

Predation

Edward Deege, Master Carpenter, citizen of the free world and Dave Matthews fan, waited among the wild acacias that covered the ridge above Lake Hollywood until the twilight sky deepened and the bowl of the lake was dim and purple. The shadows would hide him from the police.

He had watched them work the murder site for most of the day, until the fading light had forced them to stop. Two patrol officers, one man, one woman, had been left to preserve the scene, but they seemed more interested in each other than in walking the yellow tape.

Edward had no knowledge of the murdered girl, no interest in the crime scene, and no wish to be questioned by the police. His interest was simpler: dinner. Restaurants dotted the strip malls at the foot of the mountain, where well-fed people could be depended upon to part with a dollar or two. An hour's panhandling, and Edward could purchase fresh double-A batteries for his Discman, then stroll to the food stands along Ventura Boulevard, where he might choose between a Black Angus hamburger, perhaps, or a *carne asada* burrito, or Vietnamese spring rolls. The choices were limitless.

Later, having fed, he would enjoy the climb back up to the shack he'd fashioned for himself above the lake. There, his interests would shift to partaking of a bit of the evil weed, jotting thoughts on the world eco-balance in his journal, and a satisfying bowel movement.

Now, however, Edward stayed among the trees until he was past the radio car, then worked his way down the spiderweb of roads through the neighborhoods that spilled down the mountain. He knew these neighborhoods well, walking them several times each day on his way to panhandle the traffic lights and freeway exits during the cooler parts of the day, returning to the lake at night, and when the day grew warmer.

Edward, behind his evening schedule because of the

saturation of police at the lake, was anxious not to miss the prime panhandling hour. Lost time meant lost wages. He took the fast route down, headphones in place, matching his pace to Mr Dave Matthews's frenetic, multiworld beat. Edward slipped between two houses, skidded downhill along a watercourse, and emerged behind a gutted house that was being remodeled. He had come this way a hundred times, and thought nothing of it. The house sat on a cul-de-sac, most of the houses there hidden by shrubs or walls. Eyeless houses. Edward often wondered if anyone really lived in them, or if they were movie facades that could be struck and moved at will. Such thoughts creeped out Edward, and he tried to avoid them. Life was uncertain enough, as is.

He was hurrying around a great blue Dumpster, expecting to see absolutely nothing, the same empty dark street that he'd seen a hundred times before, and was surprised when he saw the four-wheel-drive truck idling in the lightless street. He stopped, his first thought to run, but the hour was late, and his hunger gave him pause.

The truck was familiar. It took a moment for Edward to realize that this was the same vehicle he had earlier described to the two men looking for the jogging girl.

Run, or not run?

Hunger got the better of him. So did base greed.

Edward averted his face and plowed forward, hoping to slip past the truck and vanish between the houses before whoever was within could interfere. He was doing a good job of it, too, until the man with the sunglasses stepped out from behind the wheel. Here it was night, but he still wore the dark glasses.

'Edward?'

Edward quickened his pace. He did not like this man, whose muscular arms glowed blue in the moonlight.

'Edward?'

Edward walked faster, but the man was suddenly beside him, and jerked him roughly behind the Dumpster.

Edward's headphones were pulled askew, and Dave Matthews's voice became tinny and faraway.

'Are you Edward Deege?'

'No!'

Edward raised his hands, refusing to look into the bottomless black glasses. Fear burned brightly in his stomach, and blossomed through his veins.

The man's voice softened, and grew calm. 'I think you are. Edward Deege, Master Carpenter, no job too small.'

'Leave me alone!'

The man stepped closer then, and Edward knew in that crazy, insane, heat-stroked moment that he was going to die. This man glowed with hostility. This stranger was awash in rage.

One moment, on his way to earn an honest wage; the next, at the precipice of destruction.

Life was odd.

Edward stumbled back, and the man came for him.

Powered by a triple shot of adrenaline, Edward gripped the Sony Discman and swung it at the man's head as hard as he could, but the man caught his arm, twisted, and Edward felt the pain before he heard the snap.

Edward Deege, Master Carpenter, threw himself backward and tried to scream –

– but by then the man had his throat –

– and crushed it.

CHAPTER 7

John Chen on the case

The next morning, when John Chen ducked under the yellow police crime scene tape that sealed the trail leading down to Lake Hollywood, the pencil caddy in his shirt pocket fell into the weeds, scattering pens and pencils everywhere.

'Shit.'

Chen glanced back up the road at the two uniformed cops leaning against the front of their radio car, but they were looking the other way and hadn't seen him. Good. There was a guy cop and a girl cop, and the girl cop was pretty good-looking, so John Chen didn't want her to think he was a dork.

John gathered up the Paper-Mate Sharpwriter pencils that he collected like a dust magnet, then jammed the caddy back into his pocket. He thought better of it, and put the caddy into his evidence kit. He'd be bending over a lot today and the damned caddy would keep falling, making him look like a world-class geek. It didn't matter that once he was down at the crime scene no one would be around to see. He'd feel like a geek all the same, and John had a theory that he tried to live by: If you practiced being not-a-geek when you were alone, it would eventually rub off and you would become not-a-geek when you were around good-looking babes.

John Chen was the junior criminalist in the LAPD's Scientific Investigation Division, this being only the third case to which he'd been assigned without a supervisor.

Chen was not a police officer. Like everyone else in SID, he was a civilian employee, and to be just a little on the nose about it (as John was), he couldn't have passed the LAPD's physical aptitude requirements to win a blow job from the Bunny of the Month. At six feet two, one hundred twenty-seven pounds, and with an Adam's apple that bobbed around with a life of its own, John Chen was, by his own merciless description, a geek (and this did not even include the horrendously thick glasses he was doomed to wear). His plan to overcome this handicap included working harder than anyone else in SID, rapid advancement to a senior management position (with the attendant raise in salary), and the immediate acquisition of a Porsche Boxster, with which Chen was convinced he could score major poontang.

As the criminalist assigned to the case, Chen's responsibility was any and all physical evidence that would help the detectives identify and convict the perpetrator of the crime. Chen could have rushed through his inspection of the Garcia crime scene yesterday, tagging and bagging everything in sight and leaving it to the detectives to sort out, but, in the failing twilight after Karen Garcia's body had been removed, he had decided to return today and had ordered the site sealed. The detectives in charge had closed the lake, and the two uniformed officers had spent the night guarding the site. As the male uniform had a hickey on his neck that was not in evidence yesterday, Chen suspected that they had also spent the night making out, that suspicion confirming what he believed to be an undeniable fact: Everybody was getting some but him.

Chen grimly put the good fortune of others out of his thoughts and continued along the trail until he came to the little clearing where the vic had been murdered. The wind had died sometime during the night, so the trees were straight and still, and the reservoir was a great pool of glass. It was as quiet as the proverbial tomb.

John put down his evidence kit (which looked like a

large tackle box, but weighed more) and leaned over the lip of the bluff to see where the body had been. He had photographed the site yesterday before the body was moved, and had taken a sample from where the vic's blood had dripped onto a bed of olive leaves. A little metal wire with a white flag now stood at that spot. He had also tried to isolate and identify the various footprints around the body, and he believed he had done a pretty good job of separating the prints of the two men who discovered the vic (both were wearing cleat-soled hiking boots; one probably Nautica, the other probably Red Wing) and of the cops and the coroner investigator who had walked around the area like they were on a grade school field trip. The goddamned coroner investigator was supposed to be cognizant of the scene, but, in fact, didn't give a damn about anything but the stiff. Chen, however, had dutifully marked and measured each shoe print, then located it on a crime scene diagram, as he had located (and oriented) the body, the blood evidence, a Reese's Pieces wrapper and three cigarette butts (which he was certain were irrelevant), and all necessary topographical features. All the measuring and diagramming had taken a long time, and by the time he had moved up here to the clearing at the top of the draw – where the shooting occurred – he had only had time to note the scuff marks and broken vegetation where the vic had fallen. It was at this point that he had dropped a flag on the play and suggested to the detectives that he come back today. If nothing else, his coming back might score points when promotions rolled around, putting him that much closer to the 'tang-mobile.

Standing at the top of the bluff, John Chen imagined the vic at the water's edge where he had first seen her, then turned his attention to the trail. The lip of the bluff had crumbled where the vic had fallen, and, if Chen backed up a step, he could see a bright scuff at the edge of the trail. The vic had probably taken the bullet there, her left toe dragging as she collapsed, the lip giving way as she tumbled down toward the lake. He noticed something white at the edge of the trail by the scuff, and saw that it was a triangular bit of white plastic, maybe a quarter inch on a side, and soiled by what appeared to be a gray, gummy substance. It was probably nothing – most of what you found at a crime scene was nothing – but he took a marking wire from the evidence kit, marked the plastic, and noted it on his evidence diagram.

That done, he considered the trail again. He knew where the victim had been, but where was the shooter? From the wound, Chen knew that the shooter had been directly in front of her, on the trail. He squatted in the trail to try to pick out where the shooter had been standing, but couldn't. By the time the vic was discovered, by the time the police sealed the area and Chen arrived, an unknown number of walkers and runners had come by and damn near obliterated everything. Chen sighed as he stared at the trail, then shook his head in defeat. He had hoped for a shoe print, but there was nothing. So much for coming back the next day. So much for fast advancement and a poontang Porsche. His supervisor would probably raise hell about wasting overtime.

John Chen was listening to the wind and wondering what to do next when a soft voice behind him said, 'To the side.'

Chen jumped up, stumbling over his own feet as the diagram fell into the weeds.

The man said, 'We don't want extra prints on the trail.'

The man himself was standing off the trail in the weeds, and Chen wondered how he'd gotten here without Chen having heard. The man was almost as tall as Chen, but roped with lean muscle. He wore dark glasses and short military hair, and Chen was scared to death of him. For all John knew, this guy was the shooter, come back to pop another vic. He looked like a shooter. He looked like a psychopath who liked to pull the trigger, and those two damned uniforms were probably still making out, the girl

64

slurping hickies the size of Virginia all over her partner's neck.

Chen said, 'This is a police crime scene. You're not supposed to be here.'

The man said, 'Let me see.'

He held out his hand and Chen knew he meant the diagram. Chen passed it over. It didn't occur to him not to.

First thing the man said was, 'Where's the shooter?'

Chen felt himself darken. 'I can't place him. There's too much obscuration.' He sounded whiny when he said it, and that made him even more embarrassed. 'The police are up on the road. They'll be down any minute.'

The man stayed with the diagram and seemed not to hear him. Chen wondered if he should make a run for it.

The man handed back the diagram. 'Step off the trail, John.'

'How'd you know my name?'

'It's on the document form.'

'Oh.' Chen felt five years old and ashamed of himself. He was certain he would never get that Porsche. 'Do you have any business being here? Who are you?'

The man bent close to the trail, looking at it from a sharp angle. The man stared at the scuff mark for a time, then moved up the trail a few feet where he went down into a push-up position. He held himself like that without effort, and Chen thought that he must be very strong. Worse, Chen decided that this guy probably got all the poon he could handle. Chen was just beginning to think that maybe he should join a gym (this guy obviously lived in one) when the man stepped to the side of the trail, and looked in the brush and weeds.

John said, 'What are you looking for?'

The man didn't answer, just patiently turned up leaves and twigs, and lifted the ivy.

John took one step closer and the man raised a finger, the finger saying: Don't.

John froze.

The man continued looking, his search area growing, and John never moved. He stood frozen there, wondering if maybe he should shout for help, sourly thinking that those two up in the radio car were so busy huffing and puffing that they'd never hear his cries.

The man said, 'Your evidence kit.'

John picked up his evidence kit and started forward.

The man raised the finger again, then pointed out a long half-moon route off the trail. 'That way.'

John crashed through the low brush where the man told him, ripping his pants in two places and picking up a ton of little scratches that pissed him off, but when he arrived, the man said, 'Here.'

A brass .22 casing was resting under an olive leaf.

John said, 'Holy jumpin' Jesus.' He stared at the man, who seemed to be staring back, though John couldn't tell for sure because of the dark glasses. 'How'd you find this?'

'Mark it.'

The man went back to the trail, this time squatting. John jammed a wire into the ground by the casing, then hurried to join him. The man pointed. 'Look. Here to the side.'

John looked, but saw nothing. 'What?'

'Shoe.' The man pointed closer. 'Here.'

John saw little bits and pieces of many prints, but couldn't imagine what this guy was talking about. 'I don't see anything.'

The man didn't say anything for a moment.

'Lean close, John. Use the sun. Let the light catch it, and you'll see the depression. A three-quarter print.' His voice was infinitely patient, and John was thankful for that.

John rested with his belly in the brush alongside the trail, and looked for the longest time where the man pointed. He was just about to admit that he couldn't see a goddamned thing when he finally saw it: Three-quarters of a print, partially obscured by a runner's shoe print, and so shallow on the hard edge of the trail that it couldn't have been more than three grains of dust deep. It appeared to have been made by a casual dress shoe of some kind, like that worn by a cop, but maybe not.

John said, 'The shooter?'

'It's pointing in the right direction. It's where the shooter had to be.'

John glanced back toward the shell casing. 'So you figured an automatic? That's why you looked over there?' An automatic would eject to the right, and would toss a .22 casing about four feet. Then John thought of something and squinted at the man. 'But what if the guy had used a revolver? A revolver wouldn't leave anything behind.'

'Then I wouldn't have found anything.' The man cocked his head almost as if he was amused. 'All the people around, and no one heard it. Can't silence a revolver, John.'

John felt a blush creeping up his face again. 'I know that.'

The man moved along the trail, dropping into his push-up position every few feet before rising and moving on. John thought that now would be an ideal time to run for the two uniforms, but instead jammed a wire into the ground to mark the print, and followed the man to a stand of leafy scrub sumac at the edge of the little clearing just up the trail. The man circled the trees, first one way, then another, twice bending low to the ground.

'He waited here until he saw her.'

John moved closer, careful to stay behind the man, and, sure enough, there were three perfect prints in the hard dirt that appeared to match the partial by the shell casing. As before, the prints were slight, and damn near invisible even after the man pointed them out, but John was getting better at this.

67

By the time John had taken it all in, the man was moving again. John hurried to wire the site before hustling to catch up.

They came to the chain-link fence that paralleled the road, and stopped at the gate. John guessed that the paved road would be as far as they could go, but the man stared across the road as if the slope on the other side was speaking to him. The radio car was to their left at the curve, but judging by the way the two cops were wrestling around in the back seat, they wouldn't notice an atom bomb going off behind them. Sluts.

The man looked up at the ridge. Off to their left were houses; to their right, nothing. The man's gaze went to a little stand of jacaranda trees at the edge of the road to their right, and then he was crossing and John was following.

John said, 'You think he crossed there?'

The man didn't answer. Okay. He wasn't talkative. John could live with that.

The man searched the slope in front of the jacarandas and found something that made his mouth twitch.

John said, 'What? C'mon?'

The man pointed to a small fan of loose dirt that had tumbled onto the shoulder of the road. 'Hid behind the trees until people passed, then went through the gate.'

'Cool.' John Chen was liking this. Big time.

They climbed the slope, the shooter's prints now pronounced in the loose soil of the side hill. They worked their way to the ridgeline, then went over the top to a fire road. John hadn't even known that a fire road was up here.

He said, 'I'll be damned.'

The man followed the fire road about thirty yards before he stopped and stared at nothing again. John waited, biting the inside of his mouth rather than again asking what the man was looking at.

But finally he couldn't stand it and said, 'What, for chrissake?'

'Car.' The man pointed. 'Parked here.' Pointed again. 'Coolant or oil drips here. Tire tread there.'

John was already marking the spots with wire.

The man said, 'Off-road tread. Long wheelbase.'

'Off-road? Like a Jeep?'

'Like that.'

John wrote notes as fast as he could, thinking that he'd have to call his office for the things he'd need to take a tire impression.

'He parked here because he's been here before. He knew where he was going.'

'You think he knew her?'

The man looked at John Chen then, and Chen reflexively stepped back. He didn't know why.

'Looked to be about a size-ten shoe, didn't it, John?'

'Uh-huh.'

'Pretty deep on the hard pack, which makes him heavier than he should be.' Pretty deep. Three grains of dust. 'You can use the shoe size and his weight to build a body type. An impression of the shoe print will give you the brand of shoe.'

'I know.' John was annoyed. Maybe John wouldn't have found any of this evidence on his own, but he wasn't an idiot.

'Take an impression of the tires. Identify the size and brand. From that, you get a list of makes.'

'I *know.*'

The man stared down at the lake now, and John wondered what could be going on behind those dark glasses.

'You one of the detectives from downtown?'

The man didn't answer.

'Well, you gotta tell me your name and badge number for the report.'

The man angled the glasses back at him. 'If you tell them this came from me, they'll discount it.'

John Chen blinked at him. 'But . . . what do I tell them about all this?'

'I was never here, John. What does that leave?'

'*I* turned the evidence?'

'If you'll play it that way.'

'Yeah. Well, sure. You bet.' His palms were damp with excitement. He felt his heart speed.

'Get the make of the tires and the list of cars. I'm going to call you. There won't be a problem with that, will there, John?'

'No, sir.' Automatic.

The man stared at him for a time, and then said something that John Chen would recall from time to time for the rest of his life, and wonder what the man had meant, and why he had said it. 'Never turn your back on love, John.'

The man slipped downhill through the brush, gone almost before Chen knew he was leaving.

John Chen slowly broke into a huge white smile, and then he was running, crashing down through the brush, tripping, stumbling, rolling once, then coming to his feet as he ran past the radio car to his SID van as fast as he could, yelling for those horny fuckers to knock off the lip lock.

Suddenly, advancement seemed a lot closer.

Suddenly, the 'tang-mobile was already parked in his garage.

Coming out a second day had paid off after all.

CHAPTER 8

Parker Center is an eight-story white building in downtown L.A., just a few blocks from the *Los Angeles Times* and two dozen bars. The bars are small, and see most of the cop business after the shift changes; their reporter business is steady throughout the day. Letters on the side of Parker Center say POLICE DEPARTMENT – CITY OF LOS ANGELES, but the letters are small, and the sign is obscured by three skinny palm trees like maybe they're embarrassed.

The lobby guard gave me a visitor pass to clip to my lapel, phoned up to Robbery-Homicide, and four minutes later the elevator doors opened. Stan Watts peered out at me like I was eye boogers.

'Hey, Stan. How's it going?'

Watts ignored me.

'Look, no reason for us to get off on the wrong foot.'

He pushed the button for the fifth floor.

When we got up there, he led me to a large, brightly lit room, centered on a long rectangle of cubicles occupied by men with at least fifteen years behind a gold shield. Most were on phones, some were typing, and damned near everyone looked at home in the job. Krantz was talking with an overweight guy by the Mr Coffee. Williams was leaning against a desk, laughing about something. You'd never think that twelve hours ago they were swatting blowflies off a dead girl.

Krantz frowned when he saw me, and yelled, 'Dolan! Your boy is here.'

The only woman at the table was sitting by herself at

the corner desk, scribbling on a yellow legal pad. She slid the pad into her desk when Krantz called, locked the drawer, and stood. She was tall, and looked strong, the way a woman who rowed crew or worked with horses might be strong. Other women worked the room, but you could tell from how they carried themselves that they weren't detectives. She was it. Guess if I were her, I'd lock my desk, too.

Dolan glared at Krantz as if he were a walking Pap smear, and glared at me even harder.

When she came over, Krantz said, 'Dolan, this is Cole. Cole, this is Samantha Dolan. You're with her.'

Samantha Dolan was wearing a stylish gray pants suit with a cameo brooch and dark blond hair that was cut short without being mannish. I made her for her early forties, but she might've been younger. When Krantz said the name, I recognized her at once from the stories and interviews and dozens of times that I'd seen her on TV.

I said, 'Pleased to meet you, Dolan. I enjoyed your series.'

Six years ago, CBS had made a television series about her based on a case in which she'd almost been killed apprehending a serial rapist. The series had lasted half a season and wasn't very good, but for a short period of time it had made her the most famous Los Angeles police officer since Joe Wambaugh. An article about her in the *Times* had focused on her case clearance rate, which was the highest ever by a woman, and the third highest in department history. I remembered being impressed. But then it dawned on me that I hadn't heard of her since.

Samantha Dolan's frown turned into a scowl. 'You liked that TV series they made about me?'

I gave her the friendly smile. 'Yeah.'

'It sucked.'

I can always tell when they like me.

Krantz checked his watch. 'We'll brief you in the conference room so this doesn't waste anybody else's time. Think about that, Cole. Right now the murderer could be getting away because one of our detectives is thinking about you instead of following up a lead.'

'You're a pip, Krantz.'

'Yeah. Get him down there, Dolan. I'll be along in a minute.'

Dolan led me to a small conference room where Watts and Williams were waiting, along with a tall thin detective named Bruly and a Hispanic detective named Salerno. Bruly whispered something to Salerno when we walked in, and Salerno smiled. Dolan took a seat without introducing me, or saying anything to the others. Maybe she didn't like them, either.

Williams said, 'This is Elvis Cole. He represents the family. He gets to keep an eye on us in case we fuck up.'

'I've already told'm about you, Williams.' I thought I might win them over with clever repartee.

Salerno grinned. 'You catch a lot of grief with that name?'

'What, Cole?'

Salerno laughed. You see about the repartee?

Krantz steamed in with a mug of coffee and a clipboard. 'You people want to keep wasting time, or you want to knock off the bullshit?'

Salerno stopped smiling.

Krantz had some of the coffee as he read over the clipboard, then said, 'Here's what we have: Karen Garcia was murdered at approximately ten A.M. Saturday morning by an unknown assailant or assailants at the Lake Hollywood Reservoir. We have recovered and impounded her car, which was located in a parking lot on Barham Boulevard. We believe the perpetrator fired one shot from a small-bore pistol at close range. Her body was discovered by two hikers the following day. We have their initial interviews in hand. We are also questioning other people known to have been at the lake on Saturday, or who live nearby, as well as people associated with the victim. Detectives from Rampart, Hollywood, West L.A., and Wilshire divisions are assisting in this effort. We have no suspects at this time.' Krantz sounded like Jack Webb.

'Is that it?'

Krantz flexed his jaw, pissed. 'The investigation's only twenty hours old. How much do you want?'

'I wasn't criticizing.'

I took out two sheets that I had typed, and slid them across the table. Krantz didn't touch them.

'This is everything that Frank Garcia told me about his daughter's activities on that Saturday, as well as everything I learned when I was trying to find her. I thought it might help. Pike and I spoke to some kids at a Jungle Juice stand who knew Karen's pattern. Their names are here, too.'

'We've already talked to them, Cole. We're mobilized. Tell that to the vic's father.' Like he couldn't be any more annoyed.

'We found a homeless man named Edward Deege below the lake. Deege claims he saw a female runner approached by a red or brown SUV. He's flaky, but you might want to question him.'

Krantz glanced irritably at his watch, like we were wasting more time than he'd allowed. Three minutes. 'Pike told us about this stuff last night, Cole. We're on it. Now, is there anything else?'

'Yeah. I need to attend the autopsy.'

Krantz and Watts traded raised eyebrows, then Krantz smiled at me. 'You're kidding me, right? Does her father want pictures?'

'It's like me going up to the lake. He just wants someone there.'

'My God.'

Watts had never stopped looking at Krantz. He cleared his throat. 'County's got a backlog down there. They got bodies stacked up, waiting two, three weeks. We're trying to get a rush, but I don't know.'

Krantz and Watts stared at each other some more, and then Krantz shrugged. 'I don't know when the autopsy's going to happen. I don't know if you can be there. I have to find out.'

'Okay. I want to see copies of any witness statements and the criminalist's report.'

'The criminalist's report isn't in yet. He's still working the scene. So far there aren't any witness statements except for the two guys who found the body.'

'If you have transcripts, I'd like to have copies.'

Krantz crossed his arms, and tipped back in the chair. 'You want to read the stuff, you can read it, but you're not making copies and you're not taking anything out of this building.'

'I'm supposed to be copied. If you've got a problem with that, we're going to have to call the A-chief, and ask him.'

Krantz sighed. 'Then we'll have to ask him. I hear you want the reports, Cole, but we don't have any reports to show you yet. As for getting copies, I'm going to have to talk that over with Bishop. If he says fine, then okay.'

I could live with that. 'Who's keeping the book, you or Watts?'

Watts said, 'Me. Why?'

'I'd like to see it.'

'No way.'

'What's the big deal? It'll save everybody time.' The murder book was a chronological record of all the facts of the investigation. It would include notes from participating officers, witness lists, forensic evidence, everything. It would also be the easiest way for me to stay up to date with their casework.

Watts said, 'Forget it. We get to trial, we'll have to explain to a defense attorney why a civilian was screwing around with our notes. We can't find something, he'll argue that you screwed with our evidence and we're so incompetent that we didn't know any better.'

'C'mon, Watts. I'm not going to take it home. You can

75

even turn the pages, if you want. It'll be easier on everybody.'

Krantz checked his watch again and pushed up out of the chair.

'No book. We got a couple hundred people to interview, so this briefing is officially over. Here are the rules, Cole. As long as you're in this building, you're with Dolan. Anything you want, ask her. Any questions, ask her. If you gotta take a leak, she waits outside the door. You do anything without her, it violates the agreement we have with Montoya and you're history. You got it?'

'I still want to read the transcripts.'

Krantz waved at Dolan. 'Dolan will take care of that.'

Dolan glanced at Watts. 'I'm supposed to talk to the two uniforms who rolled out when her body was found.'

Krantz said, 'Salerno can talk to the uniforms. You stay with Cole. You can handle that, can't you?'

'I'd rather work the case, Harvey.' She said his name like it was another word for 'turd'.

'Your *job* is to do what I say.'

I cleared my throat. 'What about the autopsy?'

'I said I'd find out about it, and I will. Jesus Christ, we're trying to catch a killer and I've got to babysit you.'

Krantz walked out without another word. Except for Dolan, his detectives went with him. Dolan stayed in her seat, looking angry and sullen.

I said, 'Who'd you piss off to get stuck with me?'

Dolan walked away, leaving the door open for me to follow or not. Krantz didn't want me wandering around on my own, but I guess she didn't mind.

No one had touched the two typed pages with the information I'd brought, or even looked at them. I gathered them together, and caught up with her in the hall. 'It won't be so bad, Dolan. This could be the start of a beautiful friendship.'

'Don't be an asshole.'

I spread my hands and followed, trying not to be an asshole.

When Dolan and I got back to the squad room, Krantz and Watts were talking with three men who looked like Cadillac salesmen after a bad month. One of the men was older, with a snow-white crew cut and sun-scorched skin. The other two gave me eye burn, then turned away, but the Buzz Cut stared like a worm was in my nose.

Dolan said, 'Take this chair and put it over there.'

She shoved a little secretarial chair at me and pointed at the wall near her desk. Sitting against the wall, I would look like the class dunce.

'Can't I use a desk?'

'People work at their desks. You don't want to sit there, go home.'

She stalked the length of the squad room, taking hard fast strides saying that if you didn't get out of her way, she'd knock you on your ass. She stalked back with two files, and slapped them down onto the little chair. 'The guys who found the vic are named Eugene Dersh and Riley Ward. We interviewed them last night. You want to read them, sit here and read them. Don't write on the pages.'

Dolan dropped into the seat behind her desk, unlocked the drawer, and took out her yellow pad. She was putting on quite a show.

Inside the envelopes were the transcribed interviews with Dersh and Ward, each being about ten pages long. I read the opening statements, then glanced at Dolan. She was still with the pad, her face gray with anger.

'Dolan?'

Her eyes came to me, but nothing else moved.

'As long as we're going to work together, we might as well be pleasant, don't you think?'

'We're not working together. You're here like one of the roaches that live under the coffee machine. The sooner you're gone, the faster I can go back to being a cop. We clear on that?'

'Come on, Dolan. I'm a nice guy. Want to hear my Boris Badenov impression?'

'Save it for someone who cares.'

I leaned toward her and lowered my voice. 'We can make faces at Krantz.'

'You don't want to read those things, you're wasting my time.'

She went back to the pad.

'Dolan?'

She looked up.

'You ever smile?'

Back to the pad.

'Guess not.'

A female Joe Pike.

I read both interviews twice. Eugene Dersh was a self-employed graphic designer who sometimes worked for Riley Ward. Ward owned a small advertising agency in West Los Angeles, and the two had met three years ago when Ward hired Dersh as a designer. They were also good friends, hiking or jogging together three times a week, usually in Griffith Park. Dersh was a regular at Lake Hollywood, had been up there the Saturday that Karen Garcia was killed, and had convinced Ward to join him Sunday, the day they discovered her body. As Dersh told it, they were following the trail just above the lake when they decided to venture down to the shoreline. Ward didn't like it much, and found the going hard. They were just about to climb back to the trail when they found the body. Neither man had seen anyone suspicious. Both men realized that they had disturbed the crime scene when they had searched Karen Garcia for identification, and both men agreed that Ward had told Dersh not to, but that Dersh had searched her anyway. After Dersh found her driver's license, they located a jogger with a cell phone, and called the police.

I said, 'You guys ask Dersh about Saturday?'

'He went for his walk on the opposite side of the lake at a different time of the day. He didn't see anything.'

I didn't remember that in his interview, and flipped back through the pages. 'None of that's in here. Just the part about him being up on Saturday.'

I held out the transcript for her to see, but she didn't take it.

'Watts covered it after we took over from Hollywood. You finished with those yet?' She held out her hand.

'No.'

I read the Dersh interview again, thinking that if Watts questioned Dersh about Saturday, he had probably written up notes. If Watts was keeping the murder book, he had probably put his notes there.

I looked around for Watts, but Watts had left. Krantz wasn't back yet, either.

'How long can it take to find out about the autopsy?'

'Krantz is lucky to find his ass. Relax.'

'Tell me something, Dolan. Can Krantz hack it?'

She didn't look up.

'I made a few calls, Dolan. I know you're a top cop. I know Watts is good. Krantz looks more like a politician, and he's nervous. Can he hack running the investigation, or is he in over his head?'

'He's the lead, Cole. Not me.'

'Is he going to follow up on Deege? Is he smart enough to ask Dersh about Saturday?'

She didn't say anything for a moment, but then she leaned toward me over the pad and pointed her pen at me.

'Don't worry about how we work this investigation. You wanna make conversation, make it to yourself. I'm not interested. We clear on that?'

She went back to the pad without waiting for me to answer.

'Clear.'

She nodded.

A muscular young guy in a bright yellow bowling shirt

pushed a mail cart through the double doors and went to the Mr Coffee. A clip-on security badge dangled from his belt, marking him as a civilian employee. Like most police departments, LAPD used civilians whenever they could to cut costs. Most of the slots were filled by young men who hoped the experience would help them get on the job. This guy probably spent his days answering phones, delivering interoffice memos, or, if he was lucky, helping out on door-to-door searches for missing children, which was probably as close as he would ever come to being a real cop.

I glanced over at Dolan. She was staring at me.

'Okay if I get a cup of coffee?'

'Help yourself.'

'You want one?'

'No. Leave the transcripts on the chair. Stay where I can see you.' *Sieg heil!*

I strolled over to the Mr Coffee and smiled at the civilian. 'How is it?'

'The shits.'

I poured a cup anyway and tasted it. The shits.

His ID tag said that his name was Curtis Wood. Since Curtis was around all day, going from office to office and floor to floor, he probably knew which desk belonged to Stan Watts. Might even know where Watts kept the book. 'That Dolan is something, isn't she?' The professional detective goes into full-blown intelligence-gathering mode, furtively establishing rapport with the unsuspecting civilian wannabe. I was thinking I could work my way around to Watts and the murder book.

'They made a television series about her, you know?'

'Yeah, I know. I liked it.'

'I wouldn't mention it. She gets kinda weird if you bring it up.'

I gave Curtis one of my friendliest smiles and put out my hand. 'Already made that mistake. Elvis Cole.'

'Curtis Wood.' His grip said he spent a lot of time in the

gym, probably trying to get in shape for the physical. He glanced at my pass.

'I'm helping Dolan and Stan Watts with the Garcia investigation. You know Watts?' The trained professional smoothly introduces Watts to the conversation.

Curtis nodded. 'Are you the guy who works for the family?'

These guys hear everything. 'That's right.' Note the relaxed technique. Note how the subject has proven receptive to the ploy.

Curtis finished his coffee and squared around to look me in the eye. 'Robbery-Homicide has the smartest detectives in the business. How's some dickhead like you come off thinking you can do better?'

He pushed the cart away without waiting for an answer.

So much for furtive intelligence gathering.

I was still standing there when Krantz steamed through the double doors, saw me, and marched over. 'What are you doing?'

'Waiting for you, Krantz. It's been an hour.'

He glowered at Dolan, who was leaning back in her chair. 'You letting him just walk around like this?'

'For Christ's sake, Harvey, I'm right here. I can shoot him if I have to.'

I said, 'I had a cup of coffee.' Like it was a federal case.

Krantz calmed down and turned back to me. 'Okay, here's the deal. We're still not sure about the autopsy, but I'll let you know this afternoon.'

'I had to wait here an hour for that?'

'You don't have to be here at all. Bishop says you can have the reports, so when they come in tomorrow we'll copy you on them. That's it.'

Stan Watts appeared in the hall, the Buzz Cut with him, but not the other two guys. Stan said, 'Harve. We're ready.' The Buzz Cut was still staring at me like I owed him money and he was trying to figure a way to get it.

Krantz nodded at them. 'Okay, Cole, that's it for today. You're out of here.'

'If I can have the reports, can I take copies of Dersh's and Ward's interviews?'

Krantz looked around for Dolan. 'Run off the copies for him.'

'You want me to suck his dick, too?'

Krantz turned red. Embarrassed.

'She's something, Krantz.'

'Get him the goddamned copies, then get him out of here.' Krantz started away, then stopped and came back to me. 'By the way, Cole. I'm not surprised you're here by yourself. I knew Pike didn't have the balls to come down here.'

'You didn't look so tough up at the lake when he stood in your face.'

Krantz stepped closer. 'You guys are in on a pass. Remember that. This is still my shop, and I'm still the man. Remember that, too.'

'Why'd Pike call you Pants?'

When I said it, Krantz flushed hard, then stalked away. I glanced over at Dolan. She was smiling, but when she saw that I was looking at her, the smile fell away. She said, 'Hang on and I'll make those copies.'

'I can make'm. Just show me where.'

'You have to enter a code. They don't want us running off union flyers or screenplays.'

Cops.

A few minutes later Dolan gave me copies of the two interviews.

'Thanks, Dolan. I guess that's it.'

'I've got to walk you out.'

'Fine.'

She brought me out to the elevators, pushed the button, and stared at the doors while we waited.

I said, 'I gotcha, didn't I?'

She looked at me.

'There at the end, with Krantz. I made you smile.'
The elevator doors opened. I got in.
'See you tomorrow, Dolan.'
She answered as the doors closed.
'Not if I see you first.'

In the Matter of Officer Joe Pike

Detective-Three Mike McConnell of the Internal Affairs Group was certain that he'd gotten a bad clam. He'd had lunch at the Police Academy's cafe some two hours ago where the special of the day was New England clam chowder, and ever since he could feel it rumbling through his intestines like the LAPD's battering ram. He'd been terrified that the Unmentionable would occur crossing the always crowded lobby here in Parker Center, where the Internal Affairs Group had their offices, or, worse still, riding up that damned elevator which had been jammed with the entire LAPD top command, not to mention most of the goddamned mayor's staff.

But so far so good, and Mike McConnell, at fifty-four years of age and two years away from a thirty-year retirement, had made it to his office for the case file, and now to the interview room, where, as senior administrative IAG officer, he could hurry that officious prick Harvey Krantz through the interview before he crapped his Jockeys.

When he walked in, Detective-Two Louise Barshop was already seated at the table, and inwardly McConnell frowned. The lead investigator on this case was that putz Harvey Krantz, whom McConnell hated, but he'd forgotten that the third IAG was a woman. He liked Louise fine, and she was a top officer, but he was having the Lord's Own rotten gas with the clam. He didn't feel comfortable farting in front of a woman. 'Hi, Louise. How's the family?'

'Fine, Mike. Yours?'

'Oh, just fine. Fine.' He tried to decide whether or not to warn her of his flatulence or just take things a step at a time and see what passed, so to speak. If he had a problem, maybe he could act like Krantz was responsible.

McConnell took his seat and had decided on the latter strategy when Krantz entered, carrying a thick stack of case files. Krantz was tall and bony, with close-set eyes and a long nose that made him look like a parrot. He had joined IAG less than a year ago after a pretty good run in West Valley burglary, and would be the junior detective present. Because it was his case, he would also handle the bulk of the questioning. Krantz made no secret that he was here to use IAG as a stepping-stone to LAPD's upper command. He had left the uniform as fast as he could (McConnell suspected the street scared him), and had sniveled his way into every stepping-stone job he could, invariably seeking out the right ass to kiss so that he could get ahead. The sniveling little prick never passed up an opportunity to let you know that he'd graduated from USC with honors, and was working on his master's. McConnell, whose personal experience with college was pulling riot duty during the late sixties, had joined the Marines right out of high school, and took great pride in how far he had risen without the benefit of a college diploma. McConnell hated Harvey Krantz, not only for his supercilious and superior manner but also because he'd found out that the little cocksucker had gone over his head two months ago and told McConnell's boss, the IAG captain-supervisor, that McConnell was mishandling three cases on which Krantz was working. The prick. McConnell had vowed on the spot that he would shaft the skinny bastard and fuck his career if it was the last thing he did. This, even though Mike McConnell only had to sweat out two more years before retiring to his beachside trailer in Mexico. Jesus, even looking at the little skeeze made McConnell's skin crawl. A human parrot.

Krantz nodded briskly. 'Hello, Louise. Mr McConnell.' Always with the 'Mr', like he was trying to underline the difference in their ages.

Louise Barshop said, 'Hi, Harvey. You ready to go?'

Krantz inspected the empty witness chair with his parrot eyes. 'Where's the subject?'

McConnell said, 'You talking about the officer we're going to question?' You see how he did? The subject, like they were in some kind of snooty laboratory!

Louise Barshop fought back a smile. 'He's in the waiting area, Harvey. Are we ready to begin?'

'I'd like to go over a few things before we start.'

McConnell leaned forward to cut him off. Something loose was shifting in his lower abdomen and he was getting a cramp. 'I'm telling you right now that I don't want to waste a lot of time with this.' He riffled through his case file. 'This kid is Wozniak's partner, right?'

Krantz looked down his parrot nose and McConnell could tell he was pissed. Good. Let him run back and bellyache to the boss. Get a rep as a whiner. 'That's right, Wozniak. I've developed this investigation myself, Mr McConnell, and I believe there's something to this.' He was investigating a uniformed patrol officer named Abel Wozniak for possible involvement in the theft and fencing of stolen goods. 'As Wozniak's partner, this guy must certainly know what Wozniak's up to, even if he himself isn't involved, and I'd like your permission to press him. Hard, if necessary.'

'Fine, fine, whatever. Just don't take too long. It's Friday afternoon, and I want to get out of here. If something presents itself, follow it, but if this guy's in the dark, I don't wanna waste time with it.'

Harvey made a little oomping sound to let them know he wasn't happy, then hurried out to the waiting room.

Louise said, 'Harvey's quite a go-getter, isn't he?'

'He's a prick. People like him is why they call us the Rat Squad.'

Louise Barshop looked away without responding. Probably exactly what she'd been thinking, but she didn't have the cushion of twenty-eight years on the job to say it. In IAG, the walls grew ears, and you had to be careful whose ass you kicked today because they'd be waiting their turn on you tomorrow.

The interviewee was a young officer named Joseph Pike. McConnell had read the officer's file that morning, and was impressed. The kid had been on the job for three years, and had graduated number four in his Academy class. Every fitness report he had received since then had rated Pike as outstanding. McConnell was experienced enough to know that this, in and of itself, was no guarantee against corruption; many a smart and courageous young man would rob you blind if you let him. But, even after twenty-eight years on the job, Mike McConnell still believed that the men and women who formed the police of his city were, almost to a person, the finest young men and women that the city had to offer. Over the years he had grown to feel that it was his duty – his obligation – to protect their reputation from those few who would besmirch the others. After reading Officer Pike's file, he was looking forward to meeting him. Like McConnell, Pike had gone through Camp Pendleton, but unlike McConnell, who had been a straight infantry Marine, Pike had graduated from the Marine's elite Force Recon training, then served in Vietnam, where he had been awarded two Bronze Stars and two Purple Hearts. McConnell smiled as he looked at the file, and thought that a smug turd like Krantz (who had managed to avoid military service) didn't deserve to be in the same room with a kid like this.

The door opened, and Krantz pointed to the chair where he wanted Pike to sit. The three IAG detectives were seated together behind a long table; the interviewee would sit opposite them in a chair well back from the table so as to increase his feelings of isolation and vulnerability. Standard IAG procedure.

First thing McConnell noticed was that this young officer was strac. His uniform spotless, the creases in his pants and shirt sharp, the black leather gear and shoes shined to a mirror finish. Pike was a tall man, as tall as Krantz, but where Krantz was thin and bony, Pike was filled out and hard, his shirt across his back and shoulders and upper arms pulled taut. McConnell said, 'Officer Pike.'

'Yes, sir.'

'I'm Detective McConnell, and this is Detective Barshop. Those glasses gotta go.'

Pike doffed his sunglasses, revealing brilliant blue eyes. Louise Barshop shifted in her seat.

Pike said, 'Do I need an attorney present?'

McConnell turned on the big Nagra tape recorder before answering. 'You can request consultation with an attorney, but if you do not answer our questions at this time, which we are hereby ordering you to do – and we ain't waitin' for some FOP mouthpiece to mosey over – you will be relieved of your duties and brought up on charges of refusing the administrative orders of a superior officer. Do you understand that?'

'Yes, sir.' Pike held McConnell's gaze, and McConnell thought that the boy looked empty. If he was scared, or nervous, he hid it well.

'Do you wish an attorney?'

'No, sir.'

Louise Barshop said, 'Has Detective Krantz explained why you're here?'

'No, ma'am.'

'We are investigating allegations that your radio car partner, Abel Wozniak, has been or is involved in a string of warehouse burglaries that have occurred this past year.'

McConnell watched for a reaction, but the boy's face was as flat as piss on a plate. 'How about that, son? How you feel, hearin' that?'

Pike stared at him for a moment, then shrugged so small it was tough to see.

Krantz barked, 'How long have you been partnered with Officer Wozniak?'

'Two years.'

'And you expect us to believe you don't know what he's doing?'

The blue eyes went to the parrot, and McConnell wondered what on earth could be behind those eyes. Pike didn't answer.

Krantz stood. He was given to pacing, which annoyed McConnell, but McConnell let him do it because it also annoyed the person they were questioning. 'Have you ever accepted graft or committed any act which you know to be in violation of the law?'

'No, sir.'

'Have you ever witnessed Officer Wozniak commit an act which you know to be in violation of the law?'

'No, sir.'

Louise Barshop said, 'Has Officer Wozniak ever mentioned committing such acts to you, or done or said anything that would lead you to conclude that he had?'

'No, ma'am.'

Krantz said, 'Do you know Carlos Reena or Jesus Uribe, also known as the Chihuahua Brothers?' Reena and Uribe were fences operating out of a junkyard near Whiteman Airport in Pacoima.

'I know who they are, but I don't know them.'

'Have you ever seen Officer Wozniak with either of these men?'

'No, sir.'

'Has Officer Wozniak ever mentioned them to you?'

'No, sir.'

Krantz fired off the questions as fast as Pike answered,

and grew increasingly irritated because Pike would pause before answering, and each pause was a little longer or shorter than the one before it, which prevented Krantz from working up a rhythm. McConnell realized that Pike was doing this on purpose, and liked him for it. He could tell that Krantz was getting irritated because he began to shift his weight from one foot to the other. McConnell didn't like fidgeters. His first wife had been a fidgeter, and he'd gotten rid of her. McConnell said, 'Officer Pike, let me at this time inform you that you are under orders not to reveal that this interview has taken place, and not to reveal to anyone what we have questioned you about. If you do, you will be brought up on charges of failing to obey a lawful administrative order, and fired. Do you understand that?'

'Yes, sir. May I ask a question?'

'Fire away.' McConnell glanced at his watch and felt a cold sweat sprout over his skin. They had been at this only eight minutes, and the pressure in his lower gut was building. He wondered if anyone else could hear the rumble going on down there.

'Do you suspect that I'm involved?'

'Not at this time.'

Krantz glared at McConnell. 'That's still to be determined, Officer.' Krantz actually stalked around the table and leaned over so the three of them could have a little huddle, Krantz whispering, 'Please let me drive the questions, Mr McConnell. I'm trying to create a certain mood with this man. I have to make him fear me.' Saying it like McConnell was just some incompetent old fuck standing in the way of Harvey Krantz driving in the game-winning run so he could be elected Chief of Police of the Lord Jesus Christ Amen!

McConnell whispered back, 'I don't think it's workin', Harvey. He don't look scared, and I wanna finish up.' McConnell was certain that if he didn't find a way to *pass some gas soon, he was gonna have a major explosion back there.*

Krantz turned back to Pike and paced the length of the table. 'You don't expect us to believe this, do you?'

The blue eyes followed Krantz, but Pike said nothing.

'We're all police officers here. We've all ridden in a car.' Krantz fingered through his stack of files. 'The smart way to play this is to cooperate. If you cooperate, we can help you.'

McConnell said, 'Son, why did you become a police officer?'

Krantz snapped an ugly scowl his way, and McConnell would've given anything to slap it off his face.

Pike said, 'I wanted to do good.'

Well, there it is, McConnell thought. He was liking this boy. Liking him just fine.

Krantz made a hissing sound to let everybody know he was pissed, then snatched a yellow legal pad from the table and started barking off names. 'Tell us whether or not you know anything about the following places of business. Baker Metalworks.'

'No, sir.'

'Chanceros Electronics.'

'No, sir.'

One by one he named fourteen different warehouses scattered around the Ramparts Division area that had been burglarized, and after every location, Pike answered, 'No, sir.'

As Krantz snapped off the names, he paced in an ever-tightening circle around Pike, and McConnell would've sworn that Pike was following Krantz with his ears, not even bothering to use his eyes. McConnell reached under the table and rubbed his belly. Christ.

'Thomas Brothers Auto Parts.'

'No, sir.'

'Wordley Aircraft Supply.'

'No, sir.'

Krantz slapped the tablet in frustration. 'Are you telling us you don't know about any of this?'

'Yes, sir.'

Krantz, red-faced and eyes bulging, leaned over Pike and shouted, 'You're lying! You're in on it with him, and you're going to jail!'

McConnell said, 'I think we've walked far enough down this road, Harvey. Officer Pike seems to be telling the truth.'

Harvey Krantz said, 'Bullshit, Mike! This sonofabitch knows something!' When he said it, Krantz jabbed Pike on the shoulder with his right index finger, and the rest happened almost too fast for McConnell to see.

McConnell would later say that, for a guy who looked so calm that he might've been falling asleep, Pike came out of the chair as fast as a striking snake. His left hand twisted Krantz's hand to the side, his right clutched Krantz's throat. Pike lifted Krantz up and backward, pinning him against the wall a good six inches off the floor. Harvey Krantz made a gurgling sound and his eyes bulged. Louise Barshop jumped backward, scrambling for her purse. McConnell jumped too, shouting, 'Step back! Officer, let go and step back!'

Pike didn't let go. Pike held Harvey Krantz against the wall, Krantz's face turning purple, his eyes staring at Pike the way deer will stare at oncoming headlights.

Louise Barshop shouted, 'Leave go, Pike. Leave go now!' She had her purse, and McConnell thought she was about to pull her Beretta and cut loose.

McConnell felt his stomach clench when Pike, who hadn't let go, whispered something to Krantz that no one else could hear. For years afterward, and well into his retirement, Detective-Three Mike McConnell wondered what Pike had said, because, in that moment, in that lull amid the shouting and the falling chairs, they heard the drip-drip-drip sound and everybody looked down to see the urine running from Krantz's pants. Then the most *awful smell enveloped them, and Louise Barshop said, 'Oh, God.'*

Harvey Krantz had shit his pants.

McConnell said, as sternly as he could muster, 'Put him down, now, son.'

Pike did, and Harvey hunched over, his eyes filling with rage and shame as the mess spread down his pants. He lurched knock-kneed out of the room.

Pike returned to his seat as if nothing had happened.

Louise Barshop looked embarrassed and said, 'Well, I don't know.'

Mike McConnell retook his seat, considered the young officer who had just committed a dismissible offense, then said, 'He shouldn't have laid hands on you, son. That's against the rules.'

'Yes, sir.'

'That's all. We'll contact you if we need to see you again.'

Pike stood without a word and left.

Louise said, 'Well, we can't just let him leave like that. He assaulted Harvey.'

'Think about it, Louise. If we file an action, Harvey will have to state for the record that he shit his pants. Do you think he'd want to do that?' McConnell turned off the Nagra. They'd have to erase that part of the tape to protect the boy.

Louise glanced away. 'Well, no. I guess not. But we'd better ask him when he returns.'

'That's right. We'll ask him.'

Harvey Krantz would choose to let the matter drop, but Mike McConnell wouldn't. As he and Louise waited awkwardly for Krantz's return, it occurred to McConnell just how he could fuck the arrogant, supercilious little prick for going over his head the way he had. In less than six hours, McConnell would be playing cards with Detective Lieutenant Oscar Munoz and Assistant Chief Paul Winnaeker, and everyone knew that Winnaeker was the biggest loudmouth in Parker Center. McConnell was already planning how he would let the story slip, and he was already enjoying how the word of Harvey's 'accident' would spread through the department like, well, like shit through a goose. In the macho world of the Los Angeles Police Department, the only thing hated worse than a fink was a coward. McConnell had already chosen the name he would dub the little prick: Shits-his-pants Krantz. Wait'll Paul Winnaeker got hold of that!

Then McConnell felt his own guts knot and he knew that the goddamned clam had finally gotten the best of him. He rocked to his feet, told Louise he was going to check on Harvey, then hurried to the men's room with his cheeks crimped together tighter than a virgin's in a whorehouse, barely making it into the first available stall before that goddamned clam and all of its mischief came out in a roar.

As the first wave passed, he heard Harvey Krantz in the next stall, sobbing with shame. 'It's okay, boy. We'll keep the lid on. I don't think this will hurt your career too badly.'

The sobbing grew louder, and Mike McConnell smiled.

CHAPTER 9

I spent the afternoon at my office, waiting for Krantz to call about the autopsy, then went home and waited some more. He still hadn't called by the time I went to bed, and I was getting irritated about it. At nine-forty the next morning, I still hadn't heard anything, so I called Parker Center and asked for Krantz.

Stan Watts said, 'He's not available.'

'What does that mean, Watts? He said he would call.'

'You want to know every time we wipe our asses?'

'I want to know about the autopsy. It's going on three days since she was murdered, and I'm supposed to be there. Did you get it moved up or not?' Giving back some of the irritation.

'Hang on.'

He put me on hold. LAPD had installed one of those music-while-you-wait systems. It played the theme from *Dragnet*.

I was on hold for almost ten minutes before Watts came back. 'They're making the cut this afternoon. Come on over, and I'll have someone bring you down.'

'Good thing I asked about it.'

At ten forty-five, I once more parked in the sun at Parker Center, presented myself to the lobby guard, and claimed a visitor's pass. This time when the guard phoned RHD, they let me ride up on my own. Maybe they were starting to trust me.

Stan Watts was waiting when the doors opened.

'You my guide today, Stan?'

94

Watts made a snort. 'Sure. You're all I got to do with my time.'

The RHD squad room was quieter than yesterday. The only face I recognized was Dolan's. She was talking on the phone at her desk with her arms crossed, and she was staring at me, almost as if she had been waiting for me to come through the doors.

I stopped, and Watts stopped with me. 'Dolan again?'

'Dolan.'

'I don't think she likes me.'

'She doesn't like anyone. Don't take it personally.'

Watts brought me over. 'I'll leave you two lovebirds alone.'

Dolan cupped her receiver. 'C'mon, Stan. How about I follow up on these calls I got? Can't someone else take him?'

Watts was already walking away. 'Krantz says you.'

Her mouth pruned and she cupped the receiver. 'Fuckin' Pants.'

Watts laughed, but he didn't turn around.

I said, 'Hi, Dolan. Long time no see.'

She pointed at the little secretarial chair, but I didn't sit.

Dolan thanked whoever she was talking to for their cooperation, asked them to call her if they remembered anything else, then hung up. She hung up hard.

I said, 'Looks like today's going to be another good day, doesn't it?'

'Speak for yourself.'

The drive from Parker Center to the L.A. County coroner's office takes about fifteen minutes, but the way Dolan launched out of the parking garage I thought we might make it in five, even in the busted-out detective ride she drew out of the motor pool. Dolan turned off the unit's mobile two-way with an angry snap as soon as she was behind the wheel, and tuned to an alternative rock station that was blaring out L7's 'Shove'. L7 is an L.A. chick band known for their aggressive, in-your-face lyrics.

I said, 'Kind of hard to talk with the radio that loud, don't you think?'

We careened out of the parking lot, leaving a smoking rubber trail. Guess she didn't agree.

L7's singer screamed that some guy just pinched her ass. The words were angry; the music was even angrier. So was Samantha Dolan. Everything in her manner said so, and said she wanted me to know it.

I cinched the seat belt, settled back, and closed my eyes. 'Too on the nose, Dolan. The music should be counter to your character, and then the statement would be more dramatic. Try Shawn Colvin.'

Dolan jerked the sedan around a produce delivery truck and blasted through an intersection that had already gone red. Horns blew. She flipped them off.

I made a big deal out of yawning. Just another day at the demolition derby.

We roared past a crowd of short, stocky people trying to cross the street to catch a bus. We missed them by at least two inches. Room to spare.

'Dolan, throttle back before you kill someone.'

She pressed the pedal harder and we rocketed up the freeway on-ramp.

I reached over, turned off the ignition, and the car went silent.

Dolan screamed, 'Are you out of your mind?!'

She hit the brakes, wrestling the dead power steering as she horsed the car to the side of the ramp. She got the car stopped and stared at me, breathing hard.

'I'm sorry you've got to eat shit from a hack brownnoser like Krantz, but it's not my fault.'

The horns started to go behind us. Something that might've been hurt flickered in Dolan's eyes, and she took a breath.

'I guess maybe you should be the lead on this case. I guess it's hard accepting the fact that you aren't.'

'You don't know me well enough to say something like that.'

'I know Krantz is scared of you, Dolan. He's scared of anyone who threatens him, so you get stuck doing the work that no one else wants to do. Like babysitting me, and running off copies, and having to sit in the back seat. I know you don't like it, and you shouldn't have to, because you're better than that.' I shrugged. 'Also, you're the woman.'

She stared at me, but now she wasn't glaring. She had lovely hands with long slender fingers, and no wedding band. She wore a Piaget watch, and the nails were so well done that I doubted she'd done them herself. I guess the television series had been good for her even if it sucked.

Dolan wet her lips, and shook her head. Like she was wondering how I could possibly know these things.

I spread my hands. 'The finest in professional detection, Dolan. I see all, I hear all.'

She gazed out the window, then nodded.

'You want to get along, we can get along.'

Grudging. Not confirming anything I'd said. Not even putting it on Krantz. She was some tough cookie, all right.

Dolan started the car, and ten minutes later we pulled down into the long curving drive that led to the rear parking lot of the L.A. County medical examiner's office behind County-USC Medical Center.

Dolan said, 'You been here before?'

'Twice.'

'I've been here two hundred times. Don't try to be tough. If you think you're going to barf, walk out and get some air.'

'Sure.'

The rear entrance opened to a yellow tile hall where the smell hit us like a sharp spike. It wasn't terrible, like bad

97

chicken, but you knew you were smelling something here that you wouldn't smell any other place. A combination of disinfectant and meat. You knew, on some primitive level deep in the cells, that this meat was close to your own, and that you were smelling your own death.

Dolan badged an older man behind a counter, who gave us two little paper masks. Dolan said, 'We've gotta wear these. Hepatitis.'

Great.

After we put on the masks, Dolan led me along the hall through a set of double doors into a long tile cavern with eight steel tables. Each table was surrounded by lights and work trays and instruments, not unlike those you see in a dentist's office. Green-clad medical examiners were working on bodies at each table. Knowing that they were working on human beings made me try to pretend that they weren't. Denial is important.

Krantz and Williams were clustered at the last table with the Buzz Cut and his two buddies. The five of them were talking with an older, overweight woman wearing lab greenies, surgical gloves, and a Los Angeles Dodgers baseball cap. She would be the medical examiner.

Karen Garcia was on the table, and even from across the big room I could see that the autopsy was complete. The medical examiner said something to two lab techs, one of whom was washing off Karen Garcia's body with a small hose. Blood and body fluids streamed along a trough in the table and swirled down a pipe. Her body had been opened, and a blue cloth fixed to cover the top of her head. The autopsy had happened without me.

The Buzz Cut saw us first, and tipped his head. Krantz turned as we approached. 'Where the hell were you, Cole? The cut was at nine. Everybody knew that.'

'You were supposed to call me. You knew her father wanted me here.'

'I left word for you to be notified. No one called you?'

I knew he was lying. I wasn't sure why, or why he

didn't want me at the autopsy, but I was as sure of it as I've ever been sure of anything. 'What am I supposed to tell her family?'

'Tell'm we fucked up. Is that what you want to hear? I'll explain it to her father myself, if that's what you want.' He waved at the body. 'Let's get out of here. This stink is ruining my clothes.'

We went back into the tile hall, where we pulled off the masks. Williams gathered the masks from everybody and tossed them in a special can.

I stepped up to the Buzz Cut. 'We haven't met. I'm Elvis Cole, employed by the family. Who are you?'

The Buzz Cut smiled at Krantz. 'We'll wait in the car, Harvey.'

The Buzz Cut and his two friends walked away.

I turned back to Krantz. 'What's going on with you, Krantz? Who are those guys? Why didn't you want me here?'

'Our lines got crossed, Cole. That's all there is to it. Look, you wanna go back in there and inspect the body, help yourself. You wanna talk to the ME, talk to her. The girl died of a .22 just like we thought. We recovered the bullet, but it's probably too deformed to give a rifle pattern. I don't know yet.'

Williams shook his head. 'No way. There won't be a pattern. Trust me.'

Krantz shrugged. 'Okay, the expert says no way. What else you want to know? There was no sign of a struggle or of any kind of sexual assault. We lasered the body for prints and fibers, but it was a wash. Look, Cole, I know you were supposed to be here, but you weren't, and what were we supposed to do? We lose our turn, it might be another three, four days before we can work into the schedule again. You wanna go see the bodies they got stacked in the cooler?'

'I want the autopsy report.'

'Sure. You want the report, fine. Might be tomorrow or the next day.'

'I want the crime scene report, too.'

'I already said you could have that, didn't I? We'll print out a copy for you when we get the autopsy report. That way you'll have everything. I'm really sorry about this, Cole. If it's a problem for the old man, I'll tell him I'm sorry, too.'

'Everybody's sorry, that it?'

Krantz grew red in the face. 'I don't need lip from some freelance like you. All you are is a peeper. If you'd been a cop, you'd know we're busting our asses. Bruly and Salerno are knocking on every door up at the lake. No one saw anything. We've interviewed two dozen people so far, and no one knows anything. Everybody loved this girl, and no one had a motive to kill her. We're not just sitting around.'

'Did you ask Dersh about the SUV?'

'C'mon, Cole. Get off of that.'

'What about the homeless guy? Anyone question him?'

'Fuck you. I don't need you telling me how to do my job.'

Krantz and Williams walked away.

'This is bullshit, Dolan, and you know it.'

Dolan's lips parted as if to say something, then closed. She didn't seem angry now. She looked embarrassed, and I thought if they were keeping secrets, she was part of it.

We drove back to Parker Center at the same furious pace, but this time I didn't bother asking her to slow down. When she let me off in the parking garage, I walked up to my car, where it had spent the noon hour parked in the sun. It was hot, but at least nobody had slashed the interior. Even parked at the police station, that can happen, and does.

I pulled out of the lot and drove exactly one block, then pulled to the curb in front of a taco shop, and used the pay phone there to call a friend of mine at the Department of

Motor Vehicles. Five minutes later I had Eugene Dersh's home and work addresses, and his phone number. The addresses were the same.

I called him, and said, 'Mr Dersh, my name is Elvis Cole, calling from Parker Center. Be all right if I dropped by and asked you a couple of follow-up questions about Lake Hollywood? It won't take long.'

'Oh, sure. Are you working with Stan Watts?' Watts had been the one who interviewed him.

'Stan's down here at Parker Center, too. I was just talking with him.'

'You know how to get here?'

'I can find it.'

'Okay. See you soon.'

If Krantz wouldn't ask him about the SUV, I would.

Dersh lived in a small California bungalow in an old part of Los Feliz just south of Griffith Park. Most of the homes were Spanish stucco with faded tile roofs, and most of the people in the neighborhood appeared to be older, but as they died off, younger people like Dersh would buy their homes and renovate them. Dersh's house was neatly painted in bright Sante Fe earth colors, and, from the looks of the place, he had put a lot of work into it.

I left my car at the curb, went up the walk, and pressed the buzzer. Some of the yards still showed ash from the fire, but Dersh's was clean. He must've come out and swept. A welcome mat at the front door read *Welcome Aboard*.

A short, stocky guy in his late thirties opened the door and smiled out at me. 'Are you Detective Cole?'

'I'm the detective.'

He put out his hand. 'Gene Dersh.'

Dersh led me into an attractive room with bleached oak floors and brightly colored modern paintings over white walls. 'I'm having coffee. Would you like a cup? It's Kenyan.'

'No, thanks.'

The room opened into another at the back of the house. It was fixed with a large art table, jars of brushes and colored markers, and a high-end PowerMac. Classical music came from the back, and the house smelled of Marks-a-lots and coffee. His home felt comfortable. Dersh was wearing pressed chinos and a loose knit shirt that showed a lot of chest hair, some of it gone gray. Ink smudges tattooed his fingers. He'd been working.

'This won't take long, Mr Dersh. I only have a couple of questions.'

'Call me Gene. Please.'

'Thanks, Gene.' We sat on an overstuffed taupe couch.

'Don't feel you have to rush. I mean, what a horror for that poor girl, murdered like that. If there's any way I can help, I'm happy to do it.' He'd been like that in the interview with Watts, anxious to cooperate. Some people are like that; thrilled to be a part of a criminal investigation. Riley Ward had been more tentative and clearly uncomfortable. Some people are like that, too.

He said, 'You aren't the first today. When you called, I thought you were more of the TV people.'

'The TV people called you?'

He had some of the coffee, then put his mug on the table. His eyes were bright. 'A reporter from Channel 4 was here this morning. Channel 7 called, too. They want to know what it was like, finding her body.' He tried to make himself sound disapproving, but you could see that he was thrilled that newspeople with cameras and lights had come to talk with him. He would dine out on these stories for years.

'I'll check it out this evening. See if I can catch you.'

He nodded, smiling. 'I'm going to tape it.'

'You were up at the lake on Saturday as well, weren't you, Gene?'

'That's right.'

'You recall seeing a red or brown SUV up there, like a

Range Rover or a Four-Runner or one of those things? Might've been parked. Might've been coming in or going out?'

Dersh closed his eyes, thinking about it, then shook his head, looking disappointed. 'Gee, no, I don't think so. I mean, so many people drive those things.'

I described Edward Deege. 'You see a guy like that up there?'

He frowned, thinking. 'On Saturday?'

'Saturday or Sunday.'

The frown turned into a squint, but then he shook his head again. 'Sorry. I just don't remember.'

'I knew it was a long shot, Gene, but I was just wondering.'

'Did that man or the car have anything to do with what happened?'

'Don't know, Gene. You hear things, you have to follow up, you know?'

'Oh, sure. I just wish I could help you.'

'You know anyone else who might've been up there on Saturday?'

'Uh-uh.'

'Mr Ward wasn't with you on Saturday, was he?' If Ward was there, I could ask him, too.

'No. Riley came with me on Sunday. He'd never been up to the lake before. Can you believe that? Here's Riley, a native for chrissake. He lives, what, two miles from the lake, and he's never been there.'

'I know people who've never been to Disneyland.'

Dersh nodded. 'Amazing.'

I stood, and thanked him for his time.

'That's all you wanted?'

'Told you it wouldn't take long.'

'Don't forget. Channel 4.'

'I'll watch.'

Dersh brought his mug of Kenyan coffee to the door.

'Detective Cole? Are you going to be, ah, seeing the girl's family?'

'I will be. Yes.'

'Would you tell them how sorry I am? And give them my condolences?'

'Sure.'

'I thought I might drop around sometime, since I was the one who discovered her body. Me and Riley.'

'I'll tell her father.'

Dersh sipped at his coffee, frowning. 'If I remember anything else, I'll be sure to call. I want to help you. I really want to help catch the person who did this.'

'If you remember anything, give Stan Watts a call. Okay?'

'Stan, and not you?'

'It'd be better if you called Stan.'

I thanked him again, then went out to my car. I hadn't really expected that Dersh would have seen the SUV, but, like I told him, you hear something, you have to run it down. Especially when the cops won't.

I said, 'What was so hard about that, Krantz? It took fifteen minutes.' The detective, talking to himself.

I worked my way out of the foothills south to Franklin, then east toward Hollywood. Traffic was terrible, but I was feeling better about things, even though I hadn't learned much. Doing is better than watching, and now I felt like a doer, even though I wasn't supposed to be. I thought that I might phone Dolan and tell her that Krantz needn't go back to Dersh about the car. I could probably sound pretty smug when I said it, but Dolan probably wouldn't be impressed. Also, they would find out I'd gone to see Dersh sooner or later. I thought my telling them would make Krantz a little less apoplectic, but you never know. I was hoping it would make him worse.

I left Franklin trying to get away from the traffic, but the roads stayed bad. Another sinkhole had appeared in Hollywood like an acne crater brought on by the subway construction, and Cal Trans had several streets blocked. I turned down Western to pick up Hollywood Boulevard, found the traffic even worse, then cut onto one of the little side streets there, hoping to work my way around the worst of it. That's when the same dark blue sedan that I'd been seeing in my rearview since I'd left the hills turned in behind me.

At first I thought it was nothing. Other cars were turning to get away from the traffic, too, but those cars hadn't been floating behind me since Franklin.

Cars were moving a little better on Hollywood. I passed under the freeway, then turned north and pulled to the curb in front of a flower kiosk with huge signs printed in Spanish. *Rosas $2.99.*

The sedan pulled past, two men in the front, both with sunglasses and both yucking it up and doing their best to pretend that they weren't interested in me. Of course, maybe they weren't. Maybe all of this was a coincidence.

I copied their tag number, then bought a dozen red roses for Lucy. Serendipity should not be ignored.

I waited for a short Salvadoran man to finish with the pay phone outside the flower stand, then called my friend at the Department of Motor Vehicles. I asked her to run the tag, and waited some more.

She came back in a few seconds. 'You sure about this?'

'Yeah. Why?'

'It came back "No ID". You want me to run it again?'

'No, thanks. That's fine.'

I hung up, took the roses to my car, and sat there.

'No ID' is what you get when the car is registered to the Los Angeles Police Department.

CHAPTER 10

The sun was settling over the city like a deflated balloon when I got to Lucy's apartment. I had stopped for groceries after the flower stand, and then a liquor store, all the while watching my rearview. The blue sedan didn't return, and if anyone else was following me, I didn't spot them. Just the kind of paranoid experience you want before a romantic evening.

When Lucy saw the roses, she said, 'Oh, they're lovely.'

'Do you see their tears?'

She smiled, but looked confused. 'What tears?'

'They're sad. Now that they've seen you, they know they're not the prettiest things on earth.'

She touched the flowers, then sighed playfully. 'They'll just have to get used to it, I guess.'

Lucy brought a small overnight bag as we went down to my car.

'Ben get off to camp okay?'

'Once he met a couple of the other kids he was fine. I set my call-forwarding to ring at your place. I hope you don't mind.'

'Of course not. You sure you don't want to take your own car?'

'This is more romantic. My lover is spiriting me away for a night of passion at his love nest in the mountains. I can come back for my car tomorrow.'

I had never thought of my house as a love nest, but there you go.

'What's in the bag?'

She smiled at me from the corner of her eye. 'Something you'll like. A surprise.'

Maybe having a love nest wasn't so bad.

It felt good to be with her, and good to be with her alone. We had been together a lot since Lucy moved to L.A., but always with Ben or other people, and usually with the major part of our time spent in the necessary tasks of moving them into their new apartment. Tonight was just for us. I wanted that, and knowing that she wanted it, too, made it all the more special. We drove in silence, rarely speaking, though smiling at each other in that way lovers do. She held the roses in her lap, occasionally lifting one to touch her nose.

When we got to the love nest, Joe's Jeep was parked in front.

Lucy smiled at me. Prettily. 'Is Joe staying over, too?'

Ha-ha. That Lucy. What a kidder, huh?

We brought the groceries and the roses in through the kitchen. Pike was standing in my living room. Anyone else would've been sitting, but there he was, holding the cat. When the cat saw Lucy, it squirmed out of Joe's arms, ran to the stairs and growled.

Lucy said, 'How nice. Always the warm welcome.'

Joe looked at the roses, and the grocery bags. 'Sorry. I should've called.'

'It couldn't hurt.'

Lucy went over and kissed his cheek. 'Don't be silly. Just don't plan on staying too long.'

The corner of Pike's mouth twitched.

Pike said, 'Got a copy of the criminalist's report. I thought you'd want to see it.'

I stopped with the bags.

'Krantz told me it wouldn't be ready until tomorrow.'

Pike nodded toward the dining-room table.

I left the bags on the kitchen counter, then went to the table and found a copy of a Scientific Investigation Division criminalist's report signed by a guy named John

Chen. I flipped through a couple of pages, and saw that the report detailed the evidence found at Karen Garcia's murder site. I looked at Joe, then back at the report. 'Where'd you get this?'

'The man who wrote it. Got that copy this morning.'

'Something odd is going on here, Joe.'

Lucy said, 'Something odd is always going on here. It's Los Angeles.' She took a bottle of Dom Pérignon from one of the bags. Eighty-nine ninety-five, on sale. 'Very nice, Mr Cole. I think I may purr.'

I waved my hand like it was nothing. 'Standard fare at the love nest.'

Pike said, 'Love nest?'

I frowned at him. 'Try not to spoil the fantasy.'

Pike went to the fridge, took out a bottle of Abita beer, and tipped it toward me.

'Sure.'

He tipped the bottle at Lucy.

'No, sweetie, but thank you.' Joe Pike being called sweetie. Amazing.

Joe took out a second bottle, and brought it to me. Abita beer is this terrific beer they make in south Louisiana. Lucy brought five cases when she moved.

I said, 'Luce, you mind if I read this?'

'Not at all. I'll put away the food and pretend we're doing it together. I'll pretend some nice romantic music is on the stereo, and you're reading poetry to me. That way I can pretend I'm about to swoon.'

I looked at Joe. He shrugged.

The report was direct and easy to read because of its clarity. Two detailed drawings noted body position, bloodstains, and the location of physical evidence. The first drawing was the lower site, where Garcia's body had been found, the second was of the trail area at the top of the bluff, where the shooting had occurred. Chen noted that he had discovered several Beeman's gum wrappers, an as yet unidentified triangular bit of white plastic, a Federal Arms .22 caliber Long Rifle shell casing, and several partial and complete shoe prints. Tests were being run on the wrappers, the plastic, and the shell casing, but from the size of the shoe print Chen had estimated the shooter's body weight. I read this part aloud. 'Shooter wears a size eleven shoe with an estimated body weight of two hundred pounds. Photographs of the sole imprint have been forwarded to the FBI in Washington for identification of brand.'

Lucy said, 'My, that's romantic.' She came out and sat next to me, her foot touching mine beneath the table.

Chen had followed the tracks to tread marks left by a parked vehicle on a fire road above the lake. He had made castings of the tread marks, and had taken soil samples containing what appeared to be oil drips. All of this he had also sent along to the FBI for brand identification. He determined the tire type as F205 radials, matching any number of American and foreign SUVs. These particular F205s showed uneven wear on the front tires, indicating that the front-end camber was out of alignment.

I put down the report and looked at Joe. 'Tell you the truth, I thought Deege was making it up, him saying the car looked like yours and you were the driver.'

Pike shrugged.

'So he saw something, then had fun with it.' I glanced at the report again. 'Wow. This guy Chen does good work.'

Pike's mouth twitched.

'What?'

'Nothing.'

I tapped the pages. 'Krantz didn't lie to me only about this.' I told them how Krantz had given me the runaround about the autopsy. 'I'm sure Krantz knew when it was scheduled the whole time. Five people were at the table when we arrived, and Williams was grousing about how long the cut had taken.'

Lucy said, 'That isn't necessarily odd. You said he

doesn't like you. Maybe he kept you out of the autopsy just to annoy you.'

'After the autopsy I went to see Dersh. When I left Dersh, two guys in a blue sedan were on me. It was an LAPD license.'

Pike thought about it. 'You sure they didn't follow you from Parker Center?'

'Nobody knew I was going to see Dersh, so that means they were already there. Only why would they be sitting on Dersh?'

Pike nodded. 'Now we're talking odd.'

'Yeah.'

Lucy touched my arm and traced her fingers to my hand. She tangled her feet with mine and smiled.

Joe stood. 'Guess I'll be going.'

Lucy realized what had happened and took back her hand, blushing. 'I was teasing before, Joe, really. You're welcome to stay for dinner.'

Joe's mouth twitched again, then he left.

Lucy groaned and covered her face. 'God. He must think I'm a slut.'

'He thinks you're in love.'

'Oh, sure. I'm pawing at you like I'm in heat.' I had never seen Lucy that red.

'He's happy for us.'

'Mr Stoneface? How can anyone tell what he's thinking? God, I'm so embarrassed.'

We stared at each other then, not speaking. The depth and movement that glimmered in her eyes held me until I said, 'Wait.'

The Dom wasn't as cold as I wanted, but that was okay. I filled two flute glasses, and brought them out. I put Natalie Merchant on the CD player, singing 'One Fine Day', and then I opened the big glass doors. The canyon was still. The early evening air was cooling, and the smell of summer honeysuckle was sweet. I offered Lucy my hand, and she stood. I offered a glass of the champagne. She took it.

Lucy glanced at her overnight bag, still on the floor in the kitchen, and her voice came out husky. 'I want to change. I've got a surprise for you.'

I touched her lips. 'You're my surprise, Lucille.'

Her eyes closed as she rested her head on my chest.

I thought for a moment of dead girls, heartbroken old men, and things that I did not understand, but then those thoughts were gone.

Natalie sang sweetly about a love that was meant to be. We danced, slowly, our bodies together, floating on an unseen tide that carried us out to the deck, and finally up to my bed.

Forged

The boy sat in a green world. The broad, furry elm leaves that sheltered him caught the afternoon light like floating prisms, coloring him with a warm emerald glow. Hidden there, staring between the mask of leaves at the small frame house that was his, the boy felt safe. Three black ants crawled on his bare feet, but he did not feel them.

Joe Pike, age nine. Tall for his age, but thin. An only child. Wearing shorts cut off just above the knee, and a striped tee shirt long since grimed to a murky gray. Known as a thoughtful, quiet boy at school. A bright child who kept to himself and, some teachers thought, seemed moody. In the third grade now. His first-grade teacher had asked to test the boy to see if he was retarded. The teacher then was a young man fresh from an out-of-state teachers college. Joe's father had threatened to beat him to death and cursed him as a faggot. Joe didn't know what a faggot was, but the teacher had paled and left the school midway through the year.

Joe sat cross-legged beneath the young trees at the edge of the woods, low branches cutting his line like breaks in a jigsaw puzzle as he watched his father turn into the yard and felt the same rush of fear he felt every day at this time.

The blue Kingswood station wagon stopped by the front porch, gleaming as if he had just driven it off the showroom floor. Joe watched a short, powerfully built man get out of the wagon, climb the three wooden steps to the front porch, and disappear into the house.

Daddy.

Joe's father built the house himself, three years before Joe was born, on a plot of land at the edge of the small town in which they lived, only two miles from where Mr Pike worked as a shift foreman at the sawmill. Not much out here except some woods and a creek and some deer. It was a modest clapboard design of small unimaginative rooms sitting on a raised foundation. The house was painted a bright clean yellow with white trim, and, like the car, gleamed spotlessly in the bright sunlight. It looked like such a happy home. Every Wednesday afternoon, when Joe's father got home from work, he washed the house. Three times every week, he washed the Kingswood. Joe's father worked hard for his paycheck, and believed in taking care of the things that he had. You took care of things by keeping them clean.

Five minutes later, Joe's mother came out onto the porch and called him to supper. She was a tall woman with heavy hips, dark hair, and anxious eyes. She was almost as tall as her husband. She would have supper on the table at four o'clock on the dot because that's when Joe's father wanted it. He went to work early, came home after a long day of busting his ass, and wanted to eat when he wanted to eat. They ate at four. He would drink himself to sleep by seven.

Mrs Pike walked to the lip of the porch and called without direction because she did not know that her son was watching her. 'You come in now, Joseph! We'll be having supper soon.'

Joe didn't answer.

'Suppertime, Joe! You'd better get home!'

Even as she said it, Joe could feel his heart quicken as the fear spread through his arms and legs. Maybe tonight would be different and nothing would happen, but he couldn't count on that. He just never knew, and so Joe waited silently until she went back into the house. He never went when she first called. He got home from school at three, but got gone fast, and stayed out of the house until the last possible minute. In the woods was better. Safe from the fear was better.

But ten minutes later his mother reappeared, and now her face was pinched and anxious. 'Goddamnit, boy, I'm warning you! Don't you make your father wait! You get your butt in here!'

She stalked back into the house and slammed the door, and only then did Joe slip between the branches.

Joe could smell the booze in the air as soon as he opened the door, and the smell of it and what it meant made his stomach knot.

His father was sitting at the kitchen table, feet up, reading the paper, and drinking straight Old Crow whiskey on the rocks from a Jiffy peanut butter jar. The table was set for dinner, but Mr Pike had pushed the plates to the side so he could put his feet up. His father watched him come in, finished what was in the glass, then jiggled the ice in the glass to draw Joe's eye. 'Fill 'er up, sport.'

Joe's big job. Filling his father's glass with Old Crow.

Joe got the bottle from the cabinet under the kitchen sink, pulled out the cork, and poured a little bit into the glass. His father scowled. 'That ain't even a swallow, boy. Give a man a fit highball and people won't think you're cheap.'

Joe filled the glass until his father grunted.

His mother said, 'You ready to eat?'

Mr Pike's answer was to take down his feet and pull his plate closer. Joe and his father didn't look anything alike. Where Joe was tall and thin for his age with a lean, bony face, his father was shorter than average, with heavy forearms and a round face. Mr Pike said, 'Christ, can't you say hello to your old man? A man comes home, he wants his family to give a damn.'

'Hi, Daddy.'

Mrs Pike said, 'Get the milk.'

Joe washed his hands at the kitchen sink, then got the milk from the refrigerator and took his seat. His mother was working on a highball of her own, and smoking a Salem cigarette. His mother told Joe that she drank just to keep some of the booze from his father. Joe also knew that she poured out some of the whiskey and refilled it with water, because he'd seen her do it. His mother had told him, 'Joe, your father's a damned mean drunk.'

And Joe guessed that his father was.

Mr Pike rose at four every morning, knocked back a couple of short ones to 'get his feet under him', then went to the mill. His father didn't drink in bars, and almost always came straight home unless he'd picked up a second job doing carpentry, which he sometimes did. If there wasn't the second job, the old man was home by three-thirty, pouring his first one even before he'd opened the paper, knocking back two or three before supper. After supper, he'd turn on the television, settle back in his EZ Boy to watch the news, and drink until he fell asleep.

Unless something set him off.

If something set him off, there would be hell to pay.

Joe knew the signs. His father's eyes would shrink into hard, tiny pits, and his face would glow bright red. His voice would get louder, letting everyone know he was about to let go, but Joe's mother would shout back at him curse for curse. That was the scariest part to

Joe, the way his mother did that. It was like his father was giving them fair warning, letting them know he was losing control of himself, that there was still time to settle him down, only Mrs Pike just couldn't seem to see it. Joe was only nine, but he could see it coming as fearfully as you could see a hundred-car freight train bearing down on you if you were strapped to the tracks. Joe would see the signs, and watch with horror as his mother ignored them, just kept digging at the old man in that way she had as if she wanted to set him off, when all Joe wanted was for her to stop, was to say and do the things that would calm the old man, was just get the hell out of there and run into the woods where he could hide and be safe.

But no.

His mother was blind to it, and Joe would watch as she pushed harder and harder, Joe getting so scared that sometimes he cried, begging her to leave Daddy alone, none of it doing any good until the old man finally had had enough and jumped up, shouting, 'There's gonna be hell to pay.'

His father said it every time.

That's when he started to hit.

Mrs Pike brought a roast beef to the table for her husband to carve, then went back to the stove for mashed potatoes and string beans. His mother and father weren't looking at each other, and barely spoke, and that had Joe worried. Things had been tense between them since Saturday, when his father was watching the Game of the Week with Pee Wee Reese and Dizzy Dean. His mother was vacuuming the floor around the television, which had the old man pissed off enough, but then she'd run over the antenna wire with the vacuum and screwed up the reception at the bottom of the eighth inning in a three-two game. It had been building every day since then, with both of them retreating into silence and hostility until the air in the house seemed charged with fire.

Nine-year-old Joe Pike, the only child in this house, could feel their building anger, and he knew with terrified certainty what was coming as surely as the coming of the full moon.

Mr Pike took another slurp of his whiskey, then set about slicing the roast. He cut two pieces, then frowned. 'What kind of cheap meat is this you bought? There's a goddamned vein right through the middle.'

Here we go.

Joe's mother brought potatoes and string beans to the table without answering.

His father put down the carving knife and fork. 'You forget how to speak American? How you expect me to eat something that looks like this? They sold you a piece of bad meat.'

She still didn't look at him. 'Why don't you just calm down and eat your supper? I didn't know there was a vein. They don't put a label, this meat has a vein.'

Joe knew his mother was scared, but she didn't act scared. She looked angry and sullen.

His father said, 'I'm just saying is all. Look at this. You're not looking.'

'I'll eat the goddamned vein. Put it on my plate.'

Mr Pike's face began its slow, inexorable crawl to red. He stared at his wife. 'What kind of comment is that? What's that tone in your voice?'

Joe said, 'I'll eat it, Daddy. I like the veins.'

His father's eyes flashed, and they were as small as steel shot. 'Nobody's eating the goddamned veins.'

Mrs Pike took the roast. 'Oh, for Christ's sake, this is a helluva thing to argue about. I'll cut out the vein and then you don't have to see it.'

Mr Pike grabbed the plate from her and slammed it on the table. 'I've already seen it. It's garbage. You wanna see what I do with garbage?'

'Oh, for Christ's sake, stop.'

Her husband jumped to his feet, scooped up the roast, kicked open the kitchen door, and threw it into the backyard. 'There's what I gotta eat. Garbage. Like a dog in the yard.'

Joe seemed to grow smaller in the chair, and wished that he was. That he would shrink smaller and smaller and finally disappear. The freight train was caving in the sides of the house, coming for them now, and no one could stop it.

His mother was on her feet, too, face red, screaming, 'I'm not cleaning it up!'

'You'll goddamned clean it up, else there'll be hell to pay.'

The magic words. There'll be hell to pay.

Joe whimpered, 'I'll clean it up. I'll get it, Daddy.'

His father grabbed his arm and jerked him back into his seat. 'My ass you will. Your goddamned mother's gonna do it.'

Mrs Pike was shouting now, her own face livid. She was shaking, and Joe didn't know if it was because she was scared or angry or both. 'YOU threw the boy's supper out the door! YOU clean it up. I'll let it stay there for everybody to see.'

'I'm telling you, there's gonna be hell to pay.'

'You hate it here so damned much, maybe you oughta leave. Go live somewhere they don't have veins!'

His father's eyes shrank to wrinkled dots. Arteries bulged in his red face. He charged across the kitchen and punched his wife in the face with his fist even as Joe shrieked, knocking her into the kitchen table. The Old Crow bottle fell, shattering in a splash of glass and cheap whiskey.

His mother spit blood. 'You see what kind of man your father is? You see?'

His father punched her again, knocking her to her

knees. His father didn't slap. He never slapped. He used his fists.

Joe felt liquid fire in his arms and legs, as if all the strength and control drained from them and he couldn't make himself move. His breath came in deep gasps, tears and snot blowing out of his nose. 'Daddy, don't! Please stop!'

His father punched her in the back of the head then, and she went down onto her stomach. When his mother looked up again, her left eye was closing, and blood dripped from her nose. She didn't look at her husband, she looked at her son.

Mr Pike kicked her then, knocking her onto her side, and Joe saw the fear flash raw and terrible in her eyes. She cried, 'Joe, you call the police. Have them arrest this bastard.'

Nine-year-old Joe Pike, crying, his pants suddenly warm with urine, ran forward and pushed his father as hard as he could. 'Don't hurt Mama!'

Mr Pike swung hard at the boy, clipping the side of the boy's head and knocking him sideways. Then he kicked, the heavy, steel-toed work boots catching Joe on the thigh and upending him with an explosion of nerve-shot pain.

His father kicked him again, and then the old man was over him, pulling off his belt. The old man didn't say anything, just doubled the thick leather belt and beat the boy as his mother coughed up blood. Joe knew that his father couldn't see him now. His father's tiny red eyes were lifeless and empty, clouded by a rage that Joe did not understand.

The thick belt rose and fell again and again, Joe screaming and begging his father to stop, until finally Joe found his feet and bolted through the door, running hard for the safety of the trees.

Nine-year-old Joe Pike ran as hard as he could, crashing through the low sharp branches, his legs no longer a part of him. He tried to stop running, but his legs were beyond his control, carrying him farther from the house until he tripped over a root and fell to the earth.

He lay there for what seemed like hours, his back and arms burning, his throat and nose clogged with mucus, and then he crept back to the edge of the woods. Shouts and cries still came from the house. His father kicked open the door again and threw a pot of mashed potatoes into the yard before going back into the house to curse some more.

Joe Pike sat hidden in the leaves, watching, his body slowly calming, his tears drying, feeling the slow burn of shame that came every time he ran from the house and left his mother alone with his father. He felt weak before his father's strength, fearful before his rage.

After a time, the shouting stopped and the forest grew quiet. A mockingbird chittered, and tiny flying bugs spiraled through shafts of dimming sunlight.

Joe Pike stared at his house, and seemed to float free of time and place, simply being, existing invisible and unseen here at the edge of the woods, hidden.

Here, he felt safe.

The sky grew red and the forest darkened, and still Joe Pike did not move.

He took the hurt and the fear and the shame and imagined himself folding them into small boxes, and placing those boxes away in a heavy oak trunk at the bottom of a deep stair.

He locked the trunk. He threw away the key. He made three promises:

It won't always be this way.

I will make myself strong.

I will not hurt.

As the sun set, his father emerged from the house, got into the Kingswood, and drove away.

Joe waited until the Kingswood disappeared, and then he went back to his house to see about his mother.

I will make myself strong.
I will not hurt.
It won't always be this way.

CHAPTER 11

Light from the morning sun shone through the glass steeple that is the back of my house and filled the loft. Lucy was naked, sleeping on her belly, her hair tangled from the hours before. I snuggled against her, fitting myself to the line of her hip, enjoying her warmth.

I touched her hair. Soft. I kissed her shoulder. The salty warmth good on my lips. I looked at her, and thought how lucky I was to have this view.

Her skin was a dark gold, the line of her legs and back strong even in sleep. Lucy had attended LSU on a tennis scholarship, and worked hard to maintain her game. She carried herself with the easy grace of a natural athlete, and made love the way she played tennis, with aggression and passion, yet with moments of shyness that moved me.

The cat was perched on the guardrail at the edge of the loft, staring at her. She was in his spot, but he didn't look upset. Just curious. Maybe he also liked the view.

Lucy murmured, 'Go back to sleep.'

Her eyes half opened, drowsy with sleep.

Hearing her, the cat bolted down the stairs and growled from the living room. You just have to ignore him.

'We never got to your surprise.'

She snuggled closer. 'You can look forward to it tonight.'

I touched my tongue to her back. 'I'm looking forward to it right now.'

She giggled. 'You're insatiable.'

'For you.'

'I've got to go to work.'

'I'll call and tell'm you're busy making love to the World's Greatest Detective. They'll understand. They always do.'

She pushed herself up on her elbows. 'Always?'

'A slip of the tongue. Sorry.'

'Not half as sorry as you're going to be.'

She jumped on top of me, but I wasn't sorry at all.

Later that morning, I took Lucy back to her car, then drove down to Parker Center without letting Krantz know I was coming. I thought he would raise nine kinds of hell because I'd gone to see Dersh, but when I pushed through the double doors, he said, 'Hope you didn't get in trouble about the autopsy screw-up.'

'No, but the family wants the report.'

'We'll have it for you in a few minutes. You ready for the brief?' Like we were buddies, and he was only too happy to include me on the team.

'Sure. By the way, you get the criminalist's report yet?'

'Should be soon. Get you both at the same time.'

Then he smiled and disappeared down the hall.

Maybe someone had slipped him Prozac. Maybe his good humor was a ploy to get me into the briefing where he and Watts and Williams would beat me to death for having seen Dersh. Whatever the case, he was still lying to me about the report.

We assembled in the conference room where Stan Watts gave the brief, telling me that they had checked out the ex-husband (playing softball in Central Park at the time of Karen's murder), finished canvassing the homes surrounding Lake Hollywood (no one had seen or heard anything), and were in the process of questioning those people with whom Karen worked and attended school. I asked Watts if they had developed a theory about the shooter, but Krantz answered, saying they were still working on it. Krantz nodded at every point Watts ticked off, more relaxed than at any other time I'd seen him, and still none of them mentioned my visit to Dersh. They had to know, and I found that even more odd than Krantz's behavior.

I said, 'When can I expect the reports? I'd like to get out of here.'

Krantz stood, reasonable, but all business. 'Dolan, see if you can chase down that paper. Get Mr Cole on his way.'

Dolan flipped him off behind his back as she left.

After the briefing, I went back to the squad room looking for her, but she wasn't at her desk. Krantz wasn't the only one in a good mood. Bruly and Salerno high-fived each other at the Mr Coffee and walked away laughing. Williams and the Buzz Cut came through the double doors, Krantz offering his hand and the Buzz Cut taking it. The Buzz Cut was smiling, too.

When I was here before, the fabric of the room had been stiff with tension, as if the place and the people were caught in the kind of electrified field that made their hair stand on end. But now something had happened to cut the juice. A sea change had occurred that had freed them from electric hair, and let them overlook the fact that I had interfered with their investigation by visiting Dersh. That is no small thing to overlook.

I got a cup of coffee, sat in the dunce chair to wait for Dolan, and wondered about it until the kid with the mail cart pushed his way in through the doors. Bruly slapped the kid a high five, the two of them laughing about something I couldn't overhear. Salerno joined the conversation, and the three of them talked for a few minutes before the kid moved on. When he moved on, he was smiling, too, and I wondered if he was smiling about the same thing as everyone else.

When he pushed the cart past, I said, 'Hey, Curtis. Can I ask you a question?'

He eyed me suspiciously. The last time I tried to milk Curtis Wood for information it hadn't gone so well.

'First, you were right when you told me that these guys are the best in the business. I've got a whole new respect for them. They really get results.'

'Uh-huh.'

'I was wondering if you hear what they say about me.'

Now he wasn't looking so much suspicious as confused.

'What do you mean?'

'I guess it's just a professional consideration, you know? I've really grown to respect these guys. I want them to respect me, too.'

I watched him hopefully, and when he understood what I was driving at, he shrugged. 'They think you're okay, Cole. They don't like it that you're around, but they've checked up on you. I heard Dolan say that if you were half as good as people say, your dick would be a foot long.'

'That Dolan is a class act, isn't she?'

'She's the best.'

This time it was going better. I had established rapport, and put our conversation on an intimate basis. Soon, I would have him eating out of my hand.

'It's good you're telling me these things, Curtis. With all the whispering today, I thought they were cracking jokes about me.'

'Nah.'

I gave a big sigh as if I were relieved, then made a show of looking around at Bruly and Salerno and the others. 'With all the grinning around here, they must've made a breakthrough in the case.'

Curtis Wood turned back to his cart. 'I don't know anything, Cole.'

'Anything about what?' Mr Innocent.

'You're so obvious, Cole. You're trying to pump me for information I don't have. If you think something's going on, have the balls to ask someone instead of just sneaking around.'

He shook his head like he was disappointed, then pushed the mail cart away, muttering.

'Foot long, my ass.'

Shown up once again by the civilian wannabe. Maybe next time he'd just shoot me.

Dolan came out of the copy room a few minutes later and handed me a large manila envelope without meeting my eyes. 'These are the reports Krantz wants me to give you.'

'What's going on around here, Dolan?'

'Nothing.'

'Then why do I get the feeling I'm being kept out of something?'

'You're paranoid.'

So much for the direct approach.

I went down to my car, raised the top for the sun, and waited. Forty minutes later, the Buzz Cut nosed out of the parking garage behind the wheel of a tan Ford Taurus. He made his way to the Harbor Freeway, then drove west through the center of Los Angeles, then north on the 405 into Westwood. He didn't hurry, and he was easy to follow. He was relaxed, too. And smiling. I copied his tag number to run his registration, but I needn't have bothered. I knew what he was as soon as he turned onto the long, straight drive of the United States Federal Building on Wilshire Boulevard.

The Buzz Cut was FBI.

I cruised past the Federal Building to a little Vietnamese place I know for squid with mint leaves. They make it hot there, the way I like it, and as I ate, I wondered why the FBI would be involved in Karen Garcia's homicide. Local police often call in the Feebs to use their information systems and expertise, but the Buzz Cut had been around at almost every step in the dance. I thought that odd. Then, when I introduced myself at the autopsy, he'd refused to identify himself. I thought that odd, too. And now the Feeb was smiling, and they don't smile for very much. You make one of those guys smile, you'd need something pretty big.

I was pondering this when the woman who owns the restaurant said, 'We make squid you like?'

'Yes. It's very nice.' The woman was small and delicate, with a graceful beauty.

'I see you in here very much.'

'I like the food.' The conversation I could do without.

The woman leaned close to me. 'Oldest daughter make this food you like. She think you very handsome.'

I followed the woman's eyes to the back of the restaurant. A younger imitation of the woman was peeking at me from the kitchen door. She smiled shyly.

I looked at her mother. Mom smiled wider and nodded. I looked back at the daughter, and she nodded, too.

I said, 'I'm married. I've got nine children.'

The mother frowned. 'You no wear ring.'

I looked at my hand. 'I'm allergic to gold.'

The mother's eyes narrowed. 'You married?'

'I'm sorry. Nine children.'

'With no ring?'

'Allergies.'

The woman went to the daughter and said something in Vietnamese. The daughter stomped back into the kitchen.

I finished the squid, then drove home to read the reports. Some days you should just eat drive-thru.

The autopsy protocol held no surprises, concluding that Karen Garcia had been killed by a single .22 caliber bullet fired at close range, striking her 3.5 centimeters above the right orbital cavity. Light to moderate powder stippling was observed at the wound entry, indicating that the bullet had been fired at a distance of between two and four feet. A cut-and-dried case of homicide by gunshot, with no other evidence having been noted.

I reread the criminalist's report, thinking that I would call Montoya to discuss these things, but as I thought about what I would say to him, I realized that the white plastic was missing.

When I read the report that Pike brought last night, I recalled that Chen had recovered a triangular piece of white plastic on the trail at the top of the bluff. He had noted that the plastic was smudged with some sort of gray matter and would have to be tested.

In this new report, that piece of plastic was not listed.

I checked the page numbers to make sure all the pages were there, then found Pike's copy and compared them. White triangle in Pike's report. No white triangle in Krantz's report.

I called Joe. 'You get the report you brought over directly from John Chen?'

'Yes.'

'He gave it to you himself?'

'Yes.'

I told him about the missing plastic.

'That sonofabitch Krantz doctored this report. That's why he delayed giving it to me.'

'If he left something out of Chen's report, I wonder what he left out of the autopsy.'

I was wondering that, too.

Pike said, 'Rusty Swetaggen might be able to help.'

'Yeah.'

I hung up and called a guy I know named Rusty Swetaggen at his restaurant in Venice. Rusty drove an LAPD radio car for most of his adult life, until his wife's father died and left them the restaurant. He retired from the cops the same day that the will was read, and never looked back. Dishing out fried cheese and tap beer was more fun than humping a radio car, and paid better. Rusty said, 'Man, it's been forever, Elvis. Emma thought you'd died.' Emma was his wife.

'Your cousin still work for the coroner?' I'd heard him talk about it, time to time.

'That's Jerry. Sure. He's still down there.'

'A woman named Karen Garcia was cut two days ago.'

'The one belongs to the tortilla guy? The Monsterito?'

'His daughter. I'm on the case with Robbery-Homicide, and I think they're keeping something from me.'

Rusty made a little whistling sound. 'Why does Robbery-Homicide have it?'

'They say it's because the tortilla guy owns a city councilman.'

'But you don't think so?'

'I think everybody's keeping secrets, and I want to know what. An ME named Evangeline Lewis did the autopsy. Another report these cops gave me was doctored, so I'm thinking maybe the autopsy protocol was altered, too. Could your cousin find out about that?'

'He doesn't work down in the labs, Elvis. He's strictly front office.'

'I know.'

I waited, letting Rusty think about it. Six years ago he had asked me to find his daughter after she'd run away with a crack dealer who'd wanted to bankroll his business by putting Rusty's little girl in the gang-bang sex business. Without telling her. I had found his daughter and destroyed the tapes, and now his daughter was safe, and married to a nice young guy she'd met in her recovery group. They had a baby. Rusty never let me pay for a drink, never let me pay for food, and after I stopped going to his place because I was embarrassed by all the free stuff, I'd had to beg him to stop sending it to my home and office. If there was a way to help me, Rusty Swetaggen would do it.

'Jerry would have to get into the case files, maybe. Or the ME's personal files.' He was thinking out loud.

'Would he do that and talk to me?'

'Who's the ME again?'

'Evangeline Lewis.'

'He'll talk to you or I'll beat him to death.' Rusty said

that with an absolute lack of humor. 'I'll give him a call, but I can't say when I'll get through to him.'

'Thanks, Rusty. Call me at home.'

'Elvis?'

'Yeah, Rusty.'

'I still owe you.'

'You don't owe me anything, Rusty. You say hi to Emma. Give my love to the kids.'

'Jerry will do this for you if I have to strangle him.'

'It won't go that far, Rusty. But thanks.' You see what I mean?

I spent the next hour cleaning the house, then went out onto the deck to work my way through two *asanas* and two *katas*. As I worked, I thought about Rusty's need to repay something that didn't need to be repaid. Psychologists would speculate that Rusty wanted to vicariously participate in his daughter's salvation, as if he were somehow struggling to recapture the manhood he had lost by the violation of his daughter. I thought not. I knew Rusty Swetaggen, and I knew men like him. I believed that he was filled with such a terrible and powerful love for his daughter, and for me, that the great pressure of that welling love had to be relieved or it would kill him. People often die from love, and this is a secret we all keep, even from ourselves.

When I went back inside there was a message waiting. It was Rusty, telling me to meet his cousin before the day shift began at five the next morning at a place called Tara's Coffee Bar. He had left the address, and he had given directions.

I knew it would be like that.

CHAPTER 12

I left the house at fifteen minutes after four the next morning, leaving Lucy warm in my bed.

Earlier that night, when she had come to me after work, we decided that she would live with me for the two weeks that Ben was away. We had gone down the mountain to her apartment, and brought back clothes and the personal items she would need. I watched Lucy place her clothes in my closet, and her toiletries in my bath, letting myself toy with a fantasy of permanence. I had lived alone for a long time, but sharing my house with her seemed natural and unforced, as right as if I had shared myself with her my entire life. If that's not love, it's close enough.

We ate take-out from an Italian place in Laurel Canyon, drank red wine, and listened to the swing sounds of Big Bad Voodoo Daddy on the stereo.

We made love on the living-room couch, and after that, as she traced the scars on my body in the bronze glow of candlelight, I felt a wetness on my back. When I looked, she was crying.

'Luce?' As gentle as a butterfly's kiss.

'If I lost you, I'd die.'

I touched her face. 'You won't lose me. Am I not the World's Greatest Detective?'

'Of course you are.' I could barely hear her.

'You won't lose me, Lucille. You won't even be able to get rid of me.'

She kissed me then, and we snuggled close and fell asleep.

*

I worked my way down the dark mountain curves under a sky that was clear and bright and empty of stars. No fire now. No heat now. The heat was waiting for later.

When I first came to Los Angeles, I was fresh out of the Army and accustomed to using the constellations to chart my passing. The L.A. skies are so bright with light that only the most brilliant stars are visible, and those are faint and murky. I used to joke that it was this absence of stars that caused so many people to lose their bearings, but back then, I thought answers were easy. Now I know better. Some of us find our way with a single light to guide us; others lose themselves even when the star field is as sharp as a neon ceiling. Ethics may not be situational, but feelings are. We learn to adjust, and, over time, the stars we use to guide ourselves come to reside within rather than without.

Man. I'm something at four A.M.

At four-forty I left the freeway for empty downtown streets and a pool of yellow light called Tara's Coffee Bar. Two uniformed cops sat at the counter, along with a dozen overweight, tired men who looked like they worked in the printing plant for the *Times*. Everyone was scarfing eggs and bacon and buttered toast, and no one seemed worried about cholesterol or calories.

The only man there wearing a suit said, 'You're Cole, right?' Soft, so that no one else could hear.

'That's right. Thanks for meeting me.'

Jerry Swetaggen hunched over his coffee as if it were a small fire, keeping him warm. He was a big guy like Rusty, with a pink face and ash-blond hair. He looked younger than he probably was, sort of like a bloated fourteen-year-old who'd been dressed in a hand-me-down suit. The suit looked as if it hadn't been pressed in weeks, but maybe he'd been up most of the night.

'Did you get the Garcia file?'

He glanced at the two cops. Nervous. 'I could lose my ass for this. You tell Rusty. You guys owe me big for this.'

'Sure. Coffee's on me.' You'd think I was asking for government secrets.

'You got no idea. Oh, man, you don't even come *close* to having an idea.'

'So far, the only idea I'm getting is that I could've slept in. You get me a copy of the Garcia file?'

'I couldn't get the file, but I got what you want, all right.' Jerry's hand floated to his lapel as if something lived up under the rumpled jacket and he wanted to let it out. He glanced at the cops again. Their backs were made broader by the Kevlar vests they wore under their shirts. 'Not in here. Get the coffee, and let's walk.'

'What's the big deal? What's up with Karen Garcia that has everybody so weird?'

'Get the coffee.'

I put two dollars on the table and followed him out. A warm breeze had come up, pinging us with tiny bits of grit.

'I didn't get a copy for you, but I read it.'

'Reading it won't help. I wanted to compare it with another copy I have.'

'You already got a copy? Then why'd I have to risk my ass?'

'The copy I got might have been doctored. Maybe something was left out, and I want to know what. Might just be a little thing, but I don't like it that somebody's jerking me around.'

Now he was disappointed. 'Well, Jesus. You want numbers? You want charts and graphs? I can't remember all the shit in Lewis's report.'

'What I want is to know if there was anything about her murder that the cops would want to hide.'

Jerry Swetaggen's eyebrows arched in surprise. 'You don't know?'

'Know what?'

'I figured you were already on to this, coming after Garcia. Rusty owes me, man. You owe me, too.'

'You've said that. What do we owe you for?'

'The skin section identified fourteen separate particulates at the entry wound. They're running a spec analysis now – it takes forty-eight hours to cook through the process – so Dr Lewis won't have the results until tomorrow. But everybody already knows they're gonna find the bleach.'

'The bleach?' Like I was supposed to know what that meant.

'The plastic gives them that. It's always on the plastic.'

I stared at him. 'White plastic.'

'Yeah.'

'They found white plastic in her wound.' There was no mention of plastic particulates in the autopsy report I'd read. No mention of bleach.

'The plastic comes from a bleach bottle that the shooter used as a makeshift silencer. They'll probably find adhesive from duct tape on it, too.'

'How do you know what they're going to find?'

Jerry started for the lapel again, but the two uniformed cops came out. He pretended to brush at something, turning away.

'They don't even know we're alive, Jerry.'

'Hey, it's not your ass on the line.'

The shorter cop shook himself to settle his gear, then the two of them walked up the street away from us. Off to fight crime.

When the cops were well down the street, Jerry brought out a sheet of paper that had been folded in thirds. 'You want to know what they're hiding, Cole? You want to know why it's so big?'

He shook open the page and held it out like he was about to blow my socks off. He did.

'Karen Garcia is the fifth vic murdered this way in the past nineteen months.'

I looked at the paper. Five names had been typed there,

along with a brief description of each. The fifth was Karen Garcia. Five names, five dates.

I said, 'Five?'

'That's right. All done with a .22 in the head, all showing the white plastic and bleach and sometimes little bits of duct tape. These dates here are the dates of death.' Jerry smacked his hands together as if we were back East someplace where the temperature was in the thirties, instead of here in the eighties. 'I couldn't sneak out the report because they're kept together in the Special Files section, but I copied the names and this other stuff. I thought that's what you'd want.'

'What's the Special Files section?'

'Whenever the cops want the MEs to keep the lid on something, that's where they seal the files. You can only get in there by special order.'

I stared at the names. Five murders, not one murder. Julio Munoz, Walter Semple, Vivian Trainor, Davis Keech, and Karen Garcia.

'You're sure about this, Jerry? This isn't bogus?'

'Fuckin' A, I'm sure.'

'That's why Robbery-Homicide has the case. That's why they came down so fast.'

'Sure. They've had a Task Force on this thing for over a year.'

'Is there any way I can get a copy of the file?'

'Hell, no. I just told you.'

'Can I get in to read the reports?'

He showed me his palms and backed away. 'No way, man. And I don't care how much Rusty threatens. Anybody finds out I've said this much, it's my ass. I'm out of it.'

I watched him walking away, and called to stop him.

'Jerry.'

'What?'

Something with hundreds of sticky feet crawled along my spine.

'Are the five vics connected?'

Jerry Swetaggen smiled, and now his smile was scared. The smirk was gone, replaced by something fearful. 'No, man. The cops say they're random. Totally unconnected.'

I nodded.

Jerry Swetaggen disappeared into the murky light that precedes dawn. I put the sheet in my pocket, then took it out and looked at the names again.

'The cops were keeping secrets, all right.'

I guess I just needed to hear a human voice, and even my own would do.

I put away the sheet, then tried to figure out what to do. The sheer size of it was as impossible to grasp as it is to put your arms around the Goodyear blimp. This explained why the FBI were involved, and why the police didn't want me around. If the cops were keeping their Task Force secret, they probably had good reasons, but Frank Garcia would still ask what the police were doing about his daughter's murder, and I would still have to answer. I didn't want to tell him that everything was fine if it wasn't. If I told him what Jerry Swetaggen had just told me, nothing would be secret anymore, and that might hurt the police efforts to nail the shooter. On the other hand, Krantz had kept the truth from me, so I didn't know what they had, or where they were in the investigation. I could take their efforts on faith, but Frank Garcia wasn't looking for faith.

And it was his daughter who had been killed.

I went back into the diner, found a pay phone at the rear by the bathrooms, and called Samantha Dolan's office number. Sometimes the day-shift people come on early, but you never know.

On the fourth ring a guy with a smoker's voice said, 'Robbery-Homicide. Taylor.'

'Is Samantha Dolan in yet?'

'Nah. You wanna leave a message?'

'I'll call back. Thanks.'

I bought a cup of coffee to go, then drove over to Parker Center, where I parked across from the entrance in the coral light of the approaching dawn.

I tried again to figure out what I could do and how I would do it, but my thoughts were jumbled and uneasy, and left little room for solutions.

Someone had been stalking people in the streets of Los Angeles for almost two years. If the vics are connected, you call the shooter a hit man. If they're random, there's another name.

Serial killer.

CHAPTER 13

Little by little, the night shift drifted away, and the day shift arrived. Samantha Dolan turned in driving a dark blue Beemer. Her license plate frame read I WANNA BE BARBIE, THAT BITCH HAS EVERYTHING. Most of the other cops were driving American sedans or pickup trucks, and almost all of their vehicles had a trailer hitch because cops like boats. It's genetic. Dolan didn't have a trailer hitch, but none of the other cops had Beemers. Maybe that made them even.

I followed her down, and parked next to her. She saw me as I parked, and raised her eyebrows, watching me as I got out of my car, then climbed into hers. The Black Forest leather went nicely with her Piaget watch. 'Guess the TV series wasn't so bad, Dolan. Nice car.'

'What are you doing here this early, for chrissake? I thought you private guys slept in.'

'I wanted to talk to you without Krantz around.'

She smiled, and suddenly looked very pretty. Like the bad girl next door.

'You're not going to talk dirty to me, are you? I might blush.'

'Not this time. I read through those reports you gave me and saw that some facts are missing, like the little bit of plastic the criminalist found and the white particulates that the ME IDed in Karen Garcia's wound. I was hoping maybe you could help get me the real reports.'

Dolan stopped smiling. A maroon leather daybook was in her lap, along with a briefcase and a Sig Sauer 9-millimeter. The Sig was in a clip holster, and had probably been under her front seat. Most cops carry Berettas, but the Sig is an easy gun to shoot, and very accurate. Hers had glow-in-the-dark sights.

I said, 'Do us both a favor and don't say you don't know what I'm talking about. It would make you look ordinary.'

Dolan abruptly took a cell phone from the center console and put it in her purse. 'I gave you the reports Krantz gave me. If you've got a problem with that, you should talk to him. You may not remember this, but I work for him.'

'And who does Krantz work for, the FBI?'

She continued gathering things.

'I followed the guy with the white crew cut, Dolan. I know he's FBI. I know why they're on the case, and I know what you're covering up.'

'You've been watching too much of *The X-Files*. Get out. I've got to get in to work.'

I took out the sheet of paper with the five names and gave it to her.

'If I'm Mulder, are you Scully?'

Dolan stared at the five names, then searched my face. 'Where did you get this?'

'I'm the world's greatest detective, Dolan. This isn't early for me. I never sleep.'

Dolan handed back the sheet as if she didn't believe this was happening, and by handing it back could pretend she hadn't seen it.

'Why did you come to me with this? Krantz is the lead.'

'I figure you and I can do this off the record.'

'Do what?'

'You guys have been feeding me bullshit. I want to know what's really going on with this investigation.'

Dolan was shaking her head before I finished, raising her hands. 'Absolutely not. I won't have anything to do with this.'

'I already know who the victims are, how they were murdered, and when. By the end of the day I'll have their life histories. I know you're sitting on Dersh, though I don't know why. I know Robbery-Homicide has been running a Task Force, that the FBI is involved, and that you've got the lid clamped.'

Dolan watched me as I said it, and something like a smile played on her lips. Not the bad-girl smile; more like she appreciated what I was saying.

When I finished she said, 'Jesus.'

'No. But almost.'

'I guess you're a pretty good investigator, Cole. I guess you're pretty good.'

I spread my hands and tried to look modest. No easy task. 'The world's –'

'– greatest. Yeah, I know.' She took a breath, and suddenly I liked her smile a great deal. 'Maybe you are. You've been a busy boy.'

'So talk to me, Dolan. Tell me what's going on.'

'You know what kind of spot you're putting me in?'

'I know. I don't want to come on like an adversary, Dolan, but Frank Garcia is going to ask me what's happening, and I have to decide whether or not to lie to him. You don't know me, and you probably think nothing of me, but let me tell you, I don't view that lightly. I don't like lying, I like lying to a client even less, and I will not do so unless there's a compelling reason. Understand this, Dolan, my obligation here isn't to you or Krantz or the sanctity of your investigation. It's to Frank Garcia, and later today he's going to ask. I'm sitting here right now so you can tell me why I shouldn't give this to him.'

'What if you don't like what I tell you?'

'We'll take it a step at a time.'

A sharp vertical line appeared between her eyebrows in a kind of scowl as she thought about what to tell me. I hadn't seen many women who looked good scowling, but she did.

'Remember David Berkowitz, the Son of Sam?'

'Sure. Shot people in parked cars back in New York.'

'Berkowitz just walked up to cars, shot whoever was inside – male, female, it didn't matter – then walked away. He got off on shooting people, and it didn't matter who. The Feebs call guys like that "random assassin killers", and they're the hardest type of killer to catch. You see why?'

'No connection to the victims. No way to predict who he might go for next.'

'Right.'

'Most killers kill people they know, and that's how they're caught. Husband kills wife. Junkie kills dealer. Like that. Most murders aren't solved by clues like you see on *Murder, She Wrote*, or forensics like you read about in a Patricia Cornwell novel. The easy truth of it is that almost all murders are solved when somebody rats out somebody else, when some guy says, "Elmo said he was gonna shoot him", and the cops go to Elmo's place and find the murder weapon hidden under Elmo's bed. It's that cut-and-dried. And when there isn't anyone to point the finger at Elmo, Elmo gets away.

'That's what we've got here, Cole. Julio Munoz was the only one of the vics with a sheet. He was a former prostitute who'd cleaned up his act and was working as a counselor in a halfway house in Bellflower. Semple was a roofing contractor who lived in Altadena. Totally unlike Munoz. No record, deacon in his church, the wife, the kids, the whole nine yards. Vivian Trainor was a nurse, a real straight arrow like Semple. Keech, a retired City Parks custodian, lived in a retirement home in Hacienda Heights. Now Karen Garcia. So we're talking about a street hustler, a Sunday-school teacher, a nurse, a retired custodian, and a wealthy college student. Two Hispanics, two Anglos, and a black, all from different parts of the city. We've gone to each of the families and floated the names of the other vics, but we haven't been able to link them. We're trying to tie in Garcia, but we're coming up empty there, too. Maybe you can help with that.'

'How?'

'Krantz is scared to press the girl's father, but we need to talk to him. Krantz keeps saying to let him cool down, but I don't think we can afford to wait. I want to run the names past him. I want to look through the girl's things.'

'You go through her apartment yet?'

'Of course. We didn't need his permission for that. But she might've left things at her father's house. I did, when I moved out.'

'What do you want to find?'

'Something that puts her with one of the other vics. Anything like that, and we're not talking random anymore. That makes this asshole a lot easier to catch.'

'I'll talk to Pike. We can make that happen.'

'This guy's smart. Five head shots, all with a .22, and none of the bullets match. That means he's using a different gun each time. He probably chucks them, so we won't find the murder weapons in his possession. Each shooting takes place in an isolated location, three of the five at night, so we have no wits. We've recovered two .22 caliber shell casings. No prints, both fired from different semiautomatics, and different brands. We've found shoe prints at three of the murder scenes, but, get this, three different shoe sizes, ten, ten and a half, and eleven. He's playing mix and match with us.'

'So he probably dumps the shoes, too.'

The scowl deepened, but now it wasn't because of me.

'Probably, but who knows. A nut like this, he might videotape his goddamned murders. Jesus, I wanna bust this scumbag.'

We sat there a while, neither of us saying anything until Dolan glanced at her watch.

'You've given me a lot of background, Dolan, but so far you haven't told me why I shouldn't level with Frank.'

'A lot of times, these guys will initiate contact, like Son of Sam with his letters, you see?'

'I'm listening.'

'Here was Berkowitz, getting away with murder, and he felt powerful because of it. He wanted to flaunt the fact that the cops couldn't catch him, so he started sending notes to the newspapers.'

'Okay.'

'Well, our guy hasn't done that. The Feebs say our guy doesn't want publicity, and may even be scared of it. That's one of the reasons we decided to keep this thing boxed. If we go public, maybe this guy changes his MO, or maybe he even moves to another town and starts all over again. You see what I'm saying?'

'But maybe if you go public, somebody feeds you a tip that lets you nail this guy.'

Her eyes hardened, irritated. She had nice eyes. Hazel.

'Well, shit, World's Greatest, that's the problem here, isn't it? There's no goddamned rule book on how to catch a shooter like this. You make it up as you go along, and hope you're doing the right thing. Don't you think we've talked about this?'

'Yeah, I guess you've talked about it.'

I thought about the change I'd seen up in Robbery-Homicide, how everyone was suddenly more relaxed, about the smiles and high fives, and even the grinning Feebs, and suddenly I knew there was more.

'Who's your suspect, Dolan?'

She stared at me as if she was deciding something, then wet her lips. 'Dersh.'

'*Eugene* Dersh?' That's why the cops were on him.

'Nuts like this, they can't stand not knowing what you know. They like to get up close and find out what you're saying about them. One of the ways they do it is to claim some connection to the crime. They pretend to be a witness or they say they overheard something in a bar, like that. The feds said we might get a break that way, and Krantz thinks Dersh is our break.'

'Because Dersh found this body.'

'It isn't just that. Krantz and a couple of Feebs flew back

142

to Quantico to talk with one of their behavioral science people. They built a profile based on the evidence we had, and Dersh pretty much matches up with it.'

I frowned. 'You're talking the talk, Dolan, but you don't seem all that convinced to me.'

She didn't say anything.

'Okay, if it's Dersh, how does Riley Ward fit in?'

'If the Feebs are right, he was just Dersh's cover for finding the body. You read their statements. Ward suggested that Dersh was directive in finding the body. When Dersh tells the story, he puts a different spin on how they went down to the lake. It makes everybody wonder which story is correct and why there are two stories.'

'In other words, you've got nothing. There's no physical evidence, and you guys are trying to hang it on Dersh because of an FBI profile.'

The hazel eyes stayed with me, but she shrugged. 'No, we're trying to hang it on Dersh because Krantz is feeling heat from upstairs. Bishop gave him the Task Force a year ago, but he doesn't have anything to show for it. The brass are screaming a shitstorm, and that means Bishop can't carry Krantz forever. If another body drops, and Krantz doesn't have a suspect, he'll be out of the job.'

'Maybe they'll give it to you, Dolan.'

'Yeah. Right.' She looked away.

I thought about Dersh and his Kenyan coffee. Dersh, with the bright paintings and his house smelling of Marks-a-lots. 'What about you? Do you think it's Dersh?'

'Krantz thinks Dersh is the shooter. I think Dersh is a legitimate suspect. There's a difference.'

I took a breath and nodded, still trying to figure out what to do. 'The criminalist's report suggests the shooter was driving an off-road vehicle or an SUV. Remember the homeless guy I told you about?'

'Krantz may be a dud, Cole, but not all of us got into Robbery-Homicide on a pass. I took a ride up there yesterday, but couldn't find Mr Deege. Hollywood Division uniforms have been told to keep an eye out.'

I suddenly felt better about Frank Garcia and what I would tell him.

'Well, okay, Dolan. I'm going to sit on it.'

'You're not going to tell Garcia?'

'No. The only person I'll tell is my partner.'

'Pike.' Her eyes suddenly sparkled, and the bad girl was back. 'Christ, wouldn't Krantz love that. Joe Pike knows his big secret.'

I held out my hand. 'Nice doing business with you, Dolan. I'll give you a call later about talking to Frank.'

Her hand was cool and dry and strong. I liked the way it felt, and felt a faraway stab of guilt that I liked it a little too much.

She squeezed once, and then I opened the door to get out.

'Hey, Cole.'

I stopped.

'I didn't like passing you those bum reports.'

'I know. I could tell.'

'That's good work you did, putting all this together. You would've made a good cop.'

I let myself out of her Beemer. She watched as I walked away.

CHAPTER 14

I reached my office just after seven, but I did not stay there. I gathered the interviews with Dersh and Ward, then walked across the street to a bagel place I like. I ordered Nova lox on a cinnamon-raisin bagel, then took a seat at a window table. An older woman at the next table smiled a good morning. I wished her a good morning back. The older man with her was reading a paper, and didn't bother with either of us. He looked snotty.

It was an ideal place in which to consider multiple homicide.

I went to the pay phone by the rest rooms, and called Joe Pike. He answered on the second ring.

'I'm at the bagel place across from the office. Karen Garcia was the fifth victim in a string of homicides going back nineteen months. The police know that, and they have a suspect.' If you're going to say it, you just have to say it.

Pike didn't respond.

'Joe?'

'I'll be there in twenty minutes.'

I reread Dersh's and Ward's interviews while I waited, all the while thinking about Eugene Dersh. Dersh didn't seem like a homicidal maniac to me, but maybe they said that about Ted Bundy and Andrew Cunanan, too.

Both Dersh's and Ward's versions of events agreed that it was Dersh who had suggested the hike at Lake Hollywood, but differed importantly about why they had left the trail to hike along the shoreline. Ward stated that it was Dersh's idea to walk along the shore, and that

Dersh picked the spot where they left the trail. The police called this being 'directive', as if Dersh was directing the course of events that led to their finding the body. But where Dersh was clear and decisive in describing their actions, Ward seemed inconsistent and uncertain, and I wondered why.

The elderly woman was watching me. We traded another smile. The elderly man was still lost in the paper, neither of them having shared a word in the entire time I had been there. Maybe they had said everything they had to say to each other years ago. But maybe not. Maybe their silence wasn't two people each living separate lives, but two people who fit so perfectly that love and communication could be derived by simple proximity. In a world where people kill other people for no reason at all, you want to believe in things like that.

When Joe Pike walked in, the old man glanced up from his paper and frowned. There goes the neighborhood.

I said, 'Let's walk. I don't want to talk about it here.'

We walked along the south side of Santa Monica Boulevard, heading east into the sun. I gave Pike the sheet with the five names.

'You recognize any of these names?'

'Only Karen. These the other vics?'

'Yeah. Munoz was first.' I went through the others, giving him everything that I'd learned from both Samantha Dolan and Jerry Swetaggen. 'The cops've been trying to connect these people together, but they haven't been able to do it. Now they're thinking the guy picks his victims at random.'

'You said there's a suspect.'

'Krantz thinks it's Dersh.'

Pike stopped walking, and looked at me with all the expression of a dinner plate. The morning rush-hour traffic was heavy, and I wondered how many thousands of people passed us in just those few minutes of walking.

'The man who discovered the body?'

'Krantz is under the gun to make a collar. He wants to think that it's Dersh, but they don't have any physical evidence putting Dersh to the killings. All they have is some kind of FBI profile, so Krantz has a twenty-four-hour watch on the guy. That's how they picked me up when I went over there.'

'Mm.'

The passing traffic was reflected in Pike's glasses.

'This thing has been top secret since the beginning, Joe, and the cops want to keep it that way. The deal I made with Dolan is that we'll respect that. We can't tell Frank.'

Pike's chest expanded as he watched the traffic. His only movement. 'Big thing not to tell, Elvis.'

'Krantz may be a turd, but Dolan is a top cop, and so is Watts. Hell, most of those guys are aces. That's why they're in Robbery-Homicide. So even if Krantz is half-cocked, the rest of them are still going to work a righteous case. I think we have to give them time to work it, and that means keeping quiet about what's going on.'

Pike made a quiet snort. 'Me, helping Krantz.'

'Dolan needs to ask Frank about the four other vics and look through Karen's things. Will you talk to him?'

Pike nodded, but I'm not sure the nod was meant for me.

We walked again, neither of us speaking, and pretty soon we came to Pike's Jeep. He opened the door, but didn't get in.

'Elvis?'

'Yeah?'

'Could I see those?' He wanted the interview transcripts.

'Sure.' I gave them to him.

'You think it was Dersh?' Like if it was, you wouldn't want to be Dersh.

'I don't know, Joe. The always reliable but overworked hunch says no, but I just don't know.'

Pike's jaw flexed once, then that, too, was gone.

'I'll talk to Frank and let you know.'

Joe Pike climbed into his Jeep, pulled the door shut, and in that moment I would've given anything to see into his heart.

Pike wanted to see Eugene Dersh.

He wanted to witness him in his own environment, and see if he thought Dersh had murdered Karen Garcia. If it was possible that Dersh was the killer, then Pike would ponder what to do with that.

Pike knew from the police interview transcripts that Dersh worked at home. All LAPD interviews started that way. State your name and address for the record, please. State your occupation. Pike's instructor at the academy said that you started this way because it put the subject in the mood to answer your questions. Later, Pike had been amazed to learn how often it put the subject in the mood to lie. Even innocent people would lie. Make up a name and address that, when you tried to contact them weeks later, you would find to be an auto parts store, or an apartment building packed with illegals, none of whom spoke English.

Pike pulled into a Chevron station and looked up Dersh's address in his Thomas Brothers map. Dersh lived in an older residential area in Los Feliz where the streets twisted and wound with the contours of the low foothills. Seeing the street layout was important because Krantz's people were watching Dersh's place, and Pike wanted to know where they were.

When Pike had the names of the streets bracketing Dersh's home, he used his cell phone to call a realtor he knew, and asked her if any properties were for sale or lease on those streets. The police would establish a surveillance base in a mobile van if they had to, but they preferred to use a house. After a brief search of the multiple listing service, Pike's friend reported that there were three homes for sale in that area, two of which were vacant. She gave Pike the addresses. Comparing the addresses with Dersh's on the map, Pike saw that one of the homes was located on the street immediately north of Dersh's, and kitty-corner across an alley. That's where the police would be.

Pike worked his way across Hollywood, then wound his way into the quiet of an older neighborhood until he came to Dersh's small, neat home. Pike noted the two-story dwelling just off the alley that would be the police surveillance site. In the flicker of time as he drove past the mouth of the alley, Pike saw the glint of something shiny in the open second-floor window. The officers roosting there would have binoculars, a spotting scope, and probably a videocamera, but if Pike kept Dersh's house between them and himself, they wouldn't see him. In a combat situation, those guys would fast be a memory.

The neighborhood was easy. Small houses set back from the street, lushly planted with trees and shrubs, showing little clear ground between the houses. No one was clipping flowers in their front yards, no housekeepers were peering from their living-room windows, no strollers were passing, no yapping little dogs.

Pike parked at the curb two houses west of Dersh, then disappeared between the shrubs of the nearest house, one moment there, the next gone. In that instant when he allowed himself to be enveloped by leaves and twigs and green, he felt an absolute calm.

He moved along the near house, staying beneath the windows, then crossed between the trees into the prickly shrubs that surrounded Dersh's house. He neither touched nor disturbed the plants, but instead moved around and between them, the way he had done since he was a boy.

Pike eased to the corner of the living-room window, snuck a fast glance into a bright room, caught movement deeper within the house, and heard music. Yves Montand, singing in French.

Pike followed the west wall of the house through a small stand of rubber trees planted with ferns and pickle lilies, passing beneath the high window of a bathroom to the casement windows of Dersh's studio, where he saw two men. Dersh, the shorter of the two, wearing jeans and a Hawaiian shirt. Had to be Dersh, because the other man, younger, was wearing a suit. Dersh moved as if this place were his home; the other moved as a visitor. Pike listened. The two men were at a computer, Dersh sitting, the other man pointing over Dersh's shoulder at the screen. Pike could hear Yves Montand, and catch occasional words. They were discussing the layout of a magazine ad.

Pike watched Dersh and tried to get a sense of the man. Dersh did not appear to be capable of the things that the police suspected, but Pike knew you could not tell by appearances. He had known many men who looked and acted strong, but had cores of weakness, and he had known men who seemed timid who had shown themselves capable of great strength and of accomplishing terrible things.

Pike drew even, steady breaths, listening to the birds in the trees, and remembering the Karen Garcia with whom he had spent so much time, and how she had died. Joe considered Dersh, noting his finger strokes on the keyboard, the way he held himself, the way he laughed at something the other man said. He thought that if Dersh had killed Karen Garcia, he might end the man. He would lay open the fabric of justice, and let it be Dersh's shroud. He could do such a thing now, even here in the daylight as the police watched.

But after a time Pike eased away from the window. Eugene Dersh did not seem like a killer, but Pike would wait to see what evidence the police produced. Seeing the evidence, he would then decide.

There was always plenty of time in which to deliver justice.

School

> 'We did eight hundred push-ups every goddamned day, some days over two hundred chins, and they ran us. Christ, we ran ten miles every morning and another five at night, and sometimes even more than that. We weren't big guys, like badass football linemen or any of that, you know, Rambo with all those pansy protein-shake muscles bulging. We were skinny kids, mostly, all stripped down and hungry, but, hell, we could carry hundred-pound packs, four hundred rounds, and a poodle-popper uphill at a run all goddamned day. You know what we were? We were wolves. Lean and mean, and you definitely did not want us on your ass. We were fuckin' dangerous, man. That's what they wanted. Recon. That's what we wanted, too.'

> – excerpt from *Young Men at War:*
> *A Case by Case Study of Post*
> *Traumatic Stress Disorder,*
> by Patricia Barber, Ph.D. M.F.C.C.
> Duke University Press, 1986

Gunnery Sergeant Leon Aimes stood on the low ridge overlooking the parched hills at Camp Pendleton Marine Training Depot just south of Oceanside, California, scanning the range with a pair of Zeiss binoculars that had been a gift from his wife. He'd been pissed as hell when he'd opened the box at his forty-fourth birthday and seen what they were because the Zeiss had set back the family three months' pay. But they were the best viewing glass in the world, none finer, and he'd gone to her later feeling like a dog to apologize for carrying on.

These Zeiss were the best, all right. He would use them hunting blacktail deer this fall, and, a year from now, after his posting as a Force Recon company instructor, when he returned to Vietnam for his fourth combat tour, he would use them to hunt Charlie.

Aimes sat in a jeep with his best drinking buddy, Gunnery Sergeant Frank Horse, the two of them wearing black tee shirts, field utilities, and Alice harnesses, both of them smoking the shitty cigars they'd bought down in TJ two months before. Horse was a full-blood Mescalero Apache, and Aimes believed him to be the finest Advanced Infantry Instructor at Camp Pendleton, as well as an outstanding warrior. Aimes, though African-American, had once been told by his grandmother that he had Apache blood (which he believed) and was the descendant of great warriors (which he absolutely knew to be true), so he and Horse often joked about being in the same tribe when they'd had a little too much tequila.

Horse grinned at him around the cigar. 'Can't see'm, can you?'

Aimes rolled his own cigar around in his mouth. Three hundred acres of coastal desert rolled out below them, dipping down into a little creek bed before rising again to another finger ridge half a mile away. Somewhere out in those three hundred acres was a young Marine that Horse thought had the warrior spirit. 'Not yet, but I'm lookin'.'

Horse smiled wider and nodded at nothing in particular. 'He's right under your goddamned nose, Leon. Hell.'

'Bullshit he is. If he's out there, I'll find him.' Leon Aimes scowled harder and imagined a huge checkerboard laid upon the land. He carefully searched each block on the board, noting clumps of manzanita and puppy grass as he ran a mental comparison to see if anything had moved in the minutes since he'd last scanned the terrain. He could find no trace of movement, yet he knew that somewhere out there a young Marine was slowly creeping toward him.

Horse drew deep on the stogy, making an exaggerated deal out of it, and blew a great plume of smoke into the breeze. 'Been here damn near two hours, pard.' Really rubbing it in. Really digging at Leon. 'You know he's good, else you woulda found him by now. We gonna keep the boy out there all day, or has this turned into something about you instead've something about him?'

Finally, Gunnery Sergeant Leon Aimes sighed and lowered the glasses. His friend Frank Horse was a wise man as well as a warrior. 'Okay, goddamnit, where is he?'

Horse's eyes crinkled, like he'd won some kinda goddamned bet with himself, and Aimes could tell from the smile that Horse liked this boy, all right. Horse pointed off to their left and ahead of them with his cigar. 'Heading three-four-zero. See that little depression about three hundred meters out?'

Aimes saw it at once without even lifting the glasses. The barest of shadows. 'Yeah.'

Horse reached behind them for the bullhorn. 'He came up through that little cut in the creek bank out there off to the right and has been working his way up.'

Aimes spit a load of brown cigar juice, pissed. 'How in hell did you see'm?'

'Didn't see shit.' Horse spit his own load, then looked over at his friend. 'That's the way I told him to come.'

Their eyes met and Aimes smiled. 'Get the boy in here, an' let's talk to him, then.'

Horse keyed the horn and called out across the range. 'This program is terminated, Private. Come to your feet.'

The little depression three hundred meters out on heading three-four-zero did not move. Instead, a loose collection of twigs and burlap and dirt slowly rose from the earth off to their right and less than two hundred meters away. Horse's cigar nearly fell out of his jaw, and Aimes burst out laughing. Aimes clapped his old friend on the back. 'Three-four-zero, all right.'

'I coulda sworn . . .'

'Lucky that boy wasn't gonna shoot our old asses.'

Then the two combat veterans were beyond the laughing, and Aimes nodded. Horse keyed the mike again. 'Get in here, Private. Triple time.'

Running up to them across the broken ground, Aimes thought that the ghillie suit made the private look like some kind of matted Pekinese dog, all its mats bouncing up and down. Aimes said, 'He in good shape?'

'Came here in good shape.'

'Farm boy?'

'Lived in the country, but I don't think they farmed.' Aimes liked boys who grew up on the land and knew its ways.

'What kind of name is that, Pike? English? Irish?'

'Dunno. He don't talk about his people. He don't talk much at all.'

Aimes nodded. Nothing wrong with that. 'Maybe he's got nothing to say.'

Now Horse was looking a little nervous, like they had come upon something in the road that didn't sit well with him and that maybe he was hoping that they wouldn't come upon. 'Yeah, well, just so you know, he don't say much. I don't think he's stupid.'

Aimes glanced sharply at his friend. 'You know better than to waste my time with an idiot.' He glanced back at the running Marine. 'Boy ain't stupid who scores as high on his tests as this one.' This boy had tested higher than most of the college boys who came through, and he stood first in every class he was required to take.

'Well, some of the DIs find him a little odd, and some of the platoon do, too. Keeps to himself, mostly, and reads. Doesn't grabass during free time, none of that. Don't think I ever seen the boy smile once since he come to me.'

That concerned Aimes. 'You can tell a lot by a man's laugh.'

'Yeah, well.'

They watched him come closer, and finally Aimes sighed. 'Got no use for a man ain't a team player.'

Horse spit. 'We wouldn't be standing here if he wasn't. Got a lot of fast twitch in that boy, but out on the course, he'll throttle back to help his mates. Did it without having to be told, either.'

Aimes nodded, liking that one just fine. 'Then what's all this business about being odd? You say he's the best young man in your training platoon, you show me a file on this boy saying he stands top of his class, then you bring me out here and we both get snaked by a boy seventeen years old same as he had three years as a Scout/Sniper.'

Horse made a little shrug. 'Just wanted you to know, is all. He ain't your standard recruit.'

'Force Recon isn't interested in standard recruits, and you and I both know that better'n anyone. I want moral young men I can turn into professional killers. End of story.'

Horse raised his hands. 'Just wanted you to know.'

'Well, all right.' Aimes chomped on the nasty cigar and watched the young Marine. 'What is it he reads?'

'Just reads, is all. Anything he can get his hands on. Novels, history. Caught him with some Nietzsche once. Found some Basho in his locker.'

'Do tell.'

'Knew you'd like that, too.'

'Yes, sir. Yes, I do.'

Leon Aimes pondered the private with renewed interest, as he believed that all the best warriors were poets. Those old Japanese Samurai proved that, and Aimes had his own theory as to why. Aimes knew that you could fill a young man's head with all the notions of duty, honor, and country you wanted, but when the shit hit the fan and the bullets started flying, even your bravest young man didn't stand there and die for little Sally back home or even for the Stars and Stripes. If he stood at all, he stood for his buddies beside him. His love for them, and his fear of shame in their eyes, is what kept him fighting even after his sphincter let loose, and even when his world turned to hell. It took a special man to stand there all alone, without the weight of his buddies to anchor him in place, and Aimes was looking for young warriors that he could train to move and fight and win alone. Die alone, too, if that's what it took, and not just any man was up to that. But poets were different. You could take a poet and fill his heart with the notions of duty and honor, and sometimes, if you were very lucky, that was enough. Aimes had learned long ago, perhaps even in an earlier life, that a poet would die for a rose.

Horse gestured with the cigar as the private came pounding up and fell in at attention before them, the monstrous ghillie suit making the boy look like a tall, skinny haystack.

Horse said, 'Belay that ghillie suit and stand at ease, Private. This here is Gunnery Sergeant Aimes, who is just about the best Marine in this man's Corps outside of Chesty Puller and myself. You will listen up to him. Is that clear?'

'Yes, Gunnery Sergeant!' the young Marine shouted.

Private Pike peeled out of the ghillie suit, stowed it in the back of the jeep, and returned to his position. Neither Aimes nor Horse spoke while he was doing this, and, after he was done, Aimes let him stand there a minute, thinking about things. Aimes recalled from the file he had read that the young man's name was Pike, Joseph, no middle initial. He was tall, maybe about six one, all lean and corded and burned tan by the Southern California sun. His face and hands were covered in cammie greasepaint, but he had the damnedest blue eyes Aimes had ever seen, real white-boy ice-people eyes, like maybe his people came from Norway or Sweden or some damn place, which was also okay by Aimes. He had enormous respect for Vikings, and considered them almost as fine a group of warriors as his African ancestors. Aimes looked into the blue eyes and thought that they were calm, holding neither guile nor remorse. Aimes said, 'How old are you, son?' Aimes, of course, knew how old the private was, but he wanted to question the boy, get a sense of him.

'Seventeen, Gunnery Sergeant!'

Aimes crossed his arms, and the large muscles there pulled the fabric of his black Marine Corps tee shirt tight. 'Your mother sign the papers to get you in early, or you fake'm yourself?'

The boy did not answer. Beads of sweat dripped down from his scalp and etched tracks along his gaunt face. Nothing else about the boy moved.

'I didn't hear you, Marine.'

The boy floated there with no response, and Horse drifted around behind his back so the boy couldn't see him smile.

Gunnery Sergeant Leon Aimes stepped very close to the private and whispered into his ear. 'I don't like talking to myself, young man. I suggest you answer me.'

The young Marine answered. 'Don't know it's any of your business, Gunnery Sergeant.'

Horse jumped into the young Marine's face faster than an M16 chambering a fresh round, screaming so loud that his face turned purple. 'Everything in this world is the sergeant's business, Marine! Are you stupid enough to embarrass me in front of a Marine I know to be a hero in two wars, and who is a finer man than you could ever hope to be on your very best day?'

Aimes waited. The boy didn't look scared, which was good, and he didn't look arrogant, which was also good. He looked thoughtful.

Then the boy said, 'My father.'

'You in some kinda trouble, that why your old man put

you in my Corps? You a car thief or a troublemaker or something like that?'

'No, Gunnery Sergeant.' The blue eyes met Leon Aimes. 'I told him that if he didn't sign the papers I would murder him.' There was no humor in the boy when he said it. None of that smart-ass attitude Aimes hated so much. The young Marine said it as simply as you say anything, but in that moment Aimes knew it to be true. And Aimes wondered about that, but it did not put him off. Violent young men often came into the Corps, and the Corps taught them how to channel that violence, else it got rid of them. So far, this young man was more than making the grade.

Gunnery Sergeant Aimes said, 'You know what Force Recon is, son?'

'Small-unit reconnaissance, Gunnery Sergeant.'

'That's right. Small units of men who go into the Valley of Death all by their lonesome little asses to gather up intelligence and/or hunt down and kill the enemy. I myself am a Force Recon warrior, which is the loftiest species of human life yet devised by God, none finer.'

Horse said, 'Fuckin'-A, bubba. None finer.'

'Recon takes a special man, and it ain't for everybody. Force Recon warriors are the finest warriors on this earth, and I don't give a rat's ass what those squid SEALs and green beanies over in the Army's Special Forces got to say about it.'

The private simply stood there, maybe seeing Aimes, maybe not, and Aimes was disappointed. Usually the spiel he just pitched got a smile out of them, but this one just stood there.

'Force Recon training is the hardest training in this man's Corps, or any other. We run twenty miles a day in full packs. We do more push-ups than Hercules. We learn how to see in the dark like a buncha muthuhfuckin' ninjas and how to kill the enemy with the power of our minds alone and I wanna know how come you ain't smilin', Private, 'cause this is the funniest shit anybody ever laid on your ass!'

Still no reaction.

Horse was behind the private, shaking his head and grinning again. *Told you so,* the grin was saying.

Aimes sighed, then uncrossed his big arms and stepped behind Pike so that he could roll his eyes. Horse was damn near busting a gut back there, trying not to laugh. 'All right, young man. I may not be Flip fuckin' Wilson, but Gunnery Sergeant Horse, who is as fine a warrior as I know, none finer, thinks you just might have what it takes to be one of my young men, and I think he might be right.' Aimes came around the other side of Pike and stopped in front of him, only now Aimes had taken anything even remotely humorous from his eyes and carefully folded it away. 'The gunnery sergeant says you're good at hand-to-hand.'

Nothing again, and Aimes wondered why this boy said so little. Maybe he just came from people who didn't say much.

Aimes unsnapped his fighting knife from its Alice sheath. He held it out handle first to the boy. 'You know what this is?'

The blue eyes never even went to the knife. 'It isn't a K-Bar.'

Aimes considered his knife. 'The standard Corps issue K-Bar fighting knife is a fine weapon, none finer, but not to a warrior such as myself.' He twirled the knife across the backs of his fingers. 'This is a handmade fighting dagger, custom-made to my specifications by a master blade maker. This edge is so goddamned sharp that if you cut yourself the asshole standing next to you starts to bleed.'

Horse nodded, pursing his lips knowingly as if truer words had never been spoken.

Aimes flipped the knife, caught its tip, then handed it to the boy, who held it in his right hand.

Aimes spread his hands. 'Try to put it in my chest.'

Pike moved without the moment's hesitation that Aimes expected, and he moved so damned blurringly fast that Aimes didn't even have time to think before he trapped the boy's arm, rolled the wrist back, and heard the awful crack as the wrist gave and the boy went down on his back.

The boy did not grimace, and he did not say a word.

Aimes and Horse both made a big deal, helping the kid to his feet, Aimes feeling just horrible, feeling like a real horseshit donut for pulling a bush stunt like that when the private put those blue eyes on him and said, 'What did you do?' Not to accuse or blame, but because he wanted to know the fact of it.

Aimes helped the young Marine into the back of the jeep, telling him, 'That was an arm trap. It's something they do in a fighting art called Wing Chun. A Chinese woman invented it eight hundred years ago.'

'Woman.' The boy almost seemed to nod, not quite but almost, thinking it through. He didn't seem bothered at all that Aimes had just broken his wrist. He said, 'You used me against me. A woman, smaller, would have to do that.'

Aimes blinked at him. 'That's right. You were driving forward. I trapped that energy and used your own momentum to roll your hand over and toward you.'

The boy looked down at his hand as if seeing it now for the first time, and cradled it.

Aimes said, 'Christ, you're fast, boy. You're so damned fast it got a little away from me. I'm sorry.'

The boy looked back up at Aimes. 'You teach stuff like that in Recon training?'

'It's not part of our normal syllabus, but I teach it to some of the men. Mostly we learn ground navigation, escape and evasion tactics, ambush techniques. The art of war.'

'Will you teach it to me?'

Aimes glanced at Horse, and Horse nodded, his job now done. He got behind the jeep's wheel and waited.

Aimes said, 'Yes, Marine. You come over and become one of my young men, I'll make you the most dangerous man alive.'

The young Marine didn't speak again until they were at the infirmary, where, in filling out the accident report, Aimes took full and complete responsibility for the injury. What the boy said to him then was, 'It's okay you hurt me.'

That evening, still feeling nauseated from guilt, Aimes and Horse practiced the art of unarmed war in the Pendleton gym with an ugly ferocity that left both men bloody as they desperately tried to burn away their shame. Later, they drank, and later still Leon Aimes confessed all to his wife, as he always did whenever one of his young men was injured and he felt responsible, and she held him until the very small hours of the dawn.

As a warrior and a man, Leon Aimes was above reproach, none finer.

Eight days later, PFC Pike, Joseph, no middle initial, completed Advanced Infantry Training even with the broken wrist, graduated with his class, and was re-assigned to the Force Recon Company for additional schooling. He was rotated to the Republic of Vietnam in the waning years of the United States' involvement in that war. Leon Aimes followed the young Marine's progress, as he did with all of his young men, and noted with pride that Private Pike served with distinction.

There were none finer, just as Leon Aimes always said.

CHAPTER 15

Pike phoned to tell me that Frank would see us at three that afternoon. I passed the word to Dolan, who said, 'I'm impressed, World's Greatest. I guess you're kinda useful.'

'Are you going to call me that, Dolan?'

'Beats some other things that come to mind.'

These cops think they're such a riot.

When I arrived, Frank Garcia's home was as still as a sleeping pit bull and just as inviting. No cop brass now, no city councilman; just a mourning old man and his housekeeper. I wondered if Frank would see the lie in my eyes, and thought that maybe I should borrow Pike's sunglasses.

I parked in the shade cast by one of the big maples to wait for Pike and Dolan. The tree and the neighborhood were so silent that if one of the fat green leaves fell you would hear it hit the street. The devil wind was gone, but I could not escape the feeling that it was only resting, hiding in the dry, hard canyons to the north to gather its strength before clawing back through the city from a surprising and unexpected direction.

Pike arrived a few minutes later, and got into my car. 'I saw Dersh.'

Anyone else would be joking, but Pike doesn't joke. 'You saw Dersh. You *spoke* with him?'

'No. I just saw him.'

'You went over there just to *look* at him.'

'Mm.'

'Why on earth did you go see him?'

'Needed to.'

'Well, that explains it.'

You see what I have to deal with?

Dolan parked her Beemer across the street. She was smoking, and dropped her butt on the street after she got out of her car. We climbed out to meet her.

'What does he know?'

'He knows what I know.' He. Like Pike wasn't there.

Dolan considered Joe for a moment, then wet her lips. 'Can you keep your mouth shut?'

Joe didn't respond.

Dolan frowned. 'Well?'

I said, 'You got your answer, Dolan.'

Dolan grinned at Pike. 'Yeah. I heard you don't say much. Keep it that way.'

Dolan walked on ahead of us toward the house. Pike and I looked at each other.

'She's on the tough side.'

Pike said, 'Mm.'

The housekeeper let us in, and led us to the living room. She glanced nervously at Dolan as we went, almost as if she could sense that Dolan was a cop and that there might be trouble.

In the living room, Frank was staring out the French doors at the pool and the fruit trees where the stone lions prowled. It had been only three days since I'd seen him, but his skin was pasty with a drunk's sweat, his hair was greasy, and the air was sharp with BO. A short glass, now empty, rested in his lap. Maybe it had to be that way when you lost your only child.

Pike said, 'Frank.'

Frank gazed at Dolan without comprehension, then looked at Joe. 'Is Karen all right?'

'How much have you had to drink?'

'Don't you start that with me, Joe. Don't you start that.'

Joe went over and took the glass. 'This is Detective

Dolan, the one I told you about. She needs to ask questions.'

'Hello, Mr Garcia. I'm sorry for your loss.' Dolan held up her gold detective's shield.

Frank squinted at the badge, then considered Dolan almost as if he was afraid to ask the thing he most wanted to know. 'Who killed my daughter?'

'That's why I'm here, sir. We're trying to find out.'

'You people been on this for a week. Don't you have any idea who did this?'

It couldn't have been more pointed than that.

Dolan smiled gently, telling him that she understood his pain, and perhaps even shared it. 'I need to ask you about some people that you or Karen might've known.'

Frank Garcia shook his head, but when he spoke we could barely hear him. 'Who?'

'Did Karen know somebody named Julio Munoz?'

'Is that the bastard who killed her?'

'No, sir. We're contacting everyone in Karen's Rolodex, but four names have outdated numbers. We want to ask about their last contact with Karen, what she might've said, things like that.' Dolan was good. She told her lie smoothly and without hesitation as if it were an absolute fact.

Frank seemed annoyed that this small reason was all there was to it. 'I don't know any Julio Munoz.'

'How about Walter Semple or Vivian Trainor or Davis Keech? Karen might've known them in school, or maybe they worked for you.'

'No.' You could see he was trying to remember, and was disappointed that he couldn't.

'Karen never mentioned them to you?'

'No.'

Dolan said, 'Mr Garcia, when I moved out of my parents' house, I left boxes of things behind. Old school things. Old pictures. If Karen left anything like that here, could I look at them?'

He wheeled just far enough around to see his house-keeper. 'Maria, take her back to Karen's room, *por favor*.'

I was following Dolan when Frank said, 'I want to see you guys for a minute.'

He waited until Dolan disappeared through the big doorway, then lowered his voice. 'She knows more than she's telling, and I'll bet my last tortilla those people she asked about aren't what she said. Keep an eye on her back there. See if you can't get her to let on what she's really after.'

I guess a man doesn't go from being a stonemason to a multimillionaire by being an idiot.

Joe stayed with Frank, but I followed the hall until I came to Maria, waiting for me outside a door.

'*Gracias*, Maria. We'll be fine.'

I stepped into what had been Karen's room, and in a way still was. A teenager's furniture froze the room in time. Books and stuffed animals and posters of bands that hadn't existed for a dozen years made the door a time portal taking me into the past. A Flock of Seagulls. Jesus.

Dolan was thorough. Except for old clothes and the knickknacks young women collect, there wasn't much left in the room, but we spent almost three hours going through high school and college notebooks, high school yearbooks, and the bits of a life that accumulate in the shadows of a child's room. Other than clothes, the closet was a floor-to-ceiling wall of board games. Parcheesi, Monopoly, Clue, Life. We opened every box.

Maria brought Mexican iced tea at one point, sweet with lime and mint. We found more boxes under the bed. Most of them held clothes, but one was filled with notes and letters from a pen pal named Vicki Quesada that Karen had had during her first two years at UCLA. We skimmed every letter, looking for the four names, but found none of them. I felt a kind of distance, reading the letters, until one of them mentioned Joe. The date put it about the time Karen was a sophomore. Vicki had written that Joe sounded really hot, and she wanted Karen to send a picture. I smiled. 'That Joe.'

'What's that?'

'Nothing.'

Dolan frowned and touched her waist. 'Oh, shit.'

'What?'

'I'm being paged. Goddamnit, it's Krantz. I'll be right back.'

Dolan took her purse and left the room.

I finished going through the letters, and found six more references to Joe, the next being that Joe was 'soooo cute' (she'd gotten the picture). The letters were organized by date, so were easy to follow, but most of the references were questions: *What's it like dating a policeman? Aren't your friends nervous around him? Does he take you for rides in the car?* The first two or three references made me smile, but the last references didn't. Vicki wrote that she was sorry things weren't working out with Joe, but that men were bastards and always wanted what they couldn't have. In the last letter that mentioned him, she wrote, 'Why do you think he loves someone else?'

I felt awkward and ashamed, as if I had peeped through a keyhole into a part of Joe's life that he had not shared with me. I put the letters back in the box, and the boxes under the bed.

Dolan came back, looking irritated. 'You find anything?'

'No.'

'I've got some good news for the old man. We're releasing the girl's body. He can have her buried, at least.'

'Yeah. He'll appreciate that.' I was still thinking about Joe.

'Here's the bad news: Krantz isn't going to stake the funeral.'

That stopped me. 'Come on, Dolan. Staking the funeral is a no-brainer.' Killers will sometimes attend their victims' burials. Sometimes they'll even give themselves away.

'I *know* that, Cole, but it isn't up to me. Krantz is scared of putting in for so much overtime when he's got a twenty-four/seven on Dersh. He says how can he justify the other when we already know who did it.'

'He doesn't have squat on Dersh. Barney Fife would stake that funeral.'

Her mouth hardened until white dots appeared at either corner. 'We'll deal with it, World's Greatest, okay? I'm going to attend. I can probably scare up a couple of the other guys to come in off the clock. I hate to ask this, considering, but you think you could help out?'

I told her that I would.

'What about Deege? Did anyone ever follow up on him, or is *that* too much overtime?'

'You're a real shit, you know that?'

'I know it's not you, Dolan. I'm sorry.'

She shook her head then, and raised her hands. Suddenly tired with it all.

'I told you the uniforms are keeping an eye out. He hasn't turned up yet, is all. Okay?'

'I know it's not you.'

'Yeah. Right.'

She frowned at the room like maybe we'd forgotten the one place to look that would give us what we need. Finally, she said, 'I guess we're done here, Cole. Hell, it's after six. You want to grab a drink or something?'

'I'm having dinner with my girlfriend.'

'Oh. Right.' She put her hands on her hips and frowned at the room again. 'Listen, thanks for the help. I appreciate you getting me in here.'

'No problemo.'

She walked out ahead of me. When Dolan was gone, Frank said, 'She didn't take anything, did she?'

'No, Frank.'

He hunched in his chair, scowling. 'You find out what she wanted?'

'Just what she said. She was looking for names.'

'That bitch was lying.'

Joe and I walked out of his house feeling like dogs.

When we got to the cars, I said, 'When we were going through her room we found some letters in a box under the bed. Some of them mentioned you. I had to read them.'

Pike took that in.

'I'm sorry it didn't work out, Joe. You and Karen. She seemed like a nice girl.'

Pike looked up into the elm trees. Their leaves were a light green canopy. As still as if they were a painting.

'What did the letters say?'

I told him some of it.

'That's all?' Like he knew what was there and wanted me to say it.

I told him about the one that said he loved someone else.

'They say who?'

'No. It's none of my business.'

Rampart Division Family Day . . . June, fourteen years earlier

The tail car was a brown Caprice, floating four cars behind in the light Sunday morning traffic, two white guys with Internal Affairs Group crew cuts and sunglasses. CIA wannabes.

They were pretty good, but Pike was better. He made them on his way to pick up Karen.

When Pike walked her out to the truck, he could not see them, but as he settled into a groove on the Hollywood Freeway, they were with him again. He wondered if they knew where he was going and thought they must. If they didn't, they were in for a surprise. Karen said, 'Do I look okay?'

'Better than okay.' He'd been watching the rearview.

Now she gave him the little look out the corner of her eye. 'How much better?'

He held up his thumb and forefinger, maybe a quarter inch apart.

She slapped his leg.

He spread his fingers as wide as they would go.

'Better.'

She slid across the Ford Ranger's bench seat and snuggled into him, oblivious to the car or the men in the car or what might happen because of that car. She was wearing a bright yellow sundress and sandals, the yellow going well with her golden skin and white smile. Her black hair glistened in the late morning sun and smelled of lavender. She was a lovely young woman, bright and funny, and Pike enjoyed her company.

When he took the Stadium Way exit off the Golden State Freeway, the tail car left him. That meant they knew where he was going, and either were content to break off the surveillance or had someone assigned to pick him up inside.

He followed Stadium Way through the manicured green lawns of Elysian Park to Academy Road, saw that cars were already parking along the road just up from the gate to Dodger Stadium, and pulled the Ranger to the curb. Karen said, 'Look at all these cars. How many people will be here?'

'Five or six hundred, I guess.' Wozniak would be here. Along with his wife and daughter. Pike wondered again if the IAG spooks would have a man out.

Pike walked around the front of the truck and helped her out. Wilt Deedle, a Rampart bunco detective who weighed almost three hundred pounds, pulled in behind the Ranger and nodded. Joe nodded back. They didn't really know each other, but they were familiar enough to nod. Deedle's wife and four kids were wedged into his car. Deedle, his wife, and three of the kids were wearing matching Hawaiian shirts. The fourth kid, a teenaged girl, was wearing a black tee shirt and looked sullen.

Families and couples were leaving their cars and walking up a little road into the canyon. Pike took Karen's hand, and the two of them followed. Karen said, 'It doesn't look anything like I expected. It almost looks like a resort.'

Pike let his mouth twitch, as much for the little girl's wonder in her eyes as the notion of the Los Angeles Police Academy as a resort. 'Not much of a resort when it's a hundred degrees and you're running the obstacle course. You never been here before?'

'I knew it was here, but the closest I've been is Dodger Stadium. It's pretty.'

The Academy was snuggled between two ridges in the foothills of Elysian Park, a point-blank pistol shot north of Dodger Stadium. The buildings were Spanish and laid out beneath mature red pines and eucalyptus trees. You could stand in the Academy parking lot and see across acres of stadium parking past the bleachers and into the first-base seats. That close. The Ramparts Division Events Officer had wisely made sure that the Dodgers were out of town before booking the Academy on this particular Sunday for the Family Day Picnic. They wouldn't have to worry about game traffic, but the police were making plenty of their own. A burglary detective named Warren Steiner and one of the senior Rampart uniforms, Captain Dennis O'Halloran, were trying to pick the lock to the Dodgers' gate so the arriving families could use the ball club's parking lot. They weren't having much luck with it.

Pike led Karen uphill past the guard shack and the armory, along a little tarmac road that ran between the pines to the target range and the Recruit Training Center. A couple of hundred people were already spread around the track field, some already having staked out positions with spread blankets, others tossing Frisbees or Nerf balls, most just standing around because they hadn't yet had enough beer to loosen up. Three long barbecue grills were set up at the far end of the field by the picnic tables, clouding the trees with smoke and the smell of burning chicken. Rampart Homicide had drawn chef duty this year, and wore matching tee shirts that said Don't ask where we got the meat.

Cop humor.

Karen said, 'Do you see anyone you know?'

'Know most of them.'

'Who are your friends?'

Joe didn't know what to say to that. He was looking for Wozniak and for faces he had seen downtown at Parker Center. He thought it possible that IAG might've worked through Rampart command for an officer to continue the surveillance, but he didn't think so. Wozniak had a lot of years on the job, and IAG wouldn't be certain where the Rampart commander's loyalties would lie.

Karen tugged at his arm and grinned at him. 'We can't just stand here. Come on!'

The Division had set up a soft-drink table in front of a cement wall painted with the Academy symbol and the LAPD's motto, To Protect and to Serve. When Pike was a recruit, his class had been doing physical training on the track field one hot winter afternoon as their PT instructor shouted that unless they got the lead out of their asses they wouldn't be fit to protect dog shit or serve hot beer. A black kid named Elihu Gimble cracked that he'd be happy to serve, but only after coffee and donuts, and the entire class had had to run an extra five miles. Five months later, when Gimble was a probationary officer on patrol in East L.A. he'd been shot in the back by an unknown assailant while responding to a see-the-woman call. The shooter was never identified.

Pike led Karen to the table, and together they stood in

line for their drinks. Karen kept her arm looped in his, and before long she was chatting with everyone around them. Pike admired her. Whereas he rarely spoke, she spoke constantly. Whereas he felt obvious, and apart from others, she fit easily with an openness that was quickly returned. By the time they had their sodas, she had found another couple with whom to sit, a pale woman with twin boys whose husband was a uniformed officer named Casey. Casey worked the evening shift, and Pike had never met him.

They were spreading their blankets when Paulette Wozniak appeared behind them. 'Hello, Joe. Is this the young lady we've heard so much about?'

Karen flashed the wide, friendly smile and put out her hand. 'Karen Garcia. And I can't imagine Joe saying very much about anything, but if he's been talking about me, I'm glad. That's a good sign.'

The two women shook, Paulette returning her own smile, which was slow and real and pure in a way that made Pike think of a clean, deep pool. 'Paulette Wozniak. I'm married to Joe's partner, Abel. Everyone calls him Woz.' She pointed across the field to the trees beyond where Homicide was burning the mystery meat. Abel Wozniak and a little girl were just coming through the trees. Pike guessed that Woz had been showing his daughter the obstacle course. 'That's him with the bow legs and the girl.'

Paulette was eight years older than Joe, with short light brown hair and soft brown eyes and even teeth. Her fair skin was beginning to line around the eyes and the corners of her mouth. She didn't seem bothered by the lines, and Pike liked that. She rarely wore makeup, and Pike liked that, too. The lines made her face interesting and knowing.

Paulette touched Joe's arm. 'Could I borrow you for a minute, Joe?' She put the smile on Karen. 'I won't keep him long.'

Karen said, 'I'll finish spreading the blanket.'

Joe followed Paulette onto the track, and noticed that she stood so that she could see her husband. Her smile was gone, and her brow knitted into a tight line. Woz had stopped to speak with a black couple. She said, 'Joe, is something going on with Woz?'

Pike didn't answer.

'Why is he working so many extra shifts?'

Pike shook his head, and felt himself falling inward.

She frowned at him, and he thought that he might do anything to stop that frown, but he didn't know what to do. He didn't think it his place to tell her things that Woz should tell her. She said, 'Please don't play the voiceless man with me, Joe. I'm scared, and I'm worried about him.'

'I don't know what to tell you.' Not a lie. He didn't.

Her eyes went back to her husband, and she crossed her arms. 'I think he has a girlfriend.' She looked back at Joe again, and there was a lot of strength in her now. The strength made him want to hold her, but as soon as he realized that, he took a half-step away. She didn't notice. 'I want to know if he has someone.'

'I don't know anything about a girlfriend, Paulette.'

'Even when he doesn't work an extra shift, he leaves the house. When he's home, he's always pissed off. That isn't like him.'

Pike glanced over at Woz, and saw that he was looking at them. The black couple moved on, but Wozniak stood there. He wasn't smiling. Pike glanced over at the drink tables again, and saw two men he didn't recognize speaking with the Division commander. Behind them, another man was aiming a long-lens camera at them. The camera might've been pointing at the DC and the two strangers, but Pike knew it was pointing at him. Getting a shot of him speaking with Wozniak's wife. Even here at the Division picnic, they were watching.

Joe said, 'Would you like me to speak with him? I'll talk to him if you want.'

Paulette didn't say anything for a time, and then she shook her head. When she touched Joe's arm again, he felt something electrical tingle through his arms and legs, and he forced himself deeper into the pool. Even more calm. More still. She said, 'Thank you, Joe, but no. This is mine to deal with. Please don't tell him that I mentioned this to you.'

'I won't.'

'He's coming now. I'll tell him that I was inviting you and your girlfriend to the house. Is that all right?'

'Yes.'

'In fact, it's true. Because you are invited.'

Paulette Wozniak squeezed his arm, her hand lingering dry and warm, and then she walked across the field to meet her husband.

Joe Pike stood on the track, watching her walk away, and wished that the secrets they had weren't about this.

Karen smoothed the edges of the blanket, and listened to Marybeth Casey carry on about her twins (one of whom was a bed wetter), her husband, Walter (who didn't enjoy being an officer, but night school was just too much for them right now), and how these Division picnics were always such fun because you got to meet new people.

As Marybeth went on to describe the fibroid tumors in her left breast, Karen found that she was no longer listening. She was watching Joe and Paulette Wozniak, together on the running track. Karen told herself that she was being entirely too Latin at the flush of fear that surged through her when Paulette put her hand on Joe's arm. They were friends. She was married to Joe's partner, and she was so much older than Joe.

Karen stared at Joe so intently that her vision seemed to telescope, zooming close to his face, so that every pore seemed to stand out, every nuance exaggerated. Joe was the most difficult man to read she'd ever known. He was so enclosed that she thought he must've put himself in some small secret box that he kept deep within himself. That was part of why she was attracted to him, she knew. She'd read enough psychology texts to know that much. That she was drawn by the mystery, that some great and needing part of her wanted to open that box, to find his secret self.

She loved him. She'd even told her friends that she loved him, though she hadn't yet told Joe. He was so silent, she was afraid that he wouldn't respond in kind. He was so contained that she couldn't be sure.

Karen watched them talk, and felt the flush of jealousy when Paulette Wozniak touched him, but Joe was as unreadable with Paulette as he was with her. 'You're being silly,' she thought. 'He is like that with everyone.'

Paulette Wozniak touched Joe's arm again, then walked across the field toward her husband, and Karen knew then that she was wrong.

A sour wash of fear jolted through her as she watched Joe staring after Paulette Wozniak. Everything she saw in Joe's face and stance told her that his heart belonged to someone else.

CHAPTER 16

On the morning that Karen Garcia was buried, I stood naked on my deck, stretching in the darkness. The sun had not yet risen, and, for a time, I watched the few stars brilliant enough to burn their way through the halo of light that floated above the City of Angels, wondering if, somewhere out there, a killer was watching them, too. I thought not. Psycho killers probably slept in.

Little by little, the stiffness of sleep faded as my body warmed, and I eased from the stillness of hatha yoga to the dynamic tension of tae kwon do *katas*, starting slowly at first, then moving faster until the movements became explosive and fierce. I finished the *katas* wet with sweat as the canyon below my house lightened with the first purple glimmers of sunrise. I let the sweat cool, then gathered my things and went inside. Once, I stayed out too long, and the woman who lives in the next house saw me and made a wolf whistle. Her husband came out onto their deck, and he made a wolf whistle, too. Life in L.A.

I was standing in my kitchen, drinking orange juice and watching eggs boil, when the phone rang. I grabbed it on the first ring so it wouldn't wake Lucy.

Samantha Dolan said, 'I've got two guys who'll be at Forest Lawn with me.'

'Two. Wow, Dolan. There won't be room for the mourners.' I was still pissed off about Krantz.

'Save the attitude and keep your eyes open. You and Pike make five of us.'

'Pike will be with Frank.'

'He can still see, can't he? We're looking for a white

176

male between twenty and forty. He may linger after, and he may approach the grave. Sometimes they leave something, or they'll take a souvenir.'

'Krantz's buddy at the Feebs tell you that?' It was typical behavior for a serial killer.

'The burial's scheduled for ten. I'll be there at nine-thirty. And, Cole?'

'What?'

'Try not to be such an ass.'

Forest Lawn Memorial Park is four hundred acres of rolling green lawns at the foot of the Hollywood Hills in Glendale. With immaculate grounds, re-creations of famous churches, and burial areas with names like Slumberland, Vale of Memory, and Whispering Pines, I have always thought of it as a kind of Disneyland of the Dead.

Since Dolan was going to get there at nine-thirty, I wanted to get there earlier. But when I turned into the grounds and found Karen Garcia's burial site, Dolan was already there, and so were a hundred other people. She was parked with an easy eyes-forward view of the crowd on the slope. A long-lens Konica camera rested in her lap. She would use it to take pictures of the crowd for later identification.

I slipped into the passenger side of her Beemer, and took a breath. 'Dolan, I know you're doing what you can. I was a jerk this morning. I apologize.'

'You were, but I accept. Forget it.'

'Just wanted to get that out. Makes me feel small.'

'That's your girlfriend's problem.'

I looked over at her, but she was staring out the window. Ouch.

'You know where Krantz is this morning?'

'On Dersh?'

'A surveillance team is on Dersh. Krantz and Bishop are

going to the service. Mills is going, too. They want to sit where Councilman Maldenado can see them.'

I couldn't do what she did. I couldn't work with guys like Krantz and Bishop. Maybe that was why I'm on my own.

'I thought you said you were coming at nine-thirty.'

'I figured you'd try to beat me, so I came earlier.'

I looked over at her, and she was smiling.

'You're something, Samantha.'

'Guess we're cats of the same stripe, World's Greatest.'

I smiled back. 'Okay. So it's me, you, and two other guys. How do you want to play it?'

She glanced up the hill toward a marble mausoleum. 'Got a guy up at that mausoleum, and another guy down below. They see anyone who looks suspicious, they'll get the license numbers.' The high man was sitting on the grass outside the mausoleum above us. A little road ran in front of it, identical to the road where we were parked. If the killer wanted to come and watch, he could park up there. People were scattered throughout the slope below us, the low man invisible among them. 'I figure you can work in close with the crowd since you know some of these people. I'll stay here snapping shots of the procession, then I'll come up.'

'Okay.'

'Right now, why don't you walk the perimeter.'

It wasn't a question.

She looked at me. 'Well?'

'Yes, ma'am.' If you're on free time, I guess you can tell everyone what to do.

As I slid out of the Beemer, she said, 'By the way, that was the first time you called me Samantha.'

'I guess so.'

'Don't let it happen again.'

But she was smiling, and I grinned as I walked away.

I spent the next few minutes drifting along the perimeter of the crowd, counting sixteen Anglo men between

178

twenty and forty. When I glanced down at Dolan, she was pointing the camera at me. I guess she was bored.

A blue Nissan Sentra came up the hill a few minutes before ten, parked where the other cars had parked, and Eugene Dersh climbed out.

I said, 'Oh, man.'

Dersh was conservatively dressed in a beige sport coat and slacks. He locked his car, and was walking up the hill when two unmarked detective rides turned in and idled by the front gate, unsure what to do. Williams was driving the second car. The first car was the same guys who had followed me.

The cop by the mausoleum stood and stared at them. He hadn't seen Dersh, but he recognized the RHD cars.

I trotted down to Dolan. 'Looks like the gang's all here.'

Dersh saw us looking at him, recognized me, and waved.

I waved back.

At a quarter after ten, four LAPD motorcycles escorted the hearse through the main gate. Three gleaming black limos followed, trailing a line of cars that had been waxed and buffed until they glittered with bits of the sun. Dersh watched them come, a kind of benign curiosity on his face.

When the line of cars reached us, a dozen people who looked like family members emerged from the limos. The driver of the lead car took Frank's wheelchair from the trunk as Joe and another man helped Frank out. Joe was dressed in a charcoal three-piece suit. The dark glasses made him look like a Secret Service agent, but since this was L.A., everyone was wearing sunglasses. Even the priest.

Councilman Maldenado and Abbot Montoya climbed out of the last limo. Bishop and Krantz and Assistant Chief Mills squeezed out of the sixth car, and hurried to fall in behind the councilman. Anxious to protect and to serve him, I guess.

Dolan and I were walking over when Krantz and Bishop saw us. 'What in hell are you doing here with Cole?'

Dolan pointed at Dersh.

Krantz and Bishop turned and saw Dersh looking back. Dersh smiled broadly and waved.

Krantz said, 'Holy shit!'

Bishop nudged Krantz. 'Wave back, goddamnit, before he suspects something.'

They waved back.

Bishop said, 'Smile!'

Krantz smiled.

Joe had pushed Frank most of the way up the hill when a news van from one of the local network affiliates tore through the gate. Vans from a second network affiliate and then Lucy's station barreled through ten seconds behind it, braking hard alongside the hearse. Their microwave dishes extended even as camera operators and on-air reporters jumped out.

Dolan said, 'This can't be good.'

Dolan and I walked faster, Krantz and Bishop after us.

The three reporters hurried toward Frank, two of them with radio mikes and one without.

I said, 'Wake up, Bishop. Have the uniforms keep those people away.'

Dolan and I put ourselves between Frank and the reporters as Krantz ran for the motorcycle cops. A good-looking red-haired woman leaned past me, reaching for Frank with her microphone. 'Mr Garcia, have the police made any progress in catching the serial killer?'

Bishop said, 'Oh, shit.'

A tall African-American reporter who had played professional football tried to press between me and one of the uniforms, but neither of us gave ground. 'Mr Garcia, do you believe a man named Eugene Dersh killed your daughter, and, if so, sir, why?'

Bishop jerked at Krantz's arm, his voice a panicked whisper. 'How in hell did these bastards find out?'

Behind us, Frank Garcia said, 'What is this? What are they talking about, serial killer? Who's this man, Dersh?'

Councilman Maldenado stepped forward, trying to turn the press away. 'Please. His child is about to be buried.'

Eugene Dersh had come to the edge of the growing crowd, too far away to hear, but curious like everyone else.

The redhead's camera operator saw Dersh and punched her in the back. He didn't tap her; he punched her. '*Sonofabitch! That's Dersh.*'

She shoved the black reporter out of the way and ran toward Dersh. The black reporter ran after her. Dersh looked as surprised and confused as everyone else.

Frank Garcia tried to see Dersh, but since he was in the chair, people blocked his view. 'Who is that?' He twisted around to Maldenado. 'Henry, do they know who killed Karen? *Did that man kill Karen?*'

Up the hill, Dersh was afraid and embarrassed as the two reporters barked questions. The mourners around the grave heard the reporters with Dersh, and began to murmur and stare.

The final reporter was an Asian-American woman who stayed with Frank. 'There were others, Mr Garcia. Haven't the police told you? Five people have been murdered. Karen was the fifth.' The reporter glanced from Frank to Maldenado, then back to Frank. 'Some maniac has been *hunting human beings* here in Los Angeles for the past nineteen months.' You could see she liked saying it because of how the words would play on the news. She pointed at Dersh. 'The police suspect that man. Eugene Dersh.'

Frank lurched higher in his chair, craning to see Dersh. 'That man killed Karen? That sonofabitch murdered my daughter?'

Maldenado shouldered in and forced the Asian-American reporter away. 'This isn't the time. I'll make a statement, but not now. Let this man bury his daughter.'

Above us, Eugene Dersh pushed past the two reporters, walking fast back down the hill to his car. They dogged him, peppering him with questions as their cameras recorded it. Dersh would be able to see himself on the news again, though he probably wouldn't be as happy about it this time.

Frank's face was the color of dried blood. He bobbed in his chair, wrestling the wheels to try to chase after Dersh. '*Is that him? Is that the sonofabitch?*'

Dersh climbed into his car, the reporters still shouting their questions. His voice carried in the still air, high and frightened. 'What are you talking about? I didn't kill anyone. I just found her body.'

Frank screamed, '*I'll kill you!*'

He twisted so hard that he pitched forward, falling out of the chair. His family gasped and two of the women made sharp sounds. Pike, Montoya, and several of the family clustered around him, Pike lifting the old man back into the chair as if he weighed nothing.

Dersh drove away, and when he sped through the gate, the two plainclothes cars quietly fell in behind him.

The priest told Frank's brothers to get the family seated as quickly as possible. Everyone was embarrassed and uncomfortable, and Frank's housekeeper cried loudly, but the crowd settled as the pallbearers gathered at the hearse. I tried to find Dolan, but she had joined Mills, Bishop, and Krantz in a frantic conversation at the edge of the crowd. Krantz saw me, and stormed over. 'You and your buddy, Pike, get your butts to Parker Center as soon as she's in the ground. We're fuckin'-A gonna figure out what happened here.' He walked away fast.

The climbing sun became a hot torch in the sky as the family took their seats, and the pallbearers delivered Karen's body to its grave. Heat soaked into my shoulders and face until I could feel the delicate tickle of sweat running out of my hair. Around me, a few people cried, but most simply stared, lost in a moment that was both sad and unsettling.

The three news cameras stood in a line below us, recording Karen Garcia's burial.

They looked like a firing squad.

CHAPTER 17

News vans lined Los Angeles Street outside Parker Center. Reporters and technicians milled nervously on the sidewalk, clustering around every cop who came out to grab a cigarette like piranha on bad meat. The city didn't allow smoking in its buildings, so addicted officers had to sneak butts in the stairwells and bathrooms, or come outside. These guys didn't know anything more about Dersh or the murders than anyone else, but the reporters didn't believe it. Word had spread big, and someone had to feed the networks' hunger for news.

The three skinny palms outside Parker Center seemed bent and fragile as Joe and I turned into the drive, two cars behind Dolan. Frank's limo was already at the curb, Frank's driver and Abbot Montoya helping him into the chair.

We parked between a silver Porsche Boxster and a taupe Jaguar XK8. Lawyers, here to cut deals. We got out, and for a moment Pike stared up at the squat building. The midmorning sun bounced hard off the seven strips of blue glass and burned down on us, mirrored in Pike's glasses.

Pike surprised me by saying, 'It's been a long time since I was here.'

'You don't want to go in, you can wait out here.'

The last time Joe Pike was here was the day that Abel Wozniak died.

Pike made his little non-smile. 'Won't be as bad as the Mekong.'

He pulled off the suit coat, unfastened the shoulder holster, and wound its straps around the .357 Python revolver. He put his jacket in the little storage bay behind the seats, then unbuttoned the vest, and put it with the jacket. He stripped off the tie and the shirt. He was wearing a white guinea tee beneath the shirt, and let it go with that. The guinea tee, the charcoal pants, the black leather shoes, countered by the cut muscles of his shoulders and chest and the brilliant red tattoos, made quite a fashion statement. A female detective coming out to her car stared.

We gave our names to the lobby guard, and Stan Watts came down a few minutes later.

I said, 'Frank Garcia go upstairs?'

'Yeah. You're the last.' Watts stood to the side of the elevator with his arms crossed, staring at Pike.

Pike stared back behind the dark glasses.

Watts said, 'I knew Abel Wozniak.'

Pike didn't respond.

'If I don't get another chance to say this, fuck you.'

Pike cocked his head. 'You want a piece, step up.'

I said, 'Hey, Watts. You really think Dersh is good for it?'

Watts didn't answer. Guess he was thinking about Joe.

We left the elevator on the fifth floor and followed Watts through the Robbery-Homicide squad room. Most of the detectives were working their phones, and more phones were ringing. They were busy because of the news coverage, but as we entered, a ripple of attention swept through the room. Eyes went to Joe, tracking him across the floor.

Behind us, a voice I didn't recognize spoke just loud enough to be heard.

'Cop killer.'

Pike didn't turn.

Watts led us to the conference room, where Frank Garcia was saying, 'I want to know why the sonofabitch is still walking around. If this man killed my daughter, how come he's not in jail?'

Councilman Maldenado stood on one side of him, arms crossed, and Abbot Montoya stood on the other, hands in his pockets. Dolan was seated as far from everybody else as she could get, just like in the briefings. Krantz and Bishop were with Frank, Krantz trying to explain. 'Dersh is the suspect, Mr Garcia, but we still have to build a case. The district attorney won't file without enough evidence to get a conviction. We don't want to leave any wiggle room here. We don't want another O.J.'

Frank rubbed at his face. 'Oh, Jesus Christ. Don't even joke about that.'

Bishop told us to take a seat. 'I know you're wondering what happened back there. We were just explaining to Mr Garcia that there's been more to this investigation than we've let on.'

Bishop was good. His voice was smooth and sure, and both Montoya and Maldenado looked a lot calmer than they had at the cemetery, though Frank was visibly shaking.

Maldenado wasn't happy. 'I only wish you had seen fit to tell us that there were things you needed to keep secret, Captain. It would've saved Mr Garcia the shock of what just happened. I mean, we're *all* shocked. *Five* people killed. A *serial* killer. And the man you say did it comes to the *funeral*.'

Krantz sat with half his ass on the table, and looked directly at Frank. 'I want the bastard who killed your daughter, Mr Garcia. I'm sorry you had to find out this way, but we made the right decision to keep this thing under wraps. Now that Dersh knows we suspect him, well, that takes away our advantage. I wish I knew how the goddamned press found out because I'd crimp his nuts but good.'

Frank said, 'Listen, I'm not pissed you didn't tell me, okay? I was pissed off at you guys at first, but maybe I was wrong. All I care about is getting the sonofabitch who killed Karen. That's all.'

Bishop said, 'Why don't you finish bringing them up to date, Harve.'

Krantz was making a good impression, and Bishop was pleased.

Krantz gave them everything, admitting that there were now a total of five murders, and that they had been running a Task Force for almost a year. Montoya asked about the first four victims and Krantz went through the names, starting with Julio Munoz.

When Krantz said their names, Frank straightened in his chair, looking at me, then Dolan. 'Those are the people you asked about.'

Krantz shook his head, certain that Frank was mistaken. 'No, sir. Cole couldn't've asked about them. He didn't know.'

Frank said, 'Not Cole. Her.'

Dolan cleared her throat, and shifted in her chair. She looked at her hands flat on the table for a moment, then met Krantz's eyes. 'Cole knew it all.'

The room stopped.

Krantz said, 'What are you talking about, Detective?'

'Cole came to me with the five vics. He knew the signature, and their identities, so I told him about the Task Force. He got me in to see Mr Garcia so I could ask about the first four.'

Krantz considered Pike, and seemed, in a way, pleased. 'If he knew, then Pike knew.'

Pike said, 'Yes.'

'I guess we know who shot off his mouth.'

Dolan said, 'That's bullshit, Harvey. They didn't say anything.'

Frank Garcia looked hurt. 'You knew this and you didn't tell me?'

Pike said, 'It was smart not to tell you. Krantz is right about that. It was better for the investigation.'

Dolan said, 'He was going to go to Mr Garcia with it,

187

but I convinced him not to, Harvey. Why the hell would he leak it to the press? There's nothing in it for him.'

Bishop said, 'How'd you find out about the other victims, Cole?'

'I'm a detective. I detected.'

Krantz slid off the table, disgusted and showing his palms to Bishop. 'You see what happens when you let people in? We're on top of this for a year, and now we're fucked because of these guys. And Dolan.'

Dolan stood then, eyes hard as bullet casings. 'Fuck you, Pants. It was the only way to play it.'

When she said it, Krantz turned purple.

Bishop cleared his throat and moved closer to Maldenado. 'We're not fucked, Harvey. We're still going to make an arrest.' Saying that for the councilman. He turned toward Dolan. 'I can't believe you compromised our investigation like this, Detective. This is a serious breach. Serious.'

I said, 'I already had it, Bishop. I had the vics, the feds, and I knew that you guys were running a Task Force. I was just trying to find out why you were putting so much into Dersh.'

Krantz squared his jaw again. 'What in hell does that mean? We're putting it into Dersh because Dersh is the shooter.'

'You've got nothing for the shooter. You're pressing Dersh because you're desperate for a collar.'

Frank pushed his chair forward, accidentally hitting Montoya. 'Waitaminute. It's not Dersh?'

Krantz said, '*Yes*. It's Dersh.'

'All they have is a profile that says the shooter is probably someone like Dersh. They don't have any evidence that it's really him. *Nada*.'

Williams leaned forward, the first of the others to say anything. 'You're off base, Cole. The Feebs said the perp would try to insert himself into the investigation, maybe by pretending to know something, and that's just what

Dersh did. You've read the interviews. Dersh dragged Ward down that slope just so they could find the vic.' Williams realized what he was saying then, and looked embarrassed. 'Sorry. Ms Garcia.'

Frank was nodding. He wanted it to make sense because he wanted to know who killed his daughter.

'So, you say this Dersh is the man, but you can't prove it?'

Krantz spread his hands, reasonable. 'Not yet. We believe he did it, but, as Cole says, we don't at this time have any direct evidence linking him to these crimes.'

'Then what are you doing to get the bastard?'

Krantz and Bishop traded a look, and then Krantz shrugged. 'Well, now that we've lost the advantage, the only thing we can do is sweat him. We'll have to get aggressive, search his residence for evidence, and keep up the pressure until he either confesses or makes a mistake.'

I shook my head. 'You're out of your mind, Krantz.'

Krantz raised his eyebrows at me. 'Good thing you're not conducting this investigation.'

Bishop watched Maldenado for a reaction. 'How does that sound, Councilman?'

'Our only concern is that the killer be apprehended, Captain. Certainly for the murder of Karen Garcia, but also for the sake of our city and the other victims. We want justice.'

Krantz tipped his head toward me and Joe. 'Before we do anything, we'd better plug the leak.'

I said, 'It didn't come from us, Krantz. It could've been some uniform who overheard something or maybe just some sharp reporter who dug out the facts. Maybe it was you.'

Krantz smiled a reasonable smile. 'I heard that your girlfriend works for KROK. I wonder if that has something to do with it.'

Everyone in the room stared at me. Even Dolan.

'I didn't tell anybody, Krantz. Not my girlfriend. Not anyone.'

Krantz took his seat on the table again, gazing pointedly at Maldenado. 'Well, we're going to find out, but right now we've got a maniac to get off the street. We've had one major leak, we can't afford to have another. It could mean the difference whether we nail this guy, or not.'

Frank looked from me to Joe. Joe was watching Frank, and I wondered what he was thinking.

Frank said, 'I don't believe they said anything.'

Maldenado maintained the eye contact with Krantz, then spread his hands. 'Frank, I think the police have proven that we can trust their efforts. I certainly hope that Mr Pike and Mr Cole weren't behind this, ah, lapse in judgment, but as long as we have confidence in the police, there's no reason we can't work with them directly.'

Frank said, 'Get Dersh.'

Krantz said, 'That's right, Mr Garcia. We've got to get Dersh. We can't afford to be distracted.'

Frank nodded again, and reached a gesture toward Joe. 'Sure. That makes sense, doesn't it, Joe? I don't believe you told anyone. But as long as the police are doing such a good job, I don't need you to waste your time staying on them, right?'

Pike spoke so softly you couldn't hear it. 'Right, Frank.'

Krantz went to the door and opened it. No one said anything as we left.

We walked out through the squad room, and out to my car. When we got there, I said, 'Is it me, or were we just fired?'

'It's not you.'

Pike's Jeep was still at the church. I drove the wrong way up the parking lane to let Pike out, pulling in across the Jeep's stern. We hadn't spoken on the ride, and I was wondering, as I often do, what he was feeling behind the dark glasses and beneath the blank mask of his face.

He had to hurt. He had to be feeling loss, and anger, and shame.

'You want to come up to the house and talk about this?'

'Nothing to talk about. We're off, Krantz is on.'

Pike took his gun from the glove box and clothes from behind the seats, got out, and drove away.

I guess I would feel those things for both of us.

CHAPTER 18

The woman who lives in the next house was standing on her slope, watering bright red ice plants. The Santa Anas were gone, but the stillness made me think that they would return. The air is never more still in Los Angeles than in those moments before the wind screams down on us again, once more torching the world into flame. Maybe the stillness is a warning.

The woman called, so far away I could barely hear her, 'How are you doing over there?'

'Hot. How're those boys?'

'They're boys. I saw you on TV.'

I didn't know what she was talking about.

'On the midday news. At that funeral. Oh, there's my phone.'

She turned off her hose and ran inside.

I let myself in through the kitchen and turned on the television, but it was soap operas. Guess my fifteen minutes had come and gone, and I had missed it.

I changed into jeans and a tee shirt, then made scrambled eggs. I ate at the sink, staring out the window while I drank milk from the carton. The floor in my kitchen is Mexican paver tiles, some of which were still loose from the '94 earthquake. When you're unemployed you have time to think about fixing things like that, only I didn't know how. I thought I could learn. It would give me something to do, and there might even be a measure of satisfaction in it. Unlike private detecting.

I stepped from tile to tile until I had stood on every tile, rocking a bit to see if the tiles were sound. Six of them were loose.

The cat came in and sat by his bowl, watching me. He was holding something in his mouth.

'What you got there?'

The something moved.

'I think I'm going to fix these tiles. You want to help?'

The cat took the something back out again. He'd seen me attempt repairs before.

By twenty minutes before five I had chipped up four of the tiles, covering the floor with little bits of cement. I turned on the TV again, figuring to let the news play while I worked on the tiles, but Eugene Dersh was standing outside his house while a dozen cops carried evidence boxes past the camera. He looked scared. I switched channels and found a taped report of Dersh being interviewed at his front door, peeking out through a two-inch crack, saying, 'I don't understand any of this. All I did was find that poor girl's body. I didn't kill anyone.' I switched channels again, and found Krantz surrounded by reporters. Every time a reporter asked a question, Krantz answered, 'No comment'.

I turned off the set. 'Krantz. You prick.'

At six-twenty, I was back to fixing the tiles when Lucy let herself in carrying a large white bag filled with Chinese food. 'I tried calling to warn you that the story was breaking.'

'I know. I was at Forest Lawn.'

She put the bag on the counter. 'What's all this on the floor?'

'I'm fixing the tiles.'

'Oh.'

She sounded as impressed as that cat.

'Elvis, do you think it's him?' Dersh was already 'him'.

'I don't know, Luce. I don't think so. Krantz wants to believe it's Dersh, and he thinks the way to prove it is to put on so much pressure that Dersh breaks. Everything we're seeing now is being fed by Krantz. He was already planning it when I left Parker Center. These reporters are saying just what Krantz wants them to say, that Dersh is guilty because it says so in the profile.'

'Waitaminute. They don't have anything specific that ties Dersh to these crimes?'

'Nothing.'

I sat in the cement dust on my floor and told her everything I knew, starting with Jerry Swetaggen but not naming him. I went through the forensics reports and the autopsy results, and every detail of the case that I remembered from Dolan's brief. As I talked, she took off her shoes and her jacket, and sat with me in the dust. Wearing a six-hundred-dollar pants suit, and she sat with me in the dust. Love.

When I finished, Lucy said, 'Did I wake up in Nazi Germany?'

'It gets better.'

'What?'

'Frank fired us.'

She gave me a look of infinite care, and touched my head. 'It's been a rotten day, hasn't it?'

'The pits.'

'Would you like a hug?'

'What are my other choices?'

'Whatever you want.'

Even when I'm feeling bad, she can make me smile.

After I vacuumed the kitchen, Lucy put Jim Brickman on the stereo as I made drinks, the two of us setting the containers of food in the oven to warm. We were doing that when the doorbell rang.

Samantha Dolan was standing there.

'Hope you don't mind my coming by like this.'

'Not at all.'

She was wearing jeans and a man's white shirt with the tail out. Her eyes glistened, but not from crying. She didn't look too steady.

When Dolan walked in, she saw Lucy, still in the kitchen, and plucked at my arm. 'I guess that's the girlfriend.'

She'd had a couple, all right.

Dolan followed me into the kitchen, where I introduced them. 'Lucy, this is Samantha Dolan. Dolan, this is Lucy Chenier.'

'You don't have to call me Dolan, for Christ's sake.' She put out her hand and Lucy took it.

Lucy said, 'Pleasure to meet you. I understand you're with the police.'

Dolan held on to her hand. 'So far.' Then Dolan saw our drinks. 'Oh, you're drinking. Don't mind if I do.'

She'd had more than a couple.

I said, 'Gin and tonic okay?'

'You got any tequila?' Call it three or four.

As I made Dolan a drink, she squinted at the tiles. 'What's up with the floor?'

'Home repairs.'

'First time, huh?'

Everyone has something to say.

Lucy said, 'We were just about to eat Chinese food. Would you like to stay?'

Dolan smiled at Lucy. 'That's some accent. Where you from?'

Lucy smiled back nicely. 'Louisiana. And you?'

'Bakersfield.'

'They raise cows there, don't they?'

I handed Dolan the tequila. 'So what's up, Dolan?'

'Krantz busted me off the Task Force.'

'I'm sorry.'

'Not your fault. I didn't have to play it the way I did, and I don't believe it was you who ratted to the press.' She tipped her drink toward Lucy. 'Not even with your friend here being one of them. Anyway, I don't blame you, and I wanted you to know.'

'So what're you going to do?'

She laughed, but it's the kind of laugh you give when your only other choice is to cry. 'Nothing I can do. Bishop put me back on the table, but he won't let it go. He says he's going to take a few days to cool off, then he's going to talk it over with the assistant chiefs and figure out the appropriate action. He's thinking about transferring me out.'

Lucy said, 'Just because you confirmed what Elvis already knew?'

'They're serious about their secrets downtown, Counselor. It's called compromising an investigation, and that's what they think I did. If I'm a good enough girl and kiss Bishop's ass, maybe he'll keep me around.'

Lucy frowned. 'If this becomes a gender-bias issue, you could have legal recourse.'

Dolan laughed. 'Honey, gender bias is the only reason I'm still there. Look, that's not why I came.' She glanced back at me. 'I agree with you about Dersh. That poor bastard is getting railroaded, but there isn't much I can do about it right now without tanking what little career I have left.'

'Okay.'

'Krantz is right about one thing in all this. Dersh and Ward are lying about something. I was behind the two-way glass when Watts interviewed them. You can see it a little bit in the transcript, but you could see it for sure in the room. That's why Krantz is so convinced.'

'I'm listening. What are they lying about?'

'I don't have a clue, but I'm sure Ward is scared. He knows something that he doesn't want to talk about. I'm not in a position to do anything about it, World's Greatest, but you could.'

I nodded. 'Yeah. Maybe I could.'

Dolan finished the drink, and put it down. It hadn't lasted long. 'I'd better go. Sorry to barge in.'

'Are you sure you wouldn't like to stay for dinner?'

Dolan went to the door, then gazed back at Lucy.

'Thanks, anyway, but there probably wouldn't be enough for both of us.'

Lucy smiled the nice smile again. 'No. There isn't.'

When I got back to the kitchen, Lucy had the containers out of the oven and was opening them.

'She likes you.'

'What are you talking about?'

'You don't think she came here just to talk about Eugene Dersh, do you? She likes you.'

I didn't say anything.

'Bitch.'

'Are you jealous?'

Lucy turned the sweet smile on me.

'If I were jealous, she'd be getting stitches.'

There isn't much you can say to that.

When Lucy spoke again, her voice was soft. 'So, are you going to do it?'

'What?'

'Try to help Dersh.'

I thought about it, and then I nodded. 'I don't think he's the shooter, Lucille. And if he isn't, then he's just some guy out there all alone with the weight of a city on him.'

Lucy came close and put her arms around me.

'I guess that's you, lover boy. The last white knight.'

That's me.

CHAPTER 19

Lake Hollywood was quiet the next morning, the air cool in the early hour. I went up just after sunrise, hoping to get the jump on newspeople and the morbidly curious, and I had. Walkers and joggers once more looped the four-mile circumference of the lake, but none of them gawked at the murder site, or even seemed aware of it.

Having opened the crime scene, the police had taken down their yellow tape and withdrawn the guards. I left my car by the chain-link gate, and followed the trail down through the brush to the place where Karen Garcia's body had been found. The ripped footprints where the coroner's people had carried her out were still there, cut into the soil. Blood marks the color of dead roses flagged her resting place.

I stared at that spot for a moment, then went north along the shore, counting paces. Twice the bank dropped away so quickly, and was so overgrown with brush, that I had to take off my shoes and step in the water, but most of the shoreline was flat and bare enough to make good time.

Fifty-two paces from the blood marks, I found a six-inch piece of orange tape tied to a tree where Dersh and Riley reached the water. The slope was steep; their long, skidding footprints still visible, winding down through a clutter of small trees. I backtracked their footprints up, and pretty soon I was pushing my way through a dense overgrowth before popping out onto the trail. Another piece of the orange tape was tied here, too, marking where Dersh had told the investigator they had left the trail.

I walked up the trail a hundred yards, then turned back past the tape for about the same distance. I could see the lake from further up the trail, but not from the orange tape, and I wondered why they had picked this spot to find their way down. The brush was thick, the tree canopy dense, and the light poor. Any kid with a couple of years in the Scouts would know better, and so would just about anyone else. Of course, maybe neither Dersh nor Ward had been a Scout, or maybe they just had to take a leak. Maybe they just figured what the hell, here was as good a place as any, even though it wasn't.

I went back to my car, drove down the hill to the Jungle Juice, and used their phone book to look up Riley Ward & Associates. I copied the phone number and address, then drove to West Hollywood.

Ward had his offices in a converted Craftsman house on what was once a residential street south of Sunset Boulevard. The Craftsman house had a lovely front porch, and elaborate woodwork that had been painted in bright shades of peach and turquoise, neither of which went with the two television news vans that were parked out front.

I parked in a little lot belonging to a dentist's office, and waited. Two people went into Ward's building, one of them being an on-air reporter I recognized because he looked like a surfer dude. They were inside maybe three minutes, then came out and stood by their van, disappointed. Ward was still refusing interviews. Or maybe he wasn't there.

A third van arrived. Two young guys got out, one Asian-American with black horned-rim glasses and the other blond with very short hair. The Asian-American guy had white streaks in his hair, going for that Euro-trash look. The new guys joined the surfer and his friend, the four of them laughing about something as a young woman got out of the other van and went over. She was wearing a bright yellow spring dress and thick-soled shoes that had to be damned near impossible to walk in, and cat's-eye glasses. Fashion slaves.   .

I went over, grinning like we were all just journalists together. 'You guys here to get Ward?'

The surfer shook his head. 'He's not having it. We'll wait him out, though.'

'Maybe he's not in there.'

The young woman in the canary dress said, 'Oh, he's in there. I saw him go in this morning.'

'Ah.'

I headed across the street.

The girl said, 'Forget it, amigo. He won't talk to you.'

'We'll see.'

The little porch opened to what had once been the living room but was now a reception area. The smell of fresh coffee was strong in the little house, hanging over a sweeter smell, as if someone had brought Danish. A young woman in a black body suit and vest watched me suspiciously from behind a glass desk with a little name plate that read Holly Mira. 'May I help you?'

'Hi, Holly. Elvis Cole to see Mr Ward.' I gave her the card, and then I lowered my voice. 'About Karen Garcia.'

She put the card down without looking at it. 'I'm sorry. Mr Ward isn't giving interviews.'

'I'm not a reporter, Holly. I'm working for the dead girl's family. You can understand how they'd have questions.'

Her face softened, but she still didn't touch the card. 'You're working for the family.'

'The Garcia family. His attorney is a man named Abbot Montoya. You can call them if you like.' I took out the card Montoya had given me and put it next to mine. 'Please tell Mr Ward that the family would appreciate it. I promise that I won't take much of his time.'

Holly read both cards, then gave me a shy smile. 'Are you really a private investigator?'

I tried to look modest. 'Well, I'm what you might call the premier example.'

Holly smiled wider. 'I know he's got a conference call soon, but I'm sure he'll speak with you.'

'Thanks, Holly.'

Two minutes later Riley Ward followed Holly out to the reception room, and now Ward was holding the cards. He was wearing a burgundy shirt buttoned to the neck, gray triple-pleated slacks, and soft gray Italian loafers, but even the nice clothes couldn't cover his strain. 'Mr Cole?'

'That's right. I appreciate your seeing me, considering what's happened.'

He bent the cards back and forth, looking nervous and uneasy. 'You wouldn't believe. It's been a nightmare.'

'I'll bet.'

'I mean, all we did was find her, and now, well, Gene isn't a killer. He just isn't. Please tell her family that. I know they won't believe me, but he isn't.'

'Yes, sir. I'll tell them. I'm not here about Mr Dersh, though. I'm trying to put some of the family's concerns to rest, if you know what I mean. About the body.' I glanced at Holly and let it drop, implying that the family's concerns were better discussed privately.

Ward nodded. 'Well, okay. Ah, why don't you come into my office.'

His office was spacious, with a large plank desk, an overstuffed couch, and matching chairs. Pictures of Ward with an attractive woman and two bucktoothed children lined a narrow table behind the desk. Ward gestured to the couch. 'Can I get you a cup of coffee?'

'No, thanks.'

Riley peeked out the window at the news vans, then took the chair facing the pictures. 'They're driving me crazy. They came to my home. They were here when I arrived this morning. It's insane.'

'I'm sure.'

'Now I have to waste my day hiring an attorney, and it's so much worse for poor Gene.'

'Yes, sir. It is.' I took out a pad as if I were going to take notes, then leaned toward him, glancing at the windows like they might have ears. 'Mr Ward, what I'm going to say here, well, I'd appreciate it if you didn't repeat it, okay? The family would appreciate it. You let this out, and it might hurt the investigation.'

Ward peered at me, his eyes nervous and apprehensive. You could almost hear him think, *now* what?

I waited.

He realized I was waiting for him, and nodded. 'All right. Yes. Of course.'

'The family thinks that the police are off base about Mr Dersh. We're not confident that they have the right man.'

Hope flashed over his face, making me feel like a turd.

'Of *course* they don't. Gene couldn't do this.'

'I agree. So the family, well, we're conducting our own investigation, if you know what I mean.'

He nodded, seeing a way out for his friend Gene.

'So I have a few questions, you see?'

'You bet. I'll help any way I can.'

Anxious now. Raring to go.

'Okay. Great. It has to do with why you left the trail.'

He frowned, and didn't look so anxious anymore. 'We wanted to see the lake.'

I smiled. Mr Friendly.

'Well, I know, but after I read your statements I went up to the lake and walked through it with the police.'

Ward pursed his lips and glanced at his watch. 'Holly, hasn't that damned attorney called yet?'

She called back, 'Not yet, Riley.'

'I found the little tape they used to mark where you left the main trail. The underbrush was pretty dense right there.'

He crossed his arms and frowned harder, obviously

uncomfortable. 'I don't understand. These are things the family wants to know?'

'I'm just curious about why you left the trail where you did. There were easier places to walk down.'

Riley Ward stared at me for a full thirty seconds without moving. He wet his lips once, thinking so hard that you could almost see the wheels and gears turning in his head. 'Well, we didn't discuss it. I mean, we didn't *research* what was the best way to get down. We just *went*.'

'Another ten yards the brush was a lot thinner.'

'We wanted to go down to the lake, we went down to the lake.' He suddenly stood, went to the door, and called to Holly again. 'Would you try him for me, please. I can't stand this waiting.' He put his hands in his pockets, then took them out and waved at me. 'Who cares why we left the trail right there? Can it *possibly* matter?'

'If you left because someone threatening scared you, then, yes, it could matter a great deal. That person could be the killer.'

Ward blinked at me, then suddenly relaxed. As if whatever was bothering him had receded to a far spot on the horizon. A smile flickered at the corners of his mouth. 'No, I'm sorry. No one scared us off the trail. We didn't see anyone.'

I pretended to write.

'So it was pretty much Gene saying let's go down to the lake right here, and you just went? That's all there was to it?'

'That's all. I wish I had seen someone up there, Mr Cole. Especially now. I'm sorry about the girl. I wish I could help you, but I can't. I wish I could help Gene.'

I stared at the notebook as if I knew there was something missing. I tapped it with my pen. 'Well, could there have been another reason?'

'I don't know what you mean.'

'A reason you had for leaving the trail at that certain

203

spot.' I looked at him. 'Maybe to do something that you didn't want anyone else to see.'

Riley Ward turned white.

Holly appeared in the door. 'Riley. Mr Mikkleson is on.'

Ward lurched as if he'd been hit with a cattle prod. 'Thank God! That's the attorney, Mr Cole. I really do have to take this.' He went behind the plank desk and picked up the phone. Saved by the bell.

I put away my pad and joined Holly at the door.

'I appreciate your time, Mr Ward. Thank you.'

He hesitated, his palm covering the phone.

'Mr Cole. Please give the family my condolences. Gene did not harm that girl. He was only trying to help.'

'I'll tell them. Thanks.'

I followed Holly back out through the reception area to the front door. The reporters were still out there, clumped in the street. A fourth van had joined the others.

I said, 'He seems like a nice man.'

'Oh, Riley's a peach.'

'Can't blame him for being nervous, I guess.'

Holly held the door for me, fighting a tiny smile. 'Well, he's had to answer a lot of delicate questions.'

I looked at her. 'What do you mean, delicate?'

'Riley and Gene are very close friends.'

She looked at me.

'*Very* close.'

I stepped out onto the porch, but she stayed inside.

I said, 'Closer than hiking buddies?'

She nodded.

'We're talking *really* close?'

She stepped out with me, closing the door behind her. 'Riley doesn't think we know, but how can you hide it? Gene went head over heels for Riley the first time he came into the office, and chased him shamelessly.'

'How long has this been going on?'

'Not long. Riley takes these walks with Gene three times a week, but we know.' She raised her eyebrows when she said it, then leaned back inside and glanced over her shoulder to make sure that no one could hear. 'I wish some good-looking guy would chase me like that.'

I gave her my very best smile. 'I think some guy is going to knock himself out for you, Holly.'

She fluttered the big eyes at me. 'Do you think?'

'Got a girlfriend, Holly. Sorry.'

'Well, if you ever decide to trade up.' She let it hang, gave me her nicest smile yet, and started back inside.

'Holly?'

She smiled at me.

'Don't tell anyone else what you just told me, okay?'

'It's just between us.' Then she shut the door and was gone.

I stepped off the porch of the pretty little Craftsman house, and crossed the street to my car, the reporters and camera people watching me. The surfer guy looked pissed. He called, 'Hey, did Ward talk to you?'

'Nope. They let me use their bathroom.'

The reporters let out a collective sigh and relaxed. Feeling better about things.

I sat in my car, but did not start the engine. Working a case is like living a life. You could be going along with your head down, pulling the plow as best you can, but then something happens and the world isn't what you thought it was anymore. Suddenly, the way you see everything is different, as if the world has changed color, hiding things that were there before and revealing things you otherwise would not have seen.

I once was close to a man, a police officer with sixteen years on the job, who was and is a good and decent man, who had been married and faithful to his wife for all of those years, had three children with her and a cabin in Big Bear and a fine and happy life, until the day he left her and married another woman. When he told me the news, I said that I hadn't known he and his wife were having problems, and he said that he hadn't known, either. His wife was devastated, and my friend was horribly guilty. I asked him, the way friends will, what happened. His answer was both simple and terrible. He said, 'I fell in love.' He had met a woman while in line at their bank and in the course of a single conversation his world turned upside down and would never be the same. Blindsided by love.

I thought about Riley Ward, and the woman and two children in the pictures in his office. I thought that maybe he had been blindsided, too, and suddenly the inconsistencies in his and Dersh's version of events at the lake, and why Riley Ward seemed evasive and defensive in his interview, made all the sense in the world, and none of it mattered a damn with the theories of cops and private operators with too much time on their hands.

Dersh and Ward had left the trail in thick cover to be hidden from other hikers. They had not wanted to see; they had wanted to be unseen.

They went down to the water's edge *because* of its impassable nature, never guessing that Karen Garcia's body was waiting in a manner that would force them to cook up a story to explain how they had come to be in such an unlikely place. They had lied to protect the worlds each had built, but now a greater lie had come to feed on their fear.

I sat in my car, feeling bad for Riley Ward with his wife and two kids and secret gay lover, and then I left to call Samantha Dolan.

The office was filled with a golden light when Dolan returned my call. I didn't mind. I was on my second can of Falstaff, and already thinking about the third. I had spent most of the day answering mail, paying bills, and talking to the Pinocchio clock. It hadn't answered yet, but maybe with another few beers.

Dolan said, 'She sounds like Scarlett O'Hara, for Christ's sake. How can you stand it?'

'I went to see Ward this morning. You were right. They were lying.'

I finished the rest of the can and eyed the little fridge. Should've gotten the third before we started.

'I'm listening.'

'Ward and Dersh left the trail because they're lovers.'

Dolan didn't say anything.

'Dolan?'

'I'm here. Ward said that? He told you that's why they left the trail?'

'No, Dolan, Ward did not say that. Ward's got a wife and two kids, and I would think he'd do damned near anything to keep them from knowing.'

'Take it easy.'

'I picked it up from someone who works in his office. It's all the talk, Dolan, and it took me about twenty minutes to find out. I guess you people didn't exactly break your asses doing the background work.'

'Take it easy, I said.'

I listened to her breathe. I guess she listened to me.

She said, 'You okay?'

'I'm pissed off about Dersh. I'm pissed off that all of this is going to come out and hurt Ward's family.'

'You want to go have a drink?'

'Dolan, I'm doing okay on my own.'

She didn't say any more for a while. I thought about getting the next beer, but didn't. Pinocchio was watching me.

She said, 'I was going to call you.'

'Why?'

'We found Edward Deege.'

'He have anything?'

'If he had anything, we won't know it. He was dead.'

I leaned back and stared out the French doors. Sometimes the gulls will swing past, or hover on the wind, but now the sky was empty.

She said, 'Some construction guys found him in a

Dumpster up by the lake. It looks like he was beaten to death.'

'You don't know what happened?'

'He probably got into a beef with another homeless guy. You know how that goes. Maybe he was robbed, or maybe he snatched somebody's stash. Hollywood Division is working on it. I'm sorry.'

'What are you going to do about Ward?'

'I'll tip Stan Watts and let him follow up. Stan's a good guy. He'll try to go easy.'

'Great.'

'It's the only chance Dersh has.'

'Great.'

'You sure about that drink?'

'I'm sure. Maybe some other time.'

When Dolan finally spoke again, her voice was quiet. 'You know something, World's Greatest?'

'What?'

'You're not just mad about Ward.'

She hung up, leaving me to wonder what she meant.

CHAPTER 20

That Day

The pain burns through him the way his skin burned when he was beaten as a child, burns so hot that his nerves writhe beneath his skin like electric worms burrowing through his flesh. It can get so bad that he has to bite his own arms to keep from screaming.

It is all about control.

He knows that.

If you can control yourself, they cannot hurt you.

If you can command yourself, they will pay.

The killer fills the first syringe with Dianabol, a methandrostenolone steroid he bought in Mexico, and injects it into his right thigh. The next he fills with Somatropin, a synthetic growth hormone also from Mexico that was made for use with cattle. He injects this into his left thigh, and enjoys the burning sensation that always accompanies the injection. An hour ago, he swallowed two androstene tablets to increase his body's production of testosterone. He will wait a few more minutes, then settle onto the weight bench and work until his muscles scream and fail and only then will he rest. No pain, no gain, and he must gain strength and size and power, because there is still murder to be done.

He admires his naked body in the full-length mirror, and flexes. Rippling muscles. Cobblestone abs. Tattoos that desecrate his flesh. Pretty. He puts on the sunglasses. Better.

The killer lies back on the weight bench and waits for

the chemicals to course through his veins. He is pleased that the police have finally found Edward Deege's body. That is part of his plan. Because of the body, they will question the neighbors. Evidence he has placed will be discovered, and that is part of the plan also; a plan that he has crafted as carefully as he crafts his body, and his vengeance.

He cautions himself to be patient.

The military manuals say that no plan of action ever survives first contact with the enemy. One must be adaptable. One must allow the plan to evolve.

His plan has already morphed several times – Edward Deege being one such morph – and will morph again. Take Dersh. All the attention on Dersh annoyed him until he realized that Dersh could become part of the plan, just like Deege. It was an epiphany. One sweet moment when, through Dersh, the plan changed from death to lifelong imprisonment. Humiliation. Shame.

Adaptability is everything.

He himself is morphing. Everyone thinks him so quiet. Everyone thinks him so contained.

He is what he needs to be.

The killer relaxes, letting his thoughts drift, but they do not drift to Dersh or the plan or his vengeance; they drift back to that horrible day. He should know better. He always goes back to that day as if to torture himself. Better to play the constant chess game of his plan than wallow in hurt, but for so many years hurt was all he had. His hurt defines him.

He feels the tears which he has never allowed anyone to see, and clenches shut his eyes. The wet creeps from beneath the sunglasses, leaving a trail of acid memories.

He feels the beating. The belt snaps against him until his skin is numb. Fists pound his shoulders and back. He screams and begs and cries, but the people who love him most are the ones who hate him most. *There's no place like home.* Running. Walking. A trip on a bus. He escapes from a place where kindness and cruelty are one and the same, and love and loathing are indistinguishable. He is outside a diner when a man approaches. A kindly man who recognizes his pain. The man's hand touches his shoulder. Words of consolation and friendship. The man cares. Comfort. The rest follows so easily. Love. Dependence. Betrayal. Revenge. Regret.

He remembers that day so vividly. He can see every image as if the movie of his life were broken frame by frame, each picture stark and clear, colors brilliant and sharp. The day the hated ones took the man from him. Took him, destroyed him, killed him. That day, after all these years and all these changes, burns so deeply that every cell is branded.

He was fucked up for years until he gained control over himself. Mastered his feelings, and life. Mastered himself, contained himself, prepared himself so that he can do this:

The tears stop and he opens his eyes. He wipes away the residue, and sits up.

Control.

He is in control.

His loss must be repaid, and he has the means for that now. No longer weak, no longer helpless.

He has a plan of vengeance against the one who hurt him the most, and a list of the conspirators.

He is killing them one by one because payback is a motherfucker, and he is the baddest motherfucker to ever walk with the angels through the streets of this city.

The military calls this 'mission commitment'.

His mission commitment is second to none.

They will pay.

He rolls off the bench and flexes his muscles in the mirror until the skin pulls tight, his veins bulge, and the bright red arrows glow hotly on his deltoids.

Dersh.

*

Pike's Dream

He ran without a trail because it was harder that way. Dead branches from fallen trees raked at his legs like claws reaching from the earth. The brown leaves that covered the forest floor made for slippery footing as he dodged and twisted around the trees and vines and sinkholes that made him work to maintain his balance. He couldn't fall into a runner's rhythm because he was climbing over deadfalls and jumping over downed limbs as much as he was running, but that was why he did it this way. The Marine Corps Fitness Manual that he bought from a secondhand bookstore called this type of running 'fartlek training', which was something the Swedish Alpine troops thought up, and was the grueling basis behind the Corps's legendary obstacle course. The Fitness Manual said tough training was necessary to build tough men.

Joe Pike, age fourteen.

He loved the smell of the winter woods, and the peace that came from being by himself. He spent as much time as he could here, reading and thinking and following the exercise dicta of the Manual, which had become his bible. There was joy in exhaustion, and a sense of accomplishment in sweat. Joe had decided to join the Marines on his seventeenth birthday. He thought about it every day, and dreamed about it at night. He saw himself standing tall in his dress uniform, or sneaking through the Asian jungles in the war that was waging half a world away (though he was only fourteen, and that war would probably end soon). He enjoyed a thousand different fantasies of himself as a Marine, but, in truth, he mostly saw himself getting on a bus that would take him away from his father. He had his own war right here at home. The one in Vietnam couldn't be any worse.

Joe was still tall for his age, and beginning to fill. He hoped that if he looked old enough when he was sixteen, he might be able to get his mother to fake the papers so that he could join the Corps even sooner. She might do that for him.

If she lived long enough.

Joe pushed himself harder as he neared the end of his run. His breath plumed in the cold air, but he was slick with sweat and didn't feel the cold even though all he wore were red gym shorts and high-top Keds and a sleeveless green tee shirt. He had followed the creek upstream for almost an hour, then turned around, and now he was almost back where he'd begun when he heard the laughter and stopped. The creek ran along the bottom of a slope beneath a gravel road, and, as Pike watched, two boys and a girl appeared at the top of the slope and made their way down a well-worn trail toward the creek.

Pike slipped between the trees.

They were older than Joe, the boys bigger, and Joe thought they might be seniors at the high school where he was a freshman. That would make them about seventeen.

The larger boy was a tall kid with a coarse red face and zits. He was leading the way, pushing low-hanging branches aside and carrying a feed sack with something in it. The other boy brought up the rear. He had long hair like a hippie, and a wispy mustache that looked silly, but his shoulders and thighs were thick. A cigarette dangled from his lips. The girl was built like a pear, with a wide butt. Her features were all jammed together in the center of a Pillsbury doughboy face, her eyes two narrow slits that looked mean. She carried a one-gallon gas can like Joe used to fill his lawn mower, and she was laughing. 'We don't have to walk all the way to Africa, Daryl. There ain't nobody around.'

When she said his name, Joe recognized the boy with the sack. Daryl Haines was a high school dropout who worked at the Shell station. For a while, he had worked at the Pac-a-Sac convenience store, selling cigarettes and Slurpees, but he'd been caught filching money from the cash register and been fired. He was eighteen, at least, and might even be older. Once, Daryl had gassed up the Kingswood, but Mr Pike discovered gas splattered on the paint. He'd gotten the red ass and raised nine kinds of hell. Now, when Mr Pike rolled into the Shell, he pumped his own gas and Daryl kept the fuck away from his car. He'd pointed out Daryl to Joe once, and said, 'That kid's a piece of shit.'

Now, Joe heard Daryl say, 'Just take it easy, baby. I know where I'm goin'.'

The girl laughed again, and her little slit eyes looked worse than mean, they looked evil. 'I ain't gonna wait all day for my fun, Daryl. Just so's you don't chicken out.'

The kid in the rear made a chicken sound. 'Bawk-bawk-bawk.' The cigarette bounced up and down when he made the sound.

Daryl hit the brakes and glared. 'You want me to hand you your ass, you dumb fuck?'

The other kid showed both palms. 'Hey, no, man. I didn't mean nothing.'

'Dumb fuck.'

Now the girl went, 'Bawk-bawk-bawk,' looking at the cigarette boy.

Daryl liked that, and they continued on the trail.

Joe let them get ahead, then followed. He moved carefully, taking his time to avoid twigs and branches, staying off leaves where possible, and, where not, working his toes under the crispy top layer to put his weight on the damp matter beneath. Pike spent so much time in the woods that he had learned its ways, easily tracking and stalking the whitetail deer that fed through the area. He found comfort in being so much a part of this place that he was invisible. Once, his father had chased him into the woods behind their house, but Joe had slipped away and his father couldn't find him. To be hidden was to be safe.

They didn't go far.

Daryl led them up the creek to a small clearing. It was a popular spot for drinking parties, the ground scarred with the remains of bonfires and beer cans. The girl said, 'Well, all right! Take it out of the bag and let's see the show!'

The kid with the cigarette said something Pike couldn't hear, and laughed. Yuk-yuk-yuk. Like Jughead.

Daryl put the sack on the ground and took out a small black cat. He held it by the scruff of the neck and the back legs, saying, 'You better not scratch me, you sonofabitch.'

Pike slipped down into the creek bed, and eased along the soft earth there to work closer. The cat was grown, but small, so Pike thought it was probably a female. It made itself smaller against Daryl, its yellow eyes wide with fear. Frightened by the bag, and these people, but by the woods, too. Cats didn't like unknown places, where something might hurt them. The little cat made a squeaking mew that Joe found sad. It only had one ear, and Pike wondered how it had lost the other.

The girl unscrewed the can, grinning as if she'd just won a prize. 'Splash it real good with this, Daryl!'

The cigarette boy said, 'Shoulda got gasoline.'

The girl snapped, 'Turpentine is better! Don't you know anything!'

She said it as if she'd done this a hundred times. Pike thought she probably had.

For the first time in two hours, Joe Pike felt the cold. They were going to burn this animal. Set it on fire. Listen to it scream. Watch it twist and writhe until it died.

Daryl said, 'Get the can. C'mon, quick, before the bastard bites me.'

Daryl held the cat to the ground as far from himself as he could, while the cigarette boy took the can and splashed turpentine on the cat. When the turpentine hit it, the cat hunched and tried to get away.

The girl said, 'I wanna light it.' Her eyes bright and ugly.

Daryl said, 'Well, Jesus, don't set me on fire.'

The cigarette kid fumbled some safety matches out of his shirt pocket, dropping most of them. The girl snatched one up, and tried to strike it on the zipper of her jeans.

Daryl said, 'Hurry up, goddamnit. I can't hold this sonofabitch forever!'

Joe Pike stared at the two larger boys and the ugly girl. His chest rose and fell as if he was still running.

The first match broke, and the girl said, 'Shit!'

She picked up a second, scratched it on her zipper, and it burst into flame.

The cigarette boy said, 'All right!'

Daryl said, 'Hurry.'

Joe pulled a deadfall limb from the mud. It was about three feet long and a couple of inches thick. The sucking sound it made coming out of the mud made them look, and then he stepped up out of the creek bed.

The cigarette boy jumped back, almost tripping over his own feet. 'Hey!'

The three of them stared at Joe, and then the moment of their surprise passed.

The match burned the girl's fingers, and she dropped it. 'Shit, it's just some kid.'

Daryl said, 'Get out of here, fuckface, before I kick your ass.'

The cat still squirmed. Joe smelled the turpentine.

'Let it go.'

The girl said, 'Fuck you, retard. You watch how this thing's gonna jump.' She bent to pick up another match.

Joe hoped they would just leave. Just set the cat free and go because they'd been caught. He stepped forward. 'Can't let you burn that cat.'

Daryl's eyes went to the stick, then Joe, and he smiled. 'Looks like you already had your ass kicked, shitball. You want, I can bust your other eye. I can kick your fuckin' guts out for you.'

The cigarette boy laughed.

Purple-and-green bruises were fading from Joe's left eye, the remains of the beating his father had given him six days ago. He thought that these big boys could probably beat him, too, but then it occurred to him that he'd been beaten so often, another beating wouldn't matter much. That struck Joe as funny, and he wanted to laugh, thought he might just roar with laughter, but all that came out was a twitch at the corner of his mouth.

The little cat's eyes found Joe, and Joe thought that his eyes might look like that when his father was beating him.

He stepped toward Daryl. 'Only an asshole picks on a helpless little cat.'

Daryl grinned wider, then glanced at the girl. 'Light it up, goddamnit. Then I'm gonna kick this turd's ass.'

The second match flared, and the girl hurried toward the cat.

The world as Joe Pike saw it receded as if he was looking through the wrong end of a looking glass. He felt calm, and absolutely at peace as he lifted the stick and ran at Daryl as hard as he could. Daryl shouted, surprised that Joe was really going to take him on, and rose to meet the charge. The cat, suddenly free, streaked between the trees and was gone.

The girl screamed, 'It's getting away!' Like her little show was over and she'd missed the best part.

Joe brought the stick down as hard as he could, but the stick was half rotten and broke across Daryl's forearms with a wet snap.

Daryl threw a wild windmill of punches, catching Joe in the forehead and the chest, and then the other boy was behind Joe, punching as hard as he could. Joe felt their blows hitting him, but oddly felt no pain. It was as if he were somewhere deep within himself, a small boy alone in a dark wood, watching the action without being a part of it.

The fat girl had gotten over her disappointment, and was now jumping up and down, pumping her fists like she was rooting for her football team to make the game-winning score. 'Kill him! Kill the motherfucker!'

Joe stood between the two older boys, punching wildly. The cigarette boy hit him hard behind the right ear, and when Joe turned to meet him, Daryl kicked him in the back of the leg, and Joe fell.

Daryl and the cigarette boy leaned over Joe, throwing a flurry of blows that rained on Joe's face and head and back and arms, but still he felt nothing.

They were big kids, but his father was bigger.

They were strong boys, but his father was stronger.

Joe rolled onto his knees, feeling their punches and kicks even as he lurched to his feet.

Daryl Haines hit him hard in the face again and again and again. Joe tried to hit the bigger boys, but more of his punches fell short or missed.

Then someone tripped him, and, again, he fell.

Daryl Haines kicked him, but his father kicked harder.

Joe climbed to his feet.

The girl was still screaming, but when Joe was once more erect, Daryl Haines had a strange look on his face. The cigarette boy was breathing hard, winded from throwing so many punches, arms leaden at his sides. Daryl was breathing hard, too, looking at Joe as if he didn't believe what he was seeing. His hands were covered in red.

The girl screamed, 'Beat him, Daryl! Beat him real good!'

Joe clawed at Daryl, trying to gouge his eyes, but missed and fell, landing on his side.

Daryl stood over him, blood dripping from his hands. 'Stay down, kid.'

'Beat him to death, Daryl! Don't stop!'

'Stay down.'

Joe pushed himself to his knees. He tried to focus on Daryl, but Daryl was hazy and red, and Joe realized his eyes were filled with blood.

'Are you fuckin' nuts? Stay down.'

Joe lurched to his feet and swung as hard as he could.

Daryl stepped outside of it, then jumped forward and hit Joe square on the end of the nose. Joe heard the crack and felt it, and knew that Daryl had broken his nose. He'd heard the sound before.

Joe fell, and immediately tried to get up again.

Daryl grabbed him by the shirt and shoved him down. 'You little shit! What's wrong with you?'

The cigarette kid was holding his side like he had a stitch. 'Let's get out of here, man. I don't wanna do this no more.'

Joe said, 'Gonna beat you.' His lips were split and it was hard to speak.

'It's over!'

Joe tried to hit Daryl from the ground, but the punch missed by a good foot.

'It's over, goddamnit. You're beat!'

Joe tried to hit Daryl again, but this time he missed by a yard.

'Not over . . . until I win.'

Daryl stepped back then, his face a raw mask of rage. 'Okay, you dumb shit. I warned you.'

Daryl reared back, kicked Joe as hard as he could, and Joe felt the world explode between his legs. Then there were stars and blackness.

Joe heard them leaving, or thought he did. It seemed like hours before he could move, and when he finally worked his way to his knees, the woods were still. His groin ached, and he felt nauseous. He touched his face.

His hand came away red. His tee shirt was splattered with drying blood. More blood streaked his arms.

It was several minutes before he smelled the turpentine again, and then he saw the one-eared cat, staring at him from beneath the rotten branches of a fallen tree.

Joe Pike said, 'Hey, cat.'

The cat vanished.

'That's okay, girl. You're okay.'

He thought she was probably scared.

He wondered why he wasn't.

After a while he went home.

Three days later Daryl Haines scowled at the envelope and said, 'Fuck this shit.'

It was five minutes before 8 p.m. at the Shell station. Daryl was sitting on the hard chair he kept out front by the Coke machine, leaning back the way he did, snug in his down jacket, but pissed off about the letter. It was a notice from the goddamned Army to report for his induction physical.

Daryl Haines, eighteen years old and without the luxury of a college deferment, was 1-A infantry material. He had to take the bus down to the city this Saturday just to have his ass poked and prodded by some faggot Army doctor so they could ship him over to Vietnam.

Daryl said, 'This sucks.'

Maybe he should join the Air Force.

Daryl's older brother, Todd, was already over there. He had a cushy job working on trucks at an air base near Saigon and said it wasn't so bad. You got to screw around a lot, smoke all the pot you wanted, and fuck good-lookin' gook women for twenty-five cents a throw. His brother made it sound like goddamned Disneyland, but Daryl figured with his rotten luck he'd probably have to carry a gun and get shot.

'Fuck.'

At eight o'clock, Daryl shut the lights, turned off the

pumps, locked the station, and headed down the street, wishing he could stop in a bar. Eighteen years old being old enough to kill gooks, but not old enough to down a beer when you were thinking about it.

Daryl was thinking that he could drown his sorrow between Candy Crowley's legs if the fat psycho bitch would ever come across. He was almost there last Sunday, when the nutty bitch got it in her head to burn a cat. You just had to shake your head sometimes, where she came up with stuff like that. But it seemed to get her righteously damp, and Daryl thought he'd finally get the old ball between the uprights, as it were, when that weird kid spoiled the deal. Another fuckin' nut. That kid had taken the best beating that Daryl Haines ever dished out, and he just wouldn't quit. Didn't cry, either, not even after Daryl scrambled his eggs for him. You'd think the goddamned cat belonged to the kid, the way he carried on, but Daryl had stolen it from Old Lady Wilbur, his next-door neighbor.

You just had to shake your head.

Daryl was still thinking about it when this voice said, 'Daryl.'

Daryl said, 'Yeah?'

The kid stepped out from behind this big azalea bush, his face swollen and lumpy with bruises. A big piece of tape covered his nose, and black stitches laced his lip and left eyebrow like railroad tracks.

Daryl, feeling righteously cranky because he'd been drafted, said, 'You want some more, you little fuck, you picked the right time. I'm goin' to Vietnam.'

But that didn't impress the kid, who suddenly had a Louisville Slugger baseball bat in his hands and hit Daryl on the outside of the left knee as if he was swinging away for the green wall at Fenway Park.

Daryl Haines screamed as he fell. It felt as if someone had sewn an M80 in his knee and touched the sucker off. Daryl clutched at his knee, still howling as the kid brought the bat down again. Daryl saw it coming and raised his hands, and then a second M80 went off in his right arm. Daryl screamed, 'Jesus Christ! Stop it! Stop! Don't hit me again!'

The kid tossed the bat aside and stared at him. The kid's face was empty, and that scared Daryl even more than all the gooks in Vietnam.

The kid kicked Daryl in the side of the head, kicked him again, then leaned over and punched Daryl three fast times in the face. Daryl's sky filled with a million little sparkly stars against a black field, and then Daryl puked.

'Daryl?'

'Uhn . . .'

'It's not over until I win.'

Daryl spit blood. 'You win. Jesus Christ, you win. I give up.'

The kid stepped back.

Daryl was crying so bad he felt like a baby. The kid had broken his leg and arm. Jesus, it hurt.

'Daryl.'

'Please, Christ, don't hit me again.' Scared the kid was gonna bash him some more.

'How could you want to hurt something so weak?'

'Jesus. Oh, Christ.'

'You ever do that, Daryl, I'll find you and kill you. That cat would kill you if it could, but it can't. I'll kill you for it.'

'I swear to Sweet Jesus I won't do that! I swear!'

The kid picked up his bat and walked away.

Twelve weeks later, after the casts were removed and the last of the stitches had come out, the Army doctors finally did their examination. Daryl Haines was determined to be 4-F due to a permanently disabled left knee. Unfit for military service.

He did not go to Vietnam.

He never tried to burn another cat.

CHAPTER 21

His eyes opened, and Pike was as alert as if it were the middle of the afternoon, not two in the morning. Sleep would not come again after the dream, so he rose and pulled on briefs and shorts. He thought for a moment that he might read, but he usually exercised after the dreams. The exercise worked better for him.

He put on the blue Nike running shoes, then buckled on a small fanny pack, not bothering to turn on the lights. He was comfortable in the dark. Years ago, the Marine doctors told him that his excellent night vision was due to high levels of vitamin A and 'fast rhodopsin', which meant that the pigment in his retinas which responded to dim light was very sensitive. Cat eyes, they called it.

He let himself out into the cool night air, and stretched to loosen his hamstrings. Even though he often ran forty miles a week, his muscles were loose from the years of yoga and martial arts, and responded well. He settled the fanny pack on his hips, then jogged out across the complex grounds, through the security door, and into the street. The fanny pack held his keys, and a small black .25 caliber Beretta. You never know.

Much of his running was done early like this, and he found peace in it. The city was quiet. When he chose, he could run on the crown of the street, or through parks or across a golf course. He enjoyed the natural feel of grass and earth, and knew these feelings were resonances from his youth.

He ran west on Washington Boulevard toward the ocean, taking it easy for the first quarter mile to let his body warm, then picked up his pace. The air was cool, and a ground fog hazed the streets. The fog caught the light and hid the stars, which he didn't like. He enjoyed reading the constellations, and finding his way by them. There was a time as a young Marine when his life depended on it, and he found comfort in the certainty of celestial mechanics. Two or three times every year, he and his friend Elvis Cole would backpack or hunt in remote terrain, and, during those times, they would test themselves and each other by navigating via the sun and moon and stars. More times, Pike would venture out alone to remote and alien locales. He had learned long ago that a compass and GPS could fail. You had to look to yourself. You could only depend upon yourself.

Images came. Flashing snapshot pictures of his childhood, of women he had known, men he had seen die, and men he had killed. Of his friend and partner Elvis Cole, of the people he employed in his various businesses. Sometimes he would ponder these images, but other times he would fold them smaller and smaller until they vanished.

He followed Washington Boulevard as it curved north through Venice, then left Main for Ocean Avenue, where he could hear the waves crashing on the beach below the bluff.

Pike increased his kick past the Santa Monica Pier, past the shopping carts and homeless encampments, extending his stride as he worked his way to a six-minute-mile pace. He sprinted past the Ivy-by-the-Shore and the hotels, feeling himself peak, holding that peak, then throttled back to an easy jog before walking to the rail at the edge of the bluff, where he stopped to look at the sea.

He watched ships, stars on a black horizon. A breeze caressed his back, inland air drawn to the warmth of the sea. Above him, dried palm fronds rustled. A lone car slid past, lost in the night.

Here on the bluff overlooking the water, there were green lawns and bike paths and towering palms. A bush to his right rustled, and he knew it was a girl before he saw her.

'Are you Matt?'

She was tentative, but not afraid. Early twenties or late teens, with short hair bleached white, and wide brown eyes that looked at him expectantly. A faded green backpack hung from her shoulder.

'You're Matt?'

'No.'

She seemed disappointed, but was completely relaxed, as if the reality that she should be frightened of a strange man in so deserted a place had never occurred to her. 'I guess you wouldn't be. I'm Trudy.'

'Joe.'

He turned back to the lights on the horizon.

'Pleased to meet you, Joe. I'm running away, too.'

He considered her briefly again, wondering why she had chosen those words, then returned to the ships.

Trudy leaned against the rail, trying to see over the edge of the bluff to Palisades Beach Road. She gave no indication of leaving. Pike thought that he might start running again.

She said, 'Are you real?'

'No.'

'No kidding, now. I want to know.'

He held out his hand.

Trudy touched him with a finger, then gripped his wrist, as if she didn't trust her first touch.

'Well, you might've been a vision or something. I have them, you know. Sometimes I imagine things.'

When Pike didn't respond, she said, 'I've changed my mind. I don't think you're running away. I think you're running toward.'

'Is that a vision? Or something you imagined?'

She stared up at him as if she had to consider which it might be, then shook her head. 'An observation.'

'Look.'

Three coyotes had appeared at the edge of the light, having worked their way up the bluff from the Palisades. Two of them sniffed at one of the garbage cans that dotted the park, the third trotted across Ocean Avenue and disappeared in an alley. They looked like thin gray dogs. Scavengers.

Trudy said, 'It's so amazing that wild things can live here in the city, isn't it?'

'Wild things are everywhere.'

Trudy grinned at him again. 'Well. That's certainly deep.'

The two coyotes suddenly came alert, looking north toward the Palisades an instant before Pike heard the coyote pack's song. Their singing rode down on the breeze coming out of the hills, and Pike guessed their number at between eight and twelve. The two coyotes by the garbage cans looked at each other, then lifted their snouts to test the air. *You're safe enough*, Pike thought. The others were at least three miles away, well up in the canyons of the Palisades.

The girl said, 'That's such a terrible sound.'

'It means they have food.'

She hitched her backpack. 'They eat people's pets. They'll bait a dog away from its home, then surround it and rip it to pieces.'

Pike knew that to be true, but still. 'They have to live.'

The singing grew to a higher pitch. The two coyotes by the garbage can stood frozen.

The girl looked away from the sound. 'They have something now. They're killing it right now.'

The girl's eyes were vacant. Pike thought she didn't seem to be within herself, and wondered if she was with the pack.

'They'll pull it to pieces, and sometimes, if too much blood gets on one of their own, the others will mistake it for the prey and kill their own kind.'

Pike nodded. People could be like that, too.

226

The singing abruptly stopped, and the girl came back to herself. 'You don't say very much, do you?'

'You were saying enough for both of us.'

The girl laughed. 'Yeah, I guess I was. Hope I didn't weird you out, Joe. I do that to people sometimes.'

Joe shook his head. 'Not yet.'

A black minivan turned off Wilshire and came along Ocean Avenue, washing them with its headlights. It stopped in the middle of the street near where the coyote had crossed.

Trudy said, 'Gotta be Matt. It was nice talking with you, Running Man.'

She hitched the backpack, then trotted to the van. Trudy spoke to someone through the passenger's window, then the door opened, and Trudy climbed in. The van had no plates, and no dealer card, though it gleamed with the newness of a vehicle just driven off the lot. In seconds, it was gone.

Pike said, 'Goodbye, Running Girl.'

Pike glanced toward the garbage cans, but the coyotes were gone. Back to their own place in the hills. Wild things lost in the dark.

Pike leaned against the rail to stretch his calves, then ran inland up Wilshire.

He ran in the darkness, away from cars and people, enjoying the solitude.

Amanda Kimmel said, 'Good riddance!'

Seventy-eight years old, loosely wrapped in skin that made her look like a pale raisin, and with a left leg that tingled as if bugs were creeping in all the little wrinkle troughs, Amanda Kimmel watched the two detectives sneak out of the house they were using to spy on Eugene Dersh and drive away. She shook her head with disgust. 'Those two turds stand out like warts on a baby's ass, don't they, Jack?'

Jack didn't answer.

'Wouldn't cut the mustard in Five-O, I'll bet. You'd have their sorry asses back on the mainland faster than rats can fuck.'

Amanda Kimmel dragged the heavy M1 Garand rifle back to the TV and settled in her BarcaLounger. The TV was the only light she allowed herself these days, living like a mole in the goddamned darkness so she could keep an eye on all the cops and reporters and nutcase lookie-loos who had been crashing around outside since they'd learned her neighbor, Mr Dersh, was a maniac. Just her goddamned luck, to live right behind the next fuckin' Son of Sam.

Amanda said, 'This is the shits, ain't it, Jack?'

Jack didn't answer because she had the sound off.

Amanda Kimmel watched *Hawaii Five-O* reruns every night on Nick-at-Nite, feeling that Jack Lord was the finest police officer who ever lived, and *Hawaii Five-O* the finest cop show that had ever been made. You could have your Chuck Norris and Jimmy Smits. She'd take Jack Lord any day.

Amanda settled back, had a healthy sip of scotch, and patted the M1 lovingly. Her second husband had brought the M1 home from fighting the Japs a million years ago and stuck it under the bed. Or was it her first husband? The M1 was as big as a telephone pole, and Amanda could barely lift the damned thing, but what with all the strangers creeping around outside these days as well as her living next to a maniac, well, a girl had to do what a girl had to do.

'Right, Jack?'

Jack grinned, and she just knew that he'd agree.

The first few days, armies of people poured through her neighborhood. Cars filled with rubber neckers and mouth breathers. Numbskulls who wanted their picture taken standing in Dersh's yard. (Get a goddamned life!) Report-ers with cameras and microphones, making God's own noise and not giving two hoots and a damn who they disturbed. She'd even caught one reporter, that horrible little man on Channel 2, tromping through her roses as he tried to get into Dersh's yard. She'd cursed him a blue streak, but he'd gone ahead anyway, so she turned on her sprinklers and hosed the weaselly sonofabitch down good.

After that first few days, the crush of reporters and numbskulls had slacked off because the cops ran out of places to search, so there wasn't much for the TV people to tape. The cops pretty much stayed on the street in front of Dersh's house, leaving when he left and coming when he came, except for the cops who sucked around the empty house next door at four-hour intervals. Amanda suspected that the reporters didn't know about the cops in the house, which was fine by her because the cops made enough noise by themselves, managing to wake her each time the shifts changed, because she slept so poorly what with the leg and all.

'Being old is hell, isn't it, Jack? Can't sleep, can't shit, and you don't get laid.'

Jack Lord punched a fat Hawaiian on the nose. Yeah, Jack knew that being old was hell.

Amanda drained the rest of her scotch and eyed the bottle, thinking maybe it was time for a little refill when a car door slammed, and she thought, 'Those goddamned cops with their noise again.' Probably forgot their cigarettes up in the house.

Amanda shut the TV, then dragged the big M1 back to the window, thinking that she just might scream holy hell at the bastards, keeping her up like this, only it wasn't the two cops.

Between the half-moon and the streetlamp, she could see the man pretty well, even with seventy-eight-year-old eyes and a belly full of scotch. He was walking from the street down along the alley toward Dersh's house, and he certainly wasn't a cop or a reporter. He was a large man, dressed in blue jeans and a sweatshirt without sleeves, and something stuck out about him right away. Here it was the middle of the night, dark as the inside of a cat's butt, and this asshole was wearing sunglasses.

Her first thought was that he must be a criminal of some kind – a burglar or a rapist – so she hefted up the M1 to draw a bead on the sonofabitch, but before she could get the gun steadied, he disappeared past the hedges and was gone.

'Goddamnit! C'mon back here, you sonofabitch!'

She waited.

Nothing.

'Damn!'

Amanda Kimmel propped the M1 against the window, then went back to her chair, poured a fresh slug of scotch, and took a taste. Maybe the guy was some friend of Dersh's (he had male friends visit at all hours, and she certainly knew what *that* meant), or maybe he was just an after-hours lookieloo (Lord knows, there'd been plenty, often dressed more oddly than this).

The short, sharp *bang* damned near knocked her out of her chair.

Amanda had never in her life heard that sound, but she knew without doubt what it was.

A gunshot.

'Holy shit, Jack! I guess that sonofabitch wasn't a lookieloo, after all!'

Amanda Kimmel scooped up her phone, called the police, and told them that Eugene Dersh had just been murdered by a man with red arrows tattooed on his arms.

PART TWO

CHAPTER 22

The morning heat brought the smell of wild sage up from the canyon. Something rumbled far away, a muffled thumping like the sound of heavy bombs beyond the horizon. I hadn't thought of the war in years, and pulled the sheet over my head.

Lucy snuggled into my back. 'Someone's at the door.'

'What?'

She burrowed her face into me, her hand sliding across my side. I liked the dry heat of her palm. 'At the door.'

Knocking.

'It's not even seven.'

She burrowed deeper. 'Take your gun.'

I pulled on gym shorts and a sweatshirt, and went down to see. The cat was squatting in the entry, ears down, growling. Who needs a Doberman when you've got a cat like this?

Stan Watts and Jerome Williams were on the other side of the door, looking like they'd been up a while. Watts was chewing a breath mint.

'What are you guys doing here?'

They stepped in without answering. When they did, the cat arched his back and hissed.

Williams said, 'Hey, that's some cat.'

'Better watch it. He bites.'

Williams went over to the cat. 'Hell, cats like me. You'll see.'

Williams put out his hand. The cat's fur stood up and the growl got as loud as a police siren. Williams stepped back fast.

'He got some kinda thing with black people?'

'He's got a thing with everybody. It's seven in the morning, Watts. Did Dersh confess? You guys ID the shooter?'

Watts sucked at the mint. 'Wondering where you were last night, is all. Got a few questions.'

'About what?'

'About where you were.'

I glanced at Williams again, and now Williams was watching me.

'I was here, Watts. What's going on?'

'Can you prove it?'

Lucy said, 'Yes, he can. But he doesn't have to.'

The three of us looked up. Lucy was standing at the loft's rail, wearing my big white terry-cloth robe.

I said, 'Lucille Chenier. Detectives Watts and Williams.'

Watts said, 'You here with him?'

Lucy smiled. Sweetly. 'I don't think I have to answer that.'

Watts held up his badge.

'Now I know I don't have to answer that.'

Williams said, 'Man. First this cat.'

Watts shrugged. 'We were hoping to be nice.'

Lucy's smile dropped away. 'You'll be nice whether you want to be or not, and unless you have a warrant, we can and will ask you to leave.'

Williams said, 'Well, for Christ's sake.'

'Lucy's an attorney, Watts, so don't get cute on us. I was here. Lucy and I went down to the Ralph's for some things, and made dinner. The receipt's probably in the trash. We rented a movie from Blockbuster. It's over there on the VCR.'

'How about your buddy Pike? When was the last time you saw him?'

Lucy had come down the stairs and was standing next to me with her arms crossed. She said, 'Don't answer him until he tells you why, and maybe not even then. Don't answer any more of his questions.' She faced me and her eyes were serious. 'This is the lawyer talking, do you understand?'

I spread my hands. 'You heard her, Watts. So either tell me what's going on or hit the road.'

'Eugene Dersh was shot to death last night. We picked up Joe Pike for it.'

I stared at him. I glanced at Williams.

'Are you guys joking?'

They weren't joking.

'Is Krantz running a number on Joe? Is that what this is?'

'Eyewitness saw him going into the house. We've got him downtown now to run a lineup.'

'That's bullshit. Pike didn't kill anyone.' I was getting excited. Lucy touched my back.

Watts spoke quietly. 'Are you saying he was here at the house with you two?'

Lucy stepped directly in front of me. 'Are you arresting Mr Cole?'

'No, ma'am.'

'Are you exercising any warrants at this time?' Her voice was all business.

'We just wanted to talk, is all.' He looked at me past her. 'We don't think you're good for it. We just wanted to see what you knew.'

Lucy shook her head. 'This interview is at an end. If you are not prepared to arrest him, or me, please leave.'

The phone rang even as I locked the door.

Lucy answered, scooping up the phone before I could get there. 'Who's calling, please?'

She was in full-blown protectress mode, still my girlfriend and the woman I loved, but now as focused as a female tiger protecting her mate; face down, concentrating on what was being said.

235

Finally, she held out the phone. 'It's someone named Charlie Bauman. He says he's a criminal attorney representing Joe.'

'Yeah.'

Charlie Bauman had been a United States attorney prosecuting federal cases until he decided to make five times the money defending the same guys he'd once tried to put behind bars. He had an office in Santa Monica, three ex-wives, and, at last count, eight children among them. He paid more in child support than I earned in a good year, and he'd represented Joe and me before.

He said, 'Who in hell is that woman?'

'Lucy Chenier. She's a friend of mine. She's also a lawyer.'

'Christ, what a ball-buster. You hear about Joe?'

'Two cops were just here. All I know is they said Dersh was murdered, and they've got an eyewitness who puts Joe at the scene. What in hell is going on?'

'You know anything about it?'

'No, I do not know anything about it.' Irritated that he would ask.

'Okay, okay. *Watch out, dickhead! Christ!*' Horns blew. Charlie was on his car phone. 'I'm on my way down to Parker Center now. They're waiting for the lineup to book him.'

'I want to be there.'

'Forget it. They'll never let you.'

'I'm coming down there, Charlie. I'm going to be there. I mean it.'

I hung up without another word. Lucy was watching me, her face grave.

'Elvis?'

I've been in war. I've faced men with guns, and dangerous stronger men who were doing their best to hurt me, but I could not recall a time when I was more afraid. My hands trembled.

Lucy said, 'Elvis? Is this man good?'

236

'Charlie's good.'

She still watched me, as if she was searching for something.

I said, 'Joe didn't do this.'

She nodded.

'Joe didn't do this. Dersh didn't kill Karen. Joe knows it. He wouldn't kill Dersh.'

Lucy kissed my cheek. There was a kindness in her eyes that bothered me.

'Call me when you know more. Give Joe my best.'

She went up the stairs, and I watched her go.

Parker Center uses the ground floor for booking and processing suspects. A few minutes after I checked in, Charlie hurried out a gray metal door.

'You just made it. Another five minutes, you'd've missed it.' Charlie Bauman is several inches shorter than me, with a lean pockmarked face and intense eyes. He smells like cigarettes.

'Can I see Joe?'

'Not till after. We get in the room, there's gonna be the witness. She's some little old lady. You let the cops do all the talking, doesn't matter what she says.'

'I know that, Charlie.'

'I'm just telling you. No matter what she says, you don't say anything. Me and you, we can't talk to her, we can't ask her any questions, we can't make any comments, okay?'

'I got it.' Charlie seemed nervous, and I didn't like that.

I followed him back along a tile hall as we spoke. The hall opened into a wide room that looked like any other corporate workplace, except this one had posters about drunk-driving fatalities.

'Have you had a chance to talk to him?'

'Enough to get the gist. We'll talk more, after.'

I stopped him. Behind us, two detectives I didn't know were positioning a black guy in front of a camera like they

237

use to take driver's license pictures, only this guy wasn't up for renewal. His hands were cuffed, and his eyes were wide and afraid. He was saying, 'THIS IS BULLSHIT. THIS THREE STRIKE CRAP IS *BULLSHIT*.'

'Charlie, do these guys have anything?'

'If the witness makes a positive ID and they write the paper, then we'll see. She's old, and when they're old they get confused. If we're lucky, she'll pick the wrong guy and we can all go home early.'

He wasn't answering me.

'Do they have anything?'

'They've already got a prosecutor coming down. He'll lay it out for us when he gets here. I don't know what they have, but they wouldn't've called him down if they didn't think they have a case.'

Krantz and Stan Watts came out of an adjoining hall. Krantz was holding a cup of coffee, Watts was holding two.

Charlie said, 'Okay, Krantz. Whenever you're ready.'

I looked at Krantz. 'What are you pulling on Joe?'

Krantz appeared more calm than I'd ever seen him. As if he was at peace. 'I can show you Dersh's body, if you want.'

'I don't know what happened to Dersh. What I'm saying is that Joe didn't do it.'

Krantz raised his eyebrows and looked at Watts. 'Stan here told me that you were at home with a woman last night. Was he wrong about that?' He looked back at me. 'Were you with Pike?'

'You know what I'm saying.'

Krantz blew on his coffee, then sipped. 'No, Cole, I don't know that. But here's what I do know: At three-fifteen this morning a man matching Pike's description was seen entering Eugene Dersh's backyard. A few moments after that, Dersh was shot to death by one shot to the head with a .357 magnum. Could be a .38, but judging from the way the head blew apart, I'm betting

238

.357. We've already recovered the bullet. We'll see what it tells us.'

'You got any fingerprints? You got any physical evidence that it was Joe, or is this another investigation like you ran with Dersh, you just working off an urge?'

'I'm going to let the prosecutor explain our case to Pike's lawyer. You're just here on a pass, Cole. Please remember that.'

Behind us, Williams appeared, saying that everything was good to go.

Krantz nodded at me. Confident. 'Let's see what the witness says.'

They led us past six holding cells into a dim room where a uniformed cop and two detectives were waiting with a shrunken woman in her late seventies. Watts gave her the second cup of coffee. She sipped at it and made a face.

Charlie whispered. 'Amanda Kimmel. She's the wit.'

Krantz said, 'You okay, Mrs Kimmel? You want to sit?'

She frowned at him. 'I wanna get this done and get the hell outta here. I don't like to move my bowels in a strange place.'

The wall in front of us was a large glass double-paned window that looked into a narrow room lit so brightly that it glowed. Krantz picked up a phone, and thirty seconds later a door on the right side of the room opened. A black cop with bodybuilder muscles led in six men. Joe Pike was the third. Of the remaining five, three were white and two were Hispanic. Four of the men were Joe's height or shorter, and one was taller. Only one of the other men wore jeans and a sleeveless sweatshirt like Joe, and that was a short Hispanic guy with skinny arms. The other three wore a mix of chinos or dungarees or coveralls, and long-sleeved sweatshirts or short-sleeved tees, and all six were wearing sunglasses. Every man in the room except Joe was a cop.

I bent to Charlie's ear. 'I thought they had to be dressed like Joe.'

'Law says it only has to be similar, whatever the hell that means. Let's see. Maybe this works for us.'

When all six men were lined along the stage, Krantz said, 'Nobody on that side of the glass can see in here, Mrs Kimmel. Don't you worry about that. You're perfectly safe.'

'I don't give a rat's ass if they can see me or not.'

'Is one of the men in there the same man you saw going into Eugene Dersh's yard?'

Amanda Kimmel said, 'Him.'

'Which one, Mrs Kimmel?'

'The third one.'

She pointed at Joe Pike.

'You're sure, Mrs Kimmel? Take a careful look.'

'That's him right there. I know what I saw.'

Charlie whispered, 'Shit.'

Krantz glanced at Charlie now, but Charlie was watching Mrs Kimmel.

Krantz said, 'Okay, but I'm going to ask you again. You're saying you saw that man, number three, walk down the alley beside your house and go into Eugene Dersh's backyard?'

'Damned right. You can't miss a face like that. You can't miss those arms.'

'And when the officers took your statement, that is the man you described?'

'Hell, yes. I saw him real good. Look at those damned tattoos.'

'All right, Mrs Kimmel. Detective Watts is going to take you up to my office now. Thank you.'

Krantz didn't look at her when he said it; he was staring at Joe. He did not look at me or Charlie or Williams or anyone else in the room. He did not watch Mrs Kimmel leave. He kept his eyes on Pike, and picked up the phone.

'Cuff the suspect and bring him in, please.'

Suspect.

The big cop handcuffed Joe, then brought him into the observation room.

Krantz watched Pike being cuffed, watched as he was brought in. When Pike was finally with us, Krantz took off Joe's glasses, folded them, and dropped them into his own pocket. For Krantz, no one else was in that room except him and Joe. No one else was alive, or mattered, or even meant a damn. What was about to happen meant everything. Was the only thing.

He said, 'Joe Pike, you're under arrest for the murder of Eugene Dersh.'

CHAPTER 23

Krantz handled the booking himself, taking Joe's fingerprints and snapping his booking photo and typing the forms. Hollywood Homicide raised a stink, trying to keep jurisdiction of Dersh's murder since it fell in their area, but Krantz sucked it into the Robbery-Homicide black hole. Related to the Dersh investigation, he said. Overlapping cases, he said. He wanted Pike.

I watched for a time, sitting with Stan Watts at an empty desk, wishing I could talk to Pike. One minute you're asleep in bed, the next you're watching your friend being booked for murder. You put your feelings away. You make yourself think. Amanda Kimmel had picked Joe out of a lineup, but what did that mean? It meant that she had seen someone who looked more like Joe than the other men in the lineup. I would learn more when I spoke with Joe. I would learn more when I heard the prosecutor's case. When I learned more, I could do something.

I kept telling myself that because I needed to either believe it or scream.

I said, 'This is bullshit, Watts. You know that.'

'Is it?'

'Pike wouldn't kill this guy. Pike didn't think Dersh was good for those killings.'

Watts just stared at me, as blank as a wall. He'd sat with a thousand people who had said they didn't do it when they had.

'What's next, Stan? The serial killer's dead, so you guys are going to declare victory and head for the donuts?'

Watts's expression never changed. 'I realize you're

upset because of your friend, but don't mistake me. for Krantz. I'll slap your fucking teeth down your throat.'

Finally, Watts took Charlie and me to an interview room where Joe was waiting. His jeans and sweatshirt had been replaced by blue LAPD JAIL coveralls. He sat with his fingers laced on the table, his eyes as calm as a mountain lake. It was odd to see him without his sunglasses. I could count on both hands the number of times I'd seen his eyes. Their blue is astonishing. He squinted, not used to the light.

I sighed. 'All the people in the world who need killing, and you've got to pick Dersh.'

Pike looked at me. 'Was that humor?'

Inappropriate is my middle name.

Charlie said, 'Before we get started, you want something to eat?'

'No.'

'Okay, here's what's going to happen. The ADA handling your case is a guy named Robby Branford. You know him?'

Pike and I both shook our heads.

'He's a square guy. A pit bull, but square. He'll be here soon, and we'll see what he's going to show the judge. The arraignment will be this afternoon over in Municipal Court. They'll keep you locked down here, then bring you over to the Criminal Court Building just before. Once we're there, it shouldn't take more than an hour or two. Branford will present the evidence, and the judge will decide if there's reasonable cause to believe you're the guy popped Dersh. Now, if the judge binds you over, it doesn't mean there's proof of your guilt, just that he believes there's enough reason to go to trial. If that's the way it breaks, we'll argue for bail. Okay?'

Pike nodded.

'Did you kill Dersh?'

'No.'

When he said it, I let out my breath. Pike must've

'You had to be doing something besides the goddamned shower. Think about it.'

Pike thought.

'I was being.'

Charlie wrote on the pad. I could see his mouth move. BEING.

'Okay. So you ate, took your shower, then sat around 'being' until you went to bed. Then you woke up a little after two and went for a run. Give us the route.'

Joe described the route he followed, and now I was writing, too. I was going to retrace his route during the day, then again at the same time he'd run it, looking for anyone who might've seen him.

Pike said, 'I stopped at the bluffs on Ocean Avenue between Wilshire and San Vicente, where you can see the water. I talked to a girl there. Her name was Trudy.'

Pike described her.

Charlie said, 'No last name?'

'I didn't ask. She was meeting someone named Matt. A black minivan arrived. New Dodge, no license or dealer tag that I could see. Custom teardrop windows in the back. She got in and they left. Whoever was inside would've seen me.'

I said, 'When was that?'

'Got to the bluffs about two-fifty. Started running again just at three.'

Charlie raised his eyebrows. 'You're sure about the time?'

'Yes.'

I said, 'That's only fifteen minutes or so before the old lady heard the shot. No way you could get from the ocean to Dersh's in fifteen minutes. Not even at three in the morning.'

Charlie nodded, thinking about it and liking it. 'Okay. That's something. We've got the girl, maybe. And all this running could give us plenty of potential witnesses.' He glanced at me. 'You're gonna get started on that?'

'Yes.'

Someone rapped at the door, and Charlie yelled for them to come in.

Williams stuck his head in. 'DA's here.'

'Be right out.'

When Williams closed the door, Joe said, 'What about bail?'

'You've got your business. You've got a home. All of that is to the good when I'm trying to convince a judge you won't run. But when you're talking murder, it depends on the strength of their evidence. Branford will make a big deal about this old lady, but he knows – and so does the judge – that eyewitness testimony is the least dependable evidence you can admit. If all he has is the old lady, we're in good shape. You just sit tight, and don't worry, okay?'

Pike put the calm blue eyes on me, and I wished I knew what was behind them. He seemed peaceful, as if far worse things had happened to him, and nothing that could happen here would be as bad. Not even here. Not even charged with murder.

He said, 'Don't forget Karen.'

'I won't, but right now you have to come first. Edward Deege is dead. He was found murdered.'

Pike cocked his head. 'How?'

'Dolan says it looks like a street beef, but Hollywood has the case. They're investigating.'

Pike nodded.

'I'll see about finding Trudy.'

'I know.'

'Don't worry about it.'

'I'm not.'

I took my sunglasses from my shirt pocket and held them out.

Pike's eyes flicked to the glasses.

'Krantz would just take them.'

246

Charlie Bauman said, 'Come on, for chrissake. We don't have all day.'

I put the sunglasses back in my pocket and followed Charlie out.

Robert Branford was a tall man with large hands and bristling eyebrows. He met us in the hall, then walked us into a conference room where Krantz was sitting at the head of a long table. A TV and VCR were in the corner, and a short stack of files and legal pads were on the table. The TV was on, showing a blank blue screen. I wondered what they'd been watching.

Even before we were all the way in the room, Charlie said, 'Hey, Robby, you meet your eyewitness yet?'

'Mrs Kimmel? Not yet. Gonna see her after the arraignment.'

'Better see her before.'

'Why is that, Charlie? She got three heads?'

Charlie made a drinking motion. 'Booze hound. Jesus, Krantz, I'm surprised you could stand being so close to her at the lineup. Damn near knocked me out when she walked past.'

Branford had gone to his own briefcase and was taking papers from different manila folders. He raised his eyebrows toward Krantz.

To his credit, Krantz nodded. 'She's a drinker.'

Charlie took a seat at the table without bothering to open his briefcase. 'Did Krantz tell you about the M1? If you're going to her place, you'd better wave a white flag before you get out of your car.'

Krantz said, 'I told him, Bauman. What does that have to do with anything?'

Charlie spread his hands, Mr Innocent. 'Just want to make sure Robby knows what he's getting into. A seventy-eight-year-old lush gives a visual on a guy she's trying to plug with an M1 Garand rifle. That's going to look real good when you get to court.'

Branford laughed. 'Sure, Bauman. You're thinking about my best interests.' Branford took a slim stack of papers from his briefcase and handed them to Charlie. 'Here's Mrs Kimmel's statement, plus the reports written by the officers responding to her call. We don't have anything in from the CI or the criminalist yet, but I'll copy you as soon as we get anything.'

Charlie flipped through the pages absently. 'Thanks, Robby. Hope you got more to offer the court than Mrs Kimmel.'

Branford smiled tightly. 'We do, but let's start with her. We've got an eyewit who puts your man at the scene, and picked him out of a line. Second, the swabs came back positive, confirming that Pike recently fired a weapon.'

I said, 'Pike owns a gun shop. He shoots every day of his life.'

Krantz leaned back. 'Yeah. And today he took one shot too many.'

Charlie ignored him. 'SID match the slug and Pike's gun?'

'SID has the weapons at the shed now, running them.'

Krantz said, 'You know how many guns we found at his place? Twelve handguns, four shotguns, and eight rifles, two of which are fully automatic assault weapons. This guy's a friggin' poster boy for gun control.'

Charlie made a hurry-up gesture. 'Yeah, yeah, yeah, and every one of those weapons is legally registered. Here's a prediction, Robby. You're not going to get a match.'

Branford shrugged. 'Probably not, but it doesn't matter. He's an ex-cop. He knows enough to dump the murder weapon. Does he have an alibi?'

Now Charlie was looking annoyed. 'Pike was in Santa Monica. At the ocean.'

'Okay. I'm listening.'

'We're locating the wits now.'

Branford didn't quite manage a smile. 'And all I've got to do is believe you.' He took the chair near his briefcase

248

and leaned back. Maybe he and Krantz had rehearsed it. 'For the motive, we've got Karen Garcia. Pike blamed Dersh for murdering his girlfriend. Here he was, inside the investigation, and it was killing him that everybody knew that Dersh was the one, but that the police couldn't put together a case.'

I said, 'Their relationship was over years ago. Talk to her father and check it out.'

'What does that matter? Men get weird when it comes to women.'

Branford brought another manila folder out of his briefcase and tossed it on the table.

'Besides that, we're not dealing with the most stable personality here, are we? Look at this guy's record. You see all the shootings he's been involved in? You see how many people he's killed? Here's a guy, he thinks nothing of using deadly force to solve his problems.'

I was watching Krantz. Krantz nodded every time Branford made a point, but so far the points didn't add up to much. Yet here was Krantz, looking assured and confident, and not at all bothered by the pissant nature of things like 'prior history'. Even Branford seemed amused, like he knew he was giving us nothing.

I said, 'I don't get how you put it on Joe.'

They looked at me.

Branford said, 'The old lady.'

'She knows Joe by sight? She called 911 and said she saw Joe Pike sneaking down the alley?'

Krantz uncrossed his arms and leaned forward. 'Figure it out, Sherlock. How many guys run around at night with the no sleeves and the tattoos and the sunglasses?'

'Somebody who was trying to look like Joe Pike, Sherlock.'

Krantz laughed. 'Oh, please, Cole. You don't have to be Einstein to figure this out.'

Charlie put the papers Branford had given him into his briefcase, then stood. 'You guys are light. Way light. Here

I was, thinking you were going to lay out real evidence like Pike's fingerprints on Dersh's doorknob, and all I'm getting is that you don't like that he's in the NRA. This is lame, Robby. I'll have the old lady saying she saw Santa Claus, and the judge is going to laugh you out.'

Robby Branford suddenly looked smug. 'Well, there is another thing. You wanna see it now?'

He didn't wait for us to answer. He went to the VCR and pressed the play button.

The flat blue screen filled with a soundless color surveillance video of the back of a house. It took me a moment to realize that it was Dersh's house. I had only seen it from the front.

Krantz said, 'This is a surveillance tape of Dersh's house. See the date down here?'

The time and date were in the lower left corner of the screen. The date showed it to be three days before Karen Garcia's burial. That would be the day I had learned the truth about the five victims. It was the day Pike had gone to see Dersh.

We could see a large picture window off Dersh's studio, and inside, two blurred figures I took to be Eugene Dersh and another man.

I said, 'That's not Pike.'

'No, it's not. Watch here, past the edge of the house where you can see the street.'

Krantz tapped the upper left side of the screen. Part of Dersh's drive was visible, and, beyond it, the street.

Krantz hit a button, and the image slowed. A few seconds later, the nose of a red Jeep Cherokee eased into the frame. When the cab was visible, Krantz hit the freeze frame.

Krantz said, 'That's Pike.'

Charlie's face drained, and his mouth formed a thin, dark line.

The picture advanced frame by frame. Joe's head turned. Joe looked at the house. Joe disappeared.

'When a jury sees this, they're going to put it together with everything else we have and think just what we think. Pike was doing a drive-by to case the area, working up his nut to pull the trigger.'

Robby Branford put his hands in his pockets, pleased with himself and his evidence. 'Looks pretty good now, doesn't it, Charlie? I'd say your boy's going to jail.'

Charlie Bauman took my arm and said, 'Come on. Let's go outside and talk about this.'

Charlie kept hold of my arm until I shook him off in the booking area. 'It's not what it seems. That was three days before Karen Garcia's funeral. Pike only went over there to see Dersh.'

'Don't talk so loud. Why'd he go see Dersh?'

'I'd just found out about the other victims, and that Krantz suspected Dersh for the killer.'

'So Pike wanted to go check out the suspect?'

'Yeah. That's pretty much it.'

Charlie led me to the elevators, making sure no one was close enough to hear. 'He go over there to talk to Dersh? Ask him if he did it?'

'No. He just wanted to look at him.'

'He just *looked* at him?'

'He wanted to see if he thought Dersh could do it.'

Charlie sighed and shook his head. 'I can see me trying to explain that to a jury. "*You gotta understand, ladies and gentlemen, my client is a goddamned swami and he was just trying to vibe whether or not the victim was a killer.*" ' Charlie sighed again. 'This really, really is gonna look bad for us.'

'Will it come up in the arraignment?'

'Sure, it's gonna come up. Look, I can tell you right now that Joe is gonna get bound over for trial. He's going to stand for this one. Our problem isn't with the arraignment judge anymore, it'll be with the jury.'

'What about bail?'

'I don't know.' Charlie took a pack of cigarettes from his jacket, and stuck one in his mouth. Nervous.

A passing cop said, 'They don't want you smoking in here. City building.'

Charlie fired up the cigarette. 'So arrest me.'

The cop laughed and went on.

'Look, Elvis, I'm not going to tell a jury that Pike just wanted to see the guy. I'll make up a better story than that, but it still looks bad.' He checked his watch. 'They're gonna transfer him to the Criminal Court Building in a few minutes. I'll go over there to talk with him again before the arraignment.'

'I'll meet you there.'

'No, you won't. You're going to look for the girl Pike saw at the beach. There's nothing you can do sitting in a room with me.'

The elevator doors opened and we went in. Two women and an overweight man were inside. The shorter of the women sniffed at Charlie's cigarette. 'There's no smoking in here.'

Charlie blew out a cloud of smoke, and waved his hand. 'Sorry. I'll put it right out.'

He didn't.

'How bad is it, Charlie?'

Bauman drew deep on the cigarette, then blew a huge cloud of smoke toward the woman.

'Can you spell *plea bargain*?'

CHAPTER 24

As I walked out through Parker Center, the voices of the people around me were distant and tinny. The world had changed. Karen Garcia, and Eugene Dersh were gone, and Frank Garcia had turned away from us. The police thought their assassin killer was gone, but even if he wasn't, it didn't matter.

There was only Joe in jail, and the need to save him.

I spent the afternoon retracing the six-mile route that Pike had run, listing every business along the way that might employ twenty-four-hour help. When I reached the part of Ocean Avenue where Pike had met the girl, I left my car and walked. Small groups of homeless people were dotted through the park, some sleeping on blankets in the hot sun, others clustered in small groups or busy searching through trash containers. I woke them if they were sleeping or interrupted them if they were talking to ask if anyone knew Trudy or Matt, or if, last night, they had seen a jogging man who wore sunglasses even after dark. Almost everyone said yes, and almost everyone lied. Trudy was tall and skinny, or short and fat, or had only one eye. The jogging man was a black guy looking to harvest the organs of unwilling donors, or a government operative bent on mind control. The schizophrenics were particularly cooperative. I didn't stop for lunch.

I worked my way through every Ocean Avenue hotel, asking for the names of nighttime staff, and when I finished I drove home hard to begin calling. Completing my first pass along Joe's route had taken almost five hours, and left me with a sense that I was falling behind.

Dersh's murder was the headline story on every four o'clock newscast in town. LAPD had released Joe's name as the suspect, and one station supered a picture of Joe with the legend VIGILANTE KILLER. Everyone reported that Dersh was the main suspect in the recent string of killings, with sources 'among the upper echelons of LAPD' saying that that investigation would remain open, though no other suspect was expected to be identified. The cat came in during the newscast, and watched with me.

At ten minutes before five, my phone rang, and Charlie Bauman said, 'The arraignment just ended. He's bound over.'

Charlie sounded hollow.

'What about bail?'

'No bail.'

I felt dull and weary, as if my frantic pace had taken its toll.

'We'll have another arraignment in Superior Court in about a month. I can argue for bail again there, and maybe that judge will swing in our favor. This one didn't.'

'So what happens now?'

'They'll let him sit in Parker for another couple of days, then transfer him to Men's Central. They'll keep him over in the safe wing because he used to be a cop, so we don't have to worry about that. All we have to worry about is building his defense. You find anyone who saw him?'

'Not yet.' I told him how I'd spent the day.

'Christ, how many names you got?'

'Between hotel people and businesses, two hundred fourteen.'

'Man. You work fast.'

It didn't seem like very much to me.

'Listen. Fax your list to my office. I'll have my secretary get on it tomorrow. That way you can keep pounding the pavement.'

'I'll make the calls.'

Charlie hesitated. When he spoke again his voice was calm. 'Don't freak out on me, Elvis.'

'What are you talking about?'

'It's after six. Businesses are closing, and the night shifts aren't on yet. Who're you going to call?'

I didn't know.

'Joe's okay for now. We've got time. Let's just do a good job, all right?' Like I was a little boy who'd lost his best friend, and he was my dad telling me everything would be okay if I just stayed calm.

'I'll fax the list, Charlie.'

'Good. We'll talk tomorrow.'

After we hung up, I sent the list, then got a beer and brought it out onto the deck. The air was hot, but the canyon was clear. Two red-tailed hawks floated in lazy circles overhead. They hung on nothing, patient, tiny heads cocking from side to side as they searched for field mice and gophers. I have seen them float like that for hours. Patient hunters are successful hunters. Charlie was right. When I was in Ranger School at Fort Benning, Georgia, they taught us that panic kills. Men who had lived through three wars taught us that if you panicked you would stop thinking, and if you stopped thinking you would die. A sergeant named Zim ran us for five miles every day carrying sixty-pound field packs, a full issue of ammunition, and our M16s. Between each cadence he made us shout, 'My mind is my deadliest weapon. Sergeant Zim says so, and Sergeant Zim is never wrong. Sergeant Zim is God. Thank you, God.'

When you're eighteen, that leaves an impression.

I said, 'Okay, moron. Think.'

If Amanda Kimmel had seen a man dressed like Joe, wearing sunglasses like Joe, and sporting tattoos like Joe, then someone was pretending to be Joe. Finding that person would be an even better way of clearing Joe than finding Trudy or Matt, but so far, all I had was something that no one else seemed to have: An absolute and complete belief that Joe Pike was telling the truth. I did not doubt him. I would not. They could have videotape of Joe walking into that house, and if Joe pointed at the television and said, 'That's not me', I would believe him.

You work with what you have, and all I had was faith. An awful lot of people have found that to be enough.

You look for connections.

Krantz came at this by looking for people with a motive to kill Dersh. He thought Pike's motive was Karen. Frank Garcia had the same motive, and had the money to have Dersh killed, but he wouldn't put it on Joe. That meant someone else, and I wondered if that someone had some true connection to Dersh, or had only used Dersh as a means to an end. Getting Pike. Maybe this wasn't about Dersh at all, but was about Pike.

I went inside for a yellow legal pad, came back out again, and made a timeline. From Karen's murder until the story broke that Dersh was the suspect took six days. From the story breaking about Dersh until his murder was only three days. I tried to imagine some guy with a grudge against Pike watching his TV. He's out there hating Pike, and he's never before in his life heard about Karen Garcia or Eugene Dersh, but he sees all this, and the world's biggest lightbulb blinks on over his head. *Hey, I can cap this guy Dersh to get Pike!* All in the span of three days.

Uh-uh.

That meant he knew of Dersh prior to the story breaking, and had time to think about it. Also, all of L.A. knew that the police had been surveilling Dersh around the clock. Yet this guy had picked a time after the surveillance had been scaled back. I wondered about that.

I brought my beer inside, poured it out, then went back onto the deck. The hawks were still up there. I had thought they were hunting, but maybe they were just enjoying the air. I had thought they were looking for prey, but maybe they were looking at each other instead, and finding joy in each other's company there above the earth. Love hawks.

Relationships are often different than they appear at first glance.

I decided that the killer was someone connected both to Joe and to Dersh. Joe was connected to Dersh the same way Frank was connected to Dersh: Through Karen. Maybe the killer was connected to Joe through Karen, also.

I went inside, dug around for Samantha Dolan's home number, and called her.

She said, 'Hey, it's the World's Greatest Everything. Callin' little ol' me.'

She sounded drunk.

'Are you okay, Dolan?'

'Jesus. Would you call me Samantha?'

'Samantha.'

'This has got to be about your buddy, right? I mean, you're not just calling to flirt?'

'It's Joe.'

'I'm out of that, remember? I'm off the Task Force, I don't know what Krantz is doing, and I don't care. Hey, from what I heard, Pike sounds good for it.'

'I know that Branford has a case against him, but I'm telling you that Pike didn't do this.'

'Oh, puh-lease. You weren't there, were you? You didn't see it.'

'I know him, is all. Pike wouldn't go into Dersh's house in the middle of the night and shoot him like that. It isn't Pike's style.'

'What style murder would he use, you know him so well?'

'The kind that can't be seen. Pike could do it and you would never know and would never even think that it might be him. They would disappear, one day here, the next day gone, and you'd be left wondering what happened, Dolan. That's the way Pike would do it, and, believe me, you would never find the body. Pike is the most dangerous man I know, and I've known more than a few. He is without peer.'

Dolan didn't say anything.

'Dolan? You still there?'

'Something tells me you could be pretty dangerous, too.'

I didn't answer. Let her think what she wanted.

Dolan sighed. 'Okay, World's Greatest. What do you want?'

'Whoever killed Dersh might be connected to Joe through Karen Garcia, and that goes back to the days Joe rode a black-and-white. Joe's partner was a guy named Abel Wozniak.'

'Sure. The cop Pike killed.'

'You don't have to say it like that, Dolan.'

'There's only one way to say it.'

'I want to find out who was around back then who might hate Pike enough to kill Dersh and frame Pike for it. I'm going to need files and records, and I can't get them without help.'

She didn't answer again.

'Dolan?'

'You got a fucking set on you, you know that? The trouble I'm in.'

She hung up.

I called her back, but she had the phone off the hook. Busy. I called every five minutes for the next half hour. Busy.

'Shit.'

Twenty minutes later I was sitting at the dining-room table and thinking about calling Dolan again when Lucy let herself in. She took off her suit coat and shoes, and went to the fridge without looking at me.

I said, 'I guess you heard about Joe.'

'I followed the story at work. We had people at the arraignment.'

'Uh-huh.'

She hadn't come out to give me a kiss, and she hadn't yet looked at me.

'Can I get you something to eat?'

She shook her head.

'Want a glass of wine?'

'Maybe in a minute.'

She was staring into the box.

'What's wrong?'

She stopped staring and closed the door.

'I never knew these things about Joe.'

The day's tension crept back into my shoulders with a dense tightness.

'I saw a tape of Branford arguing against bail. He talked about all the shootings Joe's been involved in, and the men he's killed.'

The tension turned into a stabbing ache.

'I thought of Joe as this strong, quiet man who was your friend, but now it feels like I never knew him. I don't like knowing these things. I don't like knowing a man who would do things like this.'

'You know he treats you well and with respect. You know he's good with Ben, and that he's my best friend.'

Something confused and fearful worked in her eyes. 'Branford said that he's killed fourteen men, for God's sake.'

I shrugged. 'If you can make it in L.A., you can make it anywhere.'

'This isn't funny to me.'

I tried to do something with the ache but there was nothing to be done. I wanted to call Dolan again, but I didn't. 'The men he's killed were trying to kill him, or me, or someone that Joe wanted to protect. He is not a hit man. He has never committed murder for hire, or killed someone simply to kill them. If he's killed, it's because he's put himself in situations that have required it. Just as I have. Maybe there's something wrong with both of us. Is that what you're getting at?'

Lucy came to the door but did not cross through. 'No, that isn't what I'm saying. There's just so much to assimilate here. I'm sorry. I don't mean to be like this.' She put on a smile, but it was strained. 'I haven't seen you all day and I miss you, and all of this about Joe made me miss you more. I just don't know what to think. I read the documents that Branford submitted to the court, and what was there scared me.'

'They were supposed to scare you, Lucy. That's why Branford used them to argue against bail. You know that.'

I wanted more than anything else to get up and go to her but I couldn't. I thought she might want me to, or that she wanted to come to me, but something was stopping her, too.

'Elvis?'

'What?'

'Did Joe kill that man?'

'No.'

'Are you sure of that?'

'Yes. Yes, I'm sure.'

She nodded, but then her voice came small and from far away.

'I don't think I am. I think that he could've. Maybe I even think that he did.'

We stood without speaking for a time, and then I went into the living room and put on the radio. I did not return to the kitchen.

I sat on the couch, staring out at the darkening sky, and realized that where Joe Pike sat this night, he could only see walls.

I wondered what the killer could see.

Number six

The hot breeze carries the stink of the public rest room to where the killer hides in a stand of red oleander. MacArthur Park is quiet this time of night, a perfect time for hunting.

The killer is flush with excitement at how well things are going. The Task Force still has not connected the five homicides, Hollywood Division detectives have begun turning evidence in Edward Deege's murder, and killing Dersh has proven to be inspired.

Joe Pike is in jail, and will stay there for the rest of his life, until some rat-house lifer pushes a shank between his ribs.

And won't that be fitting.

The killer smiles, just thinking about it. The killer doesn't smile often, learning that trait from Pike, from having studied Pike for so long now, Pike, whom he hates more than any other. But this is a special time, and there is plenty of hate to go around.

Pike, in perfect control.

Pike, in absolute command.

Pike, who took everything from him, and then gave him purpose.

Payback is a motherfucker.

The only possible fly in the ointment is this girl Trudy. The killer did what he could to protect himself from someone like her: He staked out Pike's home, making sure Pike was alone, waiting until the lights went out, then waiting longer still to be sure Pike was asleep before setting off to kill Dersh. The killer suspects that there is no Trudy, and that Pike is making it up, but he can't be sure, and thinks that he may have to find Trudy himself. He could run her name on the NCIC computers, and on VICAP through the FBI. And if someone beats him to her, well, he'll know as quickly as anyone. And deal with her then.

Still, the heavy lifting is done, and now all that remains is killing the rest of them, and ensuring with absolute certainty that Pike is convicted.

That means preparing for Pike's partner, Elvis Cole.

What a stupid name.

The killer is considering how he might deal with Cole when he hears Jesus Lorenzo approaching, and grips the .22 caliber pistol that he's taped into a plastic Clorox bottle. There is no mistaking Lorenzo. He is five feet ten, wearing red pumps with four-inch heels, a red satin micro-sheath, and a platinum wig. The killer has watched him cruise MacArthur Park on six separate nights at this time, waiting for this moment.

When Jesus Lorenzo disappears into the men's room, the killer steps out from the oleander and follows. No one else is around, no one is in the men's room. The killer knows this because he's been here for almost two hours.

The plan continues.

Payback, you motherfucker.

CHAPTER 25

Lucy and I started the next day with a careful hesitancy that left me uncomfortable. Something new had been introduced to our relationship that neither of us knew how to approach. We had slept together, but we had not made love. Though she appeared to sleep, I think it was feigned. I wanted to speak with her about Joe. I wanted her to be all right with him, but didn't know if that was possible. By the time I decided to plunge in, she had to leave for work.

As she was walking out, she said, 'Are you going to see Joe today?'

'Yes. Probably later.'

'Would you give him my best?'

'Sure. You could come with me, see him yourself.'

'I have to get to work.'

'Okay. I know.'

'But maybe.'

'Luce?'

She looked at me.

'Whatever Joe is, that's what I am, too.'

She probably didn't want to hear that.

'I guess what bothers me is that you're not disturbed by these things. You accept them as ordinary, and things like this aren't ordinary.'

I didn't know what to say that wouldn't sound self-serving, so I didn't say anything.

Lucy pulled the door closed and went to work.

Another fine day in the City of Angels.

I wanted to call Charlie Bauman's secretary to tell her

what I had already done, but she probably wasn't yet in the office. Charlie would tell her, but I wanted to tell her, too. I also wanted to contact both the FBI and the California State Sheriffs to access the data bank they keep on missing and runaway children. I wanted to see if I could get any hits on the first names, Trudy and Matt, and I also wanted to run the stolen vehicle reports for a black Dodge minivan. I decided to call Dolan first, and got Williams.

'Hey, Williams. Is Dolan there?'

'What's it to you?'

'I want to talk to her.'

'Haven't seen her. You wanna know what I heard Krantz say?'

'I'm not going to like this, am I?'

'Krantz says you were probably in on it with that bastard, Pike. He says if he can tie you into it, maybe you and Pike can do the IV tango together.' Williams chuckled when he said it.

'Hey, Williams.'

'What?'

'You're the whitest black man I ever met.'

'Fuck you, Cole.'

'You, too, Williams.'

I hung up, thinking that if the day got any better my cat would die.

I was on my way upstairs to take a shower when the doorbell rang. It was Samantha Dolan, looking hungover.

'I just called you.'

'Was I there?'

'You know what, Dolan? Today isn't a good day for humor.'

She walked in past me, again without being invited, and peeked into the kitchen. She was wearing a navy blazer over a plain white tee shirt and jeans, and oval Italian sunglasses. The shirt looked very white beneath the dark blazer. 'Yeah, well, I have days like that, too. You never fixed the tiles.'

'I don't want to be rude, but what are you doing here?'

'You worried the little woman's going to get jealous?'

'Do me a favor and don't call her the little woman. It's pissing me off.'

'Whatever. You think I could have some juice or water? I'm a little dry.'

I brought her into the kitchen and poured two glasses of mango juice. When I handed the glass to her, she took off her sunglasses. Her eyes were bloodshot, and I caught a whiff of tequila. 'Jesus, it's eight in the morning, Dolan. You hit it this early?'

The bloodshot eyes flashed angrily. 'Is it any of your business when I "hit it"?'

I raised my hands.

Dolan put the sunglasses back on.

'I was thinking about what you said last night. That maybe the killer is connected to Pike through Garcia. Maybe you've got something there, but I sure as hell couldn't call you from the office to talk about it.'

'That mean you'll help?'

'It means I want to talk about it.'

The cat nosed through his cat door. He got halfway inside, and stopped, staring at her.

Dolan scowled at him. 'What in hell are you looking at?'

The cat cocked his head, still staring.

'What's wrong with this cat?'

'I think he's confused. The only other person in the world he likes is Joe Pike. Maybe it's the glasses.'

Dolan scowled deeper. 'How nice for me. Mistaken for a two-hundred-pound bruiser with a butch cut and no tits.'

Dolan took off the glasses and bugged her eyes at him. 'Better?'

The cat cocked his head the other way.

'Why does he hold his head that way?'

'Someone shot him.'

Dolan squatted and held out her hand.

I said, 'Don't do that, Dolan. He bites.'

'Samantha.'

'Samantha.'

The cat sniffed. He eased toward her and sniffed again.

'He doesn't seem so mean to me.'

She scratched his head, then finished her juice.

'He's just a damned cat.'

I stared at him, then her. I had seen that cat claw a hundred people over the years, and I had *never* seen him let anyone other than me and Joe touch him.

'What?'

I shook my head again. 'Nothing.'

She took a hard pack of Marlboros from her pocket. 'You mind if I smoke?'

'Yeah, I do. If you gotta have one, we can go out on the deck.'

We went out. Yesterday's gray haze still hung in the air, but it had thinned. Dolan went to the rail and peered down into the canyon. 'This is nice. You got your chairs out here. You got your Weber.'

She fired up a Marlboro and blew a great fog of smoke to add to the haze. Inviting.

I said, 'So what were you thinking last night?'

'I wasn't on the job when that happened with Wozniak and Pike, but Stan Watts was. I asked him about it. Do you know what happened?'

'I know.'

A little girl named Ramona Ann Escobar had been seen leaving a park with a man the police believed to be a known pedophile and child pornographer named Leonard DeVille. Pike and Wozniak learned that DeVille had been sighted entering the Islander Palms Motel, and had driven there to investigate. When they entered the room, Ramona was not present. Pike had never spoken to me of these things, but I recalled from the newspaper coverage that Wozniak, the father of a young daughter, had apparently been fearful that DeVille had harmed the girl. He drew his weapon, and struck DeVille. Pike, feeling that Wozniak might endanger the suspect, intervened. A struggle followed, during which Wozniak's weapon discharged, killing Wozniak. Internal Affairs conducted an investigation, but brought no charges against Pike. What the articles I'd read didn't say is that even though IAG didn't bring charges, damn near every officer on the job at that time blamed Pike for Wozniak's death, hating him all the more because Pike had killed Wozniak defending an asshole like Leonard DeVille. A child molester.

Dolan said, 'So if you're looking for people with a grudge, you're gonna have to start with a couple of thousand cops.'

'I don't believe that.'

'I'm talking *hate*, buddy. They got cops still around who *hate* Pike for what happened to Wozniak.'

'Think about what you're saying, Dolan. You believe some random cop has been carrying a grudge so big he's willing to kill an innocent man like Dersh just to set up Pike?'

'*You* say innocent, and this is your theory, not mine. If one of these cowboys thinks Dersh is a serial killer, maybe he figures it's a no-brainer sacrifice. And if it isn't a cop, you're probably talking about one of the two or three hundred assholes that Pike arrested. That's still a pretty big suspect pool.'

I spread my hands. 'I can't go there, Dolan. There are so many variables here that if I try to deal with all of them I'll just sit home and wait for Krantz to crack the case.'

'Guess that wouldn't work for you.'

'Does it work for you?'

She smiled. 'No. Christ, that sun is hot.'

Dolan took off the blazer and draped it over one of the deck chairs. Her Sig was in a clip holster on the right hip of her jeans, and her tanned arms looked strong. The white shirt was so bright it made me squint.

I said, 'I've got to stay with what's in front of me, and that's Wozniak and Karen Garcia, and how they all came to meet. I need to find out everything I can about Wozniak and DeVille, and what happened in that room. I want the shooting team report, the incident report, and whatever Internal Affairs had.'

She was shaking her head before I finished. 'I can tell you right now you can forget the IAG documents. They're under seal. You'd need a court order.'

'I need Wozniak's personnel file and DeVille's case file. I'm going to talk to Joe and see what he says.'

'Man, you don't want too much, do you?'

'What else can I do?'

She took another deep pull on the cigarette. 'Nothing, I guess. I'll make some calls for you. It might take a while.'

'I appreciate your doing this for me, Samantha.'

She rested her elbows on the rail, looking out at the canyon. 'I've got nothing better to do. You know what Bishop has me doing? Due-diligence calls on last year's robbery cases. You know what that is?'

'No.'

'We gotta go through unsolved cases every three months just to keep the cases alive. You call the detective of record, ask if he's learned anything new, he says no, and you log it. A fucking clerk could do it. And every time I see Bishop, he shakes his head and walks away.'

I didn't know what to say.

She finished the cigarette and dropped it in the juice glass.

'I'm sorry, Samantha.'

She looked at me. 'You've got nothing to be sorry about.'

'I jammed you into coming across about the Task Force, just like I'm jamming you now. I apologize for doing that.

I wouldn't've told Krantz that I knew about it, or that we'd had that conversation in your car that morning.'

'Everything always comes out, buddy. I'm on thin ice now, but if I'd lied that day and they'd found out, I'd be underwater for sure. Like I said, maybe if I kiss enough ass, Bishop will let me stick around.'

I nodded.

She glanced over. 'I feel like a damned lush.'

'Because you had a couple this morning?'

'Because I want one right now.'

She stared at me some more.

'I didn't take the drink because of this shit with the job, you dumb ass.'

I looked at her, thinking that she didn't need to come to my house, that she could've called. I thought how she'd rung the bell just a few minutes after Lucy had gone.

Dolan was leaning on the rail, her back stretched long and taut, the white tee shirt pulled tight. She looked good. She saw me looking and shifted her weight so that her ass swayed. I looked away, but it wasn't easy. I thought about Lucy.

'Elvis.'

I shook my head.

Dolan stepped close and put her arms around my neck and kissed me. I could taste the cigarettes and the tequila and the mangoes, and I wanted to kiss her back. Maybe, for a moment, I did.

Then I took her arms from around my neck.

'I can't, Samantha.'

Dolan took a fast step back. She went a very bright red, then turned and ran back through my house. A moment later, I heard the Beemer rev to life and pull away.

I touched my lips, and stood on the deck for a long time, thinking.

Then I went inside and phoned Charlie Bauman.

CHAPTER 26

Charlie listened without comment as I told him why I wanted to speak with Pike.

When I was done, he said, 'Visiting starts at ten unless they're bringing him over to Men's Central this morning. Let me call over there to find out, then I'll get back to you.'

The cat came downstairs to the landing and looked at me while I waited. He went into the guest room, then came back into the living room, where he looked at me again.

I said, 'She's gone.'

He fell onto his side and licked his penis. Cats.

I couldn't get Dolan out of my head, and having her there made me feel a guilt unlike any I had known since the first time I killed a man. Dolan was leaning on the rail, and then she was pressed against me. I could still taste her cigarette. I went into the kitchen and drank a glass of water, but it didn't wash away the taste. The love I felt for Lucy flared into something white and fierce, and I wished she were here. I wanted to hold her, and tell her that I loved her, and hear her say the same back. I wanted her caress, and the comfort of her love. Most of all I wanted to stop wanting Samantha Dolan, but I didn't know how. It made me feel disloyal.

I stared out the kitchen window for a time, then washed the glass, put it away, and forced myself to think about what I had to do.

Charlie called back four minutes later, and told me to meet him in the Parker Center lobby at eleven.

I used the time until then to look for Trudy, calling the Department of Motor Vehicles for a transfer and registration check on all new minivans sold in the past two months, sorted by color. I told them I was only interested in black. We got twenty-eight hits. I asked if they could fax the information to me, but was told no, they'd have to mail it. The government in action. After that, I spent almost two hours on the phone talking to the FBI, the United States Marshals, and the L.A. County Sheriffs. Most of that time was spent on hold, but I learned that no current model year black minivans had been stolen in the past three months. I arranged to have the names Trudy and Matt run through the law enforcement agencies' VICAP and NCIC computers, which show outstanding fugitive warrants from around the country, and also contain a database of missing or abducted children. When they asked me why I wanted this, I didn't tell them about Pike; I told them I was working for the parents. Everyone was more cooperative that way, but everyone told me the same thing: With no last name, the odds of getting any useful information were slim.

I drove to Parker early, scanning the smokers out on the walk as I turned in for Dolan. She wasn't among them, and I wondered if she was getting the files I needed, or if she would. And then I thought that maybe I was looking for another reason, and the guilt burned like bitter coffee.

Even though I was early, Charlie Bauman was already in the lobby, waiting. He said, 'You look like hell. What's wrong?'

'Not a goddamned thing.'

'That's just what I need. Attitude.'

An overweight cop with a red face led us back along the corridor to the interview room. Charlie and I sat without speaking for the five minutes it took them to bring Joe. He was wearing the blue jumpsuit, but he'd rolled the sleeves. The veins in his wrists and forearms bulged as if he'd been exercising when they'd come for him.

The same black cop with weight-lifter arms who had brought Joe out of the lineup now led him through the door. 'You gonna be good?'

'Yes.'

Pike was wearing the cuffs and shackles. The black cop unlatched the handcuffs and pocketed them.

'Gotta leave the ankles.'

Pike nodded. 'Thanks for the hands.'

When the cop was gone, I smiled. Joe wasn't squinting anymore. He'd grown used to the light.

Joe said, 'You find Trudy?'

'Not yet.'

'So how come you haven't broken me out?'

'Too easy. I'd rather do it the hard way and figure out who set you up.'

Charlie leaned forward like he was going to dive across the table. 'Cole has an idea that maybe whoever popped Dersh is also connected to you through Karen Garcia. Maybe it's even the same guy who killed her.'

Pike looked at me. I thought he might be curious, but you never know with Pike.

I said, 'Whoever killed Dersh hates you so much that he made himself up to look like you, and even used a .357 like you. That means he knows you, or at least has made an effort to learn about you.'

Pike nodded.

'If he hates you that much, why wait until now, and why kill Dersh just to frame you? Why not just take you head-on?'

Pike's mouth flickered. 'Because he can't.'

Charlie rolled his eyes. 'I shoulda brought my waders. The testosterone is getting pretty deep in here.'

I went through what I'd been thinking about the timeline, and the coincidence of it all. 'He's been thinking about this, Joe. Since before the story broke about Dersh. Maybe even since before Karen was killed. He doesn't want to kill you. He wants to punish you. This guy's been carrying a grudge for a long time, and now he's seen a way to work it out, and that makes me wonder if he isn't connected to Karen also.'

Pike canted his head, and now the calm blue water of his eyes held something deeper.

'He wouldn't have to be connected to Karen. I arrested two hundred men.'

'If it's just some guy, then why here and why now? Just some guy, then we're spiking the coincidence meter, and I can't buy it.'

Charlie smiled like a wolf, and nodded. He was getting into it. 'Goddamned right.'

Pike said, 'Leonard DeVille.'

The man Joe and Wozniak went to arrest the day Wozniak died.

Charlie said, 'Who?'

We told him.

Joe said, 'DeVille was there at the end, but he was also why Karen and I met. Woz and I responded to a report she called in about a suspected pedophile. Woz thought it might be DeVille.'

Charlie said, 'So maybe it's DeVille.'

Joe shook his head. 'DeVille died in prison. An Eighteenth Street gang-banger cut him two years into his term.' Child molesters didn't last long in prison.

I said, 'Okay. What about Wozniak? Maybe there's something through him.'

'No.'

'Think about it.'

'Woz is dead, too, Elvis. There's nothing to think about.'

Someone knocked hard twice on the door, and Charlie shouted for them to come in.

It was Krantz and Robby Branford.

Krantz frowned when he saw Charlie's cigarette. 'No smoking in here, Bauman.'

'Sorry, Detective. I'll put it right out.' Charlie took

another drag and blew the smoke at Branford. 'You planning on talking to my client without me around, Robby?'

Branford fanned the air, annoyed.

'They knew you were here and called me. If you hadn't been here, I would've phoned. You're going to kill yourself with those things, Charlie.'

Charlie said, 'Yeah.'

I didn't like the expressions on their faces, and neither did Charlie.

He said, 'What? I'm in the middle of a conference with my client.'

Robby Branford took out a tiny leather notepad and glanced at it. 'At seven twenty-two this morning a transvestite named Jesus Lorenzo was found dead in a public bathroom in MacArthur Park. One shot with a .22, white plastic particulates have been identified in the wound. Initial time of death is about three this morning.'

He closed the pad, put it away, and looked at Pike.

'A full day after you killed Dersh.'

I leaned back and stared at Krantz. 'So Dersh didn't kill Karen Garcia or anyone else.'

Charlie Bauman said, 'What the hell does that have to do with us? You gonna charge Pike with that one, too?'

Branford shook his head. 'No, not that one. It's bad enough when somebody takes the law into his own hands to get revenge, but it's even worse when they fuck up and kill the wrong man.'

Charlie said, 'Pike didn't kill anyone.'

'We'll let the jury decide that. In the meantime I wanted to put you on notice.'

'What?'

'When we arraign in Superior Court next month, we're going for Special Circumstances. We'll ask for the death penalty.'

A tic started beneath Charlie's left eye. 'That's bullshit, Robby.'

Branford shrugged. 'Dersh's relatives might disagree. We're going to want to talk to your man after lunch. Why don't you and I get together and set a time when you're done here.'

I was still staring at Krantz, and Krantz was staring back.

'You going to charge Krantz with getting an innocent man killed?'

Branford walked out without answering, but Krantz paused in the door.

He said, 'Yeah, Dersh was the wrong man, and I'll have to live with that. But I've still got Pike.'

He walked out and closed the door.

Sunday Afternoon with the Wozniaks

Pike said, 'Hold on tight.'

Evelyn Wozniak, age nine, grabbed his outstretched hands as tightly as she could.

'Bet you can't lift me! I'm too big!'

'Let's see.'

'Don't drop me!'

Joe lifted, holding the girl at arm's length, and slowly turned in a circle. Evelyn squealed.

Abel Wozniak called from the barbecue. 'Evie, tell your mother I need more water in the spray bottle. Hurry up before I burn the goddamned chicken.'

Pike returned Evelyn to the earth, where, flushed and breathless, she ran into the house. A few minutes ago, Joe and Abel had set a picnic table on the covered patio out of the sun, while Karen and Paulette had gone inside for the place settings and fresh drinks. Now, Joe sat in the lawn chair beneath the big sun umbrella and sipped his beer. Across the lawn, Abel prodded at the chicken and cursed the hot coals.

Joe had always admired the Wozniaks' backyard. Abel

and Paulette kept it simple and neat. They lived in a modest home here in San Gabriel, where many officers and their families lived, and they both worked hard to keep the house and the yard looking nice. It showed, and Joe had always enjoyed coming to their home for a Sunday afternoon cookout.

Abel cursed the coals again, shouted that he needed the goddamned water, then covered the grill and came over to sit next to Joe. Abel had a beer of his own. He'd had several.

Joe said, 'You deal with it yet?'

'Fuck off. You don't know what you're talking about.' Abel stared at the smoke pouring out of the barbecue's vents.

'I followed you, Woz. I saw you with the Chihuahua Brothers. I saw you with that girl. I know what you're doing.'

Wozniak took a Salem from the pack on the ground next to his chair and lit up. Wozniak said, 'Why the hell are you doing this?'

'I can't let it go on.'

'I'm your goddamned partner, for chrissakes.'

Joe finished his beer and placed the empty bottle on the lawn. Paulette and Karen came out, Karen with a huge bowl of potato salad, and Paulette the spray bottle and a tray of forks and knives and napkins. Abel went over, used the water on his coals, then came back. The women stayed busy with the table.

Wozniak muttered, 'Fuckin' chicken looks like shit.'

'I mean it, Woz. I won't ride with this forever.'

Woz flicked at his cigarette. Nervous. 'I got responsibilities.'

'That's why I'm giving you the choice.'

Wozniak leaned toward him so far that the chair tipped. 'You think I like this? You think I want it to be this way? Man, I feel like I'm caught in a goddamned vise.'

Karen flashed a great brilliant smile at Joe, and Joe waved. Paulette smiled, and waved, too. They couldn't hear what the men were saying.

'I know it's a vise, Woz. I'm trying to help you with it.'

'Bullshit.'

'You don't have a choice.'

Wozniak watched the two women, then considered Joe. 'Don't think I don't know how you feel about her.'

Pike stared at him.

Wozniak nodded. 'I've seen you looking at Paulette. A great kid like Karen, and you're looking at my wife.'

Pike stood and looked down at his partner.

'You're going to resign, Woz. And it's going to be soon.'

'I'm warning you, you sonofabitch. If you don't back off, one of us is going to die.'

Paulette and Karen had gone to the grill and were frowning at the chicken. Paulette called, 'Abel! I think this chicken is dead!'

Abel Wozniak stared at Joe for a moment longer, and then he stalked back to the grill.

Pike watched Abel and Paulette and Karen, but soon he saw only Paulette. It was as if everything else had grown more and more faint until only she remained.

He had not felt such emptiness since he was a child.

CHAPTER 27

When I left Parker Center even more smokers were outside, watching the news vans arrive. From the number of cops on the sidewalk, there probably weren't many left inside, but you never know. Samantha Dolan wasn't among them, and neither was Stan Watts. Half the dicks on the walk were probably from IAG, and most of them weren't smoking. They were probably taking names of those who were.

I walked down to the covered level looking for Dolan's Beemer, found it, then walked back to the lobby pay phone, and called her. She answered on the second ring.

'Dolan.'

'It's me.'

'Listen, I'm busy right now. I don't want to talk.'

'I'm downstairs, and I want to talk to you. I need those files.'

She lowered her voice. 'I'm feeling just a little bit humiliated right now, can you understand that? I don't usually . . . I don't do what I did this morning.'

'Yeah. I get that. I'm feeling pretty awkward myself.'

'You weren't the one rejected.'

'I'm with somebody else, Samantha. I told you that.' I felt defensive, like I had to justify myself.

'The little woman.'

'Don't call her that. Lucy's tough, too, and she might kick your ass.'

Dolan didn't say anything.

'That was a joke, Dolan.'

'I know. I didn't say anything because I'm smiling.'

'Oh.'

'Maybe I'll call her out and see who's left standing.'

'Did you find out about the files I wanted?'

'It's really hard to talk right now. You know about this new vic?'

'I was with Pike when Krantz and Branford came down. Will you come down to your car? I really need your help right now, but I don't want whatever it is you feel about me to get confused with that.'

When she answered, it was frosty and cool. 'I think I can manage not to get confused. Five minutes.'

'Samantha.'

But she'd already hung up.

Dolan was standing at the mouth of the garage, watching the news vans. She wasn't smoking, but a crushed butt was by her toe. Guess I'd caught her between puffs. She also wasn't carrying the files.

She said, 'They're going to go crazy with this.'

'Yeah. How are you doing?'

The cool eyes came to me. 'You mean, has my ego survived your rejection, or am I grieving the loss of my self-esteem?'

'They don't come any tougher than you, do they?'

She turned back into the garage, and I followed her to the Beemer.

'Okay. Here's what I found out: Wozniak died so long ago that Rampart won't have his file anymore. They would've sent it down to the file morgue by Union Station.'

'None of this is on computer?'

'This is the LAPD, World's Greatest. We got shit for computers.'

I nodded.

'Internal Affairs has their own separate storage facility, with their own procedures for getting into their records.

Forget it. But the file morgue is different. We've got a shot at that.'

'Okay.'

'I talked to a detective I know over at Rampart. He said it's pretty much the same story with DeVille. Since he died in prison, the Rampart sex crimes detectives who worked that case would've boxed the file and sent it to storage. We could order it from the district attorney's case file morgue, but we won't have to do that.'

'You got a way to get at the files in storage?'

'I'm there almost every damned day with running the due diligence, but we can't just go in and sign the stuff out. You see?'

'So what do we do?'

'Steal it. You up for that?'

'Yes.'

'Glad you're up for something.'

The Los Angeles Police Department storage facility is an ancient, red brick building in an industrial area just south of the railroad yard. The bricks looked powdery, and I thought that there was probably no way the building could pass an earthquake inspection if it wasn't owned by the LAPD. It was the kind of place that, while you're in it, you're spending most of your time hoping we don't get a big temblor.

Dolan parked the Beemer well away from the other cars that were there, then led me through a plain gray door and along a short hall.

I said, 'Hot.'

'The frigging air must be out again. Listen, do us both a favor and don't say anything. I'll do all the talking.'

I didn't answer her.

'Well?'

'You said not to say anything.'

'Try not to act smart. You don't pull it off.'

An overweight civilian clerk named Sid Rogin was

reading a magazine behind a low counter. He was in his sixties and balding, with thin, wispy hair, and a glass eye. He brightened when he saw Dolan and put down the magazine. He was also sweating, and had a little fan going. The fan was pathetic. He would've gotten more air from a chihuahua wagging its tail.

'Hey, Sammy, what it is? They still got you running down due diligence?' The middle-class white man does black.

Dolan gave him a sparkling grin. I would've guessed that if anyone called her Sammy she would gun them down on the spot. 'Yeah, same old same old. We've got to run down a deceased officer and a perp he was working named Leonard DeVille, also deceased.'

Rogin turned a sign-in log toward her. 'Names and badge numbers. What kind of time frame we talking here on the perp?'

She picked up his pen and glanced at me. 'I've got it. No sweat.' She told Rogin when DeVille had died.

'You taking out the files?'

'Not if we're lucky. Just gotta look up some dates.' She flashed the bright smile again. 'Figure my partner here could look up the officer while I get the perp, save everybody some time.'

'Okay. Step around behind.'

Dolan and I followed Rogin into a series of rooms lined with industrial shelving stacked with dusty cardboard boxes.

'What's the officer's name?'

'Stuart Vincent.' She spelled Vincent.

'Good enough. Officers on this floor. You and I will have to go up to the second for the perps.'

'No problemo.'

We followed Rogin along the aisles, me thinking that all the crummy cardboard boxes looked like little crypts.

We turned a corner into a section of aisle marked *T-Z*. Rogin said, 'Here ya go, *V* as in Vincent.' Six boxes were marked with V's. He pulled down the one that would hold *Vi*. 'All you wanna do is look through the file?'

Dolan glanced at me, and nodded.

I said, 'That's right.'

Rogin had the lid off, pulling out a thick file that had been tied with a string. He frowned. 'It's awful thick, Sammy. You gotta read through the whole thing?'

'You look busy, Sid. Sorry to put you out this way.'

'Well, it's not that. They just don't like people back here.'

Dolan raised her eyebrows back at him and stiffened. 'Well, Sidney, I guess if you'd rather I go back to Parker and have them call down.' She let it drop, watching him.

'Oh, no, hell, you don't have to do that. It's just I gotta get back up and watch the front.'

I said, 'I'll be done by the time you guys get back from the second floor. No sweat.'

'You sure?'

'Absolutely.'

Dolan clapped Sid on the shoulder and grinned at him some more. 'Let's do it, Sid. Get outta this goddamned heat.'

I pretended to be interested in Vincent's file until their steps were gone, then I searched down the aisle for the W's. Twelve boxes were marked with a W, the eighth and ninth file boxes holding *Wo*.

We could have asked for Wozniak's file and signed for it, but we didn't want a written record connecting Dolan to what we were doing. She was in enough trouble, and if things went wrong I didn't want her in more.

I pulled Wozniak's file, then pushed the boxes back in their rows.

Wozniak's personnel file was too thick to shove down my pants, but most of it didn't concern me. I pulled the sheet listing his partners prior to Pike and their badge numbers, then flipped back to the beginning of his career and pulled the sheet noting his training officers. Wozniak was a top cop: He'd been awarded the Medal of Valor twice, twelve certificates of commendation, and a half dozen public service commendations for working with schools and troubled youth. The list of his arrests went on for pages, listing the arrestee, date of arrest, and charge. I jerked those pages, folded them, and put them in my jacket. The next section in the file was devoted to disciplinary actions. I wasn't even thinking to look at it except that Abel Wozniak had been called to appear before the Internal Affairs Group on two occasions six weeks prior to his death. The requesting Internal Affairs officer being one Detective Harvey Krantz.

I said, 'Damn.'

No other information was given except the notation that the inquiry was terminated, along with the date of termination.

Krantz.

I jerked that page, too, and put it with the others.

Dolan's voice came along the aisle, Dolan saying, 'Hey, buddy, I hope you're ready to go. We're outta here.'

I stuffed the remains of the file together and pushed it between the boxes, then hurried back to the V's. I picked up Vincent's file just as Dolan and Rogin came around the corner.

She said, 'You find what you need?'

'Yeah. You?'

She shook her head. Slow.

'DeVille's file isn't here.'

I raised my eyebrows. 'Where is it?'

Rogin waved his hand. 'Some other dick probably checked it out. You want me to look it up?'

I said, 'If you don't mind. Maybe I can call the guy and get what we need.'

We followed him back to the counter and waited while he fingered through a box of little index cards. He scratched his head, checked some numbers he'd written on a little pad, then frowned. 'Hell, it ain't here. If it was signed out, I woulda had the log-out card in here, but it ain't.'

'Any way to tell how long it's been gone?'

'Not without the card. Ain't this the shits?'

Dolan glanced at me again, then pulled at my arm.

'Maybe you just misfiled it, Sid. It's no big deal.'

When we were on our way out to her car, she said, 'I don't believe in coincidences.'

'You thinking someone ripped off that file?'

'I'm thinking I don't believe in coincidences. But we can still get a copy. The district attorney's office keeps a record of all their case files in their own storage facility. I can order up theirs.'

'How long will that take?'

'A couple of days. Don't be peevish, World's Greatest. What'd you get?'

'I got some names, and his collar jacket, but something else, too.' I told her about the disciplinary notation showing Wozniak had been the subject of an investigation, and that Krantz was the investigating officer.

Dolan made a hissing sound. 'That's IAG, man. You can't just ask Krantz.'

We got into her car. The leather was so hot it burned through my pants. Dolan lifted her butt off the seat.

'I never should've got black.'

She started the engine and turned on the air conditioner, but didn't put the car in gear.

I took out the pages and looked at them again. I skimmed over the arrest pages, but ended up back with the disciplinary sheet and the two meetings with Krantz. The dates were there. 'If I can't get the files, and I can't ask Krantz, maybe there's someone else I can ask.'

She held out her hand for the sheet. 'This doesn't say shit.'

'No. It doesn't.'

'It doesn't say if he was the subject, or if they wanted to question him about someone else.'

'Nope.'

She handed the sheet back, thinking, then took out her cell phone and punched a number.

'Hang on.'

She made three phone calls and spoke for almost twenty minutes, twice writing in a notepad. 'This guy might be able to help you. He was an IA supervisor when Krantz was there.'

'Who is he?'

She handed me the sheet. 'Mike McConnell. He's retired now, living out in Sierra Madre. That's his number. He owns a sod farm.'

'Sod.'

'He grows grass.'

'I know what it means.'

'I wasn't sure. Sometimes you're stupid.'

She floored the gas, spun her tires, and brought me back to my car.

CHAPTER 28

Sierra Madre is a relaxed community in the foothills of the San Gabriel Mountains to the east of Los Angeles. Mature green trees line the streets and kids still ride bikes without worrying about getting shot in a drive-by. The town has a peaceful, rural feel that Los Angeles lost when the developers took over city hall. It is also where Don Siegel filmed the exterior locations of the original *Invasion of the Body Snatchers*. I haven't yet seen a pod person there, though I keep looking. Farther west, L.A. is filled with them.

Mike McConnell's sod farm was on a broad flat plain near the Eaton Canyon Reservoir. The reservoir has been dry for years, and the property beneath it has been leased to farmers and nurseries who've put it to good use. Model airplane builders come fly their tiny machines out of the unused land, which is scrubby and dead, but the irrigated parcels are brightly alive with acre after acre of flowers and yearling plants, and sod.

I turned off the paved street and followed a gravel road between flat green fields of buffalo grass, Bahia grass, St Augustine and Bermuda grasses, and others I didn't recognize. Rainbirds dotted the fields like Erector Set scarecrows, spraying water, and the air smelled of fertilizer. I was hoping to find a field of pulsating pods, but instead I came to a service area where a trailer and a large metal shed sat surrounded by spindly eucalyptus trees. Live in hope.

Three Hispanic guys were sitting in the bed of a Ford pickup, eating sandwiches and laughing. They were soiled from working in the sod fields, and burned deep umber by the sun. They smiled politely as I pulled up and got out of my car. A thin brown dog was lying beneath the pickup's gate. He looked at me, too.

I said, 'Señor McConnell?'

The youngest guy nodded toward the trailer. A late-model Cadillac Eldorado was parked next to it between the trees. 'He's inside. You want me to get him for you?'

'That's okay. Thanks.'

McConnell came out as I was crunching across the gravel. He was in his sixties, with a large gut hanging over khaki trousers and Danner work boots. An unbuttoned Hawaiian shirt let the gut show like he was proud of it. He held a Negro Modelo beer in the dark bottle, but he offered his free hand. 'Mike McConnell. You Mr Cole?'

'Yes, sir. Please, call me Elvis.'

He laughed. 'Don't know as I could do that with a straight face.'

What do you say to something like that?

'I'd invite you in, but it's hotter in there than out here. You want a beer? All I got is this Mexican shit. Fresh out of American.'

'No, sir. But thanks.'

A slim Chicana who couldn't have been more than twenty appeared in the trailer's door and frowned out at him. Somebody had sprayed a thin cotton print dress over her body, and she was barefoot. Hot in there, all right.

She said, '*No me hagas es perar. No me gusta estar sola.*'

McConnell looked scandalized. '*Quidado con lo que dices o te regreso a Sonora.*'

She stuck out her tongue and pouted back into the trailer. The guys on the truck nudged each other.

McConnell shrugged apologetically. 'She's young.'

He led me to a redwood table set in the shade between the eucalyptus trees, and had some of the Modelo. A USMC globe and anchor was so faded on his right forearm that it looked like an ink smudge. 'Got two thousand square yards of St Augustine goin' out this evening to a Chinaman in San Marino. If you're looking for St Augustine I might not be able to help you, but I got twelve other kinds of sod. What are you thinking about?'

I gave him one of my cards. 'I'm afraid I wasn't being straight with you, Mr McConnell. I apologize about that, but I need to ask you about an IA investigation that happened on your watch. I'm hoping you'll talk to me about it.'

He read over the card, then put it on the table. He reached around behind him like he was going for a handkerchief, but came out with a little black .380 automatic. He didn't aim it at me, he just held it.

The men on the truck stopped eating.

'Lying's a poor way to start, son. You carrying?'

I tried not to look at the gun. 'Yes, sir. Under my left arm.'

'Take it out with your left hand. Two fingers only. I see more than two fingers on metal, I'll pop you.'

I did what he said. Two fingers.

'You keep holding it like that, away from your body like it smells bad. Walk on back over there and drop it in your car, then come on back.'

The hired hands were poised on the bed like swimmers on their starting platforms, ready to dive if the shooting started. Imagine: Coming north all the way from Zacatecas to get shot in a sod field.

I dropped the gun into the front seat, then walked back to the table.

'I didn't come here to make trouble for you, Mr McConnell. I just need a few answers. It's been my experience that if I warn people I'm coming, they have a tendency to be gone when I get there. I couldn't afford that you'd be gone.'

McConnell nodded.

'You always carry that little gun out here?'

'I spent thirty years on the job, twenty-five in Internal

288

Affairs. I prosecuted cops who were every bit as rotten as any thug on the street, and I made enemies doing it. More than one of'm has tried looking me up.'

I guess I'd carry the gun, too.

'I'm trying to learn about a deceased officer named Abel Wozniak. He was investigated when you were on the job as a supervisor, but I don't know why, or what came of it. You remember him?'

He gestured with the .380. 'Why don't you tell me what your interest is in this first.'

Retired Detective-Three Mike McConnell listened without expression as I told him about Dersh and Pike. If he knew anything of the headline news happening just a few miles to the west, he gave no indication. That's the way cops are. The first time I mentioned Joe's name, McConnell's eyes flickered, but he didn't react again until I told him that the investigating detective for Internal Affairs had been Harvey Krantz.

McConnell's weathered face split into a mean grin.

'Shits-his-pants Krantz! Hell, I was there the day that squiggly weasel let go!' He enjoyed the memory so much that the .380 drifted away from me. The guys in the truck relaxed then, and pretty soon they were balling up paper bags and climbing into the truck's cab. The show was over and it was time to get back to work.

McConnell said, 'So Pike's your partner now, is he?'

'That's right.'

'Pike's the one made Krantz shit his pants.'

'Yes, sir. I know.'

McConnell laughed. 'That boy damn near made me shit mine, too, the way he grabbed Krantz. Damn, that boy was fast. Lifted Pants right off the floor. I remember he was a Marine. So was I.'

I thought about that, and how humiliated Krantz must've felt. It had hurt his career, and he still carried the name.

'You remember why Krantz was investigating Woz-niak?'

'Oh, sure. Wozniak was involved with a burglary ring.'

He said it like it was nothing, but when I heard it I stiffened as if he'd reached out and flipped my off switch.

McConnell nodded. 'Yeah, that's right. Krantz developed it off a couple of Mexican fences working out of Pacoima, up in the valley. Little bitty guys named Reena and Uribe. We called them the Chihuahua Brothers, they were so short. Near as we could figure, Wozniak tipped these Mexicans whenever a business's alarm was on the fritz, or when he found out the watchman had called in sick, or whatever, and they'd send a crew over to rob the place. Auto parts, stereos, that kind of thing.'

'You're saying that Wozniak was dirty.'

'That's right.'

'You're telling me that Joe Pike's partner was part of a burglary ring.'

Like maybe I'd heard him wrong and wanted to be sure.

'Well, we weren't at a point in the investigation where we could make the case and charge him, but he was good for it. After he died we could've kept going, but I decided to let it drop. Here was this man's family, a wife and the children, why put them through that? Krantz was livid about it, though. He wanted to keep going and nail Pike.'

'Because Pike had embarrassed him?'

McConnell was about to take another sip of the beer when he paused, and considered me.

'Not that at all. Harvey believed that Pike was involved.'

Sometimes you hear things that you never want to hear, things so alien to your experience, so outlandish that it seems you've rolled out of bed into a Stephen King novel.

'I don't believe that.'

McConnell shrugged. 'Well, most people thought what you thought, that Krantz was just hot to get Pike because

Pike's the one made him shit his pants. But Krantz told me he really did believe Pike was involved. He didn't have any proof, but his feeling was how could they not be, the two of them riding together every day. I told'm if he'd spent more time in the car being a real cop instead of trying to suck ass his way into fancier jobs, he'd know. It's like being married. You can spend your whole life with someone and never know them.' He glanced out toward the field. The truck had stopped by the control station of the rainbirds. The two older guys were working there, but the younger guy was out on the sod, jumping and waving his arms and splashing around in the water.

McConnell slid off the table. 'Now what do you suppose that fool is doing?'

McConnell shouted something in Spanish, but the men couldn't hear him. The girl reappeared in the door to see why he had shouted. She looked as mystified as McConnell.

McConnell fished around in his pants for keys to the Caddie. 'Sonofabitch. I'm going to have to go out there.'

'Mr McConnell, I only need a few more minutes. If there wasn't any proof, what made Krantz think Pike was involved? Just because they were in the same car?'

'Harvey didn't believe Pike's story about what happened in that motel room. He thought they'd had a falling-out with each other because of the investigation, and that maybe Pike was worried that Wozniak was going to give him up to cut a deal. Krantz had been trying to do that, you know. Play them against each other. He was sure that Pike murdered Wozniak to keep him quiet.'

'Do you believe that?'

'Well, I never believed that we knew what really happened in that room. Wozniak lost it with DeVille and knocked him out. We know that much for sure because DeVille and Pike told the same story. But after DeVille was out, all we know is what Pike told us, and some of it didn't make sense. Here was Pike, young and strong and fresh out of the Marines, knowing all that karate stuff the way he did. It just doesn't make a lot of sense that he'd have that much trouble trying to cool out Wozniak. Krantz thought Pike was stonewalling us, and maybe he was, but what are you going to do? We couldn't make the case.'

I didn't like hearing any of this. I was getting irritated with it, and pissed off that McConnell was distracted by the guys in the field. Now the other two guys joined the younger guy in the artificial rain, jumping around with him.

McConnell said, 'Oh, this really is out of hand.'

'Do you think Krantz was right?'

McConnell shouted in Spanish again, but the men still didn't hear him.

I went around and stepped in front of him so he had to look at me instead of the men.

'Was Krantz right?'

'Krantz hadn't turned anything that we could make a case on. I figured one tragedy was enough, so I told Krantz to drop it. That's what we did. Look, I'm sorry I can't help you, but I gotta get out there. Those crazy bastards are costing me money.'

He started around me, and when he did I trapped his hand and twisted away the gun. He wasn't expecting it, and the move had taken maybe a tenth of a second.

McConnell's eyes widened, and he froze.

'What about these two fences? You think either of them might be trying to set up Joe Pike?'

'Wozniak was nothing to those two. Reena hauled ass back to Tijuana because he got into a beef with some meth-head. Uribe was shot to death at a gas station when he got into an argument.'

'Wozniak's file showed that he had received administrative punishments on five separate occasions, and twice been suspended for using excessive force. Seven complaints, and in five of those the complainant was either a pedophile or a pimp dealing in child prostitution. Do you know who the informant was who tipped Wozniak about DeVille?'

McConnell's eyes flicked to the gun, then came back to me.

'No. Wozniak probably had several. That's what made him such an effective patrol officer.'

'How could I find out?'

'The divisions keep a registered informant list. They have to do that to protect the officers. But I don't know if Rampart would still have one for Wozniak, all of that being so long ago.'

McConnell looked past me to the fields again, then shook his head. 'Goddamnit, you gonna shoot me, son, or you gonna let me go take care of my business? Look at the water they're wasting.'

I looked at the gun, then handed it back to him. I felt myself turn red.

'I'm sorry. I don't know why I did that.'

'Kiss my ass.'

He stalked toward the Cadillac. When he got to the door, he turned back to me, but he didn't look angry anymore. He looked sad.

'Look, I know how it is, your partner gets in trouble. Just so you know, I never believed that Pike had anything to do with that burglary ring. And I don't think he murdered Wozniak. If I'd thought he had, I would've stayed after him. But I didn't.'

'Thanks, Mr McConnell. I'm sorry.'

'Yeah. Right.'

McConnell climbed into his Caddie and roared away into his fields.

I went back to my car, put my own gun back in its holster, and sat there, thinking. The smell of the fertilizer was stronger now. Rainbows floated around the dancing men in the mist from the rainbirds. The Caddie skidded to a stop behind the truck and McConnell got out, pissed off and shouting. One by one the men stopped jumping and went back to work. McConnell turned off the water and the rainbirds died.

Sitting there, I reread the LAPD incident report and found the reference again: *Acting on information received from an unnamed informant, Officers Wozniak and Pike entered room #205 of the Islander Palms Motel.*

The more I sat there thinking, the more I thought about the unnamed informant, and what he might know. He or she probably didn't know anything, but when you've got nothing the way I had nothing, a long shot starts to look pretty good.

I went back through the rest of my notes and found Wozniak's widow. Paulette Renfro.

Maybe Wozniak talked about his work to his wife, and maybe she knew something about the informant. Maybe she knew something about Harvey Krantz, and how the Leonard DeVille file had come to be missing.

You look for connections.

I started my car, pulled in a wide circle, and drove back toward the highway.

Behind me, the sod had already begun to bake in the afternoon heat. Steam rose from the ground like a fog from hell.

CHAPTER 29

You're getting close to Palm Springs when you see the dinosaurs.

Driving through the Banning Pass, a hundred miles east of L.A. where the San Bernardino and San Jacinto Mountains pinch together to form a gateway to the high deserts of the Coachella Valley, you emerge into the Morongo Indian Reservation. A towering apatosaur and tyrannosaurus rex stand just off the freeway, built there by some sun-stricken desert genius long before Michael Crichton created Jurassic Park. Years ago, they were the only thing out here, monstrous full-sized re-creations standing in the desert heat as if they were frozen in time and place. You could pay a dime and walk around them, and maybe have your picture taken to send to all the folks back home in Virginia. *Look, Ma, here we are in California.* The dinosaurs have been there for years, but drunks and hopheads still stumble into the bars down in Cabazon, swearing they've seen monsters in the desert.

A few miles past the dinosaurs, I left the freeway and followed the state highway along the foot of the San Jacintos into Palm Springs.

During the winter months, Palm Springs is alive with tourists and weekenders and snowbirds come down from Canada to escape the cold. But in the middle of June with temperatures hovering at one hundred twenty degrees the town is barely breathing, its pulse undetectable as it wilts in the heat like some run-over animal waiting on the side of the road to die. The tourists are gone, and only the suicidal venture out during the day.

I stopped in a tee-shirt shop to buy a map of the area, looked up Paulette Renfro's address, then made my way straight north across the desert, one moment with dinosaurs and Indians, the next passing the science-fiction weirdness of hundreds of sleek, computer-designed windmills, their great flimsy blades rotating in slow motion to steal energy from the wind.

Palm Springs itself is a town of resorts and vacation homes and poodle groomers for the affluent, but the men and women who keep the city running live in smaller communities like Cathedral City to the south or North Palm Springs on what's considered the wrong side of the freeway.

Paulette Renfro lived in a small, neat desert home in the foothills above the freeway with a view of the windmills. Her home was beige stucco with a red tile roof and an oversized air conditioner that I could hear running from the street. Down in Palm Springs the people can afford to irrigate for grass lawns, but up here the lawns were crushed rock and sand, with desert plantings that required little water. All their money goes into the air conditioner.

I parked off the street and walked up her drive past an enormous blooming century plant with leaves like green swords. A brand-new Volkswagen Beetle was parked behind a Toyota Camry, only the Camry was in a garage and the Beetle was out in the sun. Visitor.

A tall, attractive woman answered when I rang the bell. She was wearing a nice skirt and makeup, as if she planned to leave soon or had just returned.

I said, 'Ms Renfro?'

'Yes?' Nice teeth and a pretty smile. She was five or six years older than me, but that meant she must've been younger than Abel Wozniak.

'My name's Cole. I'm a private investigator from Los Angeles. I need to speak with you about Abel Wozniak.'

She glanced inside like she was nervous about something. 'Now isn't really a good time. Besides, Abel died years ago. I don't know how I could help you.'

'Yes, ma'am. I know. I'm hoping you can answer a few questions about a case he was working on at the time of his death. It's pretty important. I've come a long way.' Sometimes if you look pathetic enough it helps.

A younger woman appeared behind her, the younger woman saying, 'Who is it, Mom?'

Paulette Renfro told me that we were letting out all the cold and asked me to come in, though she didn't look happy about it. Most people don't. 'This is my daughter Evelyn. Evelyn, this is Mr Cole. From Los Angeles.'

'I have to finish moving.' Annoyed.

'Hi, Ms Renfro.' I offered my hand, but Evelyn didn't take it.

'My name's Wozniak. Renfro was *her* mistake.'

'Evie, please.'

I said, 'This shouldn't take any more than ten minutes. I promise.'

Paulette Renfro glanced at her watch, then her daughter. 'Well, I suppose I have a few minutes. But I have things to do, and I have an appointment to show a house in less than an hour. I'm in real estate.'

Evie said, 'I don't need your help. I just need to bring in the rest of my things.'

Evie Wozniak stalked out of the house and slammed the door. She looked like a twenty-something version of her mother in the face, but where Paulette Renfro was neat and well put together, her daughter was puffy and overweight, her features pinched with a set that said most things probably annoyed her.

I said, 'Looks like I interrupted something. Sorry about that.'

Ms Renfro seemed tired. 'There's always something to interrupt. She's having boyfriend problems. She's always having boyfriend problems.'

The house was neat and attractive, with an enormous picture window and comfortable Southwestern furniture. The living room flowed through to a family-room combination with the kitchen on one side and a hall that probably led to bedrooms on the other. Beyond the family room, a small blue pool glittered in the heat. From the picture window, you could look down across the freeway and see the windmills, slowly turning, and further south, Palm Springs.

'This is very nice, Ms Renfro. I'll bet Palm Springs looks beautiful at night.'

'Oh, it does. The windmills remind me of the ocean during the day, what with their gentle movement like that, and at night the Springs can look like one of those fairy-tale cities from *A Thousand and One Nights*.'

She led me to a comfortable couch that looked toward the view.

'Could I offer you something to drink? With our heat out here, you have to be careful to keep yourself hydrated.'

'Thanks. Water would be good.'

The living room was small, but the open floor plan and a spare arrangement of furniture made it feel larger. I hadn't expected Paulette Renfro to keep any fond memories of Joe Pike, but as I waited for the water, I noticed a small framed picture resting in a bookcase among a little forest of bowling trophies. Paulette Wozniak was standing with her husband and Pike in front of an LAPD radio car that was parked in the drive of a modest home. Paulette was wearing jeans and a man's white shirt with the sleeves rolled and the tails tied off in a kind of halter.

Joe Pike was smiling.

I went over to the bookcase, and stared at the picture.

I had never seen Pike smile. Not once in all the years that I'd known him. I had seen a thousand pictures of Joe in the Marines, of him hunting or fishing or camping, pictures of him with friends, and in none of them was he smiling.

Yet here was this picture of her former husband and the man who had killed him.

Smiling.

Paulette Renfro said, 'Here's your water.'

I took the glass. She'd brought water for herself, too.

'That's Abel on the left. We were living in the Simi Valley.'

I said, 'Ms Renfro, Joe Pike is a friend of mine.'

She stared at me for a moment, holding her glass with both hands, then went to the couch. She sat on the edge of it. Perching.

'I imagine you find it odd that I would keep that picture.'

'I don't find anything odd. People have their reasons.'

'I've been reading about all that mess down in Los Angeles. First Karen, now Joe being accused of murdering this man. I think it's a shame.'

'You knew Karen Garcia?'

'Joe was dating her in those days, you know. She was a pretty, sweet girl.' She glanced at her watch again, then decided something. 'You say you and Joe are friends?'

'Yes, ma'am. We own the agency together.'

'Were you a police officer, also?' Like she wanted to talk about Joe, but wasn't sure how to go about it.

'No, ma'am. Private only.'

She glanced at the picture again, almost as if she had to explain it. 'Well, what happened to Abel happened a long time ago, Mr Cole. It was a terrible, horrible accident, and I can't imagine that anyone feels worse about it than Joe.'

Evelyn Wozniak said, 'Your child feels worse about it, Mother. Since he killed my father.'

She had come through the kitchen carrying a large cardboard box.

Paulette's face tightened. 'Do you need a hand with that?'

Evelyn continued on through the living room to disappear down a hall without answering.

Paulette said, 'It was hard on Evelyn. She's moving back home now. This boyfriend, the one who just left her, took their rent money and now she's lost her apartment. That's the kind of men she finds.'

'Was she close to her father?'

'Yes. Abel was a good father.'

I nodded. I wondered if she knew about Krantz's investigation. I wondered if she knew about Reena and Uribe and the burglaries.

'I really do have to be leaving soon. What is it that you want to know?'

'I want to know what happened that day.'

Paulette stiffened, not much, but I could see it.

'Why do you want to know about that?'

'Because I think someone is trying to frame Joe for Eugene Dersh's murder.'

She shook her head, but the stiffness remained.

'I couldn't even guess, Mr Cole. My husband didn't talk about his job with me.'

'On the day your husband died, he and Joe were tipped to the whereabouts of this man DeVille by one of your husband's informants. Would you know who?'

Paulette Renfro stood, and now she wasn't looking so much like she wanted to help. Now she was looking uncomfortable and suspicious.

'No, I'm sorry.'

'He didn't talk about that kind of thing with you, or you don't remember?'

'I don't like to talk about that day, Mr Cole. I don't know anything about it, or about my husband's job, or any of that. He never told me anything.'

'Please take a moment and think, Ms Renfro. It would help if you could come up with a name.'

'I'm sure I never knew.'

Her daughter came back through the room then, carrying empty boxes and clothes hangers.

Paulette Renfro said, 'Do you have all your things?'

'I'm going back for the last of it.'

'Do you need money?'

'I'm fine.'

Evelyn Wozniak stalked on through the living room and slammed the door. Again.

Paulette Renfro's jaw knotted. 'Do you have children, Mr Cole?'

'No, ma'am.'

'You're lucky. I really do have to be going now. I'm sorry I couldn't be more help.'

'Could I call you again if I think of something to ask?'

'I don't think I'll be any more help then than now.'

She walked me to the door, and I went back out into the heat. She didn't come out with me.

Evelyn was waiting by her Beetle. She'd put on little sunglasses, but she was still squinting from the glare. Waiting for me in this insane heat. The boxes and hangers were in her car.

'She wouldn't talk about him, would she? My father.'

'Not very much.'

'She won't talk about that day. She never would, except to defend that guy.'

'Joe?'

Evie glanced toward the windmills, but shrugged without seeing them.

'Can you imagine? The bastard kills her husband, and she keeps that goddamned picture. I used to draw on it. I've broken that goddamned thing so many times I can't count.'

I didn't say anything, and she looked back at me.

'You're his friend, aren't you? You came out here trying to help him.'

'Yes.'

'Do you know that they were investigating my father? The Internal Affairs?'

'Yeah. I know.'

'She tried to keep it from me. And so did Daddy.' Daddy. Like she was still ten years old. 'Men came to the house and questioned her, and I heard. I heard her screaming at my father about it. Can you imagine what that's like when you're a child?'

I thought that I could, but I didn't say anything.

'She just won't talk about it. She'll talk about anything else, but not that, and that's the most important thing that's ever happened to me. It ruined my whole fucking life.'

Standing on the cement drive was like standing on a bright white beach. The heat baked up through my shoes. I wanted to move, but she seemed about to say something that wasn't easy for her to say, and I thought that if I moved it would break her resolve.

'I want to tell you something, you're his friend. That man killed my father. It was like my world ended, I loved my father so much, and there is nothing I would love more than to hurt the goddamned awful man who took him from me.'

Pike.

'But there's something I want more.'

I waited.

'She's got all Daddy's things in storage somewhere. You know, one of those rental places.'

'You know where?'

'I'll have to find out. I don't know if there's anything there that will help, but you're trying to find out what happened back then, right?'

I told her that I was, but that I also wanted other things. I said, 'I'm trying to help Joe Pike. I want you to know that, Evelyn.'

'I don't care about that. I just want to know the truth about my father.'

'What if it's bad?'

'I want to know. I guess I even expect that it is, but I just want to know why he died. I've spent my whole goddamned life wanting to know. Maybe that's why I'm so fucked up.'

I didn't know what to say.

'I don't think it was an accident. I think your friend murdered him.'

Exactly what Krantz had thought.

'If I help you, and you find out, will you tell me?'

'If you want to know, I'll tell you.'

'You'll tell me the truth? No matter what?'

'If that's what you want.'

She wiped at her nose. 'It's like if I just knew, then I could go on, you know?'

We stood there for a time, and then I held her. We had been in the sun for so long that when my hands touched her back it felt as if I'd gripped a hot coal.

I watched the windmills stretching across the plain of the desert, turning in the never-ending wind.

After a time, Evie Wozniak stepped back. She wiped her nose again. 'This is silly. I don't even know you, and here I am telling you my life's secrets.'

'It works like that sometimes, doesn't it?'

'Yeah. I guess you'd better give me your phone number.'

I gave her the card.

'I'll call you.'

'Okay.'

'You can't tell her, all right? If she knew, she wouldn't allow it.'

'I won't tell.'

'Our little secret.'

'That's right, Evie. Our little secret.'

I drove back down off the mountain, Palm Springs far in the distance, shimmering in the heat like a place that did not exist.

303

Man of Action

The cell was four feet wide by eight feet long by eight feet high. A seatless toilet and a basin stuck out from the cement wall like ceramic goiters, almost hidden behind the single bunk. Overhead, bright fluorescent lamps were secured behind steel grids so the suicidal couldn't electrocute themselves. The mattress was a special rayon material that could not be cut or torn, and the bed frame and mattress rack were spot-welded together. No screws, no bolts, no way to take anything apart. The single bunk made this cell the Presidential Suite of the Parker Center jail, reserved for Hollywood celebrities, members of the media, and former police officers who had found their way to the wrong side of the bars.

Joe Pike lay on the bunk, waiting to be transferred to the Men's Central Jail, a facility ten minutes away that housed twenty-two thousand inmates. His hair was still damp from the basin bath he'd given himself after exercising, but he was thinking that he wanted to run, to feel the sun on his face and the movement of air and the sweat race down his chest. He wanted the peace of the effort, and the certain knowledge that it was a good thing to be doing. Not all acts brought with them the certainty of goodness, but running did.

The security gate at the end of the hall opened, and Krantz appeared on the other side of the bars. He was holding something.

Krantz stared at Pike for a long time before saying, 'I'm not here to question you. Don't worry about your lawyer.'

Pike wasn't worried.

'I've waited a long time for this, Joe. I'm enjoying it.' Joe. Like they were friends.

'You look bad, being wrong about Dersh.'

Pike spoke softly, forcing Krantz to come closer.

'I know. I feel bad about Dersh, but I've got the Feebs to share the blame. You hear Dersh's family already filed suit? Two brothers, his mother, and some sister he hadn't seen in twenty years. Bellying up to the trough.'

Pike wondered what was with Krantz, coming here to gloat.

'They're suing the city, the department, everybody. Bishop and the chief can't fire me without it looking like an admission that the department did something wrong, so they're saying we just followed the FBI's lead.'

'They should win, Krantz. You're responsible.'

'Maybe so, but they're suing you, too. You pulled the trigger.'

Pike didn't answer that.

Krantz shrugged. 'But you're right. I look bad. A year from now when everything's calmed down, that's it for me. They'll ship me out to one of the divisions. That's okay. I've got the twenty-five in. I might even make thirty if I can't scare up something better.'

'Why are you here, Krantz? Because I humiliated you?'

Krantz turned red. Pike could tell that he was trying not to, but there it was.

'I didn't ruin you, Krantz. You took care of that yourself. People like you never understand that.'

Krantz seemed to think about that, then shrugged. 'For the humiliation, yes, but also because you deserve to be here. You murdered Wozniak and got away with it. But now you're here, and I like seeing it.'

Pike sat up. 'I didn't murder Woz.'

'You were right in with him on the burglaries. You knew I was going to nail him, and you knew I would get you, too. You were a chickenshit, Pike, and you decided to take out Wozniak because you're an amoral, homicidal lunatic who doesn't think twice about snuffing out a human life. Which is about as much thought as you gave to Dersh.'

'All the time you spent investigating, and that's what you came up with. You really think I murdered Woz in that room to keep him quiet?'

Krantz smiled. 'I don't think you killed him because you thought he'd give you up, Pike. I think you killed him because you wanted his wife.'

Pike stared.

'You had something going with her, didn't you?'

Pike swung his feet off the bunk. 'You don't know what you're talking about.'

Krantz smiled. 'Like your asshole friend says, I'm a detective. I detected. I was watching her, Pike. I saw you with her.'

'You're wrong about that, and you're wrong about Dersh, too. You're wrong about everything.'

Krantz nodded, agreeable. 'If you've got an alibi, bring it out. If you can prove to me that you didn't do Dersh, I'll personally ask Branford to drop the charges.'

'You know there's nothing.'

'There's nothing because you did it, Pike. We've got you on tape casing his house. We've got the old lady picking you out of the line. We've got the residue results and your relationship with the girl. We've got this.'

Krantz showed Pike what he was carrying. It was a revolver wrapped in plastic.

'This is a .357 magnum. SID matches it with the bullet that killed Dersh. It's the murder weapon, Pike.'

Joe didn't say anything.

'It's a clean gun. No prints, and all the numbers have been burned off, so we can't trace it. But we recovered it in the water off Santa Monica exactly where you said you talked with the girl. That puts you with this gun.'

Pike stared at the plastic bag, and then at Krantz, wondering at the coincidence of how the murder weapon turned up at the very place where he admitted to being.

'Think about it, Krantz. Why would I admit to being there if that's where I threw the gun?'

'Because someone saw you. I think you went there to ditch the gun, and did, but then someone saw you. I didn't believe you about the girl at first, but maybe you were telling the truth about that part. Maybe she saw you there, and you were worried we'd find her and catch you in a lie if you denied it, so you tried to cover yourself.'

Pike looked at the plastic bag again. He knew that cops often showed things to suspects and lied about what they were to try to elicit a confession.

'Is this bullshit?'

Krantz smiled again, calm and confident, and in an odd way Pike found it warm. 'No bullshit. You can ask Bauman. The DA's filling him in on it right now. I've got you, Joe. I couldn't make the case with Wozniak, but this time I've got you. Branford's making all this noise about Special Circumstance, but he's full of shit. I couldn't get that lucky, Pike, you getting the needle.'

'I didn't put the gun there, Krantz. That means somebody else did.'

'That's some coincidence, Joe, you and the gun just happening to be in the same place.'

'It means they knew my statement. Think about it.'

'What I think is that we've got plenty for a conviction. Charlie is going to tell you the same thing.'

'No.'

'Bauman's already floating plea arrangements. Bet he didn't tell you that, did he? I know you're telling Bauman no plea, and he's saying sure, like he's going along with it, but he's not an idiot. Charlie's smart. He'll let you sit in Men's Central for six months, hoping you're telling the truth about this girl you claim you saw, but when she doesn't turn up he'll deal you a straight hand about taking the plea. My guess is that Branford will let you cop to twenty with the possibility of parole. Saves everybody looking bad about how we fucked over Dersh. Twenty with time off means you serve twelve. That sound about right to you?'

'I'm not going to prison, Krantz. Not for something I didn't do.'

Krantz touched the bars. He slipped his fingers along the steel like it was his lover.

'You're inside now, and you're going to stay inside. And if you're dumb enough to go to trial, and I'm thinking you might do that because you're such a hardhead, you'll be in a cage like this for the rest of your life. And I did it, Pike. Me. You're mine, and I wanted to tell you that. That's why I came here, to tell you. You're mine.'

The black jailer with the big arms came down the cellblock and stopped next to Krantz. 'Time to take your ride, Pike. Step into the center of the floor.'

Krantz started away, then turned back. 'Oh, and one other thing. You heard we found the homeless guy dead, didn't you?'

'Deege.'

'Yeah, Deege. That was kind've goofy, wasn't it, Pike, him telling you guys that a truck like yours stopped Karen, and a guy who looked like you was driving?'

Pike waited.

'Someone crushed his throat and stuffed him in a Dumpster on one of those little cul-de-sac streets below the lake.'

Pike waited.

'A couple of teenagers saw a red Jeep Cherokee up there, Joe. Parked in the middle of the street and waiting on the very night that Deege was killed. They saw the driver, too. Guess who they saw behind the wheel?'

'Me.'

'This gets better and better.'

Krantz stared at Pike a little longer, then turned and walked away.

Earlier, there had been a prisoner who made monkey sounds – oo-oo-oo – that Pike had thought of as Monkey-boy, and another prisoner with loud flatulence who had thrown feces out of his cell while shouting, 'I'm the Gasman!'

They had been taken away, and Pike had dubbed the jail cop with the big arms the Ringmaster.

When Pike was standing, the Ringmaster waved down the hall. Jailers didn't use keys anymore. The cell locks were electronically controlled from the security station at the end of the cellblock, two female officers who sat behind a bulletproof glass partition. When the Ringmaster gave the sign, they pushed a button and Pike's door opened with a dull click. Pike thought that it sounded like a rifle bolt snapping home.

The Ringmaster stepped through, holding the handcuffs. 'We won't use the leg irons for the ride, but you gotta wear these.'

Pike put out his wrists.

As the Ringmaster fit the cuffs, he said, 'Been watching you work out in here. How many push-ups you do?'

'A thousand.'

'How many dips?'

'Two hundred.'

The Ringmaster grunted. He was a large man with overdeveloped arm and shoulder and chest muscles that stretched his uniform as tight as a second skin. Not many prisoners would stand up to him, and even fewer could hope to succeed if they tried.

The Ringmaster snugged the cuffs, checked to see they were secure, then stepped back.

'I don't know if you're getting a square shake with this Dersh thing or not. I guess you probably did it, but if some asshole popped my lady I'd forget about this badge, too. That's what being a man is.'

Pike didn't say anything.

'I know you're an ex-cop, and I heard about all that stuff went down when you were on the job. It don't matter to me. I just wanted to say I've had you here in my house for a couple of days, and I read you as a pretty square guy. Good luck to you.'

'Thanks.'

The two female cops buzzed them out of the cellblock into a gray, institutional corridor where the Ringmaster led Pike down a flight of stairs and into the sheriff's prisoner holding room. Five other prisoners were already there, cuffed to special plastic chairs that were bolted to the floor: three short Hispanic guys with gang tats, and two black guys, one old and weathered, the other younger, and missing his front teeth. Three sheriff's deputies armed with Tasers and nightsticks were talking by the door. Riot control.

When the Ringmaster led Pike into the room, the younger black prisoner stared at Pike, then nudged the older man, but the older man didn't respond. The younger guy was about Pike's size, with institutional tats that were almost impossible to see against his dark skin. A jagged knife scar ran along the side of his neck, as if someone had once cut his throat.

The Ringmaster hooked Pike to the bench, then took a clipboard from the deputies.

Pike sat without moving, staring straight ahead at nothing, thinking about Krantz, and what Krantz had said. Across the room, the younger guy with the knife scar kept glancing over. Pike heard the older man call him Rollins.

Fifteen minutes later, all six prisoners were unhooked from their chairs and formed up in a line. They were led out into the parking garage and aboard a gray L.A. County Jail van, climbing through a door in the van's rear while two deputies with Mossberg shotguns watched. A third dep, the driver, sat at the wheel with the engine running. They needed the engine for the air conditioner.

Inside the van, the driver's compartment was separated from the rear by the same heavy-gauge wire mesh that covered the windows. The rear compartment where the prisoners sat was fixed with a bench running along each wall so that the prisoners faced each other. The van was set up to hold twelve, but with only half that number everyone had plenty of room.

As they climbed in, a deputy named Montana touched each man on the shoulder and told him to sit on the left side or the right side. One of the Mexicans got it wrong and the deputy had to go inside and straighten him out, holding up the process.

Rollins sat directly across from Pike, now openly staring at him.

Pike stared back.

Rollins snarled up his lips to show Pike the double-wide hole where his teeth should be.

Pike said, 'Sweet.'

The trip to the Men's Central Jail would take about twelve minutes with the usual downtown traffic delays. When the last of the six was in and seated, Deputy Montana called back through the cage. 'Listen up. No talking, no moving around, no bullshit. It's a short trip, so nobody start any crap about having to pee.'

He said it a second time in Spanish, then the driver put the van in gear and pulled out of the parking garage and into traffic.

They had gone exactly two blocks when Rollins leaned toward Pike.

'You the one was a cop, aren't you, muthuhfuckuh?'

Pike just looked at him, seeing him, but not seeing him. Pike was still thinking about Krantz, and about the case that was slowly coming together against him. He was letting himself float and drift and be in places other than this van.

Rollins poked the older black guy, who looked like he'd rather be anyplace else on the planet. 'Yeah, this muthuh-fuckuh the one. I got a nose for shit like that. I heard'm talkin' about him.'

Pike had arrested a hundred men like Clarence Rollins, and had fronted off five hundred more. Pike knew by looking at him that Rollins had been institutionalized for most of his life. Jail was home. The world was where you went between coming home.

'You a real Aryan muthuhfuckuh, ain't you, them fuckin' pale ass eyes o' yours. Lemme tell you somethin', muthuhfuckuh, it don't mean shit to me you killed some muthuhfuckuh. I killed so many muthuhfuckuhs you can't count, an' there ain't nuthin' I hate more'n a motherfuckin' cop like you. Lookie here –'

Rollins peeled back a sleeve to show Pike a tattoo of a heart with *LAPD* 187 written inside it: 187 was the LAPD's code for homicide.

'You know what that means, muthuhfuckuh? LAPD one eighty-seven? Means I'm a cop-killin' muthuhfuckuh, that's what it means. You best fear my ass.'

Rollins was working himself up for something. It was as predictable as watching a freight train round a bend, but Pike didn't bother paying attention. Pike was seeing himself in the woods behind his boyhood home, smelling the fresh summer leaves and the wet creek mud. He was feeling the steambath heat of Song Be, Vietnam, when he was eighteen years old, and hearing his sergeant's voice shouting at him across the dry scrub hills of Camp Pendleton, a voice he so wished to be his father's. He was tasting the healthy clean sweat of the first woman he loved, a beautiful proud farm girl named Diane. She had been from a proper family who despised Joe, and had made her stop seeing him.

'How come you ain't sayin' nothin, muthuhfuckuh? You goddamned well better answer me when I talk to your muthuhfuckin' ass, you know what's good for you. Your ass is trapped in here with me.' When he said that, Rollins flashed the long slender blade hidden in his sock.

The other places and people melted away, leaving only the van and Pike and the man across from him. Pike felt as peaceful as the woods behind that childhood home.

'No,' Pike whispered. 'You're trapped with me.'

Clarence Rollins blinked once, clearly surprised, then

launched off the bench, driving the blade square at Pike's chest and pushing with all the power of his legs.

Pike let the blade slip past his hands, then trapped and folded the wrist, channeling all the speed and power of Rollins's own attack in turning the knife. Gunnery Sergeant Aimes would be pleased.

Rollins was a large, strong man, and considerable force went back into his forearm. The radius and ulna bones snapped like green wood, slicing through muscles and veins and arteries as the bones exploded through his skin.

Clarence Rollins screamed.

Deputy Sheriffs Frank Montana and Lowell Carmody both jumped at the scream, bringing their Mossbergs to port arms. The three Hispanic prisoners were bunched together at the front screen, making it hard to see, but Rollins was thrashing around in the aisle like something was biting him.

The driver shouted, 'The fuck is going on back there?'

Carmody yelled, 'Knock it off! Get back in your seats!'

Pike was down in the aisle with Rollins, who kept turning over and flailing and spinning around. Rollins was screaming in a high, little girl's voice as a three-foot geyser of blood sprayed all over the back of the van.

Montana said, 'Holy fuck! Pike's killing him!'

Montana and Carmody both tried to sight past the Hispanics over their Mossbergs. Montana screamed, 'Get away from him, Pike! Get back in that seat, goddamnit!'

The Mexicans saw the shotguns and scrambled out of the way, still trying to avoid the blood. They were probably thinking about AIDS.

Pike lifted his hands away from Rollins and eased back onto the bench.

Clarence continued thrashing and rolling and screaming as if his whole body was on fire.

Montana shouted, 'Shut up, Rollins! What the hell is going on back there?'

The older black man said, 'He's hurt! Can't you see that?'

Montana shouted, *'Knock off that shit and get back in your seat, Rollins!* What the hell are you doing?'

The older man said, 'He's bleeding to death, goddamnit it. That's blood.'

Rollins kept howling, the blood spraying everywhere. The older man was squatting on his seat, trying to stay clear.

Pike said, 'I can help him. I can stop the bleeding.'

'Stay the fuck in your seat!'

Carmody peered through the mesh. 'Shit, he ain't faking it, man. He's bleeding like a stuck goat. One of these bastards musta cut him.'

The older man said, 'He ain't been cut! That's his goddamned bones stickin' out! His arm's broke. Can't you see that?'

Montana could see it even with the way Rollins was carrying on. The bones looked like pink ivory.

The driver said that they were only another ten minutes from the jail, but when he said it they were locked down in the thick traffic. The van didn't have a flash bar or siren, so there was no way to get the cars to move.

The old man yelled, 'Ten minutes in your butt! This man needs a tourniquet. We ain't got no belts or nothing back here. You just gonna let him bleed like that?'

Montana said, 'Fuck. We'd better do something.' He could see the bastard bleeding out back there, and the three of them getting sued by the ACLU.

Montana told the driver to radio their sit-rep and request a medical unit. He left his shotgun and his sidearm with Carmody because he didn't want to tempt any of these bastards with a weapon, then pulled on vinyl gloves. He just knew that bastard had AIDS. Every one of these scumbags probably had it.

'You cover my ass, goddamnit,' he told Carmody.

314

Carmody shouted at everyone to stay in their god-damned seats, trying to make himself heard over Rollins's moaning and flopping. Every time the blood squirted toward the Mexicans, they jumped in a little herd.

Montana trotted around to the rear, keyed open the door, and looked inside. Christ, there was blood everygod-damnedplace.

'Settle down, Rollins. I'm gonna help you.'

Rollins spun around on his back like he was break-dancing, kicking his feet and crying. Montana thought that Mr 187 was a big goddamned baby.

Pike was sitting to his left and the old guy was to his right and the Mexicans were all bunched together in the front on the left side. Carmody had the shotgun at port arms, and the driver had his handgun out.

Carmody said, 'Just drag his ass out of there and lock the fuckin' door. We can take care of him outside.'

That's the plan.

Pike said, 'You want help?'

'Stay on that goddamned bench and don't move a fuckin' muscle.'

Montana climbed into the van, trying to watch the prisoners and get a handle on Rollins at the same time.

Rollins rolled end over end, squirting blood on Monta-na's pants, then flopped backward up the aisle toward the Mexicans. All three jumped up on the seats in front of Carmody.

'Goddamnit, Rollins. You got the AIDS I'm gonna beat you to death, you fucker. I swear to God I'll kill you myself.'

Montana scrambled up the aisle past Pike and the older guy to where the three Mexicans were trying to kick the hysterical Rollins away.

Montana gritted his teeth, cursed, then grabbed Rollins by the leg, standing to tow him back down the aisle, when both Carmody and the driver shouted, 'Getouttatheway getouttatheway! He's running!'

Both their Mossbergs were pointing right at Montana.

Frank Montana felt an icy rush in his stomach as he dropped to the floor, spun around, and saw that Joe Pike had escaped through the open door.

CHAPTER 30

The mirrored towers of Los Angeles rose up out of the basin like an island from the sea. Reflections of the setting sun ricocheted between the buildings, making them glow hot and orange in the west, backdropped with a purple sky. The freeway was a lava flow of red lights chasing the sun. Twilight was beginning.

When you're coming to my house and reach Mulholland at the top of the mountain, you make a hard turn onto Woodrow Wilson Drive, then follow it along its winding path through the trees until you reach my little road. Wide shoulders flare off Mulholland there at the mouth of Woodrow Wilson, and are often used as parking by guests visiting the surrounding houses, so I don't usually pay attention. But tonight a boxy American sedan with a man and a woman in the front seat was the only car off the road. They looked away when I glanced at them. It was like having a neon sign that read COPS.

Five minutes later, I pulled into the cool shadows of my carport, let myself in, and knew why the cops were there.

Joe Pike was leaning against my kitchen counter in the dark, arms crossed, the cat sitting nearby, staring at him with abject worship.

Joe said, 'Surprise.'

It seemed normal and natural that he was here in my home, only there was no Jeep outside and he was supposed to be in jail. He wore a loose cotton beach shirt that showed little brown dolphins jumping free in the sea, the sleeves hiding his red tattoos, the shirt's tail out over his jeans. He was wearing the glasses again, even standing here in my dark house.

I flipped on the light.

'Don't.'

I flipped it off.

'Charlie didn't get you out, did he?'

'It was a do-it-yourself program.'

I went around the ground floor, pulling the drapes and drawing the shades.

'I'm home now. It would look odd if there weren't lights.'

He nodded, and we turned on the lights.

'There's a car on Mulholland at Woodrow Wilson. Anything else, or should you just start telling me why the hell you escaped?'

'There's another car at the top of Nichols Canyon. They probably have a third unit down below, coming up out of Hollywood. Two units are on my condo and another on the gun shop.'

'Sooner or later, the police are going to come here to question me.'

'I'll leave before then.'

'You have a place to stay? You've got wheels?'

The corner of his mouth twitched, like it was silly of me to ask.

'They're probably watching my house, too. Maybe they weren't when you got here, but they've had time to set up. Wait until it's full dark before you leave. Full dark, you can get all the way down to Hollywood and they won't see you.'

He nodded.

'Jesus, Joe. Why?'

'I'd rather be out, Elvis. Krantz has a case. Even though I didn't do it, they have a case, and they could win. Out here I can help clear myself. In there, I could only be their victim. I don't do victim.'

Pike told me what had happened, and how. As he spoke,

318

he picked up the cat and held it, and I thought that there were times when even tough men needed to feel a beating heart.

When he told me that the murder weapon had been recovered off the point where he'd met the girl, I said, 'They planted it.'

'Someone did. Else we're back to coincidences again. You hear about Deege?'

'He's dead.'

'Murdered. A couple of kids saw a red Jeep where it happened. Saw a guy who looked like me behind the wheel.'

I stared at him. I wanted to say something, but I didn't know what to say. It just kept getting deeper.

'It fits together pretty well. I killed Dersh. I killed Deege. Pretty soon it's going to look like I killed all these people.'

'Except Lorenzo. You were in jail when Lorenzo was killed.'

Pike shrugged, like maybe he thought there might be a way to pin that one on him, too.

I said, 'Krantz hates you. It all comes back to Krantz.'

'It all comes back to me and Woz and DeVille. Krantz was part of that. So was Karen.'

I said, 'Maybe it isn't just Karen and Dersh. Maybe all six victims go back to that day. Before Dersh we've got a shooter who's murdered five people. He's sent no notes, left no messages, but he used the same method to murder all five. That means part of him wants the cops to know that he's responsible.'

'A power thing.'

'His way of sticking out his tongue. The vics are killed three months apart, no one can find a connection, and everything points to a serial killer. But what if he's not a serial killer? What if he's just a murderer with a grudge, and a plan for his killings?'

Pike nodded.

'I tried pulling DeVille's file, but it was missing. I know you and Wozniak located DeVille through an informant, so I pulled Wozniak's file, too, but there was nothing in there. Do you know where he got the information?'

'No. Woz had people up and down the food chain.'

'I went to see his widow, but she didn't know, either.'

Pike stopped stroking the cat.

'You went to see Paulette?'

'Her name's Renfro now. She didn't want to talk about it, but her daughter is trying to help.'

Pike stared at me for a long time, then let the cat slip from his arms. He got two beers from the kitchen, handed one to me, then poured a little beer on the counter. The cat lapped at it.

'It's been a long time, Elvis. Leave Paulette alone.'

'She might be able to help.'

A car pulled up then, and Joe vanished into the living room, but I knew the car.

'It's Lucy.'

I opened the kitchen door, letting her in with a bag of groceries and two suits still in plastic laundry bags. I guess she'd gone by her apartment. Her face was ashen, and she moved with quick short steps, looking nervous. The cat hissed once, then sprinted through his cat door.

'Oh, shut up. Something's happened. Joe escaped custody.'

'I know. He's here.'

As I closed the door, Joe stepped out of the living room.

Lucy stopped in the center of the kitchen, looking at Joe. She was not happy to see him.

She said, 'What were you thinking?'

'Hello, Lucy.'

She put her purse and the grocery bag on the counter, but did not put down the two suits. Her face was hard; no longer nervous, but angry. 'Do you know what a bad move this is?'

Joe didn't answer.

'They've got him in a box, Luce. I don't know if this is the smart way to play it, but it's done.'

Lucy glared at me, and there was an anger in her face I did not like. 'Don't defend this. Let there be no doubt, I can assure you both that this is *not* the smart way to play it.' She turned back to Joe. 'Have you spoken to your attorney yet?'

'Not yet.'

'He's going to tell you to give yourself up. You should.'

'Won't happen.'

Lucy turned back to me. 'Did you have anything to do with this?'

It felt like Mama was angry at her two little boys, and I was liking it even less.

'No, I didn't have anything to do with it, and what's with you? Why are you so upset?'

She rolled her eyes as if I were an idiot, then draped the suits over the grocery bags. 'May I see you?'

She stalked across the living room.

When we were as far from Joe as we could get, I said, 'Do you think you could be a little less supportive?'

'I don't support this, and neither should you.'

'I don't support this, either. I'm dealing with it. What would you like me to do? Kick him out? Call the cops?'

Lucy closed her eyes, calming herself, then opened them. Her voice was measured and calm.

'I have spent the last three hours worried sick about him, and about you. I tried to reach you, and couldn't. For all I knew, you were part of this. You and the Sundance Kid over there, partners jumping off a cliff.'

I started to say something, but she held up a hand.

'Do you realize that his being here jeopardizes your license under California law? You're harboring a fugitive. That's a felony.'

'He's here because we have to work together if we're going to beat this thing. He did not murder Eugene Dersh.'

'Then let him prove that in court.'

'We've gotta have *proof* to prove it. So far, the state has a case and we don't have any way to dispute it. We're going to have to find the person who really killed Dersh, and right now I'm thinking that's the same person who killed Karen Garcia and those other five people.'

Lucy's mouth was tight, her face set in a hard mask because it wasn't what she wanted to hear.

'It's dangerous for him here, Lucy. He knows that, and I know it, too. He's not going to stay, but he can't leave until it's dark.'

'What if the police knock at your door right now? With a search warrant?'

'We'll deal with it if it happens.'

She stepped back from me.

'You're not the only one in jeopardy here.'

She steeled herself in a way that was visible. 'I am not Joe's attorney. As long as I'm living here with you, my license to practice law could be at risk. Worse, what is happening here now could call into question my fitness as Ben's mother if Richard sues for custody.'

I glanced at Joe, then back to Lucy.

Lucy kept the emotionless eyes on mine.

'If Joe stays, I have to leave.'

'He's going as soon as it's dark.'

She closed her eyes, then said it again, slowly and carefully.

'If Joe stays, I have to leave.'

'Don't ask me this, Lucy.'

She didn't move.

'I can't ask him to go.'

A long time ago in another place I was badly wounded and could not get immediate medical attention. Little bits of hot steel had ripped through my back, tearing the arteries and tissues inside me, and all I could do was wait to be saved. I tried to stop the bleeding, but the wounds were behind me. My pants and shirt grew wet with blood, and the ground beneath me turned to red mud. I lay there that day, wondering if I would bleed to death. The minutes turned to hours as the blood leaked out, and the passage of time slowed to a crawl in a way that made me think that I would always be trapped in that single horrible moment.

The time passed like that now.

Lucy and I stood by my fireplace, neither speaking, staring at each other with hurt eyes, or maybe eyes that didn't hurt enough.

I said, 'I love you.'

Lucy went back across the living room into the kitchen, snatched up her suits, and went out the door and drove away.

Joe said, 'You should go after her.'

I hadn't heard him approach, I hadn't felt him put his hand on my shoulder. He was in the kitchen, and now he was beside me.

'If it's about me, I would've gone.'

'Your chances are better when it's dark.'

'My chances are what I make them.'

He moved to the table, pulling the chair and sitting so quietly that I heard no sound. Maybe I was listening for other things. The cat reappeared and jumped onto the table to be with him.

I went back into the kitchen, and looked in the bag she'd brought. Salmon steaks, broccoli, and a package of new potatoes. Dinner for two.

Joe spoke from the dining room. 'Ever since I've known you, I've looked to you for wisdom.'

Pike was a shape in the shadows, my cat head bumping his hands.

'What in hell does that mean?'

'You're my family. I love you, but sometimes you're a dope.'

I put the food away, and went to the couch. 'If you want something, get it yourself.'

Two hours later it was fully dark. During that time, we decided what we would do, and then Joe let himself out the kitchen door, and slipped away into darkness.

Then I was truly alone.

CHAPTER 31

I sat on the couch in my empty house, feeling a tight queasiness as if I'd lost something precious, and thinking that maybe I had. After a while, I called Lucy, and got her machine.

'It's me. Are you there?'

If she was there, she didn't pick up.

'Luce, we need to talk about this. Would you please pick up?'

When she still didn't pick up, I put down the phone and went back to the couch. I sat there some more, then opened the big glass doors to let in the night sounds. Somewhere outside the police were watching, but what did I care? They were the closest thing to company that I had.

I poached one of the salmon steaks in beer, made a sandwich with it, and ate standing in the kitchen near the phone.

Lucy Chenier had been out here for less than a month. She had changed her life to come here, and now everything had gone to hell. It scared me. We weren't mad because we liked different movies, or I had been rude to her friends. We were mad because she had given me a choice between herself and Joe, and she felt I'd chosen Joe. I guess she was right, but I didn't know what to do about that. If she gave me the same choice again, I would decide the same way, and I wasn't sure what that said about me, or us.

Someone pounded hard on the front door. I thought it was the cops, and in a way it was.

Samantha Dolan swayed in the doorway with her hands on her hips, four sheets to the wind.

'You got any of that tequila left?'

'Now isn't a good time, Samantha.'

She started to step in past me just like she'd done before, but this time I didn't move.

'What, you got a hot date with the little woman?'

I didn't move. I could smell the tequila on her. The smell was so heavy it could have been leaking from her pores.

Dolan stared at me in the hard way she has, but then her eyes softened. She shook her head, and all the arrogance was gone. 'It isn't a good time for me, either, World's Greatest. Bishop fired me. He's transferring me out of Robbery-Homicide.'

I stepped out of the door and let her in. I felt awkward and small, and guilty for what happened to her, which stacked nicely atop the guilt I felt about Lucy.

I took out the bottle of Cuervo 1800 and poured a couple of fingers into a glass.

'More.'

I gave her more.

'You're not going to have one with me?'

'I've got some beer.'

Dolan sipped the tequila, then took a deep breath and let it out.

'Christ, that's good.'

'How much have you had?'

'Not nearly enough.' She raised her eyebrows at me. 'Had a little tiff with your friend?'

'Who?'

'I'm not talking about your cat, stupid. The little woman.' Dolan tipped her glass toward the kitchen. 'A purse is sitting on your counter. You aren't the only detective in the house.' She realized what she'd said, and had more of the drink. 'Well. Maybe you are.'

Lucy's purse was by the refrigerator, put there when

she'd set down the bags. She'd taken her clothes, but forgotten the purse.

Dolan had more of the tequila, then leaned against the counter. 'Pike wasn't smart, playing it this way. You talk to him, you should get him to turn himself in.'

'He won't do that.'

'This doesn't help him look innocent.'

'I guess he figures that if the police aren't going to try to clear him, he should do it himself.'

'Maybe we shouldn't talk about this.'

'Maybe not.'

'It just looks bad, is what I'm saying.'

'Let's not talk about it.'

The two of us stood there. It's always a laugh a minute at Chez Cole. I asked her if she wanted to sit, and she did, so we moved into the living room. The tequila followed us.

'I'm sorry about Bishop.'

Dolan shook her head, thoughtful.

She said, 'Pike would've been in uniform just before I came on. You know what areas he worked?'

'Did a year in Hollenbeck before moving to Rampart.'

'I started in West L.A. There weren't as many women on the force then as now, and what few of us there were got every shit job that came along.'

She seemed as if she wanted to talk, so I let her talk. I was happy with the beer.

'My first day on the job, right out of the Academy, we go to this house and find two feet sticking up out of the ground.'

'Human feet?'

'Yeah. These two human feet are sticking straight up out of the ground.'

'Bare feet?'

'Yeah, Cole, just lemme tell my story, okay? There's these two bare feet sticking up out of the ground behind this house. So we call it in, and our supervisor comes out,

327

and says, 'Yeah, that's a couple of feet, all right.' Only we don't know if there's a body attached. I mean, maybe there's a body down there, but maybe it's just a couple of feet somebody planted.'

'Trying to grow corn.'

'Don't try to be funny. Funny is another in the long list of things you can't pull off.'

I nodded. I thought it was pretty funny, but I'd been drinking.

'So we're standing there with these feet, and we can't touch them until the coroner investigator does his thing, only the coroner investigator tells us he won't be able to get out until the next morning. The supervisor says that somebody's gotta guard the feet. I mean, we can't just leave'm there, right? So the supervisor tells me and my partner to watch the feet.'

'Okay.'

She killed the rest of her tequila, and helped herself to another glass as she went on with her story.

'But then we get this disturbance call, and the supervisor tells my partner he'd better respond. He says to leave the girl with the feet.'

'The girl.'

'Yeah, that's me.'

'I'm up with that part, Samantha.'

She took another blast of the tequila and took out her cigarettes.

'No smoking.'

She frowned, but put the cigarettes away.

'So they take off, and now I'm there alone with the feet in back of this abandoned house, and it's spooky as hell. An hour passes. Two hours. They don't come back. I'm calling on my radio, but no one answers, and I am pissed off. I am majorly pissed. Three hours. Then I hear the creepiest sound I ever heard in my life, this kind of ooo-ooo-ooo moaning.'

'What was it?'

328

'This ghost comes floating between the palm trees. This big white ghost, going '*ooo-ooo-ooo, I want my feet.*' Real creepy and eerie, see, just like that.'

'Don't tell me. Your partner in a sheet.'

'No, it was the supervisor. He was trying to scare the girl.'

'What did you do?'

'I whip out my Smith and shout, 'Freeze, motherfucker, LAPD.' And then I crack off all six rounds point-blank as fast as I can.'

'Dolan. You killed the guy?'

She smiled at me, and it was a lovely smile. 'No, you moron. I knew those assholes were going to try some shit like that sooner or later, so I always carried blanks.'

I laughed.

'The supervisor drops to the ground in a little ball, arms over his head, screaming for me not to shoot. I pop all six caps, and then I go over, and say, "Hey, Sarge, is this what they mean by foot patrol?" '

I laughed harder, but Dolan took a deep breath and shook her head. I stopped laughing.

'Sam?'

Her eyes turned red, but she shook back the tears. 'I put everything I had into this job. I never got married and I didn't have kids, and now it's gone.'

'Can you appeal it? Is there anything you can do?'

'I could request a trial board, but if I go to the board, those pricks could fire me. Bishop just wants me out of Robbery-Homicide. He says I'm not a team player anymore. He says he doesn't trust me.'

'I'm sorry, Samantha. I'm really, really sorry. What happens now?'

'Administrative transfer. I'm on leave until I'm reassigned. They'll put me in one of the divisions, I guess. South Bureau Homicide, maybe, down in South Central.' She looked down at her glass, and seemed surprised that it was empty.

'At least you're still on the job.'

A kindness came to her eyes, as if I was a slow child. 'Don't you get it, Cole? Wherever I go, it's downhill. Robbery-Homicide is the top. It's like being in the majors, then having to go down to the farm team in South Buttcrack. Your career's finished. All you're doing is killing time until they make you leave the game. You got any idea what that means to me?'

I didn't know what to say.

'My whole goddamned career has been forcing men like Bishop to let me be a starting player, and now I don't have a goddamned thing.' She looked over at me. 'God, I want you.'

I said, 'Sam.'

She raised a hand again and shook her head.

'I know. It's the tequila.'

She looked into the empty glass and sighed. She put the glass on the table, and crossed her arms as if she didn't know what to do with herself. She blinked because her eyes were filling again.

She said, 'Elvis?'

'What?'

'Will you hold me?'

I didn't move.

'I don't mean like that. I just need to be held, and I don't have anyone else to do it.'

I put down my beer and went over and held her.

Samantha Dolan buried her face in my chest, and after a while the wet of her tears soaked through my shirt. She pulled away and wiped her hands across her face. 'This is so pathetic.'

'It's not pathetic, Samantha.'

She sniffled, and rubbed at her eyes again. 'I'm here because I don't have anyone else. I gave everything I had to this goddamned job, and now all I have to show for myself is a guy who's in love with another woman. That's pretty fucking pathetic, if you ask me.'

'No one asked you, Samantha.'

'I want you, goddamnit. I want to sleep with you.'

'Shh.'

Her breast moved against my arm. 'I want you to love me.'

'Shh.'

'Don't shush me, goddamnit.'

She traced her fingers along my thigh, her eyes shining in the dim light. She gazed up at me, and she was so close that her breath felt like fireflies on my cheek. She was pretty and tough and funny, and I wanted her. I wanted to hold her, and I wanted her to hold me, and if I could fill her empty places maybe she could fill mine.

But I said, 'Dolan, I can't.'

The kitchen door opened then, an alien sound that had no part in this moment.

Lucy was in the kitchen, one hand still on the door, staring at us, a terrible pain cut into her eyes.

I stood.

'Lucy.'

Lucy Chenier snatched her purse from the counter, stalked back across the kitchen, and slammed out the door.

Outside, her car roared to life, the starter screaming on the gears.

Outside, her tires shrieked as she ripped away.

Dolan slumped back into the couch, and said, 'Oh, hell.'

The ache in my heart grew so deep that I felt hollow, as if I were only a shell and the weight of the air might crush me.

I went after her.

Lucy's Lexus was parked in front of her apartment, the engine still ticking when I got out of my car. Her apartment was lit, but the glow from the pulled drapes wasn't inviting. Or maybe I was just scared.

I stood in the street, gazing at her windows and listening to her car tick. I leaned against her fender, and put my hand on the hood, feeling its warmth. One flight of stairs up to the second floor, but they might as well have gone on forever.

I climbed, and knocked softly at her door.

'Luce?'

She opened the door, and looked at me without drama. She was crying, sad tears like little windows into a well of hurt.

'Dolan came over because she was fired. She's in love with me, or thinks she is, and she wanted to be with me.'

'You don't have to say this.'

'I told her that I couldn't be with her. I told her that I love you. I was telling her that when you walked in.'

Lucy stepped out of the door and told me to come in. Boxes had been put away. Furniture had been moved.

She said, 'You scared me.'

I nodded.

'I don't mean with Dolan. I mean from earlier. I'm angry with you, Elvis. I'm hurt with you.'

Joe.

'You changed your life to come here, Luce. You're worried about Richard, and what's going to happen with Ben. You don't need to worry about me. You don't need to doubt what we have, or how I feel, and what you mean to me. You mean everything to me.'

'I don't know that now.'

I felt as if the world had dropped away and I was hanging in space with no control of myself, as if the slightest breeze could make me turn end over end and there was nothing I could do but let the breeze push me.

'Because of Joe.'

'Because you were willing to put everything that's important to me at risk.'

'Did you want me to call the cops and turn him in?' More tension was in my voice than I wanted there to be.

She closed her eyes and raised a palm.

'I guess you're mad at me, too.'

'I don't like these choices, Luce. I don't like being caught between you and Joe. I don't like Dolan coming to my house because she doesn't have anywhere else to go. I don't like what's happening between us right now.'

She took a breath and let it out. 'Then I guess we're both disappointed.'

I nodded.

'I didn't come two thousand miles for this.'

I shook my head.

I said, 'Do you love me?'

'I love you, but I don't know how I feel about you right now. I'm not sure how I feel about anything.'

It sounded so final and so complete that I thought I must have missed something. I searched her face, trying to see if there was something in her eyes that I was missing in her voice, but if it was there I couldn't find it. I wanted an emotional catharsis; her measured consideration made my stomach knot.

'What are you saying here, Luce?'

'I'm saying I need to think about us.'

'We're having a problem right now. Is it such a big problem that you'd question everything we feel for each other?'

'Of course not.'

'That's what thinking about us means. One thing happens, you don't stop being an us.'

I looked around at the boxes. The stuff of her life. This wasn't going the way I had hoped. I wasn't hearing things that I wanted to hear. And I wasn't doing a good job of saying the things I had wanted to say.

Lucy took my hand in both of hers.

'You said I changed my life to come here, but my coming here changes your life, too. The change didn't end when I crossed the city line. The change is still happening.'

I put my arms around her. We held each other, but the uncertainty was like a membrane between us.

After a time, she eased away. She wasn't crying now; she seemed resolved.

'I love you, but you can't stay here tonight.'

'Is it that clear to you?'

'No. Nothing's clear. That's the problem.'

She took my hand again, gently kissed my fingers, and told me to leave.

Sacrifice

The killer presses the needle deep into his quadriceps and injects twice the usual amount of Dianabol. The pain makes him furious, his rage causing his skin to flush a deep red as his blood pressure spikes. He throws himself onto the bench, grips the bar, and pushes.

Three hundred pounds.

He lowers the weight to his chest, lifts, lowers, lifts. Eight reps of herculean inhuman effort that does nothing to appease his anger.

Three hundred motherfucking pounds.

He rolls off the bench and glares at himself in the mirror here in his shitty little rental. Muscles swollen, chest flushed, face murderous. *Calm yourself. Take control. Put away the rage and hide yourself from the world.*

His face empties.

Become Pike to defeat Pike.

The killer takes a calming breath, returns to the bench, sits.

Pike's escape has changed things, and so have Cole and that bitch Dolan. Knowing that he's been framed, Pike will try to figure out who, and will be coming for him. Cole and Dolan have already tried to get DeVille's file, and that's bad, but he also knows they didn't get it.

Without DeVille's file they cannot follow the trail back to him, but they're getting closer, and the killer accepts that they are very close to identifying him.

He must act now. He decides to jump ahead to the final targets, and nothing must stop him. Pike is the wild card, but Cole he can account for. Cole must be distracted. Get his mind off saving Pike, and onto something else.

He believes that Dolan has always been overrated as an investigator, so the killer discounts her. But Cole is another matter. He has met Cole, and studied him. Cole is dangerous. An ex-Army guy who wears the Ranger tab, and an experienced investigator. Cole does not appear dangerous in an obvious way, but many officers respect him. He heard one senior detective say not to let the wisecracks and loud shirts fool you, that Cole can carry all the weight you put on him, and still kick your ass. The killer takes this opinion seriously.

When you are plotting against the enemy, you always look for an exploitable weakness.

Cole has a girlfriend.

And the girlfriend has a child.

CHAPTER 32

I walked down the infinite flight of steps from Lucy's apartment to sit in my car. I thought about starting it, but that was beyond me. I tried to be angry with her, but wasn't. I tried to resent her, but that made me feel small. I sat there in my open car on her quiet street until her lights went out, and even then I did not move. I just wanted to be close to her, even if she was up in her apartment and I was down in my car, and for most of the night I tried to figure out how things could go so wrong so quickly. Maybe a better detective could've found answers.

The sky was pale violet when I finally pulled away. I was content to creep along in the morning traffic, the mindless monotony of driving the car familiar and comforting. By the time I reached home, Dolan was gone. She had left a note on the kitchen counter. What it said was, *I'll talk to her if you want.*

I cleaned our glasses from the night before, put away the tequila, and was heading upstairs for a shower when the phone rang.

My heart pounded as I stared at the phone, letting it ring a second time. I took a breath, and nodded to myself.

On the third ring I picked it up, trying not to sound like I'd just run ten miles.

'Lucy?'

Evelyn Wozniak said, 'Why didn't you call?'

'What are you talking about?'

'I left a message yesterday. I said you should call no matter what time you got in.'

I had checked my message machine when Pike was still in the house, but there had been no messages. I looked at it now, again finding nothing.

'Okay. You've got me now.'

Evelyn gave me directions to the storage facility that her mother used in North Palm Springs. She had had a duplicate key made for the lock, and had left it for me in an envelope with the on-site manager. I asked her if she wanted to be there when I went through her father's things, but she said that she was scared of what she might find. I could understand that. I was scared, too.

When she was done, I said, 'Evelyn, did you leave any of this on your message?'

'Some of it. I told you the name of the place. I know it was your machine and not somebody else's, if that's what you're thinking. Who else would have a message that says they're the world's greatest human being?'

I put down the phone, then went upstairs, changed clothes, and drove to Palm Springs, wondering if Pike had heard the message, and if he'd erased it.

And why.

When I was thinking about Pike, I didn't have to think about Lucy.

Two hours and ten minutes later, I left the freeway and again made my way through the wind farms. The desert was already hot, and smelled of burning earth.

The storage facility was clusters of white cinder-block sheds set in the middle of nowhere behind a chain-link fence with a big metal gate. A cinder-block building sat by the gate with a big sign saying LOWEST RATES AROUND. Since nothing else was around, it was an easy guarantee to keep.

An overweight woman with skin like dried parchment gave me the key. Her office was small, but a Westing-house air conditioner big enough to cool a meat locker was built into the wall, running full blast and blowing straight at her. It was little enough.

She said, 'You gonna be in there long?'

'I don't know. Why?'

'Gonna be hot,' she said. 'Make sure you don't pass out. You pass out, don't you try to sue me.'

'I won't.'

'I'm warning you. I got some nice bottled water in here, only a dollar and a half.'

I bought a bottle to shut her up.

Paulette Renfro's storage unit was located at the rear of the facility. Each unit was a cinder-block shell that sprouted corrugated-metal storage spaces. There was no door on the shell, so you walked inside what amounted to a little cave to get to the individual storage spaces.

From the tarnish on the lock, it was clear that Paulette rarely if ever came here, but the key worked smoothly, and opened into a space the size of a closet. Boxes of various size were stacked along the walls, along with old electric fans and suitcases, and two lamps.

I emptied the closet, putting the unboxed things to the side, then carried out the boxes. When all the boxes were out, I went through the older boxes first, and that's where I found the notebooks that Evelyn Wozniak remembered. Her father had kept field notes much like a daybook, jotting notes about the young officers he trained, the perps he busted, and the kids he was trying to help, all dated, and crammed into seven small three-ring binders thick with pages. I was pretty sure that the most recent would be the most relevant.

I put the seven binders aside, then went through the rest of the boxes to see if anything else might be useful, but the only other things of Abel's were a patrol cap in a plastic bag, a presentation case with Wozniak's badge, and two framed commendations from when he was awarded the Medal of Valor. I wondered why the commendations were here in a box, but she had remarried. I guess over time she'd lost track of them.

I was repacking the boxes when a shadow framed itself in the door, and Joe Pike said, 'I wanted to get here before you.'

I glanced over at him, then went on with the packing.

'It's so easy to show you up.'

'Find anything?'

'Wozniak's daybooks.'

'You look through them yet?'

'Too hot to look through them here. I'll take them where it's cooler.'

'Want some help?'

'Sure.'

He put the boxes I had finished repacking back in the closet. I sealed the last two boxes, then handed them to him one by one.

'You erase Evelyn's message?'

He nodded.

'Why?'

'I wanted to make sure you didn't find anything here that would hurt Paulette.'

'I'm looking for something to help you.'

'I know. Maybe we'll get lucky.'

'But maybe there's something here that will hurt Paulette.'

Pike nodded.

I took that in, and it was like taking in volumes.

'How did you break Karen Garcia's heart, Joe?'

Pike stacked the boxes until the last box was in place, and then he went to the door and looked out toward the desert as if something might be there. All I could see past him were other cinder-block buildings with other people's memories.

I said, 'Karen loved you, but you loved Paulette.'

Pike nodded.

'You dated Karen, but you were in love with your

339

partner's wife.'

He turned back to me then, the flat lenses empty.

'Paulette was married. I kept waiting for the feelings I had for her to go away, but they didn't. We didn't have an affair, Elvis. Nothing physical. Woz was my friend. But I felt what I felt. I tried dating other people to feel other things, but love doesn't just come and doesn't just go. It just is.'

I stared at him, thinking about Lucy.

'What?'

I shook my head.

'You already know that Krantz thought Wozniak was involved with a burglary ring.'

'Yes.'

'It was true.'

I watched him.

'Krantz thinks I murdered Woz for Paulette.'

'Did you?'

The corner of Pike's mouth twitched, and he tipped the glasses my way. 'You believe that?'

'You know better. Krantz also thinks you were involved with Woz in the ring. I don't believe that, either.'

Pike tipped his head the other way, and frowned. 'How do you know that?'

I spread my hands.

'Right.'

Pike drew a deep breath, then shook his head. 'I didn't have any idea. All that time in the car with Woz, and I never knew until Krantz talked to Paulette and scared her. She asked Woz about it, and he denied it, so she asked me. That's how I found out. I followed Woz and saw him with the Chihuahuas. He'd gotten some girl pregnant, and he'd set her up in an apartment in El Segundo. He was paying for it by tipping the Chihuahuas on easy places to rob. Krantz had it all. He just couldn't prove it.' Just what McConnell had said.

'You tell Paulette?'

'Some of it. Not all. He was her husband, Elvis. They had the child.'

'So what happened?'

'I told him he had to resign. I gave him the choice, and I gave him the time to think about it. That way it was between me and him. That's why he died.'

I thought that maybe Krantz had been right about many things.

'What happened in the motel, Joe?'

'He didn't want to resign, but I didn't give him any choice. I didn't want to give him to Krantz, but I couldn't let a bad officer stay on the job. If he didn't hang it up, I would've brought in Paulette, and I would've arrested the Chihuahuas.'

'The Chihuahuas would've rolled on him.'

'If he resigned I would've found another way at them, but it never got to that. We got the call about the missing girl and DeVille, and Woz got the location. When we got over there, Woz was already short, and that's when he lost it and hit DeVille with his gun. I think he was just working up his nut, because he already knew what he was going to do. It was about me, and the box he was in, and how he was going to get out of it.' Pike stopped for a time, then went on. 'He let DeVille have it, and when I pushed him away he pointed his gun at me.'

'You shot him in self-defense?'

'No. I wouldn't shoot him. I didn't draw my weapon.'

I stared at him.

'He knew I loved his wife, and he knew she loved me. His career was over, and if Krantz could make the case he would go to jail. Some men can't take the weight. Some men break, and will do anything to stop the pressure.'

'Abel Wozniak killed himself.'

Pike touched his chin. 'Pointed the gun here and pulled the trigger, up through his chin and out the top of his head.'

341

I asked, but I had already guessed. 'Why take the blame?'

'It had to be explained. If I tell the truth, Krantz would be able to make the case, and if Woz goes out a felon, his pension and benefits could be withheld. Paulette and the girls would've lost everything. Maybe Parker Center might've felt sorry, and cut them slack, but how could I know? If he goes out a suicide, there's no insurance. The insurance we had then wouldn't pay if you capped yourself.'

'So you took the weight.'

'DeVille was going to wake up and say that Woz hit him. I just went with it. I told them that we struggled, and that's how it happened. It would fit with what DeVille was going to say, and it would explain Woz being dead.'

'Only you get marked rotten for causing your partner's death to protect a pedophile.'

'You do the best you can with what you've got.'

'Did Paulette know the truth?'

Pike stared at the cement. 'If Paulette knew, she would've told the department. Even if it meant losing the benefits.'

'Wasn't that her decision to make?'

'I made the decision for all of us.'

'So she doesn't know that her husband killed himself.'

'No.'

Pike just stood there, and I thought that this was his single lonely way of protecting the woman he loved, even if it had cost him any chance at her love, forever and always.

Pike would take that weight.

And had.

I said, 'All this time, all these cops hating you for nothing.'

Pike cocked his head, and even in the dim light of the little building the glasses seemed to glow.

342

'Not for nothing. For everything.'

'Okay. So now what?'

'She still gets his survivor benefits. I want to make sure that whatever leaves here doesn't affect that.'

'Even if it's something that could help you?'

The corner of Pike's mouth twitched. 'I didn't come this far to quit now.'

'Then let's see what we find.'

We sat in a Denny's just off the freeway for the next two and a half hours, drinking tea and going through the day books. The Denny's people didn't mind. With the heat, they didn't have much business.

We started with the most recent book and worked backward. Eight pages were missing from that book, but the rest were there, and legible. Wozniak's entries were often cryptic, but pretty soon they made sense to me.

At one point I saw that Pike had stopped reading, and asked him, 'What?'

When he didn't answer, I leaned closer and found what had stopped him.

This Pike is a sharp kid. He'll make a good cop.

Pike pulled back the book, and kept reading.

Many of the entries were about arrests that Wozniak made, with notes on crimes and criminals and witnesses that he took for future reference, but much of what he'd written was about the street kids whom Wozniak had tried to help. Whatever he had become, Wozniak had been sincere in his efforts to help the people he was sworn to protect and to serve.

In all seven books, only three names were used in a context that suggested they might be informants, and only one of those seemed a possible, that being in an entry dated five months prior to Wozniak's death.

I read that entry to Pike.

'Listen to this. "*Popped a kid named Laurence Sobek, age fourteen, male hustler. Likes to talk, so he might be a good source. Turned out by the Coopster. ID? Fucked up kid. Gonna try to get him inside."* ' I looked up. 'What's that mean, get him inside?'

'Get him into a halfway house or a program. Woz did that.'

'Who's the Coopster?'

Pike shook his head.

I stared at the page.

'Could it be DeVille?'

Pike considered it. 'Like a nickname. Coupe DeVille.'

'Yeah.'

'Thin.'

'You remember Laurence Sobek?'

'No.'

'Anything else in here look good?'

Pike shook his head again.

'Then this is what we go with.'

We paid the bill, then brought the books out to our cars. I took the notebook that mentioned Laurence Sobek with me.

'How can I reach you?'

'Call the shop and tell them you need me. I'll have a pager.'

'Okay.'

We stood in the heat and watched the trucks go by on the freeway. Behind us, the windmills churned for as far as we could see. Pike was driving a maroon Ford Taurus with an Oregon license plate. I wondered where he'd gotten it. When I finally looked over, he was watching me.

I said, 'What?'

'I'm going to beat this. Don't worry about me.'

I made like Alfred E. Neuman. 'What, me worry?'

'Something's eating you.'

I thought about telling him about Lucy, but I didn't.

'You take care of yourself, Joe.'

He shook my hand, and then he drove away.

344

CHAPTER 33

It was late when I got home, but I called Dolan anyway. I called her house twice, leaving messages both times, but by the next morning she still hadn't gotten back to me. I thought that she might be at Parker Center, clearing her desk, but when I called her direct line there, Stan Watts answered.

'Hey, Stan. It's Elvis Cole.'

'So what?'

'Is Dolan there?'

'She's over, man. Thanks to you.'

Like I needed to hear that.

'I thought she might be there.'

'She's not.'

Watts hung up.

I called Dolan again at home, still got her machine, so this time I took Wozniak's notebook and drove over there.

Samantha Dolan lived in a bungalow on Sierra Bonita just a few blocks above Melrose, in an area more known for housing artists than police officers.

I parked behind her BMW, and heard music coming from the house even out in my car. Sneaker Pimps. Loud.

She didn't answer the bell, on my knock, and when I tried the door, it was locked. I pounded hard, thinking maybe she was dead and I should break in, when the door finally opened. Dolan was wearing a faded METALLICA tee shirt and jeans and was barefoot. Her eyes were nine shades of red, and she smelled like a fresh dose of tequila.

'Dolan, you've got a drinking problem.'

She sniffed like her nose was runny. 'That's what I need today, you giving me life advice.'

I walked in past her and turned off the music. The living room was large, with a nice fireplace and a hardwood floor, but it was sloppy. The sloppy surprised me. A big couch faced a couple of chairs, and a mostly empty bottle of Perfidio Anejo tequila sat on the floor by the couch. The cap was off. An LAPD Combat Shooting trophy sat on top of the television; the room smelled of cigarettes. I said, 'Why didn't you call me back?'

'I haven't checked my messages. Look, you want me to talk to your friend, I will. I'm sorry about what happened last night.'

'Forget it.'

I tossed Wozniak's binder to her.

'What's this?' She scooped a pack of cigarettes off the floor, and fired up, breathing out a cloud of smoke like a volcanic fog.

'A day book that Abel Wozniak kept.'

'Abel Wozniak as in Pike's partner?'

'Read the pages I marked.'

She frowned through another deep drag, reading. She flipped back several pages, then read forward past the point I had marked. When she was done, she looked at me. The cigarette forgotten.

'You're thinking this kid is talking about DeVille?'

'This kid had a relationship with Wozniak, that much we know. He was turned out by someone called the Coopster. If that's DeVille, then DeVille links Sobek to Karen Garcia, too.'

Dolan squinted at me. 'You're saying Sobek killed Dersh.'

'I'm saying maybe he killed everybody. Krantz and the Feds have been chasing a serial killer, but maybe this guy isn't, Dolan. At first I thought the connection was through Wozniak, but maybe these killings don't have

346

anything to do with Wozniak. Maybe they're about DeVille.'

She shook her head, scowling and cranky. 'I was one of the cops trying to find a connection, remember? We didn't.'

'Did you check out DeVille?'

She waved her cigarette. 'Why in hell would we?'

'I don't know, Dolan. I don't know why you didn't find anything, but you ordered DeVille's file from the DA's Record Section, right? Let's check it out and see what's there.'

She took another pull on the cigarette, and stared into the cloud. I could almost see the wheels turning, weighing the odds and what all of this might mean. For her, it was a shot at getting in again. If she could turn something that advanced the case, it could keep her on Robbery-Homicide and save her career.

Dolan pushed off the couch, went to her phone, and called Stan Watts, asking him if she'd gotten anything from DA Records. When she hung up, she said, 'Give me five.'

She showered and dressed and took almost twenty.

When we went outside, she said, 'Move your car and we'll take mine.'

'No way, Dolan. You scare the hell out of me.'

'Move your goddamned car or I'll back into it.'

She powered up the Beemer as I moved my car.

We drove to Parker Center without saying very much, each of us keeping our thoughts to ourselves. She pulled into the red zone by the front door, told me not to touch anything, then hurried inside. Ten minutes later she came out with DeVille's file.

'You didn't fuck with the radio, did you?'

'No, I didn't fuck with anything.'

We parked a block away in a little parking lot. Dolan went through the file first, peeling away pages and dropping them on the floorboard.

'What's that?'

'Lawyer crap. This stuff won't tell us anything. We want the detective's case presentation.'

The lead detective in charge of the case was a Rampart Division sex crimes D-2 named Krakauer. Dolan told me that the case presentation was the sum total of the compiled evidence used in building the case, and would include witness statements, testimonial evidence, interviews; anything and everything that the detective accumulated along the way.

When Dolan had the lawyer crap separated, she took half of the detective's case presentation, gave me the other half, and said, 'Start reading. The case will be divided by subject and chronology.'

I was hoping for some indication that Sobek was connected to DeVille, and perhaps had been the informant that put Pike and Wozniak in that motel room on the day Wozniak died, but most of what I read concentrated on Ramona Ann Escobar. There were statements from her neighbors and the motel desk clerk and her parents, and a transcribed statement from Ramona describing how DeVille had paid her ten dollars to take off her clothes. Ramona Ann Escobar had been seven years old. It was uncomfortable to read, but I read in hopes of finding Sobek.

I was still searching when Dolan quietly said, 'Oh, holy shit.'

She was pale and stiff.

'What?'

She handed me a witness list that compiled the names of the people who had lodged complaints about DeVille. The list was long, and at first I didn't understand until Dolan pointed at a name midway down the list.

Karen Garcia.

Her face still ashen, Dolan said, 'Keep reading.'

They were all there, the first five victims, plus the

newest, Jesus Lorenzo. Dersh wasn't there, but he was the exception.

Dolan stared at me. 'You were right, you sonofabitch. These people weren't random. They're linked. He's killing everyone who helped put away Leonard DeVille.'

All I could do was nod.

'Maybe you're the world's greatest fuckin' detective, after all.'

Only one of the six victims actually gave testimony against DeVille, that being Walter Semple, who had seen DeVille at the park from where the little girl disappeared. The others were part of what Dolan called the clutter, people who had been questioned by Krakauer because they had lodged sex crime complaints against a man Krakauer believed to be DeVille, but not directly related to the case for which DeVille was finally prosecuted.

Dolan's breast rose and fell as we read through the rest of the file. A copy of DeVille's criminal arrest record was attached, listing several aliases, one of which was the Coopster.

I said, 'It's Sobek. It's got to be Sobek. We have to take this to Krantz. The other people on this list have to be notified.'

'Not yet. I want more.'

'What do you mean, more? This will break open the case. It's a showstopper.'

'It links Sobek with DeVille, but it doesn't prove he's the shooter. If I can bring them the shooter, Bishop's gotta let me on again.'

'You've already got something, Dolan. We've found a connection between these people, and we've got leads. You're going to turn this case around.'

'I want more. I want to put the whole thing right on the table. I want the headline, Cole. I want to push Krantz's face in it. I want it so tight that Bishop can't not take me back on the team.'

I stared at her, and thought that if I were her I would want it this badly, too. But maybe I wanted it more. If we got the shooter, then maybe that would clear Joe Pike.

'Okay, Samantha. Let's find this guy.'

We drove back to her place. It took Dolan almost two hours of phone calls, but we learned that Laurence Sobek wasn't in the adult system, and the system had no record of his present whereabouts. This meant one of two things: Either he'd straightened out and gotten his life together, or he'd moved away before the age of eighteen. Of course, he could always be dead, too. Boys who work the streets often end up that way.

While Dolan made the calls, I went into her kitchen for a glass of water. A couple of million photographs were stuck to her refrigerator with little magnets, including several of Dolan posing with the actress who'd played her in the series. Dolan looked like she could kick your ass and would enjoy doing it, but the actress looked like an anorexic heroin addict. Showbiz.

The picture that Dolan had taken of me at Forest Lawn was stuck near the handle with a little Wonder Woman magnet. Seeing it there made me smile.

I finished my water, then went back into the living room as she put down the phone.

Dolan said, 'We've got to go to Rampart.'

'Why?'

'Because that's where Sobek was busted as a juvenile. The Juvie Section there will know where to find his sheet. They might have it loaded on their system, but maybe somebody will have to dig through paper.'

'I thought you said we'd need a court order to get at the juvenile stuff.'

She frowned, annoyed. 'I'm Samantha Dolan, you idiot. Get up to speed.'

And this woman wanted to sleep with me.

The Rampart Division station house is a low-slung,

brown brick building facing Rampart Street a few blocks west of MacArthur Park, where Joe Pike had first met Karen Garcia. We parked in a small lot they have behind the place for officers, then entered the division through the back. This time Dolan didn't tell me to keep my mouth shut and try to look smart. Looking smart would be out of place in a station house anyway.

Dolan badged our way into the Juvenile Section, which was microscopic in size, just four detectives attached to the robbery table in the corner of a dingy room. Where Parker Center and the Robbery-Homicide offices were modern and bright, the detective tables at Rampart seemed faded and small, with outdated furniture that looked as tired as the detectives. Rampart was a high crime area, and the detectives there busted their asses, but the cases rarely made headlines, and no one was lounging around in six-hundred-dollar sport coats waiting to be interviewed on *60 Minutes*. Most of them just tried to survive their shift.

Dolan zeroed on the youngest detective in the room, badged him, and introduced herself. 'Samantha Dolan. Robbery-Homicide.'

His name was Murray, and his eyebrows went up when she said that.

'I know you, don't I?'

She gave him the smile. 'Sorry, Murray. Don't think we've met. You mean from the TV show?'

Murray couldn't have been more than twenty-six or twenty-seven. He was clearly impressed. 'Yeah. You're the one they made the show about, right?'

Dolan laughed. She hadn't laughed when I'd mentioned her show, but there you go. 'These Hollywood people, they don't know what being a detective really means. Not like we do.'

Murray smiled wider, and I thought if she told him to roll over and bark, he wouldn't hesitate. 'Well, that was some case you put together. I remember reading about it. Man, you were news.'

'Hey, it's just Robbery-Homicide, you know? We get the hot cases, and the press tags along. No different than what you do here.'

Dolan didn't look good playing modest, but maybe that was just me.

Murray asked how he could help her, and Dolan said that she wanted to look at an old juvie packet, but she didn't have a court order for it. When Murray looked uneasy about that, she grew serious and leaned toward him. 'Something we got down at Parker Center. Headline case, man. The real stuff.'

Murray nodded, thinking how cool it would be to work the real stuff.

Dolan leaned closer. 'You ever think about putting in for RHD, Murray? We need sharp cops who know how to make the right call.'

Murray wet his lips. 'You think you could put in a word for me?'

Dolan winked at him. 'Well, we're trying to find this kid, you see? So while we're reading his file, maybe you could run a DMV check and call the phone company. See if you can't shag an address for us?'

Murray glanced at the older detectives. 'My supervisor might not like it.'

Dolan looked blank. 'Gee. I guess you shouldn't tell him.'

Murray stared at her a moment longer, then got busy.

I shook my head. 'You're something, all right.'

Dolan considered me, but now she wasn't smiling. 'Something, but not enough.'

'Let it go.'

She raised her hands.

Twenty minutes later we had the file and an interview room, and Murray was making the calls.

Laurence Sobek had been booked seven times from age

twelve to age sixteen, twice for shoplifting and four times for pandering. The DOB indicated he would now be in his late twenties. Abel Wozniak was twice the arresting officer, first on the shoplifting charge, then later for the second pandering charge. Sobek's most recent booking photo, taken at age sixteen, showed a thin kid with a wispy mustache, stringy hair, and aggravated acne. He looked timid and cowed.

At the time of his arrests, he had lived with his mother, a Mrs Drusilla Sobek. The record noted that she was divorced, and had not come to pick up her son or meet with the officers any of the seven times.

Dolan scowled. 'Typical.'

Murray interrupted us, knocking once before opening the door. He looked crestfallen.

'Doesn't have a California driver's license and never had one. The phone company never heard of him, either. I'm really sorry about this, Samantha.' He was seeing his chance at the hot stuff fizzle and melt.

'Don't worry about it, bud. You've been a help.'

The booking sheets showed that his mother had lived in an area of South L.A. called Maywood.

I said, 'If she's still alive, maybe we can work through the mother. You think she's still at this address?'

'Easy to find out.'

Dolan made a copy of the booking photo, then used Murray's phone to call the telephone company.

As Dolan called, Murray sidled up to me. 'You really think I got a shot at Robbery-Homicide?'

'Murray, you've got the inside track.'

Three minutes later we knew that Laurence Sobek's mother was still down in Maywood.

We went to see Drusilla Sobek.

Detective Murray was disappointed that he could not tag along.

Drusilla Sobek was a sour woman who lived in a tiny

stucco house in a part of Maywood that was mostly illegal aliens come up from Honduras and Ecuador. The illegals often lived eighteen or more to a house, hot-bedding their cots between sub-minimum-wage jobs, and Drusilla didn't like it that they'd taken over the goddamned neighborhood. She made no bones about it, and told us so.

She peered at us heavily from her door, her flat face wrinkled and scowling. She was a large woman who filled the door. 'I don't want to stand here all goddamned day. These Mexicans see me here with this door open, they might get ideas.'

I said, 'These folks are from Central America, Mrs Sobek.'

'Who gives a shit? If it looks like a Mexican and talks like a Mexican, it's a Mexican.'

Dolan said, 'We're trying to find your son, Mrs Sobek.'

'My son's a faggot whore.'

Just like that.

When she'd first come to the door, Dolan had badged her, but Mrs Sobek had said we couldn't come in. She said she didn't let in strangers, and I was just as glad. A sour smell came from within her house, and she reeked of body odor. Behind the hygiene curve.

I said, 'Can you give us an address or phone number, please?'

'No.'

'Do you know how we can find him?'

Her eyes narrowed, tiny and piglike in the broad face. 'There some kind of reward?'

Dolan cleared her throat. 'No, ma'am. No reward. We just need to ask him a few questions. It's very important.'

'Then you better look somewhere else, lady. My faggot whore son ain't never even been *close* to important.'

She tried to close the door, but Dolan put her foot in its base and jammed the sill. Dolan's left eye was ticking.

Drusilla said, 'Hey! What the hell you think you're doing?'

Dolan was a little bit taller than Drusilla Sobek, but a couple of hundred pounds lighter. She said, 'If you don't get the stick out your ass, you fat cow, I'm gonna beat you stupid.'

Drusilla Sobek's mouth made a little round O, and she stepped back. Surprised.

I started to say something, but Dolan raised a finger, telling me to shut up. I shut.

She said, 'Where can we find Laurence Sobek?'

'I don't know. I ain't seen him in three or four years.' Drusilla's voice was small now, and not nearly so blustery.

'Where was he living the last time you knew?'

'Up in San Francisco with all those other faggots.'

'Is that where he's living now?'

'I don't know. I really don't.' Her lower lip trembled and I thought she might cry.

Dolan took a breath, forcing herself to relax. 'Okay, Mrs Sobek, I believe you. But we still need to find your son, and we still need your help.'

Drusilla Sobek's lip trembled harder, her chin wrinkled, and a small tear leaked down her cheek. 'I don't like being spoken to in such a rude manner. It ain't right.'

'Did you ever have an address or phone number for your son?'

'Yeah. I think I did. A long time ago.'

'I need you to go look for it.'

Drusilla nodded, still crying.

'We have his booking photo from when he was sixteen, but I'd like a more recent picture, too. Would you have one of him as an adult?'

'Uh-huh.'

'You get those things. We'll wait here.'

'Uh-huh. Please don't let in the Mexicans.'

'No, ma'am. You go look.'

Drusilla shuffled away into her house, leaving the door open. A fog of the sour smell billowed out at us.

355

I said, 'Christ, Dolan, you're harsh.'

'Is it any wonder her kid turned out screwed up?'

We stood there in the sun for almost fifteen minutes until Drusilla Sobek finally shuffled back to the door, like a sensitive child who had disappointed her family.

'I got this old address up there with the faggots. I got this picture he gimme two years ago.'

'It's a San Francisco address?'

She nodded, her jowly chin quivering. 'Up with the faggots, yeah.'

She handed the address and the picture to Dolan, who stiffened as soon as she saw them. I guess I stiffened, too. We wouldn't need the address.

Bigger, stronger, filled out and grown, and with much shorter hair, we recognized the adult Laurence Sobek.

He worked at Parker Center.

Final Action

Laurence Sobek, his true name and not the name by which he is currently known, finishes stapling black plastic over his windows. He has already nailed shut every window but the small one in the bathroom, leaving only the front door as a point of egress. It is sweltering in the converted garage.

The plan was simple and obvious once Sobek lifted DeVille's case file from the records section. There in black and white he knew all the people who had helped the Sex Crimes detectives put the Coopster into prison where he died, all the people who had lodged complaints or made statements, and fed the Coopster to the prison population like a sacrifice. Sobek designed the sequence of homicides to take advantage of the weaknesses in LAPD's system: He started with the peripheral complainants it would be impossible for LAPD to connect, intent on working steadily up the food chain until it was too late to stop him even when the Task Force finally realized what was happening.

Now, thanks to Cole and that bitch Dolan, he must spare the remaining minor players, and kill the people he holds most responsible. The lead Sex Crimes detective, Krakauer, died of a heart attack two days after he retired. (All to the good, as Krakauer was the only person with even a remote chance of tying together the names of the early victims.) Pike had arrested the Coopster, then sat in the witness chair at his trial and hammered the nails into DeVille's coffin, but Pike is now a fugitive.

That leaves one other.

The apartment now sealed, Sobek pulls DeVille's case file from its hiding place in the closet, along with the brittle, yellowed newspaper articles about DeVille's arrest. He has read these a hundred thousand times, touching the grainy photographs of the Coopster being led from the motel in handcuffs. He touches them again now. He hates Wozniak, who spotted him at a Dunkin' Donut shop that day, and manipulated him into revealing what he knew. *This asshole is using you*, Wozniak had said. *What this guy is doing to you is wrong*, he said. *Help me help you.*

The Islander Palms Motel. Arrest. Prison. Dead.

Sobek closes his eyes, and puts away whatever is left of his feelings for DeVille. He has studied Pike, and learned well. Abandon humanity. Feel nothing. Control is everything. If you are in control, then you can re-create yourself. Become larger. Control everything.

Sobek closes his eyes, steadies his breathing, and feels an inner calm that only comes from certainty. He admires himself in the mirror: jeans, Nikes, gray sweatshirt with the sleeves cropped. He runs a hand over his quarter-inch hair, and imagines that he is not looking at Laurence Sobek, but is seeing Joe Pike. He flexes. The red arrows he had painted on his deltoids are gone, but he thinks that when this is over, he will have them tattooed there permanently. He rubs at his crotch, and enjoys the sensation.

Control.

He places the dark glasses over his eyes.

He has a cut-down double-barrel shotgun that he lifted from the Parker Center evidence room, and a box of twelve-gauge shells filled with #4 buckshot. He pulls the weight bench to the center of the floor, then fixes the shotgun to it with duct tape. He runs a cord from the knob to both triggers, rigged so that the gun will go off when the door opens, and pulls back the hammers.

He lays out the evidence that he wants Cole and the police to find, then lets himself out the back window. He will never return to this place.

Laurence Sobek drives away to do murder.

CHAPTER 34

Dolan ripped away from Drusilla Sobek's house like the queen of the Demolition Derby. She was so excited she was shaking. 'We got the sonofabitch. Right under our own goddamned noses, but we got him.'

'No, Dolan, we don't have him yet. It's time to take it inside.'

She glanced at me, and I knew what she was thinking. That she'd like to snap the cuffs on him herself and cut Krantz and Bishop and their whole damned Task Force out of the bust.

'This is what you wanted, Samantha. This is going to get you back on the team, but not if you piss off Bishop even more than he already is.'

She didn't like it much, but she finally went along. 'This guy works the day shift, so he's probably at Parker Center right now. I'm putting this on Bishop's desk in person. We've got the files and Wozniak's book. I'm giving Bishop the whole load, and fuck Krantz.'

'Whatever. I've got to use a phone. Stop somewhere.'

'Use mine. It's in my purse.'

'I'd rather use a pay phone. It won't take long.'

She glanced at me like I was crazy. *'Sobek is there right now.'*

'I need a phone, Dolan.'

'You're going to call Pike.'

I just looked at her.

'I fuckin' knew it.'

She jerked the Beemer into the nearest gas station, blasting past a crowd of people waiting to board a bus. She

359

screeched up to the pay phones, and left the engine running.

'Don't take all goddamned day.'

I did the same thing I'd done before, calling Pike's man, giving him the pay phone's number, then hanging up. Pike called back in less than two minutes. From the static I could tell he was on a cell phone.

'We were right, Joe. It's Sobek.'

'Is he in custody?'

'Not yet. I wanted to tell you that we're bringing it to Bishop now. If we get lucky, Sobek will cop to Dersh. If not, maybe we'll find something that links him to it and clears you.'

'It's going to bring up Woz.'

'Yeah, it is. We've got to show Wozniak's notebook to tie Sobek to DeVille, and to Wozniak. Once the story breaks, they're going to dig into what happened between you in that room. I just wanted to warn you. After we're finished with Bishop, I'll call Charlie, then go see Paulette and Evelyn so they aren't caught flat.'

'You won't have to. I will.'

I didn't know what to say, but I smiled.

Dolan blew her horn.

Pike said, 'It's been a long time. I guess it's time we spoke.'

'Okay, but stay safe until this guy takes the weight for Dersh. You're still wanted, and we don't know what we'll get from him.'

When I was back in her car, Dolan swerved through the gas station, cut in front of the bus, and blasted toward the Los Angeles River.

'Dolan, have you ever killed anybody in this thing?'

'Cinch your belt tighter if you're scared. You'll be fine.'

I glanced at her and she was smiling. I guess I was smiling, too.

When we reached Parker Center, Dolan didn't bother going into the parking lot; she put it in the red zone out front. We trotted in, Dolan badging us past the desk guard. I looked at everyone we passed, wondering if Sobek would be standing there when the elevator doors opened, but he wasn't.

We pushed into Robbery-Homicide, Watts and Williams raising their eyebrows when they saw us. Dolan steamed straight into Bishop's office, surprising him on the phone.

Dolan said, 'We've got the shooter.'

He covered the phone, annoyed. 'Can't you see I'm on the phone?'

She put the photograph of Laurence Sobek on his desk. 'His real name is Laurence Sobek. Here's another picture when he was booked under his true name as a juvenile. He's our shooter, Greg. We got him.'

Bishop told whoever was on the phone that he'd get back in five and hung up. He leaned closer to the pictures. Sobek had gained muscle and changed his appearance, but when the pictures were side by side you could tell they were the same guy.

'This is Woody something.'

I said, 'You know him as Curtis Wood. He's a civilian employee here. He pushes the mail cart around.'

Krantz and Watts appeared in the door, Williams standing on his toes to see past them.

Krantz said, 'Is there a problem, Captain?'

Dolan laughed. 'Oh, please, Krantz. Like you could do something.'

'They say he's our shooter, Harvey.' Bishop squinted up from the pictures. 'Where'd you get this booking picture?'

I said, 'Sobek's juvenile record. We got the recent picture from Sobek's mother.'

I showed them the pages we'd copied from Abel Wozniak's notebook, pointing out the passages about Sobek and DeVille, and their relationship, then the copy of Sobek's juvenile record showing Wozniak as one of his arresting officers.

Even as I said it, Krantz made a sour face as if he'd bitten into a rotten carrot. 'All this proves is we've got someone working here under a false name. For all you know, he changed it legally because of the problems he had as a child.'

'No, Krantz, we've got more than that.'

Dolan said, 'You find a connection yet between the six vics, Harvey?'

Krantz stared at her, suspicious. You could tell he wanted to say they weren't connected, but he knew she wouldn't have asked if she weren't about to drop a bomb. Instead, he glanced at me. 'What's your connection in all of this?'

'If Sobek did the six vics, then he probably killed Dersh, too.'

Krantz scowled at Bishop. 'We're being scammed. This is just some bullshit Cole cooked up to save Pike.'

Bishop was looking dubious, but Stan Watts grew thoughtful. 'How are they connected?'

Dolan said, 'Leonard DeVille was the pedophile in the motel when Abel Wozniak was killed. Wozniak and Pike had gone in there on a tip, possibly from Sobek, looking for a little girl named Ramona Escobar.'

Watts nodded. 'I remember that.'

'Cole worked backward from Dersh, asking who'd have a motive and why would they put it on Pike.'

Krantz said, 'This is bullshit. Pike killed that man.'

Bishop raised his hand, thinking about it.

Watts looked at me. 'How'd you make the jump to DeVille?'

'I wasn't thinking the connection was through DeVille. I was thinking it had to be through Wozniak, but it turned out to be the other.'

Dolan went on. 'We tried to pull DeVille's case file out of stores, but it's missing. Sobek could've slipped in there and lifted it. I ordered this copy up from the DA's section.

This is the witness list from that case file. All six vics are on this list.'

Bishop stared at the witness list without expression for almost thirty seconds. No one else in the room moved, and then Bishop quietly said, 'Fucking-A. Goddamned fucking-A. All six victims are right there.'

As Krantz read it, Watts and Williams looked over his shoulder, Williams making a whistling sound.

Bishop said, 'Okay, this is looking good. This is major, but what have you got that locks Sobek to the killings?'

'So far just what you see here. The relationships. You'll need to bring Sobek in and sweat him. You've got more than enough for warrants to search his home and automobile.'

Williams was still with the list, shaking his head. 'This fuckin' guy I see every day. We were just talkin' about the new Bruce Willis movie.'

Krantz jutted his jaw. He hated giving anything to Dolan or me, but he could read Bishop, and he knew Bishop wanted it. 'It's good, Captain. Let's find Sobek or Wood or whatever his name is and get him in here. I can get a phone order for the search, and get that done while we're talking to him.'

Bishop picked up his phone. No one said anything while he spoke, but Stan Watts caught Dolan's eye and winked. She smiled when he did. After a couple of minutes, Bishop wrote something, then put down the phone. 'Wood didn't come in today. He didn't come in yesterday or the day before, either.'

Krantz peered at Dolan. 'I hope you didn't do anything to make him bolt.'

'We didn't go near him, Harvey, and no one could've tipped him. We didn't see his mother until twenty minutes ago, and she doesn't know how to contact him.'

Bishop said, 'Now, Harve, let's not make accusations. I think Sam's done a good job here.'

Krantz smiled, smooth and friendly, and squarely in Bishop's butt.

'I wasn't accusing you, Samantha. This is good work. This really is.' He turned to Bishop. 'But we've got to take this a step at a time now. If this stands up, and I believe it will, Samantha, then this man is a civilian employee of the Los Angeles Police Department. He was murdering people while he worked here, and he was using our information sources to do it. If we're not careful, we could have another public relations nightmare on our hands. We need to match his prints. We've got to field some physical evidence, maybe correlate the daytime homicides with the days this guy had off or missed work, that kind of thing. Then hope for something physical when we raid his home.'

He looked at Dolan, then the others, like he was trying to drive home a point. In command and on top of things.

'If he's not here, we have to find him, and that might take time. I want to move fast, but I don't want to lose this guy because we didn't get all the signatures we should've, and I don't want him tipped because word leaked out.' Krantz looked at Dolan when he said that, and she turned red.

Bishop laced his fingers, nodding. 'Okay. How do you want to play it, Harvey?'

'Let's keep it small until we know what we're dealing with. Just us, and maybe two radio cars, but let's not make a big show with SWAT. If something goes wrong, the press will be all over us. Until he's in custody, I don't want him to know we're on him. If we miss the guy, the press will have it all over the air and he could slip through our fingers.'

'Okay, Harvey, that sounds good. Set it up the way you want, and roll on it.'

Krantz clapped Stan Watts on the shoulder, then turned for the door. He looked like Errol Flynn heading off with the Dawn Patrol.

364

Dolan said, 'I want a piece.'

Everyone stopped, and looked at her.

'Captain, I earned a place here. I want this. I want to be there when we get this fucker.'

Krantz's jaw tightened, and he made the little jut. He wanted to tell her no so badly that he had cramps, but he was watching Bishop.

Bishop tapped his desk for a moment, then leaned back and nodded. 'It's Harvey's Task Force, Samantha. I never force a commander to take someone he doesn't want.'

Krantz nodded, and jutted his jaw again.

'But I think you deserve a second chance. How about you, Harve? Think you could find room for Dolan?'

It was clear what Bishop wanted, and Krantz hated it. His jaw rippled with tension, but he nodded gamely. 'We'll meet you in the parking lot, Dolan. You're welcome to come along.'

Everyone filed out as the meeting broke, Stan Watts and even Williams slapping Dolan on the back or shaking her hand. She accepted their congratulations with a wide, bright smile, sparkling eyes, and a flush of excitement that was breathtaking. Samantha Dolan was beautiful.

I would never again see her as happy.

CHAPTER 35

When we got down to her car, Dolan opened the trunk, and tossed me a bullet-resistant vest. 'Here. Gonna be small, but you can adjust the straps.'

I held it up to myself, then put it back in her trunk. 'Not my color.'

'Your call.'

Dolan stripped off her shirt right there in the parking lot until she was down to her bra, then put on her own vest. All the people out on Los Angeles Street could see her, and so could the cops coming out of Parker Center, but she didn't seem to mind.

Dolan caught me watching and grinned nastily. 'See anything you like, go for it.'

I waited in the car.

When Dolan was dressed, she got behind the wheel. 'I've been thinking about all this, hotshot, and I'm putting you on notice. I'm not giving up on you.'

I looked at her.

'I'm not calling it quits just because you've got your Southern Belle. I want you, and I always get what I want. Maybe I'll put Scarlett O'Hara on notice, too. I intend to take you away from her.'

I shook my head and stared out the window.

'Be the best you've ever had.'

'Dolan, let's just not go there, okay?'

Her voice and her eyes softened. 'I know you love her. I just gotta make you love me more.'

She looked away then, and I looked away, too.

We sat quietly after that with the air conditioner

running until Krantz and Watts rolled out of the covered parking in their D-ride, Williams and Bruly behind them. Dolan keyed a small black radio. 'I'm on.'

Watts came back, 'Okay.'

Williams said, 'Up.'

We pulled into line behind them, and eased out of the lot.

I said, 'Hey, Dolan.'

'Mm?'

I stared at her until she glanced over.

'I like you a lot. I mean a lot, you know?'

She made a gentle smile that crinkled her eyes, but she didn't answer.

The plan was simple: We would proceed directly to Sobek's address, reconnoiter the area, then withdraw to decide what to do while waiting for two Rampart Division radio cars to come in as backup units.

Two blocks from Sobek's address, Krantz slowed as we passed an AM-PM Minimart, and called us over the radio. 'We'll meet back at this minimart after we make the pass.'

Everybody rogered that.

'Dolan. You go in from this side, and we'll follow in a couple of minutes. Williams, swing up and come down from the north. We don't want to look like a parade.'

Dolan double-clicked her radio to roger, then glanced at me. 'First smart thing that airhead has said.'

'Watts probably suggested it.'

Dolan laughed.

Williams swung up a side street as Dolan and I continued on by ourselves.

Laurence Sobek, also known as Curtis Wood, lived in a converted garage apartment in a depressed residential area less than one mile from Parker Center. An undersized house like a little square box cut into a duplex sat near the street, with a driveway running along its side to a smaller box at the back of the property, which was Sobek's conversion. A stocky Hispanic woman and three small children were in the front yard of the house next door, playing with a garden hose. The neighborhood wasn't unlike where his mother lived: Rows of small stucco boxes and older apartment buildings, mostly inhabited by immigrants from Mexico or Central America. Sobek's box was run-down and sad.

I said, 'I make two doors, one facing the main duplex and another on the side. Looks like something's on the windows.'

'You see anyone in the main house?'

'Couldn't tell, but it looks quiet.'

'I didn't see a car.'

'Me neither. But it could be one of these on the street.'

We passed Williams and Bruly coming in opposite us, then took two right turns and went back to the AM-PM. The two Rampart radio cars were waiting when we got there. We pulled in beside them and left the engine and air conditioner running. Williams pulled in thirty seconds after us, and Krantz followed almost a minute after. We joined him at his car.

Krantz said, 'We got the telephonic warrant, so we're good to go with entering the property. Stan, how do you want to play it?'

Dolan nudged me. There was Krantz, giving it over to Watts again.

Watts said, 'Secure the duplex first. I want to get that woman and her children out of there. Put one of the radio cars on the house directly behind Sobek's conversion in case he makes a run out the back. The rest of us cover the doors and windows. If he doesn't answer the door, I don't want to break it down, 'cause then he'll know we were here. Maybe see if we can slip the lock, and if not maybe we can crack one of the windows.'

I said, 'How do you want to approach the house?'

Krantz frowned at me. 'Let us worry about that.'

Watts answered anyway. 'I'd say two groups, one down the drive and the other from the side yard to the north.

Again, we want to keep a low profile. If he's not home, it's best if he doesn't know we were here.'

Krantz gave the radio units their assignments, describing Sobek and giving them copies of the file shots the employment office had taken. He told them that if this guy came hauling ass through the yard they should consider him dangerous and act accordingly.

When the uniforms had gone back to their cars, Krantz turned back to the rest of us. 'Everybody got their vest?'

Dolan said, 'Cole doesn't.'

Krantz shrugged. 'Won't matter. He's going to wait here. So are you.'

'Excuse me?'

'This is as far as you go, Dolan. I was fine with letting you tag along, but this is it. This is a Task Force operation, and you're not part of the Task Force.'

Dolan charged up to Krantz so fast that he jumped back, and Williams lurched between them.

'Take it easy, Dolan!'

Dolan shouted, 'You can't do this, goddamnit! Cole and I *found* this guy!'

'I can do anything I want. It's my operation.'

I said, 'This is really chickenshit, Krantz. If you felt this way, you should've made the play in front of Bishop.'

Krantz jutted the jaw. 'I've inspected the scene and determined it's best for the operation if only Task Force members participate. We're going to look too much like an army back there as it is. If you and Dolan were there, we'd be crawling all over each other and the odds of someone getting hurt would increase.'

I smiled at Watts, but Watts was staring at the ground. 'Sure. It's a safety issue.'

Dolan's face grew as tight and hard as a ceramic mask, but her voice softened. 'Don't cut me out of this, Harvey. Bishop said I could go.'

'You did. You're here. But this is far enough. When the location is secure, you and your boyfriend can come in.'

He jutted his jaw at me, and I wondered how it'd feel to kick it. The 'boyfriend' would like kicking it just fine.

I said, 'Why are you doing this, Krantz? Are you scared she's going to get the credit for doing your job?'

Watts said, 'You're not helping.'

I spread my hands and stepped back. 'You want me out of it, fine, I'm out of it. But Dolan earned a piece of this.'

Krantz considered me, then shook his head. 'That's big of you, Cole, volunteering like that, but I don't give a shit what you want or not. I still think your partner killed Dersh, and I still think you had something to do with breaking him out. Bishop might be willing to overlook that, but I'm not.' He glanced back to Dolan. 'Here's the way it is: I run this Task Force. If you want any chance, and I mean *any*, of getting back on Robbery-Homicide, you'll sit your fanny back in that car and do exactly as I say. Are we clear on that?'

Dolan's face went white. 'You want me to be a good little girl, Harvey?'

Krantz drew himself up and tugged at his vest. It made him look bulky and misshapen, like a deformed scarecrow. 'That's exactly what I want. If you're a good girl, I'll even make sure you get some of the credit.'

Dolan stared at him.

Krantz told the rest of them they'd be going in one car – his – and then the four of them got into it and drove away.

I said, 'Jesus, Dolan, what a prick. I'm sorry.'

She looked at me as if I was confused, and then she smiled.

'You can sit here if you want, World's Greatest, but I'm going in through the back.'

I didn't think it was a smart idea, but that didn't do any good. She climbed into the Beemer without waiting for me, and it was either stand there like Krantz's toad or go with her.

Krantz had gone up the front street, so we drove up the

back, straight to where the second radio car was waiting. The two uniforms were standing against the fender, smoking while they waited for Krantz's call.

Dolan said, 'You guys hear from Krantz yet?'

They hadn't.

'Okay. We're gonna move in. Wait for the call.'

I said, 'Dolan, this isn't smart. If we surprise one of these guys, they could blow our heads off.' I was thinking about Williams, looking so hinky he'd pop a cap if someone behind him sneezed.

'I told you to wear a vest.'

Great.

The property behind Sobek's was a single-family bungalow about the size of an ice chest. Nobody was home, except for a yellow dog in a narrow wire pen. I was worried the dog would bark, but all it did was wag its tail and watch us with hopeful eyes. Dolan and I moved up the drive, and into a backyard that was separated from Sobek's by a chain-link fence overgrown by morning glories that were brown and brittle from the heat. His converted garage was close to the fence and easy to see.

Dolan made a hissing sound to get my attention, then motioned for us to go over the fence.

When we were on Sobek's side, we separated and circled the building. I listened close at the windows, and tried to see inside, but couldn't because they'd been covered by what looked like plastic garbage bags. The bags meant he was hiding something, and I didn't like that.

Dolan and I met near Sobek's front door, then moved to the side.

I whispered, 'I couldn't see anything in there. Did you?'

'Every damned window is like this. I couldn't see anything and didn't hear anything. If he ain't our guy, he's a goddamned vampire. Let's try the door.'

Stan Watts and Harvey Krantz came down the drive,

and froze when they saw us. Krantz made an angry wave for us to come over to him, but Dolan gave him the finger.

'You're cutting your own throat with that guy, Dolan.'

'He's fucked me long enough. You got your gun?'

'Yeah.'

'Let's try the door.'

Dolan went to the front door and knocked, just the way you'd knock if you wanted to ask your neighbor for a small favor. I stood three feet to her left, gun out, and ready to get on Sobek if he answered.

Stan Watts drew his gun and hurried over beside me. Krantz stayed out by the duplex. I could hear Williams and Bruly in the next yard.

Watts said, 'Goddamnit, Samantha.' But it was only loud enough for me.

Dolan knocked a second time, harder, and said, 'Gas company. We got a problem we've traced to your house.'

No answer.

She said it louder. *'We've got a gas company problem out here.'*

Still no one answered. Watts stood, and Krantz hurried over from the duplex. His face was red, and he looked like he wanted to bite someone in the neck.

'Goddamnit, Dolan, I'm going to have your ass for this.' He was whispering, but it was harsh and loud, and if anyone was inside they would've heard. 'This is *my* collar.'

I said, 'He's not here, Dolan. Pull back and let's figure out what to do.'

Krantz put away his gun and jabbed me with his finger. 'I'm going to have your ass for this, too. You, and her. Stan, you're a witness.'

The three of us were still off to the side when Dolan touched the knob. 'Hey, I think it's open.'

I said, 'Dolan. Don't.'

Samantha Dolan eased open the door just far enough to peek inside, but she probably couldn't see anything.

372

Dolan relaxed.

'We're clear, Krantz. Looks like I've done your job again.'

Then she pushed the door open and something kicked her backward with a sound like a thunderclap.

Stan Watts yelled, 'Gun!' and hit the ground, but I didn't hear him.

I pushed low through the door, firing at a smoking double-barrel shotgun even before I knew what it was. I think I was screaming.

I fired all six rounds before the hammer clicked on nothing, and then I was running back into the yard, where Watts was trying to stop the bleeding, but it was already too late.

The point-blank double load from the shotgun had blown through her vest like it wasn't there.

Samantha Dolan's beautiful hazel eyes stared sightlessly toward heaven.

She was dead.

CHAPTER 36

As Detective Samantha Dolan's blood seeps into Los Angeles' dry earth, Laurence Sobek parks his red Cherokee in the next victim's drive. He no longer carries the little .22 with his homemade Clorox suppressors; he carries a full-blown .357 magnum loaded with light, fast hollow points. When he shoots his victims now, they will blow apart like overripe avocados, with no chance for survival.

Sobek has the gun in his waist, his hand tight on its grip as he goes to the door. He knocks, but no one answers, and, after knocking again, walks around to the back, where he tries the sliding glass doors. He considers forcing the doors, but sees a Westec alarm light blinking from its control panel.

Sobek is ready to kill. He is ready to do murder, and wants to with such a ferocity that his palm is slick on the pistol's wood grip.

He goes back to the Jeep, and drives up the hill until he finds a parking place with an unobstructed view of the house.

He waits for the child.

Krantz said, 'Oh, holy Jesus. Oh, Christ.'

He dry-heaved, and turned to lean against an avocado tree. Williams and Bruly came around the corner, guns out and eyes wild, the four uniforms following with their shotguns. Someone shouted from one of the surrounding houses. The yellow dog howled.

Bruly yelled, *'Is she dead? Jesus, is she dead?'*

Watts's hands were red with Samantha Dolan's blood. 'Krantz, clear the house. Williams, clear the house, goddamnit.'

No one was paying any attention to the house. If Sobek had been in there, he could've shot the rest of us.

I said, 'It's clear.'

Watts was still shouting. 'Williams, secure the evidence. Wake up, goddamnit, and be careful in there. Do *not* contaminate the evidence.'

Williams crept to the door, gun out and ready. Watts went over to a garden spigot, washed his hands, then took out his radio and made a call.

I draped my jacket over Dolan's face, not knowing what else to do. My eyes filled with tears, but I shook my head and turned away. Williams had stopped outside the door and was staring at her. He was crying, too.

I felt her wrist, but it was silent. I rested the flat of my hand on her belly. She was warm. I blinked hard at the tears, then put Samantha Dolan and everything I was feeling out of my head to concentrate on Joe.

I went to Sobek's garage.

Krantz saw me from the tree and said, 'Stay out of there. It's a crime scene. Williams, stop him, goddamnit.'

'Fuck you, Krantz. He could be out there killing someone else right now.'

Williams went back to staring at Dolan. 'She's really dead.'

'She's dead.'

He cried harder.

Watts called, 'Cole, be careful. He could have the whole fucking thing booby-trapped.'

I went inside without stopping, and Krantz came in behind me. Bruly came to the door, but stopped there.

The air was layered with drifting gun smoke. It was intensely hot and dark, with the only light coming through the open door. I turned on the lights with my knuckle.

Sobek didn't have furniture; he had weights. A weight lifter's bench sat squat and ugly in the center of the room, black weight disks stacked on the floor around it like iron toadstools. No one walked in front of the shotgun even though smoke still drifted from both barrels. Residual fear. Articles from the *Times* about the killings and Dersh and Pike were pinned to the wall, along with a Marine Corps recruiting poster and another poster depicting LAPD SWAT snipers.

Bruly said, 'Jesus, look at this shit. You think he's coming back?'

I didn't look at him; I was looking for trip wires and pressure plates, and trying to smell gasoline, because I was scared that Sobek had rigged the garage to explode. 'You don't rig a booby trap the way he's rigged this place and expect to come back. He's abandoned it.'

Krantz said, 'We don't know that, Cole. If we can get Dolan cleaned up fast enough, we can secure the area and wait for him.'

Even Bruly shook his head.

I said, 'You're really something, Krantz.'

Bruly took a small book from a cardboard box, then a couple more. 'He's got the Marine Corps Sniper Manual in here. Check it out: The Force Recon Training Syllabus, Hand-to-Hand Combat. Man, this turd is the ultimate wannabe.'

Krantz opened the fridge and took out a glass vial. 'It's filled with drugs. Steroid products. The guy's a juicer.'

It wasn't much of an apartment, just one large room divided by a counter from a kitchenette, with a bath and closet. All I cared about and wanted was to find a slip with Dersh's address, or the clothes that Sobek used to dress as Pike – anything at all that would tie Sobek to Dersh and clear Joe.

'Over here, Lieutenant.'

Bruly found seven empty Clorox bottles in the closet,

along with three .22 pistols and some ammunition. Two of the Clorox bottles had been reinforced with duct tape.

Krantz slammed Bruly on the back. 'We got the sonofabitch!'

I said, 'Dolan got him. You just came along for the ride.'

Krantz started to say something, then thought better of it, and went to the door. He spoke to Stan Watts. Outside, a siren approached.

Leonard DeVille's original case file was spread across the kitchen counter, along with yellowed clippings about Wozniak's death, the lead detective's witness complainant list, and notes and addresses on all six victims. Karen Garcia's address was there. Her habit of running at Lake Hollywood, and notes on her route were there, as were similar notes on Semple, Lorenzo, and the others. It was creepy; like getting a glimpse inside a cold and evil mind that was planning murder. He had watched some of these people and charted their lives for months.

Krantz said, 'I've got to hand it to you, Cole. You and Dolan made a right call. That was good work.'

'See if there's anything about Dersh.'

Krantz's jaw jutted, but he didn't say anything. Maybe, just then, he thought it was possible.

We were still shuffling through Sobek's planning notes when we came to my listing in the yellow pages, and a DMV printout showing my home address and phone numbers. Dolan's home address was listed, also.

Bruly whistled. 'He has you, dude. I don't know how, but he knew you and Dolan were on him.'

Krantz fingered through the papers. 'He was all over Parker Center every day. He could've heard anything. He could've asked damn near anyone anything, and no one would've thought anything of it.'

The way Krantz said it made me think that he and Sobek had had more than one conversation.

Bruly spread more loose pages, exposing a snapshot that was so wrong to this place and moment that I almost didn't recognize it. A snapshot of three boys talking to a teenaged girl holding a tennis racket. The girl's back was to the camera, but I could see the boys. The boy on the right was Ben Chenier. Two other snapshots of Ben were mixed with the papers, all three taken from a distance at his tennis camp in Verdugo. Lucy's apartment address was scratched on a corner of the DMV printout.

Krantz saw the pictures, or maybe he saw the expression on my face. 'Who's this boy?'

'My girlfriend's son. He's away at this tennis camp. Krantz, this address is my girlfriend's apartment, this one's my home. That's the television station where Lucy works.'

Krantz cut me off to yell outside for Watts. Somewhere out on the street, the siren died, but more were coming.

'Stan, we've got a problem here. It looks like Sobek was going to shut down Cole. He might be on the girlfriend, or the girlfriend's son, or on Cole's home.'

Something sharp and sour blossomed in the center of me, and spread through my arms and legs and across my skin. I felt myself shaking.

Watts looked through the papers and photographs as Krantz spoke, and turned away with his cell phone before Krantz finished. Watts read out the addresses into the phone, requesting patrol officers be dispatched code three. Code three meant fast. Sirens and lights. Watts cupped the phone to glance back at me. 'We got the camp's name?'

I told him. I was shaking when I borrowed Bruly's phone to call Lucy.

When Lucy came on, she was hesitant and contained, but I cut through that, telling her where I was, and that officers were on their way to her, and why.

Krantz said, 'Cole, do you need me to speak with her?'

When I told her that Laurence Sobek had snapped Ben's picture, her voice came back higher and strained.

'This man was watching Ben?'

378

'Yes. He took photographs. The police are on their way to the camp now. They've dispatched the Highway Patrol.'

Krantz said, 'Tell her we have officers on the way to her, too, Cole. She'll be safe.'

Lucy said, 'I'm going to Ben. I'm going to get him right now.'

'I know. I'll come get you.'

'There's no way I could wait. I'm leaving now.'

'Luce, I'll meet you there.'

'He's got to be safe, Elvis.'

'We'll keep him safe. Stan Watts is talking to the camp, now.'

When I said it, Watts looked over and gave me a thumbs-up.

I said, 'Ben's okay, Luce. The camp people have him. He's with them right now, and we're on the way.'

She hung up without another word.

I tossed the phone back to Bruly on my way out the door, trying to ignore the tinge of accusation I'd heard in her voice.

The Verdugo Tennis Camp was a good hour east of L.A. in the rural foothills of the Verdugo Mountains. Krantz used a bubble flasher, and knocked a hundred most of the way. He left Watts to coordinate the surveillance of my home and Lucy's apartment, and spent much of the drive on his cell phone talking to Bishop. Sobek's landlady provided a license number, and both the LAPD Traffic Division and the Highway Patrol were alerted. The make and model of Sobek's Jeep were identical to those of Pike's.

Williams sat ahead of me in the front seat, crying and muttering. 'A fuckin' shotgun. He about cut her in half with that goddamned thing. Motherfucker. I'm gonna cap that sonofabitch. I swear to Christ I'm gonna cap his ass.'

I said, 'We're taking this guy alive, Williams.'

'No one asked you, goddamnit.'

379

'Krantz, we're taking this guy alive. If he's alive, he'll cop to Dersh.'

Krantz patted Williams's leg. 'Worry about yourself, Cole. My people can handle themselves, and we're bringing this asshole to trial. Right, Jerome?'

Jerome Williams stared out the window, jaw flexing.

'We're bringing this man to trial, right, Jerome?'

Williams twisted around so he could see me. 'I ain't forgot what you said. When this is over, I'm gonna show you just how goddamned black I am.'

The sheriffs were already there when we arrived, four radio cars parked on the camp's dirt-and-gravel lot. The camp administrators were talking nervously with the sheriffs, as, behind them, horses snuffled in their stables. Ben had been right: It smelled of horse poop.

Krantz hoped to spot Sobek and capture him, so he had the sheriffs park their vehicles inside the camp's barn, then spoke with the senior sheriff about setting up surveillance positions. We did all this in the camp's dining hall, a screen-walled building with unfinished wood floors. The kids were being held together in the boy's dormitory.

Other parents arrived before Lucy, collecting their children and leaving as quickly as possible. Krantz was pissed that the camp administrator, a woman named Mrs Willoman, had called the families, but there wasn't anything he could do about it. If the cops tell you that a multiple-homicide killer might be dropping around, there aren't many responsible alternatives.

Lucy arrived ten minutes later, her face strained when I went out to meet her. She took my hand, but didn't answer when I spoke to her, and didn't look at me. When I told her that we were in the dining hall, she walked so quickly that we broke into a trot.

Inside, she went directly to Mrs Willoman, and said, 'I want my baby.'

A teenage camp counselor brought Ben from the bunk

room. Ben looked excited, like this was a hell of a lot better than riding horses or even playing tennis.

Ben said, 'This is cool. What's going on?'

Lucy hugged him so tightly that he squirmed, but then her face flashed with anger. 'It isn't cool. Things like this aren't *cool*, and aren't *normal*.'

I knew she was saying it for me.

Krantz asked Lucy to stay until we received word that her apartment had been secured. After, we would follow them home to make sure they arrived safely. Krantz offered to provide twenty-four-hour protection, and Lucy accepted. She stared at Ben, rubbing his back, and said that maybe they should go back to Louisiana until this was over. When I told her I thought that might be a good idea, she went over to the screen wall and looked out.

I guess she just wanted to be someplace where she could feel safe.

We sat around a big table, sipping something red that the counselor called bug juice, Krantz and I explaining Sobek to Lucy and Ben. Lucy kept one hand on Ben, and held my hand with the other, but still did not look at me. She spoke only to Krantz, though she occasionally squeezed my hand as if sending a message she was not yet capable of saying aloud.

Finally, Krantz was paged, and checked the number. 'That's Stan.'

He called Watts, listened for a few seconds, then nodded at Lucy. 'We've secured your home. Manager let us in, and officers are on the site.'

The tension drained out of her like air from a balloon. 'Oh, thank God.'

'Let me just wrap up here, and we'll get you home. If you decide you want to leave town, let me know and we'll bring you to the airport. I'll call the Baton Rouge PD, if you'd like, and bring them up to speed.'

Lucy smiled at him like Krantz was human. 'Thank you, Lieutenant. If I decide to go home, I'll call you.'

Home.

She took my hand again, and smiled at me for the first time in a while. 'It's going to be all right.'

I smiled back, and everything seemed much better in the world.

While the counselors were getting Ben's things, I took my bug juice to the door and stared out at the tree line, searching it the way I had when I was eighteen, and in the Army. I thought about Sobek, and what we had found in his garage. His goal was to kill the people he blamed for putting DeVille in prison, and he had started with the people most removed from the prosecution, probably because it would be hardest for LAPD to connect them together. I wondered if that was the only reason. I wondered if maybe he also didn't blame them the least, which meant he was saving the people he blamed the most. Pike, for sure, but there was also Krakauer and Wozniak, though they were both dead. The more I thought about it, the more it bothered me, because he had had a personal relationship with Wozniak, and there was every possibility that it was Sobek who had been the one who had tipped Wozniak to DeVille's location that day. I stared at the stables and thought about the horses within; I couldn't see them, but I heard them and smelled them. They snorted and whinnied and talked to each other, I guess, and were real even though they were beyond my sight. Life is often like that, with realities layered over other realities, mostly hidden but always there. You can't always see them, but if you listen to their clues, you'll recognize them all the same.

Krantz was having two of the sheriffs load Ben's things when I said, 'He's not coming here, Krantz.'

Krantz nodded. 'Maybe not.'

'You don't get it. He's not coming here, or my place, or Lucy's. It's a diversion.'

Now Krantz frowned, and Lucy looked over, both hands draped on Ben's shoulders.

'Think about it, Krantz. He wants to kill the people he blames for DeVille, and he's doing that, but then he realized we're onto him. His game's over, and he knows it, right?'

Krantz was still frowning.

'He knows that it's only a matter of days before we link the vics, and when we do we'll have a suspect pool, and he's in the pool.'

Krantz said, 'Yeah, that's why he decides to take you out of the play.'

'But to what end? He can't go on working at Parker, killing another couple of dozen people. If he believes we're on to him, he's going to cut to the chase. If he's thinking that his play is over, then he's going to want to kill the people he blames the most. He can't get to Pike, Krakauer's dead, so that leaves Wozniak.'

'Wozniak's dead, too.'

'Krakauer was a bachelor. Wozniak had a wife and a child, and they're in Palm Springs. That's where I got Wozniak's daybook. That's where we should be.'

Lucy's hands tightened around Ben, as if her newfound security was falling away. 'But why would he take Ben's picture? Why would he have our address?'

'Maybe he put those things together to distract us. We're here with you now; we're not with Wozniak's widow, and that's where he's going.'

'But you're just guessing. Did you see her address there? Were there pictures of her and her daughter?'

'No.'

'We *know* he had our address. We *know* he's a killer.' She gripped my arm then, as hard as Frank Garcia had gripped me when he had begged me to find his child. 'I need you right now.'

I looked at Krantz. 'Krantz, he's going to Palm Springs.'

Krantz didn't like it, but he was seeing it. 'You got her name and address?'

'Her name is Paulette Renfro. I don't remember the address, but I can tell you how to get there.'

Krantz was already dialing his phone. 'The States can get the address. They can get a car there before us.'

Krantz frowned as he made the call, and I knew what he was seeing in his head, a couple of sheriff's deps snapping the cuffs on Sobek, the two deputies getting the headlines and being interviewed by Katie Couric.

I looked back at Lucy, and gave her my best reassuring smile, but she wasn't at home to receive it.

'That's where he's going, Luce. I can't go back with you now, but just stay here until I get back. I'll take you home when I get back.'

Lucy's eyes were distant and cold, and hurt.

'I don't need you to take me home.'

Krantz went for the door even as he worked the phone, calling to Williams. 'Jerry, let's mount up. We're going over there.'

When we left the cafeteria, I glanced back at Lucy, but she wasn't looking at me. I didn't need to see her to know what was in her eyes:

I had chosen someone else once again.

CHAPTER 37

Sobek has not moved for the better part of an hour. The desert sun has driven the temperature inside his Jeep to almost 130 degrees, and his sweatshirt is soaked, but he imagines himself a predatory lizard, motionless in the brutal heat as he waits for prey. He is armored by muscle and resolve, and his mission commitment is without peer. He will wait for the rest of the day, if necessary, and the night, and for all the days to come.

It does not take that long.

A car eases up the residential streets below and pulls into the vic's drive. Sobek fingers the .357 when the car turns in, thinking it's her, but it isn't. A man gets out and stands looking at the house in the brilliant desert light, the man wearing jeans, an outrageous beachcomber shirt with the tail out, and sunglasses.

Sobek leans forward until his chest touches the steering wheel.

It is Joe Pike.

Pike goes to the front door, rings the bell, then goes around to the back of the house. Sobek can't see him back there, and thinks Pike must be sitting on the little veranda, or that he's found a way inside.

Sobek waits, but Pike does not return.

His heart pounds as he clutches the .357 with both hands. The gun is nestled between his legs where he can feel the weight of it on his penis. It feels good there.

He allows himself to smile, the first expression of emotion he's had in days. Pike has come to him.

Control.

Sobek settles back and waits for Paulette Wozniak and her daughter to return.

Paulette picked up her daughter Evelyn earlier that morning from Banning, where Evelyn had dropped her car for service. Evelyn's Volkswagen Beetle had gone kaput, and now Evelyn was without a car. First the boyfriend, then the apartment, now the car. Paulette had taken Evelyn to her job at Starbucks, then picked her up again, and was bringing her home to wait until her car was ready at the end of the day. Evelyn, of course, wasn't happy about it. Paulette never expected to find a strange car in her drive.

Evelyn was sulky and angry, and glowering in the passenger seat like she was fit to choke a dog. The only thing she'd said that morning was to ask if Paulette had heard from Mr Cole again. Paulette hadn't, and thought it odd that Evelyn would ask.

Paulette Renfro turned onto her street thinking the old cliché was true: When it rains, it pours. What could be next?

Evelyn glared at the strange car. 'Who's that?'

'I don't know.'

A neat, clean sedan was parked to the side of her drive, leaving her plenty of room to get into her garage. She did not recognize it, and wondered if one of her friends had gotten a new car without telling her. It was so hot out that they were probably in back, waiting under the veranda, though she couldn't imagine why anyone would be waiting for her unannounced.

Paulette pressed the garage opener, eased her car inside, then let Evelyn and herself into the house through the laundry room.

She went directly to the back glass doors in the family room, and that's where she saw him, standing tanned and lean and tall in the shade on the veranda. He was waiting for her to see him. He wore a flowered shirt that looked a size too big and dark glasses, and her first thought, the very first thought that came to her after all these years was, *'He hasn't aged a day and I must look like hell.'*

Evelyn said, 'There's a man outside.'

Joe raised a hand in greeting, and Paulette felt herself smile.

Evelyn said, 'You know that guy?'

Paulette opened the door, then stepped back to let him inside.

'Hello, Joe.'

'It's good to see you, Paulette.'

She had thought of this moment – of seeing him again – in her dreams and over morning coffee and during long quiet drives across the desert. She'd imagined what she would say and how she would say it in every possible way, but all she managed to get out was so lame.

'Would you like some water? It's so hot out.'

'That would be fine. Thank you.'

Evelyn got that ugly sulk on her face, the one that said she was unhappy and everyone was supposed to know it. You had to know it and do something about it, else she'd get even sulkier.

Evelyn said, 'You called him Joe.'

Paulette knew what was coming. 'Joe, this is Evelyn. Evie, you remember Joe Pike.'

Evelyn crossed her arms, then uncrossed them. Her face grew blotched. She said, 'Oh, fuck.'

Joe said, 'Paulette, I need to talk to you. About Woz, and about something that's going to happen.'

Before Paulette could say anything, Evelyn leaned toward Joe and shrieked, 'What could you *possibly* have to say? You killed him! Mother, he's wanted! He just murdered someone else!'

Paulette took her daughter by the arms, wanting to be gentle, but wanting to be firm, too.

'Evie. Go in the back. I'll talk to you later, but I want to talk with Joe now.'

Evelyn pulled away, livid and furious from a lifetime of mourning her father. 'Talk to him all you want! I'm gonna call the police!'

Paulette shook her daughter with a fierceness she hadn't felt in years. 'No! You won't!'

'He killed Daddy!'

'You *won't*!'

Joe spoke quietly. 'It's okay, Paulette. Let her call.'

Evelyn looked as surprised as Paulette felt, the two of them staring at Joe for a moment before Evie ran back toward the bedrooms.

Paulette said, 'Are you sure? I saw on the news.'

'I'll be gone before they get here. You look good, Paulette.'

He spoke with the absolute calm at which she had always marveled, and secretly envied. As if he were so certain of himself, so secure and confident that there was no room left for doubt. Whatever came, he could handle it; whatever the problem, he would solve it.

She felt herself blush. 'I've gotten older.'

'You've grown more beautiful.'

She blushed deeper, suddenly thinking how odd this was, to be here with this man after all this time, and to blush like a teenager because of him.

'Joe, take off those glasses. I can't see you.'

He took off the glasses.

My God, those eyes were incredible, so brilliantly blue that she could just stare. Instead, she got him the water.

'Joe, I've seen the news. A friend of yours was here. What happened?'

'We can talk about it later.' He glanced after Evelyn and shrugged. 'The police are coming.'

She nodded.

'I didn't kill that man. Someone else did. The same person who killed another six people.'

'That's what your friend said.'

'His name is Laurence Sobek. He was one of Woz's

informants. When the story is out, you're going to have the press and the police bring up everything that happened on that day. They're going to dig into Woz again. Do you understand?'

'I don't care.'

'It could hurt you.'

'It can't.'

Behind them, Evelyn spoke in a voice so soft that Paulette hadn't heard it since Evie was a child.

'Why could it hurt her, and why do you care?'

Paulette turned and looked at her daughter. Evelyn was peeking around the corner like a five-year-old, her face distant and smooth.

'Did you call the police?'

Evie shook her head.

Pike said, 'Go call. Your mother and I have to talk.'

Evelyn went to the bookcase and took down the picture of her father and Paulette and Joe Pike.

'She keeps this out where anybody can see it.' She looked at Paulette. 'Why do you keep this goddamned picture? Why keep a picture of someone who killed the man you loved?'

Paulette Wozniak considered her adult daughter for a time, then said, 'The man I love is still alive.'

Evie stared at her.

Paulette said, 'Joe didn't kill your father. Your father killed himself. He took his own life.' She turned back to Joe and looked at the placid blue eyes, the eyes that made her smile. 'I'm not stupid, Joe. I figured it out years ago when I went through his notebooks.'

Joe said, 'The missing pages.'

'Yes. He wrote about the Chihuahua brothers, and that whole mess. And then, later, just days before it happened, he wrote how he felt trapped. He didn't say he was planning on it. He didn't say what he was going to do or how, but he wrote that there was always a way out, and that a lot of cops had gone that way before.'

Evie was pulling at her fingers now, pulling and twisting like she was trying to rip them off.

'What are you talking about? What are you saying?'

Paulette felt a horrible pain in her chest. 'I didn't know for sure until I went through his books after he was dead, and then, I don't know, I just didn't want you to know the truth about him. You loved him so. I took out those pages and destroyed them so you could never find them, but I know in my heart what he was saying there. Joe didn't kill your father. Your father took his own life, and Joe took the blame to protect you, and me.'

Evie shook her head, and said, 'I don't believe you.'

'It's true, honey.'

Paulette tried to put her arm around Evelyn, but Evelyn pushed her away. Paulette looked at Joe then, as if maybe he would know what to do in the sure certain way of his, but that's when a large, muscular man wearing sunglasses stepped out of the kitchen behind Joe, aimed a black pistol, and pulled the trigger.

Paulette screamed, 'Joe!'

Her shout was drowned by a deafening sound that hit her like a physical blow and made her ears ring.

Joe hunched forward, then spun so quickly that he seemed not to move at all, was just suddenly facing the man, a big gun in his own hand, firing three huge times so fast that the shots were one BAMBAMBAM.

The big man slammed backward, hitting the kitchen floor with a wheezing grunt, and then there was silence.

The moment was absolutely still until Joe hunched again, and that's when Paulette saw the blood spreading on Joe's back like some great red rose.

She said, 'OhmyLord! Joe!'

Joe winced when he tried to straighten, then looked at Paulette, and smiled. She hadn't seen that smile in so many years that her heart filled and she wanted to cry, though the smile was small and hurt.

He said, 'Gotta go now, Paulette. You take care of your baby.'

Joe Pike held her gaze for another moment, then turned away as the large man sat straight up on the kitchen floor as if rising from the dead and shot Joe again.

Joe Pike fell hard.

The two women finally arrive, and Sobek eases down the hill to Paulette's house. He knows from watching that none of the neighbors are home, so he strolls up the drive and into Paulette Wozniak's garage without fear of being seen.

He creeps through the garage past Paulette Wozniak's ticking car, and puts his ear to the utility door, but doesn't hear anything. He knows that doors like this usually open to a laundry room or a kitchen, and decides to take the chance that Pike and the others aren't poised on the other side. He turns the knob, then cracks the door, and sees a washer and dryer.

He can hear voices now, and then a woman shouts, 'What could you *possibly* have to say? You killed him! Mother, he's wanted! He just murdered someone else!'

Sobek grips the .357, pulls back the hammer, then eases into the laundry. He peeks into the kitchen. No one. He creeps through the kitchen, careful not to make any noise, getting closer and closer to the voices until they are just around the corner in the family room. Two women and the Pikester.

Sobek takes a deep breath, then another, then steps around the corner and shoots Joe Pike in the back.

Ka-Boom!

The .357 kicks harder than the little .22s, and before he can shoot again Pike has a gun in his hands and fires BAMBAMBAM. Three bricks hit Sobek in the chest all at the same time, knocking him flat on his ass, and making him see stars.

He thinks he is dead, then realizes that the Kevlar vest

he's wearing under the sweatshirt has saved him. Most cops wear lightweight vests designed to stop common rounds like the 9mm or .45, but Sobek wears the heavier model, rated at stopping anything up to and including the .44 Magnum.

Control.

He hears voices. They're talking. Pike is still alive, but wounded.

Second chance.

Sobek sits up and shoots Joe Pike again even as the younger woman screams.

Pike drops like a bag of wet laundry, and Sobek says, *'Cool!'*

The older woman falls to her knees beside Pike and grabs for his gun, but Sobek runs forward and kicks her in the ribs. He is dizzy from the hits that he's taken, but his kick is solid and upends her.

A red pool spreads through Pike's shirt.

Sobek looks at Paulette Wozniak, then the younger woman. 'Are you Abel Wozniak's daughter?'

Neither of them answer.

Sobek points the .357 at the older one, and the younger one says, 'Yes.'

'Okay. Let's get a couple of chairs, and you two sit down.'

Sobek feels disoriented and nauseated from the chest trauma, but he tapes their wrists and ankles to two wooden dining-room chairs and puts more tape over their mouths. Then he peels off his shirt and vest to inspect his wounds. The entire center of his chest is a throbbing purple bruise. The bullets probably broke some ribs. Christ, that Pike can shoot. All three bullets would've been in his heart.

Sobek spits on Pike's body, and screams, 'FUCK YOU!'

The screaming makes his head spin worse, and he has to sit or throw up. When the spinning subsides, he considers the women.

'You're next.'

He is thinking about how best to kill them when he hears a car door out front and sees two deputies strolling toward the house.

Sobek drags the two women into a back room to hide them even as the doorbell rings. He puts on his shirt, not even thinking of the three bullet holes, and hurries to the door as it rings again. He plasters on a big smile, opens the door with a surprised expression, and says, 'Oh, wow, the Highway Patrol. Are we under arrest?'

The two deps stare at him for a moment, and then the closer one smiles. Friendly and getting the joke. 'Is Mrs Renfro at home?'

'Oh, sure. She's my aunt. Did you want to see her?'

'Yes, if we could.'

'Come on in out of that heat and I'll bring you back. She's in the pool.'

The other dep smiles then and takes off his campaign hat. He says, 'Man, I could go for some of that.'

Sobek nods, and smiles wider. 'Hey, why not? I'll get you guys a beer or a soft drink, if you like.'

He holds the door and lets them step past him into the living room, then closes the door, takes out his .357, and shoots both deputies in the back, puts the gun to their heads, and shoots them again.

CHAPTER 38

Verdugo to Palm Springs was less than an hour. Paulette didn't answer when I called, which none of us liked, but I left word on her machine that she should drive directly to the Palm Springs Police Department and wait for us there.

During the drive, Krantz spoke several times on the radio, once getting a report that sheriffs had arrived on scene at Paulette's, and that everything was fine.

We left the interstate at North Palm Springs and drove directly to Paulette's house in the hills above the windmills. A clean new sedan that I didn't recognize was parked in the drive. The garage door was down, and no other cars were parked on the block. The house, like the neighborhood, was still.

I said, 'I thought the sheriffs were supposed to be here.'

'They were.'

Krantz got on his radio and told someone to confirm with the sheriffs, then have them send another car.

We parked beside the sedan, and got out.

Williams said, 'Goddamn. It's hot as hell out here.'

We didn't make it to the front door. We were passing the big picture window when all three of us saw the body in the family room, and a cold sweat broke over my back and legs even in the awful desert heat.

'That's Joe.'

Williams said, 'She-it.'

Krantz fumbled out his gun. 'Jerome, radio back. Tell'm we need cars right goddamned now. I don't care who. Tell'm to send an ambulance.'

Williams ran back to the unit.

Two swerving blood trails led out of the living room through the family room and into the kitchen. I couldn't see any other bodies, but I thought it might be Paulette and Evelyn. Then I saw that the sliding back doors were open.

'I'm going in, Krantz.'

'Goddamnit, we gotta wait for backup. He might still be in there.'

'Those people might be bleeding to death. I'm going in.'

The front door was locked. I trotted around the side of the house, popping fast peeks through every window I came to, not seeing anything unusual until I found Paulette and Evelyn in the rear corner bedroom. They were taped to chairs with duct tape covering their wrists and ankles and mouths, and struggling to get free. I tapped on the glass, and their eyes went wide. Evelyn struggled harder, but Paulette stared at me. I made a calming gesture, then spread my hands, asking if Sobek was in the house.

Paulette nodded.

I mouthed, 'Where?'

Paulette shook her head. She didn't know.

I moved along the rear of the house to the glass doors, dropped into a push-up position, and peeked inside. Joe was slumped on his side, the back of his shirt damp with blood. I was trying to see if his chest was moving when I heard a voice. The two blood trails ran past Pike through the kitchen and into the laundry room; that's where the voice came from. I looked at Pike again, and this time the tears started and my nose clogged, but I made the tears stop.

Krantz came toward me from the opposite side of the house, stopping on the other side of the doors. He had his gun out, holding it with both hands. 'I've got units and paramedics on the way.'

'Paulette and her daughter are alive in the room at the

end of the hall. I'm hearing something in the garage. You get them out of here, okay? Get them safe.'

'What are you going to do?'

'Someone's in the garage.'

Krantz swallowed, and I could see then that he heard the voice. 'Ah, maybe I should do that.'

I liked him then, for maybe the first time. 'I'm better, Harvey. I'll do it. Okay?'

He stared at me, and then he nodded.

'Just get them out of the house. Where's Williams?'

'Covering the front.'

'He got a radio?'

'Yeah.'

'Tell him we're going inside and not to shoot me, then get those women.'

I stepped through the doors. The smell of blood was thin, and raw, and the great black desert flies had already found their way into the house. Pike was out in the center of the floor, but I did not go to him. I stayed near the walls, trying to see as many doors as possible.

I whispered, 'Just us, buddy.'

The blood trails arced through the kitchen and into a laundry room, where they stopped at a closed door. The voice was behind the door. Maybe Sobek was sitting in the garage talking to the bodies. Lunatics do that.

Here's what you do: You open the door, or you walk away and wait for the Palm Springs PD. If you walk away, then whoever is in the garage bleeds to death and you have to live with that, and with knowing you didn't go in because you were scared. These are the choices.

I closed my eyes, and whispered, 'I don't want to get shot.'

Then I hammered back my pistol, took six fast breaths, and went in.

Sobek's red Cherokee was parked directly in front of me, the sheriff's car next to it, both engines ticking. The two deps were in the front seat of their car, the remains of their heads slumped together in death. The voice was coming from their radio. I looked under both cars, then glanced into their back seats. Sobek wasn't there.

I closed the utility door behind me, and went back into the kitchen. Krantz had freed Paulette and her daughter. They were behind him, just coming into the family room from the hall. I thought we were going to make it. I thought that we'd get them out of there, and safe, but that's when Jerome Williams shouted something from somewhere outside, and two fast shots cracked through the house.

Krantz shouted, 'Jerome!'

Laurence Sobek ran out of a doorway at the end of the hall and in that crazy moment might have been Joe Pike; large and powerful, and dressed as Pike used to dress, even down to the sunglasses. But not. This was a mutant Pike, an anti-Pike, distorted and swollen and ugly. He didn't look like Curtis Wood now; he looked more like the inbred villain in a slasher movie.

Paulette, Evelyn, and Krantz were in the line of fire between me and Sobek. I yelled, 'DOWN! GET DOWN!'

Krantz shoved Paulette out of the way, aimed past Evelyn, and fired twice, hitting Sobek in the big torso both times.

Sobek came off the wall firing blindly, his bullets hitting the floor and the ceiling. One of his rounds caught me under the right arm with a hard slap, knocked away my gun, and spun me into the refrigerator.

Paulette ran to her daughter, again blocking Krantz's line of fire.

I yelled, 'Head shot, Krantz! The head! He's wearing a vest!'

Sobek charged straight down the hall, and barreled into Paulette, wrapping her in his arms and knocking Evelyn aside. He was crying, and his eyes were hopping as if his brain was on fire. He put his gun to her head.

'I'm not done yet. I'm not done.'

Krantz yelled, 'Drop your gun! Put it down, Curtis!'

My arm felt wet and tingly, as if worms were crawling beneath the skin. I tried to pick up my gun, but the arm wouldn't work.

Sobek jammed his weapon harder into Paulette's neck. 'You drop your own fuckin' gun, Krantz! You put it down or I'll kill this bitch. I'll do it, you bastard. I'll do it right fuckin' now!'

Krantz backed up, his gun shaking so badly that if he fired he would as likely hit Paulette as Sobek. I think Krantz knew that, too.

I tried to pick up my gun with my left hand. Sobek didn't even seem to know I was there anymore. He was focused on Krantz.

'I MEAN IT GODDAMNIT KRANTZ I'M GONNA DO IT I'M GONNA DO IT RIGHT NOW BLOW HER BRAINS OUT AND THEN I'M GONNA KILL MYSELF I DON'T CARE I DON'T CARE!'

It is against LAPD policy for an officer to give up his or her weapon. They teach that at the Academy, they live by it, and it is the right thing to teach and live by. You give up your weapon, and you're done.

But if you don't do what Laurence Sobek says, and someone dies, you will always wonder. It is another choice and another door, and you won't know what lies behind it until you go there.

He was going to kill her.

'Okay, Curtis. Just let her go and we'll talk. I'm putting the gun down like you want. Just don't hurt her, Curtis. Please do not hurt her.'

Krantz put his gun on the floor, and for the second time that day I liked Harvey Krantz.

I spoke quietly. 'Sobek? Why'd you kill Dersh? He wasn't part of this?'

Crazy eyes danced to me. 'Pike killed Dersh. Don't you watch the news?'

Krantz said, 'Shut up, Cole. Curtis, put down the gun. Please.'

Sobek walked Paulette closer to Krantz, shaking his head. 'I'm not done yet. They're going to pay for the Coopster. They're going to pay for that.'

Behind Sobek, Pike moved.

I said, 'Tell us about Dersh, Sobek. Tell us why you set up Pike.'

Sobek pointed his gun at me, and cocked the hammer. 'I didn't.'

Pike's eyes opened.

Krantz said, 'Damnit, Cole, shut up. Curtis, don't kill him. Let this woman go.'

Pike pushed himself up. His face was a mask of blood. His shirt was wet with it. He picked up his gun.

Sobek said, 'She's gotta die, and Wozniak's kid is gonna die, too. But you know what, Harvey?'

'What?'

Sobek aimed his .357 point-blank at Harvey Krantz.

'You're gonna die first.'

I said, 'DeVille isn't dead.'

Laurence Sobek stopped as if I'd hit him with a board. His face filled with rage, he aimed his gun at me again, then brought it back to Krantz. I could see his gun hand tighten.

He said, 'This is for killing my father.'

Krantz yelled, 'NO!'

Sobek was squeezing the trigger when Joe Pike brought up his weapon and fired one round through the back of Laurence Sobek's head. Sobek collapsed in a heap, and then there was silence.

Pike fell forward onto his hands, and almost at once tried to push himself up again.

Paulette said, 'Joe, lie down. Please lie down.'

Krantz just stood there. I could hear the sirens far away now, but drawing closer.

I struggled to my feet and went to Joe. Blood ran down my arm and dripped from my fingers.

'Stay down, Joseph. Got an ambulance on the way.'

Pike said, 'No. If I go down now, I'll spend the rest of my life in prison. Right, Krantz?'

Krantz said, 'You're going to bleed to death.'

Pike found his feet and stood, using Paulette to steady himself. He put his pistol into the waistband of his pants, then looked at me. 'You're shot.'

'You're shot twice.'

Pike nodded. 'It's so easy to show you up.'

He staggered then, but I caught him.

Paulette said, 'Please, Joe.' She was crying.

Pike was looking at me. 'Maybe there'll be something at Sobek's to put him with Dersh.'

'There wasn't.'

Pike looked tired. He took a handkerchief from his pants, but the blood had soaked through and it was red.

Paulette Wozniak said, 'Oh, damn.'

She pulled off her shirt and used it to wipe his face. She was wearing a white bra, but nobody looked or said anything, and I thought in that moment I could love her myself, truly and always.

The corner of Joe's mouth twitched, and he touched her face. 'Gotta go.'

Paulette blinked at the tears.

Joe let his fingers linger. 'You really are more beautiful.'

Then he turned away for the door, leaving his fingerprints in blood on her face.

Krantz said, 'I can't let you go, Pike. I appreciate what you did, and I'll stand up at your trial, but for now it's over.'

Krantz had his gun again. He was pale, and shaken, but he had the gun.

I said, 'Don't be stupid, Krantz.'

'It's over.'

Pike kept walking.

Krantz aimed his gun, but it was shaking as badly now as when he was aiming at Sobek. 'I mean it, Pike. You're a wanted man. You are under arrest, and you're going to stand trial. I won't let you leave this house.'

Krantz steadied the gun with his second hand, and pulled back the hammer, and that's when I twisted the gun away from him with my good hand. I shoved him against the wall.

Krantz screamed, 'You're interfering with an officer, goddamnit! You're obstructing justice!'

Pike walked out the front door without closing it, and then he was gone.

I said, 'Goodbye, Joe.'

Krantz slumped to the floor and put his face in his hands. The sirens were working their way up the hill and would soon arrive. They would probably pass Pike on their way up, and I wondered if any of them would notice the car driven by the bloody man. Probably not.

Krantz said, 'You shouldn't've done that, Cole. You aided and abetted his escape. I'm going to arrest you. It's going to cost your license.'

I nodded.

'You didn't help him, you asshole. He's going to bleed to death. He's going to die.'

The sirens arrived.

CHAPTER 39

Of the two shots Sobek fired at Jerome Williams, only one connected, nipping an artery in his thigh. He would make it. My own wound was a bit more complicated. The bullet had torn through the outside of my right pectoral muscle, clipped the third lateral rib, then exited through my right latissimus dorsi. One of the hospital's resident surgeons came down to take a look, and said, 'Hmm.'

You have to worry when they say that.

'I can clean you up,' he said. 'But you're going to need some reconstructive surgery to the muscle group. Your pectoris attacher tendon is partially sheared, and the anterior joint capsule needs to be repaired.'

'How long will that take?'

'Four hours, tops.'

'Not how long will the surgery take. How long would I have to be here?'

'Three days.'

'Forget it.'

'Just want you to know the score. I gotta put you out anyway to take care of this.'

'Just give me a local. You're not putting me anywhere, and I'm not going out.' I wanted to be awake to find out about Pike. I figured they'd find him bled out on the side of a road. I wanted to be awake when the word came because I wanted to go to him.

'It's going to hurt like a sonofabitch with just a local.'

'Pretend you're a dentist and shoot me up, for chrissake.'

He gave me about two thousand injections, then cleaned the wound, and stitched the muscles and skin. It hurt worse than he said, but maybe it wasn't just the shoulder.

When he was done, he said, 'I'm giving you a Percocet script for the pain. You're going to need it. When the anesthetic wears off you're going to hurt even worse. This is strong stuff, so be sure you take just what I'm writing here. You need to see your own doctor tomorrow.'

'I'll be in jail.'

He sighed again and handed me the prescription. 'Take twice as much.'

He used thirty-two stitches to close the wound.

Krantz officially arrested me in the Palm Springs Hospital emergency room while Williams was in surgery. Stan Watts had driven out, and he stood there with a blank expression as Krantz read me the rights. Krantz said, 'Stan, I'm having him brought to County-USC so they can look at him. Maybe they'll want to book him in the jail ward there, and keep him overnight.'

Watts didn't answer.

'I want you to be there when they look at him. If they give him a pass, bring him over to Parker for the booking. I'll take care of it myself when I get back.'

Watts didn't answer again; he just kept staring at me with the blank look.

Krantz walked away to talk to the press.

When Krantz was gone, Watts said, 'I spent the whole ride out trying to figure out whether to blame you for Dolan.'

'I've been doing some of that myself.'

'Yeah, I imagine you would. But I know Dolan more than ten years, and I know what she was like. When she was hit, I saw how you went in. You didn't know what was in there, but you went right in. I saw how you covered her with your jacket.'

He stood there for a time like he didn't know what else

403

to say, then put out his hand. I gave him my left, and we shook.

I said, 'Any word on Pike?'

'Not yet. Krantz said he was hit pretty bad.'

'Yeah. Bad. You guys finish going through Sobek's garage?'

'Most of it. SID's there now.'

'You see anything that clears Pike?'

Watts shook his head. 'No.'

I considered the Percocet script, wondering if it could take away this kind of hurt.

Watts said, 'C'mon, I'll take you back.'

'Krantz called a radio car.'

'Screw the radio car. You can ride with me.'

We didn't say ten words between Palm Springs and L.A. until we were approaching the exit for the County-USC Medical Center, where Krantz had ordered him to bring me.

'Where's your car?'

'Dolan's.'

'You drive with that arm?'

'I can drive.'

He continued past the County-USC exit without a word and brought me to Dolan's. We pulled into her drive, and sat there, staring at the house. Someone would have to go back to Sobek's garage for her Beemer. Someone would have to bring it home.

'I'm not going to book you tonight, but you gotta come in tomorrow.'

'Krantz will be pissed.'

'You let me worry about Krantz. You gonna come in or am I gonna have to go look for you?'

'I'll come in.'

He shrugged like he hadn't expected anything else, and said, 'I'll bet she's got a pretty good bottle of tequila in there. How about we tip one for her?'

'Sure.'

Dolan kept a spare house key beneath a clay pot in her backyard. I didn't ask Watts how he knew. When we got inside, Watts knew where she kept the tequila, too.

Her house was as quiet as any house could be, as if something had vanished from her home when she died. Maybe it had. We sat and drank, and after a while Stan Watts went back into her bedroom. He stayed there for a long time, then came out with a small onyx box, and sat with the box in his lap, and drinking. When he'd had enough to drink, he opened the box and took out a small blue heart. He slipped the heart into his jacket pocket, then put his face in his hands and cried like a baby.

I sat with him for almost an hour. I didn't ask him about the heart or the box, but I cried with and for him, and for Dolan, too. And for Pike, and me, because my life was falling apart.

The human heart is worth crying for, even if it's made of onyx.

After a while I used Dolan's phone to check my messages. Joe hadn't called, and neither had Lucy. The news of Laurence Sobek's identification and the events in Palm Springs had broken, and I hoped she would've called, but there you go.

I thought that I should call her, but didn't. I don't know why. I could shoot it out with Laurence Sobek, but calling the woman I loved seemed beyond me.

Instead, I went into Dolan's kitchen for the photograph she'd taken of me at Forest Lawn. I stared at it for a long time, and then I took it. It was right there on the refrigerator, but I hoped that Watts hadn't seen it. I wanted it to be between me and Samantha, and I didn't want it between Watts and her.

I went back into the living room and told Watts that I had to leave, but he didn't hear me, or, if he heard, didn't think I was worth answering. He was someplace deep within himself, or maybe in that little blue heart. In a way, I guess he was with Dolan.

I left him like that, got my prescription filled, then drove home, wishing I had a little blue heart of my own. A secret heart where, if I looked real hard, I could find the people who were dear to me.

CHAPTER 40

My home felt large and hollow that evening. I phoned the guys who work for Joe, but they hadn't heard from him, and were upset by the news. I paced around the house, working up my nut to call Lucy, but thinking of Samantha Dolan. I kept seeing her earlier that morning, telling me she was going to stay after me, that she always got what she wanted, and that she was going to make me love her. Now she was dead and I would never be able to tell her that she already had.

My shoulder throbbed with a fierceness I didn't think possible. I took some of the Percocet, washed my hands and face, then called Lucy. Even dialing the phone hurt.

Ben answered on the third ring, lowering his voice when he realized it was me.

'Mom's mad.'

'I know. Will she speak to me?'

'You sure you want to?'

'I'm sure.'

I waited for her to come to the phone, thinking about what I would say and how I would say it. When Lucy picked up, her voice was more distant than I'd hoped.

She said, 'I guess you were right.'

'You heard about Joe?'

'Lieutenant Krantz called. He told me that Joe left the scene wounded.'

'That's right. I took away Krantz's gun so that Joe could leave. Officially, I'm under arrest. I have to go down to Parker Center tomorrow and turn myself in.'

'They call that aiding and abetting.'

I felt slow and stupid and sick to my stomach. My entire right side hurt.

'That's right, Lucy. I took Krantz's gun. I interfered. I committed a felony, and when I'm convicted I'll lose my license, and that's that. I'll get a job as a rent-a-cop, or maybe I can re-up with the Army. Be all I can be.'

Her voice softened. 'Were you going to tell me that you were shot?'

'Krantz tell you that?'

'Oh, Elvis.'

Sounding tired, she hung up.

I stood at the phone for a time, thinking that I should call her back, but I didn't.

Eventually, the cat came home, sniffing hopefully when he eased into the kitchen. I opened a can of Bumble Bee tuna, and sat with him on the floor. The Bumble Bee is his favorite. He lapped at it twice, then came to sniff my shoulder.

He licked at the bandages, and I let him.

There isn't so much love in the world that you can turn it away when it's offered.

The next morning, Charlie brought me to Parker Center, where Krantz and Stan Watts walked me through the booking process. Neither Krantz nor Watts mentioned that I had spent the night at home. Maybe they had worked it out between them.

I was arraigned that afternoon, a trial date was set in Superior Court, and I was released without bail. I wasn't really thinking about the proceedings; I was thinking about Joe.

Paulette Renfro and Evelyn Wozniak drove in from Palm Springs for the arraignment. After, they sat with Charlie and me to discuss what had occurred between me and Krantz. Paulette and Evelyn both offered to lie on my behalf, but I declined. I wanted them to tell the truth. Charlie listened to their version of events, which matched with mine. When they were done, Charlie leaned back and said, 'You're fucked.'

'That's what I like about you, Charlie. You're inspirational.'

'You want my legal advice, take them up on their offer to lie. We can cook up a good story, then it's the three of you against Krantz in court, and you'll skate.'

'Charlie, I don't want to play it that way.'

'Why not?'

That Charlie is something.

Later, Charlie spoke with the prosecutor handling the case, a young woman named Gilstrap out of USC Law who wanted to be governor. He came back and told me that I could plead guilty to the one felony charge of interfering with a police officer, and they would drop the obstruction of justice charge. If I took the plea, I would receive probation with no jail time served. I said, 'It's copping to a felony, Charlie. It means I lose my license.'

'You fight this, you're gonna lose your license anyway. You'll also do eighteen months.'

I took the plea, and became a convicted felon.

The next day I went into the hospital to have my shoulder rebuilt. It took three hours, not four, but left me in a cast that held my arm up from my body as if my shoulder were dislocated. I told the doctor that it made me look like a waiter. The doctor said another centimeter to the left, and Sobek's bullet would've severed the nerve that controlled the small muscle groups in my hand and forearm. Then I would've looked like overcooked macaroni.

Thinking about that made me feel better about the cast.

That evening, Lucy brought flowers.

She let her fingers drift along the cast, then kissed my shoulder, and didn't look so mad anymore. A kindness came into her eyes that frightened me more than Laurence Sobek or getting shot or losing my license.

I said, 'Are we over?'

She stared at me for a long time before she shook her head. 'I don't know. It feels different.'

'Okay.'

'Let's be honest: This job was an excuse to come here. I came to Los Angeles because I love you. I changed my life to be with you, but also because I wanted to change. I had no promises or expectations about where we would go with this, or when, or even if any of it would work out. I knew what you were and what it meant the first time we met.'

'I love you.' I didn't know what else to say.

'I know, but I don't trust that love as much as I used to. Do you see?'

'I understand.'

'Don't just say that.'

'I get it, Lucy, but I couldn't have done anything else. Joe needed me. If he's not dead, he still needs me, and I will help him.'

'You're angry.'

'Yeah. I'm angry.'

Neither of us said very much more, and after a while she left. I wondered if I would see her again, or ever feel the same about her, or she about me, and couldn't believe that I was even having such thoughts.

Some days really suck.

The next morning, Abbot Montoya wheeled Frank Garcia into my room. Frank looked withered and old in the chair, but he gripped my leg in greeting, and his grip was strong. He asked about my arm, and about Joe, but after a while he seemed to drift, and his eyes filled with tears.

'You got that sonofabitch.'

'Joe got him.'

'You and Joe, and the woman who came to my house.'

'Her name was Samantha Dolan.'

His face screwed up, concerned. 'They haven't heard anything about Joe?'

'Not yet, Frank.'

'Anything you need, you let me know. Lawyers, doctors, I don't care what. Legal, illegal, it doesn't matter. My heart belongs to you now. If I can do it for you, I'll do it.'

He started to sob, and I felt embarrassed.

'You don't owe me anything, Frank.'

He squeezed my leg harder, so hard I thought the bone might break. 'Everything I have is yours. You don't have to understand that, or me. Just know that it's so.'

I thought about Rusty Swetaggen, and understood.

When they were leaving, Abbot Montoya stepped back through the door.

'Frank means it.'

'I know.'

'No. You don't know, but you will. I mean it, too. You are ours now, Mr Cole. Forever and always. That is a blood oath. Perhaps we are not so far from the White Fence, even after all these years.'

When he left I stared at the ceiling.

'Latins.'

Later that afternoon, Charlie Bauman was filling my room with cigarette smoke when Branford, Krantz, and Stan Watts dropped by.

Krantz stood at the end of my bed with his hands in his pockets, saying, 'A couple of kids found Pike's car outside Twentynine Palms.' Twentynine Palms is a barren, rugged place northeast of Palm Springs where the Marines have their Ground Combat Center. They do live-fire exercises out there, bringing in the fast movers to napalm the sand.

Charlie sat up.

I said, 'Was Pike in it?'

Branford glanced at my cast. 'Nope. Just a lot of his

blood. The whole front seat was soaked. We've got the States out there doing a sweep.'

They were staring at me like I had helped him park the car.

Bauman said, 'You're not still going to prosecute Pike for this Dersh thing, are you, Branford?'

Branford just looked at him.

'Oh, for chrissake.'

I said, 'Krantz, you know better. You saw how Sobek was dressed, just like Pike. He's who the old lady saw.'

Krantz met my eyes. 'I don't know anything like that, Cole. Mrs Kimmel saw arrow tattoos. Sobek didn't have tattoos.'

'So he painted them on, then washed them off.'

'I heard you ask Sobek if he did Dersh. I heard Sobek deny it.'

Charlie waved his cigarette, annoyed. 'You want a signed confession? What are we talking about here?'

'I want facts. We haven't been sitting on our asses with this, Bauman. We ran everything Pike said about his alibi through the system, and it came back just the way I thought it would: bullshit. No hits on a black minivan, Trudy, or Matt. We flashed Sobek's picture in a six-pack for Amanda Kimmel, but she *still* puts the finger on Pike.'

Branford said, 'We've got the murder weapon, the GSR, and the motive; that gives us Pike.'

Charlie said, 'Pike's statement wasn't a secret. Sobek could've tossed the gun off the pier to match with Pike's story. If Sobek didn't kill Dersh, why was Jesus Lorenzo killed just a few hours later? You writing that off as a coincidence?'

'I'm writing it off as something I can't ask Sobek because Sobek is dead. Look, Pike saved Krantz's life, and those two women's, but I can't just forget about Dersh because we owe him one. You give me some proof that he didn't do it, or that Sobek did, I'll think it over.'

Charlie Bauman waved his cigarette like he didn't

believe Branford for a second, then considered Krantz. 'Tell me something, Lieutenant? You really draw down on Pike after Pike saved you?'

'Yes, I really did that.'

'Even after he saved your life?'

'He murdered Eugene Dersh, and he's going to answer for it. What I feel doesn't matter.'

'Well, at least you feel something.'

No one said much after that, and pretty soon everybody left but Watts.

He said, 'We buried Samantha this morning. Had over a thousand officers in the ranks. It was nice.'

'I'll bet it was.'

'We get any word on Pike, I'll let you know.'

'Thanks, Stan. I appreciate it.'

Thinking back, I'm sure the only reason Stan Watts tagged along with Krantz and Branford that day was to share Samantha Dolan's final moment with me, and to tell me that a thousand officers had seen her off.

I don't think he would've come for any other reason.

I wish I could have been there to see her off with them.

I left the hospital the next day.

The doctors raised hell, but I couldn't take lying in bed with Joe still missing. I hoped that Joe was alive, and thought that if anyone could survive it would be him, but I also knew that if Pike had found his way into the ravines and arroyos of the desert, his body might not be discovered for years.

I took too many painkillers, but still couldn't drive with the cast, so I hired a cab to take me out to the desert. I went back to Paulette's house, then up to Twentynine Palms, and tried to imagine what Joe might've been thinking, and where he might've gone, but couldn't.

I checked all the nearby motels and service stations, and ate so many Percocet that I threw up twice.

I went back to the desert the next day, and the next, but

never found a trace. The cab fares totaled eight hundred dollars.

Perhaps if I were a better detective I could have gotten a line on him, or found his body, though not if Joe was alive and covering his tracks.

Telling myself that was better than thinking him dead.

When I wasn't at the desert I haunted Santa Monica, walking Joe's route both during the day and at night, talking to clerks and surfers and gang-bangers and body-builders and maintenance people and food vendors and the limitless armies of street people. I walked the night route so often that the hookers who worked Ocean Avenue brought home-baked pie for me and Starbucks coffee. Maybe it was the cast. They all wanted to sign it.

My friends at the FBI and the DMV ran still more searches for black minivans, and people named Trudy and Matt, and I even got them to badger their friends in other states to do the same. Nothing turned up, and after a while my friends stopped returning my calls. I guess our friendship had its limits.

Eight days after I left the hospital I phoned Stan Watts. 'Is there anything on Joe?'

'Not yet.'

'Has SID finished with Sobek's garage?'

He sighed. 'Man, you don't give up, do you?'

'Not even after I'm dead.'

'They finished, but you're not going to like it much. They got this sharp kid over there named Chen. He tied Sobek to all of the vics except Dersh. I'm sorry.'

'Maybe he missed something.'

'This kid is *sharp*, Cole. He lasered Dersh's place looking for fibers that could've come from Sobek's, but found nothing. He lasered Sobek's, looking for something that might've come from Dersh, but that was a bust, too. He doped both places, and ran gas chromes, but struck out

414

all the way around. I was hoping he'd find something that put Sobek with Dersh, too, but there's nothing.'

Chen was the guy who'd done the work up at Lake Hollywood. I remember being impressed when I'd read it. 'Think you could send over these new reports?'

'Shit, there's gotta be two hundred pages here.'

'Just the work he did on Dersh's place, and Sobek's garage. I don't need the others.'

'You got a fax there?'

'Yeah.' I gave him the number.

He said, 'You really been taking a cab out to the desert?'

'How'd you hear about that?'

'You know something, Cole? You and Dolan were of the same stripe. I can see why she liked you.'

Then he hung up.

While I waited for the fax, I reread Chen's Lake Hollywood report, and was again impressed with its detail. By the time I finished, the new reports had arrived, and I found them exhaustive. Chen had collected over one hundred separate fiber and soil samples from Dersh's home and property, and compared them with samples taken from Sobek's apartment, clothing, shoes, and vehicle, but found nothing that would tie the two together. No physical evidence tied Dersh to Joe Pike, either, but that didn't seem to bother Krantz.

I read the new report twice, but by the end of the second reading felt as if I was wasting my time – no matter how often I turned the pages, no new evidence appeared, and Chen's evidentiary conclusions remained unchanged. I was thinking that my time would be better spent looking for Trudy, or going back to the desert, when I realized that something was different between the work that Chen had done at Lake Hollywood and the work he'd done at Dersh's house.

I had read these reports hoping to find something exculpatory for Pike, but maybe what I was looking for wasn't something that was in the report. Maybe it had been left out.

I phoned the SID office, and asked for John Chen.

The woman who answered the phone said, 'May I tell him what it's regarding?'

I was still thinking about what the report didn't say when I answered her.

'Tell him it's about Joe Pike.'

CHAPTER 41

The New, Improved John Chen

John Chen had leased the Porsche Boxster – also known as the 'tangmobile – on the very day he was promoted for his exemplary performance in the Karen Garcia homicide. He couldn't afford it, but John had decided that one could either accept one's miserable place in life (even if, like John, one was born to it) or defy it, and you could defy it if you just had the balls to take action. This was the new, improved John Chen, redefining himself with the motto: *If I can take it, it's mine.*

First comes the 'tangmobile, then comes the 'tang.

Just as John Chen had had his eye on the Boxster, so had he been head over heels in heat for Teresa Wu, a microbiology graduate student at UCLA and part-time assistant at SID. Teresa Wu had lustrous black hair, skin the color of warm butter, and professorial red glasses that John thought were the sexiest thing going.

Still flush with the accolades he'd garnered for his work at Lake Hollywood, John drove back to the office, made sure everyone there knew about the Boxster, then asked Teresa Wu for a date.

It was the first time he had asked her out, and only the second time he'd spoken to her. It was only the third time he'd been brave enough to ask out *anyone.*

Teresa Wu peered at him over the top of the red glasses, rolled her eyes as if he'd just asked her to share a snot sandwich, and said, 'Oh, please, John. No way.'

Bitch.

417

That was a week ago, but part of John's new-found philosophy was a second motto: *No guts, no nookie.* John had spent the next seven days working up his nut to ask her out again, and was just about to do so when some guy named Elvis Cole called, wanting to speak with him.

Now Teresa had left for school, and John put down the phone with a feeling of annoyance. Not only had the incoming call blown today's chance at Teresa Wu, but Chen didn't like it that Cole implied he had missed something at the crime scene. Chen liked it even less that he'd allowed the guy to badger him into meeting back at the Dersh house. Still, Chen was curious to hear what Cole had to offer; after all, if Chen could make a headline breakthrough on the Dersh case, Teresa Wu might change her mind about going out with him. How could she turn down a guy with a Boxster *and* his name on the front page of the *L.A. Times*?

Forty minutes later, John Chen tooled his 'tangmobile into Dersh's drive beside a green-and-white cab. The police tape had been removed from Dersh's door, and the house long released as a crime scene. Now it was nothing more than bait for the morbid.

As Chen shut down the Boxster, a man whose arm stuck from his body in a shoulder cast climbed out of the cab. He looked like a waiter.

The man said, 'Mr Chen. I'm Elvis Cole.'

There's a dorky name for you. Elvis.

Chen eyed Cole sourly, thinking that Cole probably wanted him to falsify or plant evidence. 'You're Pike's partner?'

'That's right. Thanks for coming out.'

Cole offered his good hand. He wasn't as big as Pike, but his grip was uncomfortably hard – like Pike, he was probably another gym rat with too many Y chromosomes who played private eye so he could bully people. Chen shook hands quickly and stepped away, wondering if Cole was dangerous.

418

'I don't have a lot of time, Mr Cole. They're expecting me back at the office five minutes ago.'

'This won't take long.'

Cole started down the alley alongside Dersh's home without waiting, and Chen found himself following. John resented that: Ballsy guys lead; they don't follow.

Cole said, 'When you covered the Lake Hollywood scene, you backtracked the shooter to a fire road and found where he'd parked his car.'

Chen's eyes narrowed. He automatically didn't like this, because Pike had done the tracking and he'd only tagged along. Chen, of course, had left that part out of his report.

'And?'

'There's no mention of the shooter's vehicle in the Dersh report. I was wondering if you looked for it.'

Chen felt a flood of relief and irritation at the same time. So that was the guy's big idea; that was why he'd wanted to meet. Chen put an edge in his voice, letting this guy know he wasn't just some a-hole with a pocket caddy.

'Of course, I looked for it. Mrs Kimmel heard the shooter's car door slam in front of her next-door neighbor's house. I checked the street and the curbs there and in front of the next house for possible tread marks, too, but there was nothing.'

'Did you look for oil drips?'

Cole said it just like that, without accusation, and Chen felt himself darken.

'What do you mean?'

'The Lake Hollywood report mentions oil drips that you found at the scene. You took samples up there and identified the oil.'

'Penzoil 10–40.'

'If the shooter's car was leaking up at the lake, it probably left drops here, too. If we found them, maybe you could prove they'd come from the same vehicle.'

Chen darkened even more, his face burning at the same time he felt a grim excitement. Cole had something here. Chen could compare brand, additives, and carbon particulate concentration to match the two samples. If he got a match, it would break open the Dersh case and guarantee headline coverage!

But when they reached the street, Chen's enthusiasm waned. The tarmac had last been refreshed in the sixties, and showed pothole plugs, the scorched weathering of L.A.'s inferno heat, and a webwork of tiny earthquake cracks. In the general area where Chen reasoned that the shooter had parked, any number of drips dotted the road, and they might've been anything: transmission fluid, power steering fluid, oil, brake fluid, antifreeze, the hawked lugey of a passing motorist, or bird shit.

Chen said, 'I don't know, Cole. It's been two weeks; anything that dripped that night has been weathered, dried, driven over, maybe contaminated with other substances. We won't be able to find anything.'

'We won't know if we don't look, John.'

Chen walked along the edge of the street, kicking pebbles and frowning. The damned street was so speckled it looked like measles. Still, it was an interesting idea, and if it panned out, the benefits might be enormous. Sex with Teresa Wu.

Chen dropped down into a push-up position the way Pike had shown him and considered the light on the road's surface. He let everything blur except the light, and noticed that some drips shined more than others. Those would be fresher. Chen moved to the curb, and imagined a car parked there, an SUV like the one at Lake Hollywood. He went low again in that place, looking for drip patterns. A vehicle parked for a time would not leave a single drip, but several, the dots overlapping.

Cole said, 'What do you think?'

John Chen, lost in the street, did not hear him.

'John?'

'Huh?'

'What do you think?'

'I think it's a long shot.'

'Is there any other kind?'

John Chen went back to the Boxster for his evidence kit, then spent the rest of the afternoon taking samples, and daydreaming about Teresa Wu.

CHAPTER 42

Exactly twenty-four days after the City of Los Angeles district attorney's Office registered my conviction with the state, I received a letter from the California State Licensing Board revoking my investigator's license. In the same mail, the California Sheriffs Commission revoked my license to carry a firearm. So much for the Elvis Cole Detective Agency. So much for being a detective. Maybe I could become a sod farmer.

Two days later the doctors cut off my cast, and I began physical therapy. It hurt worse than any physical pain I'd ever felt, even worse than being shot. But my arm worked, and I could drive again. Also, I no longer looked like a waiter.

I drove to my office for the first time since the desert, walked up the four flights, and sat at my desk. I had been in that office for over ten years. I knew the people who worked in the insurance office across the hall, and I used to date the woman who owned the beauty supply company next door. I bought sandwiches from the little deli in the lobby, and did my banking in the lobby bank. Joe had an office there, too, though it was empty. He had never used it, and now perhaps never would.

I watched Pinocchio's eyes move from side to side, and said, 'I guess I could hang you in the loft.'

When the phone rang, I said, 'Elvis Cole Detective Agency. We're out of business.'

Frank Garcia said, 'What do you mean, out of business?'

'Just a joke, Frank. How you doing?' I didn't want to get into it.

'How come you haven't called? How come you and that pretty lady haven't come see me?'

'Been busy. You know.'

'What's that pretty lady's name? The one works for Channel 8?'

'Lucy Chenier.'

'I want you two to come have dinner. I'm lonely, and I want my friends around. Will you?'

'You mind if it's just me, Frank?'

'Is something wrong? You don't sound so good.'

'I'm worried about Joe.'

Frank didn't say anything for a while, but then he said, 'Yeah, well, some things we can control, and some we can't. You sure you're all right?'

'I'm fine.'

I spoke to Lucy every day, but over time our calls grew shorter and less frequent. I didn't enjoy them, and felt worse after we had spoken. It was probably the same for Lucy, too.

Stan Watts called, time to time, or I called him, but there was still no word about Joe. I phoned John Chen on eight separate occasions to see if he'd gotten anything from the tests he'd run, but he never returned my calls. I still don't know why. I stayed in touch with Joe's gun shop, and went through the motions of searching for the mysterious girl in the black van, but without real hope of finding anything. After a time, I felt like a stranger in my own life; all the things that had been real to me were changing.

On Wednesday of that week, I phoned my landlady and gave up my office. The Elvis Cole Detective Agency was out of business. My partner, my girlfriend, and now my business were gone, and I felt nothing. Maybe when I lost my license I had gone, too, and that was why I didn't feel anything. I wondered if they were hiring at Disneyland.

On Thursday, I parked in Frank Garcia's drive, and

went to the door expecting dinner. Abbot Montoya answered, which surprised me.

He said, 'Frank and I had a little business, and he invited me to stay. I hope you don't mind.'

'You know better than that.'

He led me into the living room, where Frank was sitting in his chair.

I said, 'Hi, Frank.'

He didn't answer; he just sat there for a moment, smiling with a warmth that reached all the way into my heart.

He said, 'How come I gotta find out from other people?'

'What?'

'You weren't kidding about being out of business. You lost your license.'

'There's nothing to be said for it, Frank. How'd you find out?'

'That pretty lady, Ms Chenier. She called me about it.'

'Lucy called you?' That surprised me.

'She explained what happened. She said you lost it helping Joe get away.'

I shrugged, giving his own words back to him. 'There's things we can control, things we can't.' I wasn't comfortable talking about it, and didn't want to.

Frank Garcia handed me an envelope.

I held it back without opening it. 'I told you. You don't owe me a nickel.'

'It's not money. Open it.'

I opened it.

Inside, there was a California state investigator's license made out in my name, along with a license to carry a concealed weapon. There was also a brief, terse letter from a director of the state board, apologizing for any inconvenience I might've suffered for the temporary loss of my licenses.

I looked at Frank, then at Abbot Montoya. I looked at the license again.

'But I'm a convicted felon. It's a state law.'

A fierce pride flashed in Abbot Montoya's eyes then, and I could see the strength and the muscle and the power that had been used to get these things. And I thought that maybe he was right, maybe he and Frank weren't so far from the White Fence gang-bangers they'd been as younger men.

He said, '*Temos tu corazón y tu el de nosotros. Para siempre.*'

Frank gripped my arm, the same fierce way he had gripped me before. 'Do you know what that means, my friend?'

I couldn't answer. All I could do was shake my head.

'It means we love you.'

I nodded.

'That pretty woman, she loves you, too.'

I cried, then, and couldn't stop, not for what I had, but for what I didn't.

CHAPTER 43

Two days later I was hanging a framed copy of the new license in my office when the phone rang. My first thought was that it was John Chen or Stan Watts, but it was neither.

One of the guys who worked in Joe's gun shop said, 'You know who I am?'

My heart rate spiked. Just like that, and a cold sweat filmed my chest and back.

'Is this about Joe?'

'You ever been to the old missile control base above Encino? The one they turned into a park? You'll like the view.'

'Is Joe okay? Did you hear from him?'

'No way. Joe's probably dead. I just thought we might get together up at the park, maybe raise one for an old friend.'

'Sure. We could do that.'

'I'll give ya a call sometime. Bring a six-pack.'

'Anytime you want.'

'Sooner the better.'

He hung up.

I locked the office, and drove hard west through the city, and up to Mulholland.

It was a beautiful, clear Friday morning. The rush hour had passed, letting me make good time, but I would've made the time even if the streets had been crushed. It had to be Joe, or word of him, and I drove without thinking or feeling, maybe because I was scared the word would be bad. Sometimes, denial is all you have.

The government had built a missile control base high in the Santa Monica Mountains during the Cold War years. Then it was a top secret radar installation on the lookout for Soviet bombers coming to nuke Los Angeles. Now it was a beautiful little park that almost no one knew about except mountain bikers and hikers, and they only went on weekends.

When I reached the park, a Garcia tortilla company truck was parked off the road. I left my car behind it, hurried into the park, and made my way up the caged metal stairs to the top of the tower. The observation tower had once been a giant radar dome, and from it you could see south to the ocean and north across the San Fernando Valley.

Joe Pike was waiting on the platform.

He stiffened even though I didn't hug him hard. He was pale, and thinner than I'd ever seen him, though the white Garcia bakery shirt made him seem dark.

I said, 'Took you long enough to call, goddamnit. Can you spell "worry"?'

'I was down in Mexico, getting better.'

'You got to a hospital?'

Pike's mouth twitched. 'Not quite. How's the arm?'

'Stiff, but it's okay. I'm more concerned about you. You need anything?'

'I need to find Trudy.'

'I've been looking.' I told him what Watts had reported, and what my own searches had confirmed. Nothing on a black minivan or Trudy or Matt existed anywhere in the system. I also told him that I had no leads.

Pike took that in, and went to the rail. 'The police are on my house and the gun shop. They've frozen my accounts, and flagged my credit cards. They've been to see Paulette.'

'Maybe you should go south again. Sooner or later I'll get a hit that we can work with.'

427

Pike shook his head. 'I won't go south to hide, Elvis. I'm going to live it out here, one way or the other.'

'I'm not saying go south to hide. Go to stay free. Coming up here is too big a risk.'

'I'm willing to risk it.'

'And go back to jail?'

Pike's mouth flickered in an awful way. 'I'll never go to jail again.'

Then he looked past me, and straightened in a way that made my scalp prickle. 'They're on us.'

A flat blue detective sedan and an LAPD radio car slid to a stop by the Garcia van. A second radio car barreled in from the opposite direction, stopping in the center of the road. We didn't wait to see who they were or what they were planning.

Pike went low fast, and snaked down the twisting metal stair toward the ground. I was right behind him. We couldn't see the stair from the platform, or the ground from the stair, but if we could get away from the observation tower, the park opened onto miles of undeveloped mountains that stretched south to Sunset Boulevard and west to the sea. If Pike could get into the sage, there was no way the police could follow him without dogs or helicopters.

As we banged down the stairs, I said, 'There's a trail works south through the mountains to a subdivision above the Sunset Strip.'

'I know it.'

'If you follow the trail down, I can pick you up there later.'

It was planning done for nothing.

When we reached the bottom of the stair, Harvey Krantz and two SWAT cops with M16s were waiting.

The SWAT cops covered Joe Pike like he was a coiled cobra. They spread to the sides for crossing fire, their black rifles zeroed on Pike's chest even from ten feet away. Behind them, a cop shouted our location to the people on the road.

Krantz wasn't holding a gun, but his eyes were on Pike as if he were a down-range target. I expected him to start with our rights, or tell us we were under arrest, or maybe even gloat, but he didn't.

Krantz said, 'Go for it, Pike. Shoot it out, and you might get away.'

The SWAT cops shifted.

Pike stood with his weight on the balls of his feet, hands away from his body, as relaxed as if he were in a Zen rock garden. He would have a gun somewhere, and he would be wondering if he could get to it, and fire before the SWAT cops cut loose. Even wounded and weak, he would be thinking that. Or maybe he wasn't thinking anything at all; maybe he would just act.

Krantz took a step forward, and spread his hands. 'I don't have a gun, Pike. Maybe you'll get me.'

I looked from Krantz to Joe, and knew in that moment that something more than an arrest was happening. The SWAT cops traded an uncertain glance, but didn't lower their guns.

'What's wrong with you, Krantz?' I put up my hands. 'Raise your hands, Joe. Goddamnit, *raise them*!'

Pike didn't move.

Krantz smiled, but it was strained and ugly. He took another step. 'Time's running out, Joe. More officers are on the way.'

'Raise your hands, damnit! If you don't, then Krantz *wins*!'

Pike took a single breath, then looked past Krantz to the SWAT cops, talking to them now. 'My hands are going up.'

He raised them.

'Gun in my waistband under my shirt.'

Krantz didn't move.

One of the SWAT cops said, 'Krantz, get his damned gun.'

Krantz took out his own gun.

Stan Watts trotted up the path, breathing hard, and stopped when he saw us.

The SWAT cops said, 'Hey, Watts, get this bastard's gun.'

Stan Watts took Pike's gun, then took mine, and he stared at Krantz, standing there with his gun at his side. 'What in hell's going on, Krantz? Didn't you tell them?'

Krantz's jaw rippled as if he were chewing hard candy, and still his eyes didn't leave Pike. 'I wanted Pike to spook. I was hoping he'd give us the excuse.'

I said, 'Take his gun, Stan. Please take his gun.'

Watts stared at Krantz, then the gun Krantz held. Krantz's fingers worked at the gun like they had a life of their own. They kneaded and gripped the gun, and maybe wanted to raise it. Stan Watts went over and pried the gun away, and then pushed Krantz back hard.

'Go wait in the car.'

'I'm your superior officer!'

Watts told the SWAT cops they were done, then told us to put our hands down. He wet his lips like his mouth was dry. 'You're not under arrest. Branford's dropping the charges. You hear that, Pike? Branford's with your attorney right now. SID put Sobek's vehicle at Dersh's house. That's enough to get you off the hook.'

I gripped Pike's arm, and held it. John Chen had come through.

Krantz pushed past Watts and jabbed his finger at Pike. It was exactly the same move he'd made at Lake Hollywood the first time I saw him. 'I don't give a rat's ass what SID says, Pike; you're a murderer.'

Watts said, 'Stop it, Harvey.'

Krantz jabbed again.

'You killed Wozniak, and I still believe you killed Dersh.'

Krantz jabbed again, and this time Pike grabbed his finger so quickly that Harvey Krantz did not see him move. Krantz shrieked as he dropped to the ground, screaming, 'You're under arrest, goddamnit! That's assaulting an officer! You're under arrest.'

Pike and Watts and I stared at him there on the ground, red-faced and screaming, and then Watts helped him up, saying, 'We're not going to arrest anyone, Harvey. Go back to the car and wait for me.'

Krantz shook him off, and walked away without another word.

I said, 'Get him off the street, Watts. He came up here to murder Pike. He meant what he said.'

Watts pursed his lips, watching until Krantz was gone, then considered Pike. 'You could make a complaint, I guess. There's grounds.'

Pike shook his head.

I said, 'That's it? We're just going to forget what happened here?'

Watts put the frying pan face on me. 'What happened, Cole? We came up to give you the word, we did.'

'How'd you know we were here?'

'We've been running taps twenty-four/seven on phones Pike's employees are known to use. The wire guys heard Pike's boy tell you about this place, and figured it out.'

Watts glanced back to the road where Harvey Krantz was waiting in their car, alone.

Watts handed back our guns, holding on to Pike's as Pike reached for it. 'What Krantz said about hoping you'd give us an excuse, that's bullshit. He's just upset. I don't play it that way, and he wouldn't either. Bauman said you hadn't been in touch, so we figured if there was a shot at reaching you up here, we should take it.'

I said, 'Sure, Watts.'

'Screw you, Cole. That's the way it is.'

'Sure.'

Watts followed after Krantz, and pretty soon the police

mounted their cars, and left great brown clouds of dust as they drove away. I guess Harvey Krantz hated Pike so much he had to believe Pike was guilty no matter what. I guess that kind of hate can make you do things you ordinarily wouldn't do.

'Watts can say whatever he wants, but Krantz wanted it. You don't bring tactical officers to tell some guy he's off the hook. You don't even roll out. If Krantz didn't want it, he could've put the word through me and Charlie and the guys at your shop. You would've heard.'

Pike nodded without comment, and I wondered if he even gave a damn. Maybe it was better not to.

I said, 'What are you going to do?'

'Call Paulette.'

'Does it bother you, what Krantz said about Wozniak? That you're still carrying the blame?'

Pike shrugged, and this time I knew he didn't give a damn.

'Let Krantz and everyone think what they want. What I think, and do, is more important.'

Pike took a deep breath then, and cocked the dark glasses my way.

'I missed you, Elvis.'

That made me smile.

'Yeah, Joseph, I missed you, too. It's good to have you back.'

We shook hands then, and I watched him walk down to the Garcia bakery truck and drive away. I stood in the hot wind for a time, telling myself that it was over, that Pike was home, and safe, but even as I told myself these things, it was without a sense that any of it was finished, or resolved.

We were different now. The world had changed.

I wondered if our lives would ever be the same, or as good, and if we were less than we had been.

The devils take their toll, even in this angel town.

Maybe here most of all.

*

I have lived in my house for many years, but it wasn't my house anymore. It wasn't the cozy A-frame that wrapped me in warm woods and copper sunset light, hanging there off the side of a mountain. It had become a great cavern that left me listening to echoes as I walked from room to room searching for something I could not find. Climbing to the loft took days. Going into the kitchen weeks. Funny, how the absence of a friend can do that. Funny, how it takes a woman three beats of a heart to walk out a door, but the man she's walking away from can't make that same trip in a lifetime.

Guess that's why you're smiling, Cole. It's so damned funny.

That night, I locked my door, and worked my way down the crooked mountain streets into Hollywood. It gets dark in the canyons first, shadows pooling in the deep cuts as the high ridges hide the sun. Here's a tip: If you leave the canyons you can find the light again, and get a second chance at the day. It doesn't last long, but nobody said second chances will wait for you.

The Sunset Strip was a carnival of middle-aged hipsters rat-racing Porsches, and goateed Val-dudes smoking twenty-dollar Cubano Robustos, and a couple of million young women with flat bellies flashing Rodeo Drive navel rings. I didn't see any of it. Shriners from Des Moines were lined up outside House of Blues like catalog models for JCPenney. Yellow-haired kids clumped outside Johnny Depp's Viper Room, laughing with LAPD motorcycle cops about the latest acid casualty. Didn't see it; didn't hear it. Twilight faded to full-on night, and the night grew later. I drove all the way to the water, then north through the steep mountain passes of Malibu, then back along the Ventura Freeway, just another mass of speeding metal. I felt edgy and unsettled, and thought that maybe if I drove long enough I might find a solution.

I love L.A.

It's a great, sprawling, spread-to-hell city that protects

433

us by its sheer size. Four hundred sixty-five square miles. Eleven million beating hearts in Los Angeles County, documented and not. Eleven million. What are the odds? The girl raped beneath the Hollywood sign isn't your sister, the boy backstroking in a red pool isn't your son, the splatter patterns on the ATM machine are sourceless urban art. We're safe that way. When it happens it's going to happen to someone else. Only thing is, when she walks out of your door, it isn't someone else. It's you.

I let myself off the freeway at the top of the Santa Monica Mountains and turned east along Mulholland. It's quiet up there, and dark; a million miles from the city even though it lies in the city's heart. The dry air breezed over me like sheer silk, and the desert smells of eucalyptus and sage were strong. A black-tailed deer flashed through my headlights. Coyotes with ruby eyes watched me from the grass. I was tired, and thought I should go home because this was silly, all this aimless driving. Just go home and go to sleep and get on with my life. You can save the world tomorrow. Find all the answers you want tomorrow.

After a time I pulled off the road, cut the engine, and stared at the lights that filled the valley floor. Two million people down there. Put them end to end and they would wrap around the moon. Red taillights lit the freeways like blood pumping through sluggish arteries. An LAPD helicopter orbited over Sherman Oaks, spotlighting something on the ground. Another opera I didn't want to be part of.

I got out of my car and sat cross-legged on the hood. The barrel shape of an owl sat atop a power pole, watching me.

The owl said, 'Who?'

You get that from owls.

A month ago, I had almost been killed. My best friend and partner had almost died, too, and I'd spent every day since then thinking that he was gone. Today, he came very close to dying again. Samantha Dolan was dead, my girlfriend had walked out on me, and here I was sitting in the dark with an owl. The world had changed, all right. Some great large place inside me was empty, and I didn't know if I could fill it again. I was scared.

The air was sultry, and felt good. When I first came here, I fell in love with this place. During the day, Los Angeles is a great playful puppy of a town, anxious to please and quick with a smile. At night, it becomes a treasure chest filled with magic and dreams. All you have to do is chase your dreams. All you need is the magic. All you have to do is survive, but it's that way anywhere. That's what I found here when I first came; that's what more and more people find here every day, always had and always would. It's why they come; that treasure chest of hope.

I could make it right with Lucy. I could pull my life together again and fill that empty place.

The owl said, 'Who?'

I said, 'Me.'

I climbed back in the car, but I didn't go home. I turned on the radio and made myself comfortable. I didn't need to go home anymore. I was already there.

L.A. isn't the end; it's the beginning.

So was I.